Freedom Earned

Ronald Price

NEWMAN SPRINGS PUBLISHING
320 Broad Street
Red Bank, NJ 07701

First originally published by Newman Springs Publishing 2020

ISBN 978-1-64801-361-4 (Paperback)
ISBN 978-1-64801-362-1 (Digital)

Printed in the United States of America

Introduction

The new twin towers were here and America was at its most historical crisis. The loss of the twin towers opened the eyes of the world to Islam, and America found itself in the crosshairs of a tyrannical Islamic faction that wanted to make the world an Islamic one. The people did not see what was coming or the entanglements of the changes that lay ahead.

The administrations would change from party to party, and many would find the America they knew to be weakened and guided into a reformed form of communism that would be called the new progressives. But those with open eyes and the party itself would still be known as the Democratic Party and would insist it was still the people's party and the only one capable of guiding America into the new America, unharmed and free to all who would venture to pass her borders with the insight of free medical care. No one would be left behind and no one would be left hungry—these are among the top priorities of the Democratic Party and its self-proclaimed leaders.

With the advent of all illegal aliens given amnesty, the ranks of voters for the party have been captured, and they knew no other party would ever be able to vote them out of power for they had the control and they felt nothing and no one would ever have the ability to change the dynamics they had put in place, for both houses of the Congress were firmly in their control. Any and all who would embrace the party would be taken care of. To ensure the changes, the government slowly increased the taxes and the takeover of major businesses was slow but deliberate and without hesitation. One feared to move against any government official for fear they would be seen as an uncooperative citizen and they would be without any friends

3

to help them. Once the medical industries were taken over and the health care became a single payer, the lives of the young and middle age were assured, but the elderly found themselves on rationed health care and that meant many would die earlier than needed because of the high cost of the health-care programs in place.

The government had accepted and ratified the United Nations (UN) gun control legislation, and the government had allowed the United Nations to enter the country and remove all privately owned guns. For the hunter, they had to belong to a government-controlled hunting club, and the rifles used were owned and controlled by them. The people were too late to change the dynamics of the government and found themselves in alignment with the world's dominating socialists. Islam was still inflicting damage to many countries, but they had been controlled mostly in the Middle East and Africa but were still a threat to all of earth's societies, more so in the European Union. However, they were slowly moving into Central and South America with Mexico becoming the staging area for them to move silently into the borderless United States.

However, there were many Americans—Democrats, Republicans, and Independents—secretly working to save the country and then the world, for they had not forgotten the rights of their forefathers and they were determined to return them to the people. The return of constitutional rights was paramount for their survival. Those who pretend to be friends of the people and planned to enslave them would find the real American waiting and willing to fight for their freedom, for freedom is earned, not bought or taken for granted, but earned through faith and determination of each patriot's love for his country.

CHAPTER 1

Hostility and Friendship

Wednesday, May 27

A deep purring from far away got louder and louder until it pounded and rang in Tork's ears. His eyes blinked wide open, and he cursed the damn phone for making such a racket. He grabbed the handset and yelled into the mouthpiece, but the sound that came out was a very sleepy, "Yeah, what da ya want?" The reply echoing in his ear and begging for help was from someone he had not seen in years—well, it seemed like years, yet it was only one or two. Considering how he felt, time was unimportant right then.

"Tork, it's Cal. I need your help. I'm in real trouble and you're the only one I can turn to."

"Cal, what the hell? Oh, never mind, what's the problem? What have you gotten yourself into this time?" He had not heard from Cal Varner for a couple of years, and every time he did, it was about money. Cal had an unquenchable need for money. "How much do you need and where the hell are you? The last time I sent you any money, it was to Bolivia, Cal, and when are you going to repay me?"

The phone was silent for a moment. Tork could hear Cal's heavy breathing like he was very tense, almost like he was afraid to move. He could sense him looking around, as if they were watching him.

"Tork, I've stumbled onto something big, and I don't know who to turn to. I just do not know what to do. You've got to help me, somehow. Please! Can you help?"

Ever since they were children, Tork was always getting Cal out of trouble. If it wasn't a woman, it was his big mouth. "Cal, where are you?"

"Sausalito. I'm being followed, and I slipped in off the freeway to call you. I think I lost him, but I'm not sure."

He seemed to be calming down and starting to use his brain. His thinking was coming back and he seemed to be breathing normally, and the panic in his voice was gone. It appeared he was more rational than he was before. Tork could get down to business now and find out what was going on and how he could help Cal out of another mess he had gotten into. Normally he is a very quick-witted guy, so Tork thought something had to really scare him, for him to be in such a panic.

"Cal, just what have you found? What's bothering you? You're not making any sense. Can I meet you somewhere in Frisco?"

"Tork, I don't know how to start. I was driving back from Vegas yesterday, and I drove to Boulder City to see Jack Peterson. You remember him?"

"Yeah," Tork said.

"Well, he was out of town, so I took Highway 95 to Needles. I didn't want to return to Vegas, so I thought I'd pick up I-40 and come into LA that way. It was late afternoon when I started, and it was getting late when I arrived in Needles. I grabbed a cola and a quick pee stop there and headed on out." Cal hesitated, listening.

"Are you there, Cal? Don't hang up on me."

"I was about fifty or sixty miles past Needles when the car started to act up, probably got bad gas when I fueled up in Nevada," Cal continued. "The car started to buck and jerk so badly I decided to pull off at the next exit. I pulled off and started north toward some place called Kelso. It was getting late, and I figured I could find something open to get the car fixed or a motel to spend the night. But there was nothing, so I headed back toward I-40 hoping to find something at the next exit. The car's bucking and jerking were getting worse, so I started looking for a side road. Thought maybe a rancher or farmer might be available to help. As I drove, I spotted a side road. It looked like the closest road to civilization, so I took it. I had gone about five or six miles when I hit a washout.

"The gully was too deep to go across, and I figured it was a summer flash flood that caused it. They're common here this time of year. I slowed and was trying to figure a way around it when I noticed another side road just to the right of the washout. I swung the car over so I could see it better and hoped it would take me around the gully. A broken destination sign was lying on the ground, and I got out of the car to read it. I needed to see if it would get me to a town or someplace to get the car repaired. I got back in and coached my heap on. If it wasn't for bad luck, I guess I wouldn't have had any at all. Like in Vegas, it was just rotten."

"Cal," Tork interrupted, "get to the point, will you, please?"

"Sorry, Tork, but I almost have to give you all the details."

Boy, Tork thought, *this is going to take all night.* Cal continued and Tork decided to be patient and let him finish.

"Where was I?" Cal said, "Oh yeah. The road was getting worse and worse, and I felt like I was going to be out there forever. As I drove, the road got narrower and narrower, so close the bushes were scraping the side of the car. It didn't look like anyone had been out there for years. I was about to look for a place to turn around when I suddenly noticed the road start to widen ahead of me. I approached the wider part of the road, and I could see in my headlights what seemed to be new asphalt ahead of me. I couldn't figure out what was going on. Everything looked okay to me, but still looked wrong. I just couldn't put my finger on it. There I was, in the middle of nowhere heading nowhere, totally lost with a bad running engine and a great road appearing out of nowhere. I was beginning to wonder if I was going nuts or if I was just tired. It didn't figure. I was driving through a thickly overgrown road, and suddenly there appears new asphalt on the highway. I was right. As the car picked up on the new pavement, the ride was suddenly very smooth, and the road widened out. It was if someone had built a new road and forgot to tell anyone about it. Nowhere in sight could I see other cars, nor could I see any farmhouses or lights of any kind around me. I don't mind telling you, I was starting to feel better, figuring that a town was very close."

Tork thought for a moment and said, "Look, Cal, I don't mean to be pushy, but could you maybe, just maybe, get a little closer to the point, huh?"

Cal, taken aback by Tork's prompting, wiped the sweat from his face. In addition, his nerves were getting the best of him, and although it was a hot night, he could almost feel a chill starting. Cal continued, "Well, I hadn't gone more than a mile when I realized I was not on a road. I could see no cat's-eyes or centerlines out there anywhere, and I had that feeling again."

Suddenly, Cal went silent. Tork could hardly hear him breathing over the phone. Tork become suddenly alert. "What's wrong?" he asked. "What's wrong?"

Very quietly, Cal said, "Tork, I think they've found me. I've got to go. Meet me at Mo's. I'll try to get there by daylight. Please, buddy, I need your help."

Cal had Tork scared and worried. His tone of voice and the unfinished story had him wondering just what Cal had gotten into. Tork looked at the clock. It was just past three thirty in the morning. He got up and hurriedly showered, dressed, and got out his 9mm automatic. He checked the magazine, picked up a spare clip, and dropped it into his pocket. Then he tucked the automatic into his waistband knowing the penalty for having a gun in his possession was hazardous to his health.

Since the merger between the United States, Canada, and Mexico had divided the country into three geological sections known as North America and Congress had eliminated the constitution by merging together and erasing all borders, constitutional rights were transferred to the UN Mandate of Articles. It made the ownership or possession of a weapon or a firearm of any kind illegal. This had created the night of guns for peace when the new Congress permitted the UN forces to enter the country and homes to confiscate all weapons in all three sections. The new country had now been subjected to the indignity of being serfs.

Tork had crossed the Oakland Bay Bridge to Frisco and was on his way to Mo's Place, a rather out-of-the-way all-night diner, a friendly place. Mo's Place was on a backstreet, an all-night diner frequented by night workers and insomniacs. It had good food, coffee, and friendly people. The best food was there. Mo Brodrick owned it, an old friend of Tork and Cal's. The diner was a favorite of the local constabulary, a frequent stop for the beat cops and a safe place for them to meet. Cal knew he would be safe there if he could make it in one piece. With the country virtually police-controlled, it paid to know them.

Tork pulled up in the small parking lot and looked for Cal's car. It wasn't there. He had hoped Cal would have made it before he did, for he was closer than Tork. Also, Tork had to shower and dress before leaving.

When Tork arrived, he went in looking for Cal and thought maybe he might have parked on the street and walked down to Mo's.

"Hi, Charlene," Tork called out to the redheaded server. "How yah been, ginger? Still my sweetie?"

Charlene smiled, winked, and replied, "Sure, sweetheart, and yer still the kidder. What brings you out this early in the morning?"

"Oh, just meeting Cal. Have you seen him?"

"No," was her reply. "I haven't seen him for some time, but Mo just said he thought he saw his car go by. He told me it seemed odd. Said Cal usually parked in the rear and comes in from there."

"Thanks, Charlene. Which direction was he going?"

"Toward the bay," she replied.

It concerned Tork for he hoped he had arrived in time. If Cal was headed for the bay, he was going to come around back and park behind Mo's. He had to go up two blocks and circle back to the parking lot in the rear. Tork went to the back of the diner and opened the door. Just as the door opened, he saw two men pulling Cal from his car. One of them held a gun in his left hand and tried to pull Cal out of his car with his right. The second guy kept getting in the way of his partner.

It was the edge Tork needed. He slipped up behind them both and cracked one of the men across the head with his 9 mm. He went down quickly. The other turned to see what had happened. Tork shoved the gun deep in his gut and said, "Drop it, stupid, or I'll blow your spleen all over the parking lot."

He was good, and he was fast. Before Tork could pull the trigger, the man had let go of Cal. Sidestepping and grabbing Tork's gun, he pushed himself back and with his gun in hand slapped Tork across the head. Tork dropped as fast as the other guy. He found himself on his knees trying to protect himself and to see where he had gone wrong when he was hit a second time. Everything slowly started to fade. Grays became blacks. He could hear someone in that black spinning pit calling his name. As they called, the name got louder and closer. Then a blurred image started to take shape and blackness.

"Tork, Tork, wake up! Wake up! Are you okay?"

Another voice was saying something. Tork wasn't sure who it was, but it was somehow familiar. His eyes opened, and as his senses returned, he could feel the pounding in his head. *Boy*, he thought, *I need a big bottle of Lortab right now.*

Why couldn't it have been simply, "I need money," when Tork asked Cal what he needed when he called him? No, nothing's that simple with Cal. Tork guessed that's what friendship was for. Tork got stuck with all the bumps and bruises and Cal gets out of trouble.

A dark void suddenly changing to multicolored lights, echoing sounds, and noises enveloped him. Stars and waving colored ribbons were all around him. He felt himself drifting off as the noises and sounds around him faded in and out. Then the waving colors slowly drifted into blackness.

Tork lay there unconscious, as Cal and Charlene turned him over. Cal took his pulse and breathed a sigh of relief when he felt a strong and steady pulse. "He's okay," he said. "Just out like a light."

Charlene felt the strain release and the tears flowed across her cheeks. A little "thank God" escaped her lips.

Others in the restaurant had heard the commotion and came out in time to see a car leave the area and Charlene and Cal kneeling over Tork. Charlene picked up Tork's gun and put it under her apron.

Realizing the police would soon be there, Cal said, "Quick, Charlene, give me the gun before the cops get here." Cal quickly stuffed the gun in his waistband in the middle of his back. He knew what could happen if the police caught anyone with a gun. It could mean years in a federal or a UN prison.

The new laws allowed for the UN to build prisons and staff them with their own personnel. The host country then paid for them out of tax money. It was part of the UN law that a previous president signed and was never ratified by Congress until this administration took over. It also meant that the new American soldiers or civilian had no rights anywhere in the world including all of North America. Americans were now under foreign control—UN control to be exact.

CHAPTER 2

Waiting for the Prey

Wednesday, May 27

"I send you on a simple job and both of you blow it." The elderly man was obviously chastising both men for failing to complete their assignment.

"I'm sorry, Colonel. We almost had him. He was putting up a good fight, and we would have collared him if this other guy hadn't shown up. We suspected he was a cop. He hit Thomas with an automatic, and I had it in my gut before I knew it. If I hadn't moved when I did, he probably would have fired. As it was, I managed to hit him and stun him enough to hit him a second time and knock him out."

"If you knocked him out, why didn't you grab your target?"

"He pulled loose from me when I—"

"I don't need excuses," the colonel said. "Both of you get out there and find the guy. If the other one is with him, bring them both in. Understand?"

"Yes, sir," they replied.

"Pick up another car. They've probably made the one you were using. This time, get him or them and bring them back here."

"Yes, sir."

"Another thing, keep the network surveillance on him. Keep on your toes this time, Thomas, or do you enjoy getting slapped across the head with automatics?"

With that remark burned into his head, Stewart T. Thomas and Marvin A. Prackett departed for Frisco with determination and resolve.

Col. Donald D. Duncan, North American air force commander of operations, was busy calling his superiors. "I know it's a setback, sir! The intruder stumbled in on the strip and turned around and started back before we could intercept him... Yes, sir, we got his license number from one of our road cameras and have identified him... Yes, sir. I sent two men out to get him and bring him in.... No, sir, nothing serious. We'll keep him incognito here... Yes, sir. Until the operation is completed... Will do, sir. Goodbye."

All the best laid-out plans and all it takes is one unknown to screw it up. Colonel Duncan picked up the phone, hit a patch number, and said, "Ops, has that stealth reported in yet?... I want to know the minute it does, and I want it patched in directly to me. Understand?... Thank you!"

The colonel sat back in his chair, picked up a half cup of cold coffee, and started to think about the mission and why. *What is the price of freedom? They, the administration, had destroyed the family, and we the American people kill more babies each year than Hitler did during the war. Border jumpers have more rights than our citizens. We reward our citizens when they loot, burn, and kill with more legal benefits than they deserve. Foreign nations are doing their best to break us up and destroy our economy and seem to be succeeding. Leading congressmen from the Border States are firmly in the president's pocket.*

Duncan's mind raced through past events that led to these thoughts. *All we need is a return to our independence. A country like ours cannot survive as a service country. We need to build and produce with national pride for all of our citizens. We must regain our companies and control our destiny without outsiders doing it for us. We have many other ways to help people without bankrupting them or forcing all the major corporations out of the country with higher taxes. If Canada and Mexico wished to remain as part of the United States, it would need to be by referendum in the United States first and then in each of the two countries.*

The direction they were going was correct in his mind. *Yes, he thought, we must eliminate the liberal processes and greed that have overtaken the industry and politics. We must shut the door on any who will sell us off for silver or gold. The laws they enacted to control corporate greed paid off for a time—only now our industries have moved to overseas locations where the laws here are of little use. We must control the moneymakers and remove those left-wing liberal and mammy-pammy judges. All the people have a right to this country's heritage. We are not just European, Native American, African, or Asian. We are Americans.*

He muttered aloud, "If we can pull this off, maybe, just maybe, we can bring some sanity back to this country." He knew they must restore the constitution, defeat the liberals, and stop the new world order at all costs. His mind relaxed, his eyelids were heavy, and he slipped into sleep, tired from the pressure of the day's events.

*****

As Tork regained consciousness, two men stepped out of a police car and hurried over to the group. "What's going on here?" one man shouted.

The other held up his hand to him. "Everyone, please stay where you are. I want you and you"—pointing to Charlene and Cal—"to tell me what happened."

Cal started to explain that the two men were trying to rob him when Tork started to focus in on those around him. Tork's head reminded him of the day's events. He opened his eyes and looking down on him was Cal, Charlene, and several cops he knew. Det. Sgt. Roland Tempelton, San Francisco Police Department, was holding a cold compress on Tork's head that a waitress had handed him.

"Okay, Tork, what's going on? And don't tell me its siesta time in the parking lot."

Tork tried to smile, but it hurt and he winced from the pain. He gazed around and his eyes fell on Cal. "Well, this is another fine mess you got me into, Ollie."

Cal smiled and knew Tork was going to be okay.

"Sorry, Sergeant, but when I saw those two guys trying to get Cal, I had to do something. I just didn't figure on coming out second. I had no gun, so I tried to help Cal the best way I could."

"Yeah, Sarge," Cal said. "I asked Tork to meet me here this morning. I needed a hand and knew Tork could help me out. I figure a couple of hoods with guns you guys missed decided they would pick up a few extra bucks."

"Okay, I guess I can buy that. You know how the law is now. Down on anything that may injure a fellow member of the New Order. You get my drift?"

"Yeah, Sarge," both Tork and Cal replied in unison.

They helped Tork up, and feebly, he got into Mo's for a much needed cup of coffee and an ice bag. After sitting in the booth and sipping a cup, he started on Cal. "Okay, Cal, now what's this all about? You're on an old road that turns into a new road. What's strange about that?"

"Look, Tork. I drove a good ten miles or farther down that road, scratched the hell out of my car, and probably destroyed the steering with all the chuckholes I hit. I'm telling you I was lucky to get through to the new section. I drove down the new part of the road about a mile or so not seeing a thing. Figured I should have been in or close to a town, or some lights, or something. But nothing was out there, so I decided to turn around and go back.

"The car was starting to run a little better and I was hoping whatever the trouble was, it started to clear itself up. After I turned around and headed back toward the old road, I glanced in my rearview and saw moonlight shining on something coming up behind me. As I watched, it grew bigger. I realized then it was a vehicle closing on me with no lights on. I don't know how but he was coming up real fast. It scared the hell out of me, so I kicked the pedal to the metal. The car bucked a couple of times and the good Lord was with me and cleared whatever was fouling up the injectors. They let go and I took off. I hit that old stretch of road doing a good seventy and kept it there until I hit the main highway and headed home with them following me all the way."

Tork thought for a moment and then said, "I think we need to drive down there. We should start early enough so you can look for it at night. If we leave this afternoon, we should get their early in the morning before daybreak, and hopefully you can find your Indian gift shop sign and the road. Once we find the road, we'll follow it and see where it goes."

"I don't know, Tork. I think my lights tipped them off," said Cal. "Going in with our lights on may be a mistake."

"Cal, I'm hoping you're right. If we're going to find them, we need to let them know where we are. To do that, we need to set them up ourselves."

"What have you got in mind, Tork?"

"Cal, trust me."

CHAPTER 3

Concern

Washington DC
Tuesday, May 28

A very influential member of Congress was on the phone with a highly placed member of the revolutionary council, busily trying to mend a breach in a high-level security activity that could save America.

"I spoke with Colonel Duncan yesterday, and he assures me he will have the intruder in custody by tonight. He has two intelligence officers working on it right now, and I do not think we have anything to worry about."

Senator Forthright put down the phone and turned to his aide. "Michael, call Emory and have him get my plane ready. We'll be flying to California tonight. I have to make sure nothing goes wrong. Too many errors are showing up to suit me."

Michael Poncie nodded his head, went into his office, and dialed a private number.

The phone rang several times before a gruff voice answered, "Yeah?"

"Is Emory there?"

"Yeah, just a minute," he replied.

"Hello, Emory Watson. May I help you?"

"Emory, Michael here. How soon can you have the Falcon ready to fly with long-range tanks? We have a long trip ahead of us."

"It's all ready to go, Mike. Give me an hour for in-flight preparations and we can take off."

Emory didn't particularly like Michael, so he took advantage of calling him Mike whenever he could. He knew Michael detested it, and it made Emory feel good when he could put one over on the pompous bureaucrat.

Michael had told him before that his name was Michael, not Mike, or Mickey, or Mick. It was Michael and he would not stand for anything less.

Well, then, thought Emory, *Mike it will be. Yes, sir, Mike it is.*

Emory pulled back on the Falcon's throttles and the four jet engines started to whine as the turbine's RPM increased. The plane began to move down the runway as the plane's airspeed picked up rapidly. The wings began to move up as air under and above the wings started to lift it into the heavens. Just as Emory felt her rise up, he reached over and pushed the switch to raise the landing gear.

You could hear the hydraulics whining as the wheels came up, the wheel well doors closed, and the closed door light came on. The plane increased its altitude to its assigned airspace and headed west. Destination? Somewhere in Southern California.

*****

The senator reached over and pushed the intercom button.

Emory responded immediately, "Yes, Senator."

"Patch me through to Duncan."

A few minutes later, the intercom next to the senator buzzed. "Yes," the senator answered. Duncan was on the line. "Have you taken care of that problem yet, Colonel?"

"No, sir. My two operatives are still on it. Seems Mr. Calvin Varner has disappeared. They are checking the area now and hope to have a lead soon. We have found his girlfriend and have her under surveillance as we speak."

"Colonel, I don't have to tell you the serious consequences we may encounter if this fails. I'm airborne and will give you our ETA in about an hour from now. Mark the time and have the scrambler on. Our destination is the strip. Be there when we arrive!"

"Yes, sir. How many are in your party?"

"There'll be myself, Emory, and Michael." Then as an afterthought, the senator said, "Out," to end the conversation.

The colonel reached over and pushed his intercom button. "Get me Stewart and Maps on the scrambler and make it pronto."

Within a few minutes, Stew answered, "Colonel, Stewart here."

The colonel asked, "Were you able to locate the targets?"

Stew answered, "Yes, sir. We were able to find out they had left early this afternoon.... No, sir. At this time, we have no idea where they were headed.... Yes, sir. From what we found out, it's a man by the name of Marion 'Tork' Albertson. We ran a make on him. He was a Special Forces officer during the Iraqi War. He is a fully qualified gunship pilot, who they decorated during four special assignments behind enemy lines. We have ordered his records from the records archives and should have them soon, sir.

"We believe they are moving south to investigate what happened to Mr. Varner at the strip. So we might be seeing them early in the morning if they are headed that direction. You should have security on alert and put out some perimeter personnel sensors around both the compound and the detention center. That's the area they saw Varner in when we started following him. Also, sir, we have completed our investigation in Frisco and are en route home now. We just fueled in Modesto and should reach home plate as planned. Colonel, next time, we go by air. We wasted a lot of time on this trip, sir."

"Roger. Keep me informed of any unusual incidents that may occur on your return. By the way, what was Mr. Albertson's military rank when he was released from active duty?"

"He mustered out as a captain, sir."

The colonel called out to the orderly. "Check with communications and see if we have Stewart and Maps on satellite tracking."

"Yes, sir."

"Also let me know when you get the ETA on the Falcon."

"Yes, sir."

The colonel rose from his chair, stretched, yawned, and looked at the surveillance monitor and then to the distant mountains. For a short time, he watched the waves of heat rising off the desert floor. In deep thought, his mind started to wander as he looked out. The soaring temperatures had shot up to 120 degrees. The night would be just as cold.

Soon some of the country's born and bred marauders and wheeler-dealers will feel the heat of labor. They will then appreciate what the American people have been going through. Thoughts of the past and the foreseen future came to mind.

The doors will soon be closed and America can start rebuilding her economy, giving back the people their jobs, their factories, and their dignity. Made in America will mean in America and not when they assemble it here and make it elsewhere. Yes, the colonel thought, *now is the time. Yes, now is most definitely the time.*

Colonel Duncan called the main control center in the compound and gave the man on duty an order. "Get me security immediately. Have him come directly to my office?"

"Yes, sir."

Within minutes, the chief of Security entered the colonel's office.

"Yes, sir?"

"I want proximity sensors set up around the compound and the detention center. We may have guests coming, and we wouldn't want them to get lost, would we? Also make sure the VIP quarters are ready for guests. The senator and his party will be here soon, expecting three in all. Oh yes, we have two guests that will be coming by way of our sensors. Make them comfortable in the detention center until we can interrogate them."

"Yes, sir. We have surveillance systems in operation now, ground sweep radar and sensors at a hundred yards."

"That's fine. However, we are dealing with a Special Forces intruder. I would feel better if you had another sensor line out at least another a hundred yards…. Okay, thanks."

The security officer picked up the phone, barked a few orders into it, and reassured the colonel the sensors would be in put in place.

CHAPTER 4

Arrival

Bakersfield, California
May 28
Late evening

Tork and Cal had stopped in Bakersfield for food and fuel and to make a plan. Problem? Yes. Tork did not know any more now than he knew when Cal called him. He had no idea what was going on or why two men were after Cal. None of it made any sense. Cal had no idea either. He just made a bad turn because of car trouble. Now two armed men were after him.

While Tork was not sure what was going on, he did know only the military, drug dealers, crooks, and police carry guns and go looking for people. Both of them thought Cal had mistakenly stumbled into a drug drop off. The new asphalt and the long run it made convinced Cal it was being used as an airstrip for small planes. It made sense to him; it was drug runners trying to shut Cal up.

Tork said, "When we find the new road you spoke of, we'll park off the road out of sight. I brought a tarp to throw over the Jeep once we've hid it. We'll pack in and follow the road for about ten meters so we have time to duck if any vehicles are roaming around. Also, they may have sensors monitoring the road. Any vehicles passing may set them off. That may have been how they spotted you the first time."

Cal was uptight with enthusiasm and ready to go. They ticked him off about the chase and he wanted to get even for the licks Tork had taken for him.

"I'm ready. Let's go get them. I don't care how bad they are. Let's go."

Tork and Cal finished by fueling the Jeep, and Tork picked up a few specialty items that Cal couldn't figure out why.

"What are you doing, Tork?

"Oh, just a little insurance policy," replied Tork.

CHAPTER 5

Command Concern

Orinda, California
May 28

Diana Richmond had just returned home from shopping at the Pleasant Hills Mall. It had been a fruitful shopping spree, and she was looking forward to sharing her booty with her mother. She had planned to go with Marion this morning, but he had called saying Cal was in trouble again and he and Cal would be going to Southern California for a few days. He said he would call when he returned or sometime tonight if he got the chance to.

"Mom, I'm home!"

"Oh, hi, darling. Thought I heard you come in."

"Hi, Mom. Come and see what I have bought Marion."

Cheryl Richmond knew how much Tork hated the name Marion. Nevertheless, he loved Diana, so she was the only one that could call him Marion.

"Where is Tork today, Di?"

"He and Cal went to the desert for a couple of days. Cal has gotten himself in another bind, and Marion is helping him out. He's supposed to call me tonight sometime. If he does call and I'm not home, get his number and the name of the motel they're staying in. Okay, Mom?"

"Well, all right, hon, but aren't you staying home this evening?"

"Yes, I intended to but I may be going down to Lafayette. Carol has to pick up her car from the dealership. I told her I would take her down if she went, and if I'm not back when Marion calls, I want to make sure I can call him back later. Remember to get his number please. He should have his cell phone with him, and I don't have his new number yet."

"Okay, darling. I'll get it for you, if he calls."

With that, Diana called Carol.

*****

"Cal, turn off at the truck stop or whatever, okay? We need fuel and I have to call Di and let her know we're on our way."

"Count on me. I could use a pit stop myself."

"If you're getting tired, Cal, I can pick up on the driving," Tork replied.

"Thanks, Tork, but I'm all okay. A cold cola would be great though."

Cal continued thinking quietly and then said, "Tork, I've been thinking and I just can't figure out why they were after me. There wasn't enough moonlight to see anything. The car's headlights only picked up the road, and I was too occupied with the engine to pay attention to anything else. Just why they came after me really bothers me. If they were drug runners, why didn't they shoot?"

Tork shrugged his shoulders. "Don't know, Cal, but if they wanted you dead, they had the chance to do it. I don't think it was a drop, and if I were, there should have been some kind of activity going on, you know, plane, trucks, cars, or something. Cal, you didn't see anything out there."

"But they came on me fast and without lights on. Then they followed me all the way to the main road. I didn't figure it."

"Well, chances are they were using night-vision devices and could follow you all the way to the highway. Oncoming headlights would have blinded them if they continued after reaching the road. So they backed off. Too big a chance of having an accident. It gave you a little edge, but it looks like they caught up with you anyway. I suspect they got close enough to get your plate number. With help from friends, police, or whatever, they were able to track you. That's why they caught you in Sausalito. Chances are, all they had to do was monitor your movements until the time was right to pick you up. That was when I stepped in at Mo's Place. It looks to me like it's a 'government' job and on a large scale. We're going to be walking on those proverbial eggs before it's all over. Just what have you done to piss off the government enough for them to chase you?"

Cal looked at Tork, a little bewildered, and said, "Tork, I'm sure you're aware of what you're doing, because I'm not."

Tork replied, "Look, the very first thing we do is look for any unusual rocks, posts, or plants that are out of place. We find that and we find sensors. We find sensors and I'll lay you odds it's strictly a government operation. Could be you fell into a sting operation and they wanted you on ice until it's over. If that's the case, no problem. If it's a top secret operation, we might have a real opportunity on our hands. Best we can do is to wait and see and hope."

"Yeah, I guess you're right. They could have just killed me at Mo's, right?"

"Well, Cal, that's what I thought."

"Look, up ahead. Looks like a truck stop."

Cal's never-ending appetite and thirst were as good as the best GPS system in the country. Cal pulled into the truck stop and after moving around several big rigs found the gasoline pumps for the cars and cussed at the three bucks a gallon price tag plus the one fifty UN tax the president agreed on. Cal thought, *What a guy! Yes, sir, what a guy.*

Cal pulled up and stopped. He looked around and started to cuss. "Blasted attendants are never here when you want them."

Tork looked up. "Cal, this is a self-service pump island. If you want gas, you pump it. I'll meet you inside. I need to call Di. I'll grab a booth for us. Come on in when you're finished."

Tork moved swiftly to the restaurant and asked the hostess for a quiet booth.

"Hello." It was Di's mom on the line.

"Mrs. Richmond, this is Tork. Is Di home?"

25

"No, Tork. She went into Lafayette with Carol to pick up Carol's car. I suspect they went out to eat or maybe to a movie. I expected her back by now, but you know those girls."

"Yeah, I know. Tell her I'll call her later tonight when we check into a motel and get settled. Okay?"

"Okay, Tork. I'll tell her. By the way, she needs your new cell number."

Tork gave her the number, and she said goodbye and hung up. He then ordered two large Cokes from the hostess and waited for Cal. A few minutes later, Cal came in sat down. "Well, were fueled and ready to roll. Let's eat."

Tork and Cal resumed their trek. Cal picked up the driving, and Tork tried to figure out where they stood. He thought to himself, *The men hunting Cal could have been ahead of him all the way. Could be when I stepped in, it threw them a curve. They hadn't expected anyone else to enter the game. Could be they had gotten instructions or something else? Well, I'll be ready for them. Yes, I'll be ready for them.*

Tork drifted into restless sleep. Everything were jumbled up in his mind, inconsistencies mixed with facts, men with guns that fired big *bang* flags, almost a nightmare. Suddenly Cal reached over and shook Tork, waking him out of a sound sleep. "Uh…who? Who? Who…what's happened? Oh yeah, where we at, Cal?"

Coming out of his sleep and realizing they had stopped, Tork came up in his seat and looked around. They were in a restaurant parking lot. Cal had been driving for hours and was tired, ready to eat, and rest again.

"Let's go eat. I'm starved." With that, Cal opened his door and got out. "It's only four miles to the turn off, Tork. We're almost there."

After a snack and coffee, Tork laid out his plan. "The way I see it, we need a base of operation where we can come and go and have access to a telephone. You were on your way back from Vegas when you turned off right? Okay, then we go back toward the Nevada border and retrace your way back. You look for anything that's familiar so we can find the right turn off, okay?"

After their rest and meal, the mission was once again moving forward.

Cal took the wheel so he could recall anything he had seen the previous night. At the state line, they turned around and headed back and started looking for the right turn off. It was difficult trying to find a familiar place you had only seen once before, when suddenly Cal let out a cry, "That's it, Tork! That's it! Coming up on the right, the turn off, that's it. I know it is."

*****

Emory reached over and hit the landing gear switch, and the whining of the plane's hydraulic motor could be heard and the gears started to lower. Emory was on his approach to the field, and no lights had come on. He had come in low dropping down and flying under cover of the local airport's radar. As his onboard radar searched ahead of him, he cut his two outboard engines and was taking it in on the two inboard ones. *Thank God they had modified these birds years ago and added the other two engines.* It made the bird stronger, faster, and quieter when dropping two engines off line. Suddenly the darkness lit up ahead of him. The dazzling approach lights and then the runway lights were on.

Emory had to touch down quickly before they put out the lights. Seconds later, his wheels were on the ground. He gently brought the nosewheel down into contact with the runway. He started to brake with his engine thrusters and then his brakes. The plane rapidly slowed, and no sooner had he slowed when they turned the runway lights off.

He was in the dark; nothing but his instrument lights illuminated his panel with an eerie glow. Emory reached up and started turning off unneeded systems. Just as he was about to bring the ship to a stop, a vehicle appeared before him. A sign lit up on the back of the unit. The words started moving across it. It was like one of those roadside signs that print up bargains in stores as you go by them. This one was saying, "Follow me. Leave your lights off. Maintain radio silence. We'll have you under cover shortly." The sign continued to repeat the message.

The vehicle was leading them through aprons and hardstands.

Suddenly the sign changed to, "Continue ahead slowly. You are entering a hangar. There will be a slight decline." Within a minute, Emory could feel the plane descending an incline, and he could hear the engines pitches grow louder. He knew he was inside the hangar. After moving slowly, he heard a rumbling behind him. The vehicle ahead of him flashed *stop* on the board. He stopped the plane, and the rumbling noise stopped. The whole area then flooded with light.

They were safely in the underground hangar, and the doors were closed to stop any light leaking out to the outside world. They had arrived.

Emory went back into the cabin. The senator was getting ready to deplane. "Nice flight, Emory. Thanks."

Michael piped in with, "Yeah, thanks. Nice and smooth."

"You're welcome, Senator. You too, Mike."

Michael started to say something to Emory and then changed his mind. Probably planned to dress him down again and had second thoughts with the senator there.

Emory went over to Special Operations to set up for departure and have the plane refueled and serviced. He would need the plane's refrigerator filled and in-flight rations put on board for the return trip.

Michael left everything to Emory knowing Emory would set everything up right.

Emory entered the operations room as a security personnel covered him. "ID please," said the one in command.

Emory pulled out his card and gave it to him. "Thank you, sir," Emory approached the counter. "I need all tanks full, rations replaced, and the fridges filled as soon as possible. We may be leaving soon."

"Yes, sir," he replied. "We have already started refueling. In-flight will be over when your tanks are full, and you'll be ready for a turnaround within thirty minutes if you need it."

Emory looked out into the hangar. He figured they were about sixty feet underground.

He could see the gradual slope of the ramp coming in and several other aircraft sharing the same hangar. It was amazing they had brought him in and parked him in the dark with the other aircraft so close. Two other birds were sharing the hangar, one other Falcon and a helicopter painted in commercial colors, both marked with the Freedom Earned logos, blue and white stripes, strictly company colors. There were sixteen of these hangars underground, with most of them housing gunships, fighters, and light bombers. In addition, a large number of Special Forces and special ops personnel were quartered in the barracks.

The company was getting closer to Freedom Earned with just a few loose ends to tie up before it began. One loose end had brought the senator out here. It must have been important to take him out of Washington this close to zero hour. *Well, all I can do*, he thought, *is to get ready for the ride back.* His thoughts were interrupted when the special ops officer called to him. "Your bird's ready to go whenever you are."

"Thanks, appreciate the effort," he replied.

*****

They took the senator directly to Colonel Duncan's office. Time was critical, and he wasted no time on him.

"Well, Duncan, have you found our missing intruder and his friend?"

The senator was very troubled; they were on the eve of Operation Freedom Earned, and this had to happen. Before they could go on, all the loose ends had to be tied up. It was of the essence they completed everything by the 30th or they could lose the initiative. It would be some time before they would have another window of opportunity.

"No, Senator. We have two crews out now looking for them, and our forces are on alert. They seem to have dropped out of sight, but we do have the girl. They picked her up this afternoon in Lafayette and should be arriving soon. A chopper is shuttling them down now. Maybe we can get something out of them when they arrive."

"I don't have to tell you how important this is," the senator said. "Everything at this moment hinges on stopping them from reporting any of this to the police. If any of this gets out, it could set us back years. We must protect it at any cost, Colonel. When they arrive, call me. I'll be in my quarters. One other thing, has the stealth data come in yet?"

"No, sir. We are still waiting for touchdown. When it's on the ground, I'll call you."

"Have you reported this to Alpha One yet?"

"No, sir. We haven't."

"Sir, don't you—"

The senator held up his hand, stopping him midsentence. "Colonel, I'll decide when it's time to bring the council and Alpha One in on what's happened. It's my responsibility, not yours."

"Yes, sir." Duncan knew when it was time to hold back. He would give the senator a little more time. Then he would alert both Alpha One and the council about the problem. Right now though he needed a little more time for his crew to find Calvin Varner and Marion Albertson. Hopefully the girl would help.

The colonel leaned back, lit his cigar, and started going over his emergency notification list, ticking off the numbers of the alert crews and support base commanders. If anything went wrong, the abort phase would need to be started immediately. He reached over and pulled his computer keyboard to him. He opened his alert channel and keyed in his security codes. Once inside, he brought up the pre-programmed dialing list and started entering the numbers. Within seconds of being activated, they would notify the support bases and they would begin the abort phase.

The colonel thought for a moment. *If we wanted the country back so decent people could walk the streets again at any hour, be it man, woman, or child of any race or creed, if we expected to receive good health, food, and decent jobs, well then, we have to succeed.*

A knock on the door brought the colonel out of his thoughts. "Yes?"

"Colonel, we have installed all the proximity sensors in the areas you requested. I set up a couple of TV cameras on the southeast and southwest perimeters as requested. Although we didn't think we would ever need them there, but with an imminent threat looking at us, well, I thought that being safe sir might be prudent."

"Thank you and especially for your attention to details," replied Colonel Duncan. "Call me when the senator arrives. I'll be in my quarters."

"Yes, sir."

CHAPTER 6

The Decision

Revolutionary Council, Command Center
Washington DC

"Gentlemen, Colonel Duncan has notified us of a serious problem. Infiltrators may have compromised the integrity of our California base. I have had Senator Forthright on the hotline from there, and he has advised us to put our initial implementation date on hold until they can clear up this problem."

"General, what exactly do you mean by 'serious' problem, and if it is serious, don't you think it would be prudent to move our dates up and not back? We have come too far to turn back now. The country is in a state of near anarchy. We must be ready to fight if we expect to win. Those liberals in all parties on the hill are giving us away faster than we can count to ten."

Perry Newcomb, senior member of the House of Representatives and one of several conservative Democrats serving in the House, was an old FDR and Harry Truman fan.

"Perry, we have the situation under control and are working on the problem. We don't want to move before all our forces are in place. What we are doing is as close to treason as we can get. At this time, we must take control immediately, if we are to succeed. To move ahead now could cause us to fail. No, we need a little more time to bring this to a head."

He was a staunch Democrat of the old school and was appalled by the excessive attitude of the House and what had happened to the country and the constitution. Their lust to give and give and give without those receiving to repay or contribute was appalling. He knew the only way to restore the country's constitutional rights was to move against the administration and the Congress. He could see it was the only way to free the people and regain the eroded world leadership. It was decided—establishing a new order within was necessary. The new world order could not be a part of the country or the American people. All borders must be reestablished and then a referendum taken to settle the inclusion of both foreign nations as a part of the United States of America. If any one nation voted against the issue, it would become null and void, and the borders would be reestablished as before. At that point, all illegal aliens would be turned back from the borders and all found in the country deported. America and her people must come first.

America must reopen her factories with jobs available for all. Perry was in this to liberate the country from the foreign domination that was taking place and to restore law and order. He was a man convinced. They were tearing the country apart, and no one cared. Well, he and the council did. If the Congress, the administration, and judicial branches didn't care, well, then they would have to go.

Perry questioned the general. "General, if this is a very serious problem, will we be in jeopardy from the military? Installations in the surrounding areas could affect our efforts."

"No, all the installations in that area believe there is a special testing facility that is top secret, and they will pass all incoming aircraft through without hindrance."

"Also," the general continued, "we have managed to assign top operatives at each installation and assault personnel to take command when we reach zero hour."

Perry was making notes of the general's remarks and listening intently as the general continued. "As you know, we have many personnel ready to act when the time comes. We have scrutinized, planned all phases, and planned again to ensure our success. Gentlemen, we cannot fail. We are too close. Too many people are involved now, and it is imperative we remain on our present schedule, provided of course nothing else goes wrong."

The general reached over and picked up his computer board. He typed in his personal code and opened a modem link to California and started typing. A few minutes later, he turned to his colleagues and said, "Gentlemen, I have sent Senator Forthright and Colonel Duncan authorization to start our strike plan after they have cleared up this problem, provided we have no serious leaks. But in case the media or some small-time police agency gets involved, I have instructed them to move in a subteam and escort those involved to their base camp. They will make them comfortable until phase 1 is complete. Is everyone in agreement?"

No one moved for a few minutes, one by one, after much thought, all agreed it would be the best thing to do.

"Gentlemen, we have much to do. We are getting close, and the country will need each and every one of us. So let's go on back and make sure everything is ready to go. Count down will start soon. Keep your computer links and smartphones on line. Should any one of them fail, you must call for a backup unit. We have them ready and preprogrammed. You know the number. Remember, freedom must be earned."

The members of the board silently got up and left the conference room. The top men in government from both parties, military generals from all services, and members of the president's own cabinet returned to their lives, with a true belief they would be saving the country and restoring democracy. In most of their minds, they knew from the lowest levels of government to the highest, they were manipulating the people and taking advantage of both the government and big business. America needs big business and most of all she needs the little guys too. They're what made America what it is.

America's ability to let the small entrepreneur create and grow was something that had been lost. The yoke of outrageous medical costs put on the neck of small business to control them was bankrupting the people at an alarming rate. The hospitals were reeling in excessive wealth with the high cost of service. Most doctors lined up patients like cattle, moving from room to room, seeing, diagnosing within three or four minutes, and not being able to remember a patient's name without the aid of a patient's file. It boiled down to no money, no cure. If you needed government help, you had to lose everything for Medicaid to work.

Drug costs had skyrocketed in this country, but in others, the costs were way below the American market, and they came from the same factories. Congress had changed bankruptcy laws in favor of the banks and credit card companies. It had become a joke. Congress had established a fee on all e-mail delivered to computers that went directly to the Postal Service, a fee that was unearned, fees that paid them for their inefficiencies. That too riled the new American public.

Yes, this government was in need of a complete overhaul. These were just a few of the problems the committee was concerned with— maybe not big to some, but they were the ones with which the population was concerned, health, jobs, homes, decent drug costs, nourishing food to eat, and a safe country to live in without fear of a child being kidnapped or assaulted and having teachers they could trust and a moral society for all to believe in. They all wanted to go back to decency. God knows what a mess it's in now.

CHAPTER 7

Kidnapped

Lafayette, California

Diana Richmond had just left Carol at the local Ford dealership and had started home when a light-colored van pulled in behind her and followed her. She pulled into a supermarket to pick up a few things for her mother and was getting out of the car when the van pulled up beside her. As she moved to the back of the car, the van driver got out and moved in behind her when she turned toward the market entrance. The back doors of the van opened, and another man stepped out, grabbed Diana, and pulled her to the open van doors. The first man grabbed her, and between them, they pulled her into the van, hands clamped over her mouth to stifle any cries. They slammed the van doors; a waiting woman inside reached over, and before Diana could move, she thrust a needle into her arm. Dianna slid silently into unconsciousness. No one had seen a thing, and in less than several seconds, it was over. The van backed out of its parking place and drove away.

The two men were in the front of the van while the women remained in the back with Diana. They drove up the freeway and headed east toward Walnut Creek and then went south toward San Ramon. Several miles down the road, the driver turned down onto a back road and went several miles. He turned left into a secluded pasture, pulled up under an old oak tree, turned off his engine, and waited. Both men and the women remained silent, each to their own thoughts. Suddenly from the radio, a load and sharp voice spoke, "Alpha One, this is Apple Jack 4. Over."

Maps reached over, picked up the mic, and replied, "Alpha One. Over."

"Alpha One, we are two minutes from touchdown. Do you have the assigned cargo? Over."

"Roger," Maps replied. "The cargo is ready to be loaded. Your turnaround time shouldn't take more than three at the most. Over."

"I have you in sight, Alpha One. Over."

The sound of a chopper slowly became louder as it descended and touched down. Maps and Stew picked up Diana and carried her to the helicopter. The woman opened the side door and they laid Diana down and strapped her in, and the woman entered and sat beside her. The bird slowly lifted up off the ground and departed.

Apple Jack 4 was airborne—their destination, a small airport fifteen minutes from its pickup point where a Falcon executive jet was waiting for them.

Stew and Maps went back to the van. Stew picked up the cellular phone and punched in a number. The phone rang only once.

"Northern Control," came the answer.

"The cargo's airborne. Alert Duncan. Out," Stew responded. He turned the phone off and they headed south toward home.

The bird was airborne a short time when the pilot radioed ahead, "We're coming in. ETA, twelve minutes. Is the Falcon ready for transfer? Over."

"Roger. Everything is ready. Over," he replied.

Colonel Duncan and Senator Forthright had just sat down to discuss the update they had received from the Council Command Center when the call came through. Colonel Duncan picked up the phone and listened, hung it up, and spoke to the senator. "They have the girl and are on their way. Should be here in a couple of hours. Maybe now we can find out where our elusive friends are and what they are up to."

The senator nodded in approval. Both then returned to the message received from the council.

CHAPTER 8

Fate

Cal sat silently looking out the windshield when he spoke, "Tork, why don't we rent a couple of motorcycles? Might be easier to move around on dirt bikes."

Tork thought for a moment and then answered Cal. "The ground around here is very sandy and loose, and there's a lot of hard rocky stuff as well. A good four-wheel might come in handy if we have to cut across country, and we wouldn't have any room for our equipment. Besides, we'll have water and food if we have to hide in the desert. I think maybe we should stay with the Jeep."

"That sign we just passed, Tork, it looks like the same one I saw the other night. Yeah, I'm almost positive. No, damn it. I am positive. That's where we turn when we come back. It's the one that will take us to that new road I told you about."

Tork reached down and reset the trip meter. "Well, we'll be able to find it easier when we return."

As they pulled into Shoshone, Tork started looking for a small motel, no frills, just some place to use as their headquarters. They didn't want to draw any attention to themselves, and he thought it would be safer if they were kind of out of the way—incognito as the word he wanted to use.

*****

The phone rang and an orderly picked it up. "Freedom Corporation."

"We've spotted them north bound, and we have surveillance cars on them. They're driving a green four-wheel. Looks pretty loaded. We will try to implant a sensor on them, if we get the chance to. We will advise you if successful."

The caller hung up, and the orderly redialed his phone.

It rang only once when the colonel answered, "Yes, what is it?"

"Colonel, the two men are heading north. Looks like they may have missed us. Maybe Mr. Varner can't find the turn off again. We'll continue to maintain surveillance."

"Thank you. Be sure I am made aware of their movements at all times. Understand?"

"Yes, sir," he replied.

The senator looked over to Colonel Duncan and spoke, "Colonel, with the two men located, I think it's time I returned to Washington. Please have Emory prepare our plane. Upon my return, I will be reporting to the committee. It looks like we can continue the count down. Let me know when you have them both in custody."

"Yes, sir. I'll let you know." The senator picked up the phone and dialed the operator.

"Yes?" came the reply. "May I help you?"

"Get me Emory Watson. He should be in the VIP quarters."

"Just a moment please."

The phone rang several times and a heavy voice answered, "Hello?"

"Emory, Senator Forthright. How soon can you have the plane ready for our return flight to Washington?"

"The plane's ready now, Senator. Shouldn't take more than a half hour for me to preflight her. Maybe less. Everything was ready when I put her to bed. How soon would you want to leave?"

"I'm ready now. Have you had enough rest, Emory?"

"Yes, sir. I'll call you when we're ready to leave."

When Emory opened the door to the operations room, he could see the returning Falcon through the windows of the underground hangar. The door to the aircraft opened and two men holding up a frightened girl came out. They helped her down a short ladder to the ground.

She looked unsteady, almost like they doped her up or something.

"May I help you?" Emory looked toward the Ops counter. A tall, smiling redhead looked at him and asked again, "May I help you?"

"Yes, the Falcon on the left. We'll be leaving within half an hour. I would like to make sure it's been serviced and in-flight is on board. I'll be back in twenty minutes to do a preflight on it. Okay?"

"Yes, sir. We'll have it ready for you."

Emory went to the desk, sat down, and pulled out his charts. He prepared a flight plan for the return flight, double-checked it, and took it to the attendant. "Like this filed for an immediate takeoff."

He then checked his charts a third time and recalculated his speed required to meet the deadline. It was essential he be back in Washington on time. Freedom Earned was getting closer, and nothing could happen to cause a delay at this crucial period. Far be it for him to be the cause of something going wrong at this point.

The attendant returned with the flight plan and nodded. Only thing left was to call the senator and tell him they were ready.

*****

It was just past midnight when Tork and Cal left their motel and headed south. It was a cool night with little traffic on the roads. As Tork drove, he went over his plans with Cal. It was important they were together on what might happen.

If the men that had chased Cal were there or someone else were to intervene, they would need to be ready to react quickly.

"Cal, I brought a camouflage tarp and a mountain tent. They're in the back. I'd like to set up an observation point on high ground so we can watch what goes on both at night and during the day. We have rations enough to cover us for a few days and plenty of water. It'll be hot, so we need to see if we can find a gully to pitch the tent and hide the Jeep. We're going to need to spread out and look for a place before daybreak if we want to be in position before the sun comes up. And we must be well hidden. I'd like to observe the area, the roads, and anything else we can before first light. Remember, we can see more under cover during the day than we can at night."

"What about weapons, Tork? Do we have any?"

"No, I thought it best we don't have anything that could go against us if this is a government project you stumbled into. Remember, they weren't trying to hurt you. Not once have we been shot at. Only when I tried to intervene and then they could have shot me, but they only knocked me out. No, they weren't trying to do that. Killing wasn't in their game plan. There is definitely something else going on, a real involvement of some kind."

"There, to your right, about two hundred yards up. Yeah, that's it, our turn off. I'm sure off it. Turn off there, Tork."

Tork checked his trip meter. Cal was right.

In the headlights, Tork could see the road start to narrow as Cal had described it to him. Tork turned off his headlights as they slowed, almost crawling as their vehicle cleared the brush. Tork suddenly felt the ride turn from a bumping hard one to a smooth one, almost like a new asphalt highway feels when you first drive on it.

"Boy, that's smooth. Hard to see in this light, but it looks like it's getting wider. We had better get off the road and park before we go any farther. And look for those sensors I suspect are out there. If they are, we can expect company real soon."

Cal said, "Well, I figured I had gone at least a mile when I decided to turn around. We haven't gone that far yet, so maybe we haven't tripped any of their sensors?"

Tork pulled off the road, engaged the four-wheel drive, and felt it dig in as they started into the sand. He was going slowly to keep the sound of the engine low. "Okay, Cal, we'll get out here and start looking for a place to hide the truck and ourselves."

Cal started getting his gear together, flashlights with a red filter lens, compass for each, canteens, shelter covers, sleeping bags, binoculars, night glasses, and some army MRE field rations.

"Tork, where in the world did you get the field rations?" Cal asked.

"Picked them up at a survival store in Concord. Thought I would be using them when I went hiking. Didn't expect to use them this way."

Tork and Cal dismounted from the vehicle and started looking for a good observation point on high ground if available. Both men started in opposite directions moving slowly, stopping at intervals, eyes straining to find what they needed. It was taking time. Both feared the unknown.

As Cal moved in toward what he thought was their meeting place, he felt a slight downward movement on his legs. He tried seeing ahead, but the red light could not give him any distance. He knew he was moving down. Suddenly he lost his footing, dropped to his knees, and started sliding down. He caught himself and realized he was in a deep depression in the ground. He stopped, stood up, and could see from the skyline he was about six to eight feet below ground level. It looked like a good place to park the Jeep, if there was an easy access in and out.

Cal checked his compass and started toward the rendezvous area. As walked, he could feel the gradual incline start, and he walked straight up into the area above him. He looked in the direction of the Jeep and tried to see it in the darkness. Then Cal hesitated to move. It was so still. Suddenly he could hear the sound of someone moving through the brush and sand, moving toward him. Cal lay down on the ground so he could use the dark sky as a focal point to see above. He could hear the movement getting close, and though straining his eyes, he could see nothing. Suddenly he felt his ribs caving in as a heavy weight fell on him, and a "damn it" in a familiar voice came to his ears.

"Get off me, Tork," he cried.

"Hell of a fall when you don't expect it," Tork replied.

Cal told Tork about his find and how they could move the truck down out of sight.

Tork looked around using his red light and felt Cal was right. *This could be a good place to hide the Jeep before daylight.*

Cal and Tork returned to the Jeep and moved it down into the gully, put the camouflage tarp over it, and started looking for an observation post where they could survey the entire area.

After an hour of searching, they found a knoll that set them up high enough to see completely around them. They dug in and piled rocks around their position with observation openings. It was tight, but it would do. They would need to lie down, and it would be difficult to turn, so facing in opposite directions was necessary.

They had everything they needed from the Jeep and both exhausted from their work required rest and sleep. Cal fell asleep, and Tork lay their thinking about the day's events and what lay ahead. Soon he would have the answers to their quest. Whatever spooked them should be revealed during their reconnaissance the next day. Tork looked up at the sky, clear, and bright with stars, a really black desert night. He yawned, and the day's excitement flooded in on him. His eyes shut and he was sound asleep.

CHAPTER 9

Conference

It was the sudden traffic in Emory's ears that brought him back to reality. Some airliner was asking permission to climb to a higher altitude so his passengers could be comfortable. Emory scanned his instruments, made a few minor changes to his controls, and rechecked his time and airspeed to ensure a timely arrival. He activated his autopilot, and all systems were operating normally. He got up and went aft to the passenger cabin.

"Everything okay, Emory?" the senator asked when he saw him enter the cabin.

"Senator, everything is fine. We should meet our ETA as planned."

The senator's laptop computer was open and all he needed to do was finish a code and hit enter on his keyboard. The modem would hum, and a coup d'état would begin.

Key commanders would act in unison at strategic bases scattered across the country, simultaneously moving into position with all the might and force at their command, deploying specially trained troops to intervene in state and federal agencies. They would put National Guard commanders that were not reliable under house arrest in all the selected states and sections. The House and Senate would be closed, and all members in both the House and Senate outside the coup would be placed under arrest as well. They would detain all at highly classified detention centers in a southwest state, arid and desolate, well out of harm's way. C-5 Galaxy and C-17 Globemaster

II aircrafts waited to transport them safely to the detention centers. Dividing them up would be necessary. Placing them into separate centers and commingling the weak with the hard-liners would be necessary to control them.

The council would step in and declare a state of siege and, for the good of the country, place it under military control. They planned to suspend all constitutional rights temporarily and then implement the new powerful laws, returning the country to the people.

They would relocate the United Nations out of the United States, and diplomatic ties with all nations would be temporarily suspended. All foreign-dominated industries would be seized. Controlling interests would be negotiated.

A specially trained drug task force would be hitting the drug czars where it hurt the most, right in their own backyards. Any intervention from the host government would bring massive retaliation from the rebel-led United States.

All known members of drug rings would be arrested along with their lawyers and jailed. The world would learn they meant business. The news would be censored, and the gangs in all our major cities would find it hard to operate working on chain gangs.

All subversive would be picked up and held in holding camps until the country is stable. It was time to act. After all freedom is earned, and it's something everyone has to work for to keep. Elements that were against the people and the disposed constitution would need to be returned with all amendments plus one. That one would guarantee it forever.

The senator's thoughts were interrupted when Emory announced, "Senator, we will be arriving soon another forty-five minutes if this light traffic keeps up a slight overcast with light rains in DC. We'll start our descent in about twenty minutes. Is there anything I can do for you now?"

"No, everything is fine. Please contact Michael on the scrambler and have him take over the doomsday alert status for me. Buzz me when he's up and online so I can shut down. Then get me the counsel coordinator. I need to set up a meeting when we arrive in Washington."

"Yes, sir." Emory grabbed a cold drink from the fridge and returned to the cockpit, scanned his instruments, and put on his earphones. He then listened to the air traffic controllers doing their thing as he approached his destination.

Michael had stayed at the base to interrogate the woman they had brought in to decide if a situation was developing that could jeopardize the plan. It was inherent all loose ends were tied up if they were going to be successful. His concentration was interrupted when the phone rang. He reached down and picked up the handset.

"Yes, I'll be right there. Make her comfortable. See that she's fed."

Michael put on his tie, sprayed a little cologne on, and slipped a 9 mm Smith and Wesson into his shoulder holster and then went out the door. It was time to see how much this pretty young woman knew.

CHAPTER 10

A Call to Arms

Lt. Comm. Eric Pride was completing his preflight when the voice from the open cockpit distracted him. "What was that, sailor?"

"Sir, change in your flight plan. You need to refile at Ops. They want you there. Pronto."

Pride secured his panels, unhooked his harness, and climbed out of his F-22 Raptor and headed for Operations. *This had better be good*, he thought. *I just wasted enough time to get me halfway to San Diego. Wonder what the change might be about.* It never occurred to him that it might be the beginning of the takeover, although he and many of his contemporaries were well involved in the change to restore the country to its true values and preserve the lost moral code due to the intervention of the United Nations.

They had recruited him several years earlier, and he was ready for a change. The country was becoming too socialistic, and it had to change. He knew they'd lost their freedom.

He walked into Operations and Bill Holland motioned him to the corner. "Looks like this might be it, Eric. Just received this from the courier." Bill handed Eric an envelope.

Eric opened it up and inside was a single piece of paper with two words on it, "Freedom earned." Eric nodded and left Operations, and he went directly to his quarters where he opened a briefcase in his locker and took out a sealed envelope.

Opening the envelope, he scanned the contents and went to a designated pay phone to make a local call. He let the phone ring three times and then hung up. Seconds later, his phone rang. A voice said, "Upon arrival at San Diego, you will be contacted with a destination. Follow instructions to the letter, and good luck." The phone went dead.

Eric looked up at the pale blue sky and a bright sun. *Perhaps today will be the rebirth of America*, he thought. Eric knew that across America, in every state, the word had gone out. He was ready. *Yes*, he thought, *everyone is ready*. The rebirth of a great nation was about to start. *God bless America, and God bless all of us*, he thought.

*****

Michael pulled up a chair and waved the security guard away. "Well, young lady, I hope everything is all right and you have been well taken care of?"

Diana Richmond looked at him. She was afraid and bewildered at what had happened to her. "Where am I? Why have I been kidnapped? Who are you people? I've done nothing wrong."

With panic in her voice and tears in her eyes, Michael knew there was nothing to fear from Diana, just an unfortunate citizen caught in the middle. "Relax, young lady. You have nothing to fear. We just need you to answer a few questions for us, and we'll arrange to take you home, okay?"

After a half hour of questions and tears, Michael was satisfied the intruder stumbled into the base area, and if they had not chased him, nothing at all would have happened. Now however, both of them would be found and held until Operation Freedom Earned was completed. Michael had read the dossier on Albertson, and he was very impressed. He had no doubts they were up against a highly trained individual with determination and resolve. *Yes*, he thought, *Albertson has guts*. He knew somewhere out there he was stalking them.

Michael picked up the phone and dialed.

"Control, Ted Johnson. May I help you?"

Michael spoke, "Have you picked up any unusual or strange occurrences on your sensors this evening, Ted?"

"No, sir. Just the usual animal activities out near the old highway."

"What kind of activity?" Michael asked.

"We only have a few sound sensors out there. It's desolate and sometimes we can hear small animals moving around. Nothing big though."

"Well, anything at all, animals or not, check it out!"

Ted replied, "Yes, sir," and hung up.

CHAPTER 11

The Net Tightens

Council Command Center
Washington DC
May 28

Admiral Sandini, a staunch muscular man, six feet and two inches in height, considered one of the nation's finest admirals, commander, First Central Atlantic Revolutionary Fleet (CFCARF), entered the room with two aides following closely behind him. "Good morning, gentlemen. Good to see you. Have we had any news yet on our missing infiltrators?"

"No, sir," an aide replied across the room. "We have lost contact with them. Duncan reports they are close to the desert base but is not sure just where they are at this point in time, sir."

The admiral replied, "Before I can move naval units into position, I must know if we have been compromised in any way. All naval deployments must appear normal. The movement of a carrier group must be done at the right time to avert suspicion and give us the edge we need. It's taken us a year to move all of our people into that group to ensure we have absolute control."

A senior council member looked up and spoke, "We know, Admiral. We've all had to work miracles this last year to help restore the country. Since the last election, we've had no choice but to plan on the restoration, not since Hitler has such a liberal socialistic government been elected to power anywhere in the world. I've almost

50

come to believe the administration and Congress will start regulating how we dress next, and they have already dictated our daily menus. It's like working for a brick wall. No matter what you do, that lop-sided House and Senate pass laws revoking our rights. Yes, gentlemen, we must make sure at all costs. There must never be a compromise, now or ever."

A senior member of the House spoke up, "Yes, I truly believe that old Frank and Harry would roll over in their graves if they knew what happened to the party."

Another member retorted. "I'll bet ole Ronnie's there with them, all shaking their heads in disbelief, especially after the merger with Canada and Mexico."

His remark was followed by laughter, and one member remarked, "Yes, and I'll bet there's a jar of jelly beans sitting on the table."

The door to the council opened. A young woman, Lieutenant Sanders, Naval Intelligence, entered and spoke, "Gentlemen, I just received a message from October One. The New Mexico base is fully operational with the detainee's quarters ready and waiting for their guests."

Senator Forthright cleared his throat and said, "Gentlemen, we are very close to saving the union. As they saved it once before through a great civil war, so can it be saved again? We must keep in mind that we are involved on a highway of civil war. As the South saw fit to break away from the union, we are trying to unite the union and return us to a God-fearing republic that has a government of the people, by the people, and for all the people—a government ruling the people. When we make laws making it a felony to have school prayer and one that legalizes the killing of unborn babies, we lose and our losses are our inability to control our freedom and to decide for ourselves as a representative republic what we want, not what the government dictates. Keep in mind, there should be no question as to where our destiny lies, and we therefore should not have to rely on the government to make all of our decisions for us. It is time to move the country forward as our Founding Fathers envisioned. 'To victory with freedom for all,' so to speak. Gentlemen, the time to tell the people is now. If all goes well in California, Operation Freedom

Earned will begin to forge ahead. The call to arms has been made, and all are waiting to move forward."

The senator looked at the admiral and said, "Admiral, do we have those squadrons of F-18 available? And can we rely on all the men?"

"Yes, sir. All of our men and women are ready. All are operational. Reserve and National Guard organizations are waiting for the word to move. All active-duty units were moved into launch position. We now have two carrier groups and two submarine squadrons ready to move on their initial targets. One carrier group is on station, and other submarines are on stationed in both the Atlantic and Pacific areas. Only a few of us have the full details to maintain complete secrecy. All units are tuned in to our new crypto codes and will operate only using them when we activate the coup. We are relatively safe on exposure at this time. In fact, we believe it is completely safe."

Looking over the assembled group, the senator spotted Tony Calbreath, head of the Arrest and Confinement group. "Tony, are you ready?"

"Yes, sir. As you heard, the base in New Mexico is ready and waiting. I have a fleet of cars ready for the initial retrievals here in Washington, with special groups ready to pick up those members that are out of the Washington area. We have three senators that are out of the country, and we have handpicked military groups there to retrieve and fly them to New Mexico. The infiltration is complete now."

"Thank you, Tony. Next item, I want those two loose gongs in California apprehended and questioned. At this point, we can't take chances. I want to know immediately when you have them in custody."

*****

Tork was between fantasy and reality, half asleep and half awake, struggling with the hard ground and fatigue, dozing and waking, looking at his watch only a few minutes from the last time he looked. He knew it was going to be a long hard day.

"Hey, Tork!" Cal was nudging him in the ribs. Dawn was just coming up over the mountain, and light was beginning to illuminate the valley floor.

Tork cried out to Cal in a low voice, "I thought I caught some movement at three o'clock." They earlier decided to use the clock to determine their position if they saw anything. The twelve would be north, the three would be east, the six would be south, and the nine would be west. Cal faced twelve o'clock and Tork faced six o'clock.

"It's moving to the right, about three o'clock. Should be moving around us. You might be able to see them in a few minutes. It was about 150 meters out. I couldn't make it out, but it looked like a small land vehicle," Cal continued.

Tork concentrated on his right side, straining his ears and eyes, hoping to see whatever it was. He picked up his night glasses and looked.

He saw nothing. He started to think Cal was seeing things and was about to say so when he saw them. There were three vehicles moving slowly, moving about fifty feet and stopping for a second or two, and then going on. He couldn't quite see what was going on. Then he realized the vehicles were not behind one another; they were about a hundred feet apart, running parallel together. The question in his mind was, *What are they doing?*

The vehicles continued to move across his line of vision toward their right side, slowing, stopping, and moving ahead. Tork was uneasy. Something about those vehicles troubled him. As they moved away, the sun came up over the mountain.

Tork was scanning the distant landscape and mountains for anything unusual, and he was coming up empty-handed. Cal had his binoculars trained on a distant object. It was blurred, but familiar, just a little too far to identify.

"Boy, what I wouldn't do for a satellite picture of that little sucker out there."

"What was that?" Tork asked, lost in thought.

"Tork, I have movement at three o'clock but just can't make it out." Cal blinked to clear his vision. "It is gone now. Looked like a large cylinder had come up out of the ground and then went down again. The heat waves are distorting everything, making it hard to focus."

Tork was having the same problems. The heat waves were so bad it was almost impossible to focus on any one object too long before you started getting dizzy from the dancing heat. "We're going to be out of water by tonight, Cal. We'll need to go down to the Jeep and fill our water jugs. It'll be a good time then to look at the object you saw. Did you get a fix on it?"

"Sorry, Tork. I lost it before I could get a distance. Just know the direction."

"Keep looking for it and get a compass reading if you can. Finding it will be easier."

"Okay, Tork," replied Cal. With his glasses on a short tripod, Cal aligned them to the last area he thought he saw the object. He then set his compass in line with it so he could get a true reading when they spotted it. "God, it's hot," he cried.

Tork rolled over on his back and wiped the sweat from his eyebrows. "Yeah, it's hot, Cal. If we can't come up with anything today, we'll go looking for those vehicles we've seen. I'm a little curious about what they were up to."

*****

Colonel Duncan entered the equipment garage looking for the security team they had sent out early in the morning. As he started crossing over to the office, a tall man in desert dress hailed him. "Colonel, just a moment please."

The colonel stopped and turned. He was in luck as the man shut the door on a Humvee and walked over to him. "Colonel, we set up ground bugs every meter in three rows so they all intersect each other, about a meter apart. Believe me, sir, there is no chance in hell they can slip by us from the old road all the way to the strip and the access doors and entrances. We've run a zigzag. If they manage to get by one of them, they'll walk right into the other one in front."

Colonel Duncan looked at the security officer. "What happens when you pick them up?"

"Well, Colonel, we'll be able to pinpoint their direction of travel, and the computer will predict their possible destination, and we'll be there when they arrive."

The colonel looked pleased. "I want to know the minute you get a reading. No matter where or what I'm doing, you call me. Understand?"

"Yes, sir," he replied.

*****

Night had fallen and the cool night air from the desert was starting to chill Tork's bones. "Cal, it looks like we're in luck. Little light from the big cheese tonight."

"Yeah, I've had to use my night glasses to see anything at all," replied Cal.

Earlier Cal had been scanning for the cylinder he had seen during the day, and his vigilance had paid off. It was almost dark when it came out of the ground again, and this time the earth had cooled enough for him to see through the heat waves and pinpoint the target. It was about two hundred meters out and had stayed up more than two minutes, just enough time for a bearing check and distance.

Tork crawled out from under the enclosure and stood up, stretching out the kinks and looking around the area at the same time. "Come on, Cal. Let's move out. Maybe we can spot that cylinder of yours and find out what those vehicles were up to."

Cal secured his gear, grabbed the night glasses, and stood up. He too stretched out the kinks from the long day and got his bearing from his compass. Turning toward the direction of the cylinder, he said, "Tork, I figured it to be about three to four hundred yards, just to the right of my position. We should be able to walk right up to its location. It should be easy to find, whatever it is. I think it's sitting down in the ground and raised hydraulically. We should find a good part of it sticking up just out of the ground when we find it."

Tork grunted in approval and started toward the last area they had seen the vehicles earlier in the day. Now maybe they could find out just what they were up to and what all that stop and starting was about. "Come on, Cal. Let's check the trucks we saw first, and then we can see what that cylinder is."

The two of them spread out about fifty feet apart and started walking toward the area they had seen the trucks. Carefully, and with their night glasses on, they scanned ahead hoping they would not run into a trip wire or another sensor out there waiting for them. Tork found the first set of tire tracks and motioned Cal over to them. They walked slowly along the tracks and could see where the vehicles had stopped and they started again. It appeared no one had dismounted from the vehicles; they just seemed to stop and then start again.

They had gone about hundred yards and Tork spoke, "Cal, I'm going to move over to the next set of tracks. We've only seen this set and they've been made by only one vehicle. We saw three out here this morning. I'm guessing they were abreast and not in line. Just seemed to look that way to us. Give me a few minutes to find them, and then we can follow them together."

Cal had walked another hundred yards seeing nothing unusual when he spotted a canister just to his left, sticking up out of the ground. It looked like a can at first, and then he noticed what looked like an antenna sticking out of the top of it. He stopped and adjusted the focus on his night glasses. It was not a can. He walked up to it and could see it was some kind of a device he hadn't seen before. He turned and made sure his flashlight had its red cover over the lens, and then he flashed it toward Tork.

Tork had been scanning around him and had been unable to see anything unusual when he saw Cal's red light flashing on and off. He stopped and then crossed over to Cal. "What's up, Cal? Find something?"

"Yeah, look down here by my feet. What do you make of it, Tork?"

"Damn," Tork almost shouted out the word. It's a radio-controlled prox sensor, probably infrared and sound-detecting. "So that's what they were doing. They were planting sensors around the perimeter. We better get out of here fast. No doubt they know we're here, and right now they know where we are. Let's move toward your cylinder area. It's away from these sensors and we can lose them in that direction."

Tork and Cal turned toward the location of the cylinder Cal had seen and started walking keeping low and in the shadows of the night.

The night had cooled considerably, and they both were starting to feel the desert night chill. The sky was clear and the heavens were filled with stars. Cal looking up and could see the enormity of the heavens and couldn't help commenting on its beauty to Tork.

Tork looked up and saw the majesty of them all. "Cal, you really surprise me from time to time. In the most desperate times of your life, you always seem to find the good. Here we are in the middle of the desert looking for God knows what and you take the time to look over the sky, when you should be looking over this cold empty desert."

"Yeah, I know, Tork. Just can't help but see great things when they are staring me in the face. You know, Tork, it's cold and were tired and we don't seem to be getting what we want, but I can still smile and smell the fresh air out here. And with all my troubles, I have you as a friend. Thanks, Tork."

"Yeah, well I…kind of like you too, Cal. Now let's find these renegades and fix this problem. We're running out of time and we don't know who is after you, do we?"

*****

Security had picked them up almost as soon as the coming out of the ground, as they started walking toward the sensor line. Radar operations had brought up a ground sweep radar unit to track them, and they were now being followed electronically. Every step was monitored, and the information was being fed into the computer. There, every move was anticipated. Tork and Cal were being careful, moving slowly, deliberately. You could see the blip on the screen stop, pause, and then move again.

Yes, they had two very cautious bleeps on the radar screen.

The officer looked over to the sergeant and in a low, polite, unrestrained voice filled with confidence said, "Call Colonel Duncan.

Tell him they're on their way and ask him if he would like to be at the observation cylinder when we apprehend them."

"Yes, sir," he replied.

The colonel was just getting ready to call Washington when the phone rang. "Yes.... Very good. I'll be right there. Don't do anything until I arrive. Understand?"

The sergeant returned to the operations room and informed the officer in charge the colonel was on his way and to do nothing until his arrival. The officer nodded and watched the progress of the two bleeps on the screen as they moved across ground toward the observation post.

The colonel arrived and said, "Raise the observation post up just out of the ground, just enough for them to stumble over it or see it so they can look it over. Have the external mic on and two men armed in the post. As soon as they look it over, raise it up and have the men apprehend them and bring them to me. I'll be in my office. Then find their transportation and equipment and impound it."

"Yes, sir," he said.

They watched and charted Tork and Cal's movements, observing each step they took. They were within feet of the cylinder, and the solider watching the RadarScope raised his arm, hand closed, and his first finger pointing up. Suddenly he dropped his hand and exclaimed in a load voiced, "Now!" A hand activated a switch button, and hydraulics started to hum. The cylinder with occupants moved up to catch the prey.

*****

Tork and Cal moved very carefully across the sand in the direction of the cylinder. Tork had been searching ahead, looking for more sensors, finding none. He felt they were safe, hoping the observers had seen nothing more than rabbits moving around their sensors.

Cal spoke, "We should be getting close, Tork. And if my calculations are correct, we should see something soon."

Just as Cal had finished speaking, Tork suddenly fell forward. "What the hell was that?" Tork had tripped over something he failed to see in his night glasses. He stood on top of a large rock when it suddenly started to rise out of the ground, knocking him down again. This time, he rolled over and out of the way as a large cylinder rose up out of the ground.

As he looked up, startled, Cal caught a glimpse of a door sliding in on the side of the cylinder, and before he could say anything at all, someone switched on floodlights illuminating them. Two uniformed men stood there with M-16s aimed at them.

"Gentlemen, welcome. We have been expecting you. Please raise your hands and don't try anything heroic. We only want to ask you a few questions."

They handcuffed, searched, and took Cal and Tork into the cylinder.

Tork looked over at Cal and knew at this point it would be smart to play along with them. Maybe now they could get a few answers. In any case, it seemed they were getting in deeper and deeper.

Cal and Tork entered the cylinder. It was much larger than Cal had suspected; it could hold a dozen men easily. It had a small ladder going up about eight feet to a second deck above them. It looked like some kind of observation deck. Cal could hear the valves open and the pulse of the hydraulics as the cylinder began to silently move down into the earth. Well, he thought, wherever they were going, it was a plus, for that was the reason they were here. To find out just what this was all about and why they chased him all the way to the bay area.

The observation unit dropped into the earth, and the door opened. The two men ordered both Cal and Tork out. As they walked through the doorway, a stern man with purpose and obvious authority met them.

Colonel Duncan casually invited both men to follow him and then led them into an interrogation room. He had their handcuffs removed and instructed them to sit.

"What the hell is going on and why have we been taken prisoner?" Tork demanded.

Colonel Duncan spoke, "Why, gentlemen, you're not prisoners. Your guests, and while we're at it, perhaps you can tell us why you are on a military reservation without permission. As far as what the hell is going on, perhaps you can tell me."

Tork realized they were in the hands of expert military personnel and knew they had intruded into something very big.

Colonel Duncan smiled at Tork and commented, "Interesting, Mr. Albertson, that you have such an abundance of cigarette lighters hidden on you! Are you an advent smoker or did you have something else in mind? Perhaps like sabotage?

*****

Council Command Headquarters

"Gentlemen, I have good news. We have the two men in custody and are ready for action. The time draws close for our freedom. In the next few hours, everything will be ready, and we can start to return the country back to its citizens and get rid of the liberal left. If we want to remain a viable part of the world, then we must act. It's obvious that congress will do nothing more than the president and his cohorts allow them to do. All bases have reported they are ready. All combat commanders have signaled ready to go. All receiving bases have the heat on and accommodations ready for their guests.

"The time is here, gentlemen. Countdown has started. We have been assured through negotiations with big business that they will return to these shores if and when reality is here. They have given us a list of all laws that have financially forced them out of the country to manufacture their products in foreign lands. If we are successful, they will reopen their factories here and put America back to work. To do this, it will be necessary for the people to realize the need for the new laws and to see the necessity for change.

"We have organized a cohesive group who will be responsible for ensuring this information is properly given to the people. We have infiltrated the major media groups, which can be used for this purpose. Are there any outstanding problems in any area that we will need to correct before implementation? If there are, let's have them now so we can get the field teams going and resolve them. We don't want any delays or miscalculations at this point. Our teams are waiting."

No one spoke. Everyone seemed ready.

"Okay then let's meet back here at 0300 hours. By then Colonel Duncan should have his problem completed, and we should be ready for our second deployment prior to zero hour."

With those words, the group silently returned to their duties and on each of their minds, *Treason*.

CHAPTER 12

Roundup

Central Intelligence Agency
Langley, Virginia
0024 Hours

Bill Loadman, director of Internal Security, was sleeping soundly when the telephone started to ring. It had only rung several times, and he had it in his hand. "Hello, Loadman here."

"Sorry to wake you, sir. This is Mark Osborne. We have something strange going on that doesn't make sense. We need your help."

"What is it, Mark?"

"Sorry, sir. It's so big we can't trust even a secured line. You will need to come in here. I'll send a car for you, sir."

Bill hung up the phone and dressed rapidly and told his wife there was an emergency and would call her later. Bill knew it would only take fifteen minutes for the car to arrive for him, but it seemed like only minutes had gone by when there was a knock on the door. He opened it and two agents stood before him.

"The car's here, sir. Are you about ready to go?"

"Yes, let's go." Walking to the car, Bill started asking questions about the emergency.

"Sorry, sir. We don't know all the details. You'll need to get them from Mark. All we know is it's big."

The car pulled away from the curb and was headed toward CIA headquarters. The two agents were busy talking about the office, the new president's latest proclamation, and the cutbacks the agency was getting and how it was going to affect them and national security. Then the car made a detour and was headed south of the agency.

Bill looked up and realized they were heading in the wrong direction. A cold tingling sensation went down his spine, and the hair stood up on the back of his neck. Yes, something was wrong but not at Langley. It was in the car he was riding in. He slipped his hand inside his coat and onto the butt of his gun. Suddenly he felt the hard nose of an automatic sticking into his side.

"Sorry, sir. I'll have to have that. Please take it out slowly with two fingers and give it to me."

Bill pulled the gun out and gently dropped it into the agent's hand. "You want to tell me what's going on here?"

"Sorry, sir. You'll find out soon enough."

The car slowed and turned off the main road onto a winding dirt road, stopping at the end of it. There standing silently was a navy helicopter. When the men boarded the aircraft, the pilot started the engines, and within minutes, they were airborne.

*****

Diana was sitting on the edge of her bed, worried about her mother and Tork, what had happened to him, where he was, or if she would ever see him again. Who were these people and what were they up to? Question after question went through her mind. She had asked for her mother to be notified that she was all right, but not knowing what was really going on, she didn't know if they would call her. Anything to calm her mother's fears.

*****

Colonel Duncan looked at both men. "What am I going to do with you two?"

Cal looked over to Tork, smiled, and said, "Send us home!"

Tork chuckled and said, "Yeah, you know, give us the keys to the car and we'll be on our way."

"Ah, gentlemen, I wish it were that easy, but unbeknownst to you, you have stumbled on a project that will change the face of this country and return it to the people, to Americans."

Tork sat silently for a few moments. Then he stood up, faced the colonel, and said, "There is no place in this country we cannot go or anything at all we cannot do. How can you claim you are giving America back to the people? We already have it."

"Tork—May I call you Tork?" The colonel went on not waiting for Tork to reply. "This country has undergone extensive change over the past several years in all parts of it. You can travel, yes. You are, however, restricted in many ways. Your constitutional rights have been taken away. European forces have entered your country and taken by force your personal weapons. No, I don't think you already have it, Mr. Albertson. Not at all!

"In addition, the country's revenue system has forced all the most productive corporations out of the country. We have lost an immense number of jobs to this exodus, and there are millions of Americans that were once the envy of the world now living in substandard conditions. A third of our country is on Supplemental Nutrition Assistance Program (SNAP) Electronic Benefit Transfer (EBT) cards. Once the greatest country in the world, we are now on the verge of becoming a third-world economic country. I say becoming when I should say we are now a third-world country. We are only steps behind Russia and others.

"As foreign countries see us growing weaker, they prepare to move in and take over. The war on terrorism and the influx of the Arab warring nations have caused the world to see us a paper tiger with no fangs. Europe wants to control not only all of Europe but also the world, with both the EU and Islam bidding for the chance to do just that."

Colonel Duncan gazed at both Tork and Cal evaluating them carefully. Satisfied at what he observed, he continued, "We have no desire to control any nation. These factors have proven to us that we are losing ground. The president's latest concession to the United Nations has given control over this country to the United Nations with absolute power. Our total law enforcement in this country is in the United Nations' hands.

"If there is a riot in Los Angles, they will have the right to send in UN troops, and under the conditions of the law, we cannot intervene. They have integrated the US Department of Education with the United Nations to act as an example to the world of how they too can be rewarded by adhering to the United Nations' authority. The new world order has not lived up to the standards expected by the framers of the constitution. Did you know that as we talk, there is a treaty being drawn up by the president to ship American technicians and craftsman to nations such as Africa, India, and others that lack the trade and crafts to build up their nation's industries? Sounds good, doesn't it? But there's a hitch—those that go will be forced to go as a condition for their families to receive their welfare. No work, no eat. Yes, Tork, you can go where you want to now, but how about tomorrow? In-country passports are being readied for internal travel control as we speak."

Tork looked at the colonel, thinking about his statement and what had been happening over the past few years. The Congress was lopsided, and the party in power had caused most of the industrial base to move to Canada, Mexico, and China. Hell, half the Mexicans in California, Nevada, Arizona, and Utah had started moving back to Mexico for the jobs that moved south. Maybe this man had a point. Those that were staying were getting full amnesty and could stay with citizenship on the way.

"Maybe you're right and maybe not," Tork said. "I would have to see more than just trust in what you have said to join in a treasonous plot that is obviously going on here. What have you got, Colonel, a couple of hundred men here, planning and plotting? Come on, Colonel. Once the army gets wind of this, you're gone."

The colonel smiled and pushed a button on his desk.

An orderly entered the room. "Yes, sir," he said to the colonel.

"Take this young man over to the holding area and make him comfortable. Give him a room with a view."

The orderly moved over to Cal and handcuffed his hands behind his back. "Sorry, sir. Just a precaution." He then led Cal away.

The colonel looked at Tork and thought for a second. "I'm sending you to meet a very special guest of ours just to let you know we have a few more involved than you think we do. I'll introduce you to them after you have met our special guest."

He instructed the guard that had been standing by during the interrogation to take Tork over to VIP quarters, and he gave him a room number on a slip of paper that would make two people happy.

After Tork left, the colonel picked up the phone and put it on the scrambler and called Washington.

"Ah, Senator, Colonel Duncan here. I have good news, sir. Both intruders have been interrogated. As we thought, it was a fluke. One had stumbled onto the base by mistake. Had we laid low and had not attempted to apprehend him, he would have turned around and left. It seems he had car trouble and was looking for a town and a garage. Bad decision by security. We have them both now in custody and will hold them until this is over."

A curt reply and a keep all informed was made, and the game was still in play and they were moving closer to Freedom Earned.

The guards led Tork through a number of underground tunnels past a well-orchestrated group of well-trained men and women, all in civilian clothing, but they were military. Tork was looking, noting, and thinking he had made a bad estimate on strength. He knew he was off by a couple of hundred or more. This place was too big for such a small number of personnel.

They arrived at a corridor that was softly lit and paneled in a medium oak, with doors and peek holes. *This must be the VIP area*, he thought. It had crossed Tork's mind he was going to a holding cell when they told him they were on the way to the VIP quarters.

The guard stopped at a door halfway down the corridor, inserted a key, and knocked several times before he opened it. He looked inside before entering. He knew his business.

Tork could not see inside, but heard the guard say something to a woman inside. He came out, removed Tork's handcuffs, and told him to go in.

Tork looked at the man, wondering why he had joined such a perilous venture. He then walked through the door and entered a large spacious apartment. There sitting on the sofa was Diana. She looked up and seeing Tork burst into a smile, tears running down her cheeks. She was so happy to see him that she balled like a baby.

Tork took her in his arms and held her. "What happened? I left you at home, so how did you get here?"

Diana told him everything about her abduction, the injection, waking up inside a hangar, and her interrogation by the colonel. "What's going on, Tork? Who are these people?"

Tork looked at her, thinking how he was going to tell her they were the middle of a coup. "Diana, it seems Cal stumbled into a plot to overthrow the government, and now it appears we are in the middle of it. At this point, I don't know just what to think, but they do have a strong argument. And if they pull it off, the people just might buy it."

Diana looked stunned at Tork, her mouth open, unable to mutter even a sound.

Tork sat on the seat next to her and started to think. His thoughts went to the present conditions, to what was happening in California. The rights of the people were slowly being abolished as congressional changes were made. They were being made at lower levels. State, counties, and cities were all engaged in reducing the rights of each citizen. Slowly and secretly, they were taking them away. The gay marriages and other liberal changes were destroying society. A little unnoticed law is changed, and only those directly involved see it happen. It did no good to complain; the people had arrived at a conclusion that if it didn't concern them, they didn't care. Life went on.

People complained about not having jobs, listening to the president as he claimed everything was the fault of the past, and they were all working diligently to improve and make it all right again. Soon everyone would work again. They were at peace, and the world was moving toward a united world, a new world where all would be equal and all could share together. No one could point to another and say that they had more or less. Only in the old Soviet Bloc nations did you see a difference. They had lived through it and knew what freedom meant. They knew they could only earn and not take freedom for granted. They knew there could never be equality, that there would always be those who could create more for themselves, and if they couldn't do it legally, then they would do it anyway they could.

Yes, there were millions out there that were ready for a change, a change that would bring back yesterday, return the industries, and open the mills and factories. Yes, it was time investments were made by all, to bring them back and put America back in control.

The military was being used to control the hot spots in the world and to enforce the will of the United Nations. The United Nations, as usual, was ineffective and had to rely on the United States and the European Union to bring the hot spots under control. Then the United Nations moved in to police.

Tork's thoughts filled his mind. Soon the president would give them the power to police. They would be controlled by those who could not govern themselves, a council controlled by countries that were not long ago warring on one another and still unable control their own. The United States of Europe was controlling the UN General Assemblies and Security Council. They had called for and had all veto powers stripped from the members. Only the secretary-general had the veto. They had managed to control the United Nations. All wondered what was next.

A complete retreat from the laws of the land and a surrender of what was left of the constitution—not much left of it, Tork thought. It had been in the papers before all this happened. Tork remembered it, a limit on or to stop anyone from leaving the country without government approval had been passed by Congress and the president had signed it. A rider on the bill had allowed their borders to be opened through the United Nations. Anyone wishing to enter the United States only had to petition the United Nations for entry. They had given the authority to the world to enter and do what they wanted without regard to US law or its citizens. The amnesty to all who entered gave them the right to citizenship and the welfare that went with it too.

The United Nations had the power to arrest, try, and incarcerate any citizen.

They answered the question when the left-leaning leaders loaded the Supreme Court with liberals that struck down their immigration laws as unconstitutional, and they were forced to accept everyone from all nations that thought their governments were unfair. Yes, the Caribbean had flooded the east coast of Florida with Haitians. Florida had become the state of three languages. The government had decreed that English, French, and Spanish would have to be used as official languages. Many people had left the state in chaos. It was difficult for harmony to exist.

It had become a forgotten state; only the rich could afford to visit there, and their numbers were becoming smaller and smaller. No, the United Nations had control of who could enter. Once again American people were betrayed by the administration and the Congress.

Thought after thought of what was happening was going through Tork's mind. The loss of family farms, industries being forced out of the country because of law and high taxes, and mandatory health imposed on small business forced thousands of them to close, putting thousands out of work.

Tork hadn't noticed what was going on. He seldom read a paper or watched television. Subconsciously it was all collecting, coming together, bit by bit, and he was beginning to understand what these people were doing. He was thinking it might be time to join in this new American revolution, a civil war of wars.

Tork turned to Diana and began to explain everything to her. It might be time for them all to stand up and be counted. After all, they caused it with a vote, but how were they deceived? This was one answer they needed to fully understand. What had happened and why?

CHAPTER 13

A Moment of Truth

Admiral Sandini Flagship

The helicopter with America's top spy on board was approaching an aircraft carrier in the Atlantic, about 180 miles southeast of Virginia.

Bill Loadman had fallen asleep after the chopper had been airborne for a short time. He'd learned to sleep under stress, knowing the importance of rest and what it did for his strength. He yawned and started to stretch. But as his arms went up, the men watching him raised their automatics and cautioned him about any sudden movements. He was grateful for no restraints; being handcuffed would have been unbearable.

He looked out a dark window and could see the lights on the ship looming up on him and could hear the sound of the radio coming from the pilot's earphones. He couldn't tell what was said, but he knew they would be landing soon. Whatever the ship?

Whoever she belonged to, he would know soon.

The chopper came in, following the lights signaling him. As they flew closer to the ship, Loadman could see they were landing on a carrier. The only question in his mind was, *Whose?*

The chopper landed easily, and the engine was shut down as soon as she touched the deck. As the door slid open, a familiar voice spoke out to him. "Welcome, Bill, to Freedom Earned."

Loadman climbed out to greet the admiral, one of his oldest and dearest friends. "What's going on, Sandini?"

"Come with me and I'll explain it to you. It's something you and I have discussed many times, something that I could not accept, but you were preaching."

The man from the CIA looked at the admiral for a few seconds. "Okay, Admiral. What's this all about? Why have you brought me here?"

Admiral Sandini's reply was curt and to the point. "Your men brought you, Bill, and we'll discuss it in my office." The two men left the flight deck accompanied by two agents.

*****

Diana and Tork were cuddling together when the knock came at the door. Tork rose up to answer it.

Colonel Duncan and two guards were standing there. "Well, well, well, Colonel, long time no see!" Tork said.

The colonel smiled, discarding Tork's sarcasm, and entered the room with one guard staying outside. "Mr. Albertson, I would like to show you—both of you—what we are doing here and why it was necessary to apprehend the three of you, why Mr. Varner was chased across California, and why it was necessary to bring you both back here to this location."

"Well, Colonel, we just can't wait, can we, Diana?" The sarcasm was cold and cutting. "I would love to know just what Cal could have possibly learned that would cause such a shake-up and why we are being held prisoners."

"Held prisoners?" With a tone of sarcasm in his voice, Duncan continued, "No, Mr. Albertson. A guest would be more like it. After all, you were the one that trespassed, were you not? As for Mr. Varner, you might consider him a national security risk. After all, he ran from a US Air Force secured facility, didn't he? You realize we do have the right to protect this country from terrorists and saboteurs. Now, Mr. Albertson, let's get down to business, shall we? After the grand tour you both are about to take and you verbalize your opinion of what you see and learn, then and only then will we discuss your future. Until then, let's take a walk and see what we are doing here and why."

They all left the room and Colonel Duncan escorted them through the underground corridors. He pointed out different areas of interest and responsibilities of the military and some of the lesser secure systems in the complex.

He showed them the underground hangars with warplanes ready for launch. The size of the facility amazed both Tork and Diana. Tork looking closely at everything was also evaluating each and everything seen and said. As the entered the operations room, Tork could see why they were caught so easily. The surveillance monitors covered the entire wall. As a rabbit moved, you could hear each thump on the ground.

The colonel picked up on Tork's thoughts. "We heard you crawling out from under your hiding place before we saw you and followed every step you took."

Tork glanced at him. "Yeah. We found your sensors after we'd been walking. That's dirty pool, Colonel. From what I see, we are below ground level, and I suppose there's a first-class runway up there some place, right?"

The colonel motioned him to a plotting board of the United States. "In each state, you can see blue markers. Each one of these markers represents PPP. That's a person pickup point. The red, yellow, and green represent destinations. The black ones represent control points. At each control point is a pickup team and a forwarding group. When the time comes, each team will act on the PPP in their area and deliver them to the forwarding group. At this time, the PPPs will be placed aboard the aircraft and flown to the destination according to their position or office they hold.

"Mr. Albertson, they will be incarcerated until we have restored the freedoms that have been taken away from the people and a new amendment to the constitution written to ensure we cannot lose them again. In short, we are going to have a revolution."

The words stunned Tork and Diana. "You must be mad," Tork said. "How in the world do you expect to accomplish this? It's impossible."

"Tork, we have members in every government position from both parties. We have all been appalled by what has happened to us and what is coming. We can no longer stand by and watch this country be destroyed from within. No enemy has brought us to our knees. The British Empire or any other nations could subdue us, but through careful manipulation, these people have done just that. Foreign troops have entered our country and disarmed our citizens. Therefore, sir, we now stand on a pinnacle of soiled destruction. We have given up liberty after liberty, and the United Nations has more power in the country than our military.

"They run the education system from the United Nations and you can see the results of that in our streets. The time has now come for patriots to rise up and throw off the shackles that bind us. Soon we will strengthen the laws, abolish the dope trade, and remove the United Nations and foreign troops from our soil. We will restore moral values to our country.

"In addition, we will intervene in the sovereignty of every foreign country that's supporting the drug trade and the new world order. We are prepared to act on these subjects. Members of Congress that have joined us have prepared legislation that will give us the power we need. Foreign countries doing business here will reduce their control.

"The majority of all corporations will be owned by Americans. Foreign countries that own stock in any company doing business here will sell it or we will seize it. Corporate managers will follow the law. Insider dealing on any level will be a felony, and those who perpetrate it will be tried and jailed. We will require all states to pass sunshine laws. All government legislation must be in the open for all to see. There are so many facets to this it would take hours to explain and to certify. In short, we are taking back America. Freedom is earned, and we plan to earn every bit of it."

Tork had thought about this himself over the last couple of years, but like so many, he had cussed at the changes but did nothing change it back. Yes, he had often thought about doing the same thing, but he knew there was nothing he could do. Instead, he went along with all the other sheep.

He looked at the colonel and said, "How do you join this clambake?"

The colonel smiled. "Welcome aboard, Captain." He reached into his inside coat pocket and handed Tork a single sheet of paper.

Tork looked at it. "You must have been very sure of this, Colonel."

Diana looked confused. "What are you looking at, Tork?"

He handed her the sheet of paper.

Diana took it and started to laugh. "Well, Captain, welcome to the new army," she said.

They had recalled Tork to active duty and his orders read he was assigned to an army delta unit in California. "Well. No wonder we had problems with you guys. I suppose you have a couple dozen SEALS around here too," said Tork.

"Oh, we have much more than that, Captain."

Tork turned to the colonel. "What has happened to Cal? I don't want to see anything happen to him. I think we can use him. His views are the same as mine and Diana's."

The colonel turned to the guards. "Take the Captain to C Corridor so he can talk with his friend." He turned to Diana. "Please come with me, young lady, and let me fill you in on what's going on."

Diana was pleased the colonel was including her in this clambake too. It meant a lot to her.

*****

The admiral had laid out all the basic plans and had introduced Bill Loadman to the projected B plans and what was going to happen. He invited Bill to join them and become part of this restoration of freedom and rights. Bill was in full agreement, but felt he would be a traitor.

"I'm sorry, Admiral," he said. "I cannot fight against my own people. I agree something must be done, but this is too much even for me. It's madness. You will all end up in prison."

The admiral chuckled. "Bill, there is not enough prisons in the country or even in this continent to hold all of us. This project will touch almost every household in the country. It would be impossible for it to happen anywhere else but here. Remember freedom is earned and the Supreme Court stole it from us when they agreed with the merger."

The admiral looked at his friend closely. "Bill, you must consider that we have a great deal of House and Senate members that are working for us, and we expect many more to join our cause. I know how you feel, and I know that you should join with us. If you fear for you or your family, rest assured you feel no differently than the Founding Fathers did when they went to war with King George. Remember, they were Englishmen that felt the Crown had let them down. So they took it into their own hands to address what they thought was wrong. From their efforts, the greatest super power on earth emerged. Now it has been subjugated by her citizens, men and women that have sold her out to the new world order, to the United Nations.

"With or without you, we will regain this country for every citizen. We will once again provide this country with its constitution, as written by our Founding Fathers. Only those changes taking away our rights will be removed. The constitution as written and honored on September 11, 2001, will be honored. The merger with Canada will and Mexico will be repealed until the people in the United States can vote on a referendum."

At that moment, a lieutenant commander on the bridge called the admiral and reported a priority message had been received. Two words had been transmitted. The message read, "Freedom earned." The admiral smiled and said, "All is well. Carry on as instructed."

The admiral addressed Bill. "You think about it, Bill, and then you tell me you still want to work for the UN International Police, because if we lose, that's where you'll be, that is, if they decide not to put you into a dark hole in Brussels or Calcutta or another hellhole. Remember, at this moment, thousands of men and women are getting ready to do battle with your government. Anyone else wanting to get involved, well, they all know where they stand, and that to win their freedom, it must be earned. Wouldn't you feel better knowing that you'd be working with them and for them and not against them?"

Bill Loadman looked at this great admiral of the navy, and he knew he was sincere. "Admiral, I must talk with my wife, and then maybe I can make a decision that would guide us both to our destiny. You have made a strong case for this, and I need to talk it over with her."

The admiral smiled and left the good man to his thoughts. He went directly to the communications center and sent a coded message to Washington. It read, "Pick up Mrs. Loadman and transport to this location immediately."

*****

Senator Stoppell had been working late with his staff on a proposed bill to plug holes in the Federal Equality Health and Pharmacy Plan that had been passed and signed into law. It had excessive cost overruns due to abuse and lack of positive controls to save it. The senator had been working on the new bill. An advocate of the new world order, he was highly respected by the president, one of the new Americans that believed in the power of the United Nations.

The bill was designed to increase taxes to pay for it. It was easier to increase spending than to correct the abuse and prosecute the offenders. The increase in taxes would affect everyone's income. No one would be exempt. The cradle-to-grave medical care had to be preserved at all costs, no matter who was hurt. The United Nations had decreed it, the president demanded it, and the new government approved it. As the senator was getting into his car in the underground parking lot, two men approached him. As the senator closed the door, one man put up his hand and motioned the senator to lower his window so they could speak.

The senator reached over and pushed his left front window button and the window slid silently down. "Yes, gentlemen. What can I do for you?"

The one man smiled. In a soft voice, he asked, "Excuse me, are you Senator Stoppell?"

"Yes," he replied. "What can I do for you?"

"Sorry to bother you, sir, I'm agent Parker and this is agent Clarkson. We're from the bureau." Parker opened a small leather folder he was holding and let the senator see his credentials. "You have a priority emergency meeting with the president, sir. There seems to be something going on, and the president has asked the bureau to pick you up, sir, and several of your staff. Seems there's some real problems coming up on the med bill and the president wants a high-level meeting tonight. He doesn't want anything to go wrong with it at this stage. If you don't mind, sir, we have a car ready to take you over to Andrews for the flight to Camp David. If you like, sir, you can call your family from the helicopter on our way there."

"That's great, but I'm really tired. Can we do this in the morning?"

"I'm afraid not, sir. The president needs you immediately."

"Well, I've got everything with me on the new bill, and this will give me a chance to go over it with him before we finalize it. Okay, tired or not, let's go." The senator got out of his car and locked it, and the three men entered a bureau car and departed for what he thought was a ride to the base and Camp David.

All over Washington, the same scenario was going on. At each selected target, they were picked up and taken to a plane or a heli-copter for transport. Before the sun was to rise on another day, all the selected targets had to be picked up and at their destinations or on their way to the holding camps. At the same time, the chosen military units were moving into position throughout the country. State governments were being silently taken over. Selected governors were picked up by federal agents and were on their way to camps where they would be kept away from other members of the House and Senate. Naval units had moved into position in both oceans. Carrier task groups were standing offshore.

The members of the House and Senate that were part of the revolutionary council were standing together to make the announce-ment at 6:00 a.m. in Washington DC. The country would awaken to a new, free, and brighter nation.

At the precise time of the announcement, a delta assault group would be hitting three known drug cartel bases in Mexico and Latin America. They would hunt down and bring back the drug lords to the United States for trial. Special selected ground forces, air, and naval units were moved to a position just off Panama. Should the cartel's host countries try to intervene in American operations, they would be smashed. They had planned everything to the last detail.

Both air and naval units had targeted military bases and depots in each country. If need be, they would destroy them. The council was determined to stop all drug traffic into the country. The first proclamation would be to guarantee all basic constitutional rights based on the 1941 laws. They would enact all civil rights laws to protect all citizens based on their national origin, color, and gender. They would revoke all state same-sex marriage laws and allow companion laws to prevail with states granting spousal-type benefits. There would be no homosexual allowances within the military.

They would recess the Supreme Court and then hold the justices at a secret base until the revolutionary government was in complete control of the country. They expected that there would be areas that would fight to maintain the laws and the way of life as it was. The council hoped that without a governor or lieutenant governor to control the state, they would have far less opposition to worry about. With strategic bases in key areas, it was doubtful that there would be serious opposition from any state government. To ensure it, they had the commanding generals of each state's National Guard picked up that would have been a threat to them. All State National Guard levels had been reduced to token levels, so pick up would be easy to accomplish.

All members of the council were determined to restore democracy. It was thought by many that America would have fought to earn her freedom from the political chaos it had fallen into. With the country converted into a service nation with a foreign-controlled industrial base, it placed the political control of the nation in the hands of foreign nations.

Through their corporate structures in the United States, Americans were retrained from high-technical jobs to service industries and at half their former salaries and wages. Since the base realignment and the exit of essential defense companies, the Chinese out stripped the country in warship production. The country was unable to build any at all, and the replacement vessels were built in foreign countries. The Chinese navy was larger than the North

American navy. The Chinese submarine fleet was less sophisticated but larger in boats, and the Russians had made billions from them.

Despair and destitution had taken its toll on all. The time was now. The time is right to regain America. It would be a struggle. The bases were gone and the military had been depleted. The war in Afghanistan and Iraq had pulled the National Guard out of the country, leaving the states unable to support themselves in an emergency. Hurricane Katrina and massive wildfires with high levels of storms and floods devastated whole states. With the lack of troops at home, it necessitated help from other countries allowing other countries and the Mexican army to enter this country with aid. Many Americans asked, Where is that fast, deployable military that the secretary of defense had promised? It appeared it was a smoke screen to lull the people into an inert weak force that permitted the merger of America, Canada, and Mexico and the sell out to the United Nations and the European Union. Waiting in the wings was China, building, completely trained, and ready to strike. Russian Special Forces had done their job well.

CHAPTER 14

First Blood

Rebel Council Headquarters
Washington DC
0530 Hours

The council members sat behind a long table with microphones sitting front of them. They were all distinguished members of the military and Congress. Well-known members from both parties were easily recognized. Each had a copy of a prepared statement in front of them, and each had a specific statement to make.

Captain Hollister-Smyth, North American navy, put the phone on its cradle, thought for a second, and then walked over to a military member of the council and whispered in his ear, "Everything is ready, sir. The planes are airborne and should be making their first strike as the announcement is being made here. All first target areas are a go, weather conditions are excellent, and we should have our first feedback while you are on-air."

The man he spoke to was heavyset, strong, ambitious, and goal-oriented. Four bright stars graced his collar. He looked up at the captain and smiled. "Thank you," he said and jotted down a message on a notepad and then handed it to the captain. The captain read the note, returned to the telephone, and dialed a number.

"Hello.... Yes, everything is ready. The committee of information has informed the networks a special high-level announcement from the White House would be made at 0600 hours. They agreed to preempt all programming for the announcement. We have told them it's a presidential statement of major importance that involves national security. They also believe it's the president that's going to make it."

The captain hung up, turned to the group at the table, nodded his head, and left the room.

The chairman saw him nod and told the group they had informed the networks and the announcement would be made through their facilities. Once it started, they wouldn't dare cut them off. It would be too much of a headline to ignore.

The clock's second hand was moving second by second, heart-beat by heartbeat, as it moved closer to telling the world that the American people were going to take back their country, all constitutional rights were to be restored, and all borders recognized and patrolled and that all UN influences would be removed and all diplomatic ties would be broken from the United Nations and its member states.

*****

Four giant C-5 transport aircraft flew in under radar, and the Delta Forces were ready. The destination was a well-equipped facility deep in a South American jungle with a full-size runway and with fighter planes stationed there along with a battalion of regular army. The time was approaching 0600 hours, and the men were in position. A C-17 transport was ahead of them and had landed with a Delta assault team on board. They were going to take out communications, tower control, missile batteries, and security forces on duty. A special hit team would disable all aircraft on the ground.

The main force coming in would strike the drug facilities and garrison before they could mobilize. They would arrest and bring all drug dealers and workers to the new United States for trial.

"Freedom Leader One to Freedom Leader Two. Over."

Colonel S. Knipe looked at his copilot. "They're there and have started the operation." He keyed his mic and answered, "Freedom Leader Two. Over."

The reply was short. "Freedom Leader Two, you are clear to touch down, and we have the field in control. Piece of cake. Over."

"Freedom Leader One, we are three minutes out and on our way."

The whine of the hydraulics lowering the landing gear alerted the crew. The plane touched the runway with a sudden squeal.

With hands on gear and weapons at the ready, a highly trained group of men were ready to stop the flow of drugs to the United States. The plane's engines roared as it began to slow down. The officers and leading NCOs barked orders. Each man had direction and location burned into his mind.

The plane made a sharp right turn, and the engines increased in power as the huge aircraft turned itself around. At the moment the plane had touched down, the doors were opening. Now men and equipment flooded from the aircraft and separated to all points of the compass. With each team moving rapidly toward their objectives, you could hear firing as they reached their positions. With loud detonations, they moved rapidly toward the laboratories and the enemy.

From overhead, aircraft from the carriers were giving ground support when called in. The garrison of government troops threw down their weapons and put up their arms when they saw the big birds landing. The speed and accuracy of the assault were too much for them to handle.

The assault teams had destroyed the fighter planes before a pilot could get in them or a ground crew could start them. Some of them were unharmed and had little fuel in their tanks. It was a good hit. Five transports had landed, and the troops had taken their objective with fewer casualties than projected. The element of surprise had worked.

*****

Deep in a bunker under the laboratories were three men conversing in Spanish. "What the hell happened? Why hadn't your soldiers seen this coming down? I want answers."

"I don't know, *senor*. Our radar was operational, and our contacts in Washington should have let us known what was going on.

We have top-level congressmen and senators on our payroll. This should not have happened."

The head drug czar spoke, "We are paying out millions to keep the supply lines open. When this is over, and when we get out of here, I want answers. Do I make myself clear?"

The general answered, "Yes, sir, if they don't find us first."

"If they find us first, General, they will only find two of us alive."

The general looked at both drug czars and knew they meant business. If their secret bunker was found, he was a dead man.

*****

The commander of the new American forces addressed his officers. "How's it look, Colonel?"

The colonel looked at the man standing before him. A black star on his lapel, jungle camouflaged fatigues, and a black leather open holster on his side with a 9 mm automatic snugly tucked in it.

"We have their battalion commander at the command plane being debriefed by Intelligence. Seems we have everyone but two of the top cartel bosses and the federal commander. I have teams looking for them dead or alive. If they don't turn up, we'll bring in sounding equipment and start looking for them. As high tech as this place is, they probably have a bunker around here someplace. I suspect they're holding up, waiting for us to leave."

"Do we have any air surveillance monitoring for them?"

"Yes, General. We do."

Suddenly over the radio speaker came, "Rover 2 to CC1. Over."

The call broke the silence in the command plane. The operator reached over and keyed his mic. "CC1. Over."

"I have movement southwest of your position moving slowly through the brush. It's light. Looks like it might be only one person or animal moving toward you. You might want to intercept. Over."

"Roger, Rover 2. We have a reflex team on the way. Thanks for the help. Out."

The team moved into the jungle just south of the largest laboratory. They spread out along each side of the trail and waited. There was one person moving slowly and carefully. He was armed with a holstered sidearm and was dressed in a fatigue uniform. It was hard to see his rank, but by the looks of him, he appeared to be an officer.

The man moved into full view and the sergeant could see he was a general. He whispered, "Jackpot." As the general moved abreast of them, the sergeant called out in Spanish, "Alto."

The general instantly stopped and put up his hands. Two of the team members stood and, with weapons ready, covered the general. The sergeant instructed the general to unbuckle his gun belt and let it drop to the ground. The general carefully removed the buckle, and then his gun and holster hit the ground with a thud. The other troopers stood up and moved to the path covering the general, allowing no escape for him.

The sergeant saluted the general, and with all military respect, they escorted him back to the command ship.

As they approached the airfield, the general observed devastating destruction all around him. They had destroyed his entire squadron of fighters, the barracks were in flames, and the warehouses were burning. It was obvious to him that all had been lost. Hopefully, they would be merciful.

The American general looked at his counterpart. "General Lopez, where are the men in charge of the drug operation? We know they have not left the area. Where are they hiding?"

The general looked perplexed. "General, I have had to…How do you say it? I have eliminate them."

"General, you have killed them?"

"*Si*," he answered.

"They were going to blame me for your assault and the failure of my troops to stop you. I knew they would kill me after you had gone, and I had no choice but to eliminate them both."

"General, where are they? Where can we find them to identify them?"

"They are in an underground bunker a hundred meters south of the main laboratory. We managed to escape by an underground tunnel connecting the laboratory with the bunker. I shot them both while they were planning on a reprisal attack in Washington. Seems you have a number of representatives and senators that are on their payroll. Sorry, General, but how else do you think we can move the drugs into the country with ease? On one hand, you have established an interdiction program to stop us. Nevertheless, with their help, we were able to move the drugs in without detection."

"Well, General, I don't think we'll be having that problem much longer. Colonel, place the general under guard."

The sergeant turned to escort the general to the other prisoner location.

The American general continued addressing the colonel. "We'll move him out to Dessert Area II within the hour. I want the laboratories searched from one end to the other and find that bunker. I want all the evidence in there ready to move out with us."

The colonel knew that time was short. The country's government by then must have known they'd been invaded and they would most likely be getting ready for a counterattack. They must be off the ground and on the way back soon; he figured two hours at the most.

*****

It was 6:00 a.m. and all the networks were ready for the tie in with the White House communication system. The engineer was watching the clock on the wall. At exactly six, he dropped his finger and the tie-in was complete.

The picture filled the screens in the control room. Everyone was expected to see the Oval Office. Instead, it was a US senator.

"Good morning, fellow Americans. Early this morning, loyal American troops took control of the government. We have dissolved both houses of Congress and have established a revolutionary government. We have put all state governors both here and in the Canadian and Mexican regions that have not joined us under house arrest. We ask all of our citizens to remain calm at this time. Be assured we respect your constitutional rights. It was necessary to regain control of the government that has been out of control.

"We of the revolutionary council could no longer stand by and see the country overrun with foreign corporate invader and the merger between us and our friends in the north and in the south. With the stationing of troops and the control of the United Nations taken over by the European nations, we felt that saving the country was necessary as was saving the constitution from a corrupt government that had abandoned it after the so-called merger between America, Canada, and Mexico. They had moved all our high-tech manufacturing plants out of the country. Our people have become service lackeys for them all. We have had our auto plants moved south into Mexico and South America, and China leaving us with nothing more than dealerships and warehouses. They make most other manufacturing products outside the United States, and they make much of it in China, leaving you holding the bag, and that's made there too. We will return all foreign troops on American soil to their home countries immediately. We will move the United Nations out of the United States and will no longer allow their use of American forces. No foreign commander will control American troops at any time now or in the future."

The senator put his hand to the earpiece he wore, looked at the camera, smiled, and continued, "They have just announced it. We have successfully invaded the largest drug operation in the Americas. We have destroyed all the facilities, and we have informed the host country we will not tolerate any illegal drug operation that is supplying our people. All aircraft have been safely returned to their home bases and our casualties were light. We are putting the world on notice. The United States will no longer condone any country that plans to harm our people.

"Fellow Americans, we know you will be upset with what is taking place. Rest assured we will return the government to the people once we have eliminated the corruption from within. Remember, freedom is earned through deed and action. You cannot stand by and let it slip away through government or court intervention. The use of, 'We must give up some rights to be safe,' will not be supported. The country has lost too many rights when simple laws on the books could have been used.

"They should have returned illegal immigrants to their home countries long ago, not condone it by merging together. Our borders should have been closed and the army sent to patrol it. Laws enacted to search out the terrorist should never have interfered with our constitutional guarantees. Instead the merger erased the borders and the constitution. We will change the changes and reestablish our borders. The constitution will be reinstated in full without the amendments removing or restricting any of us. We will make new updates each hour on the hour. God bless you all. God save this gracious land, and God bless America."

The station engineer was dumbstruck. He looked around at his colleagues and saw no smiles, only bewilderment. One man nervously muttered, "What the hell am I going to do now? I'll die. I've got to have my stuff. Those bastards can't do this to me." They all looked at one another astonished. Suddenly the door opened to reveal the morning news commentator.

"Anyone think to call the White House and see what they're doing about this?" she asked.

"Gimme that phone. I gotta have my stuff!"

*****

The president was awakened at 0530 hours by a Secret Service agent. "Sorry, sir. We have received a call from an unknown source. Seems there is going to be a special announcement at 0600 hours. The caller said it would be in all of our best interest, especially you, sir. And if we missed it, we may be very embarrassed."

The president of the United States dressed quickly and met the others in the Oval Office. A maid brought in hot coffee and Danish rolls.

The TV was turned on and the president turned to his security officer. "What's going on? Do you have anything on this? Are we the butt end of a bizarre joke? You better have one hell of reason for all of this. If you don't, I would suggest you find out what is going on. Do I make myself clear?"

"Yes, sir. Quite clear. I have called the justice department. They've notified the FBI and the CIA. We're waiting for them now."

The president was not happy about getting up that early for some crank caller. He had a full day ahead of him and needed the rest. Big things were going on and it was time to tighten up on the loose ends. The party had control of the country. The people had to rely on the party and the government for everything. The forced health programs had eliminated small businesses, and the big corporate giants where being taxed to the hilt. The people had no choice but to reelect the party in power if they wanted to eat.

The broadcast had ended, and the president and his staff sat dumbfounded, looking at one another as if they couldn't believe what they had heard. Seconds ticked by when suddenly the phone rang and broke the silence. An aide picked it up, listened silently, and then handed the phone to John Beacon, the press secretary. "You may want to give a statement sir. This is network news."

John cradled the phone and covered the mouthpiece and turned to the president with a bewildered look.

The president spoke softly, "Tell them we will be calling a press conference within the hour to expose this phony plot for what it is."

John relayed the message. He was about to put down the phone when the president said, "Call the attorney general. I want the FBI here immediately. Also, get me the heads of all services. These guys want to play hardball, do they? Well, we're going to show them how we play for keeps."

A few minutes later, they ushered the attorney general directly to the Oval Office.

As he entered, he spoke, "Mr. President, I have prepared to declare a state of emergency and have arranged to call out the reserves and the National Guard if necessary. We still have many foreign units at Bliss and Dix. Should I call on their commander for assistance? Oh yes, I have forgotten the Luftwaffe at Holloman. They can be put on alert, sir."

The president looked at him with a wildness of anger and power. "Yeah, do that. I want every agent in the FBI out looking for these donkeys, the military alerted, all personnel recalled and ready to move at a moment's notice, all coast guard vessels put to sea, and the navy on full alert. I don't want one of them to get out of this country. Do I make myself clear? Damn. I kept our troops overseas to eliminate this problem. What happened?"

"Yes, sir, quite clear."

*****

As the country started to wake up, the word was already spreading across the nation. Many looked at the news as an answer to their problems. Men and women who had been working in salaried positions were demoted and replaced with party members, computer programmers were demoted, reassigned or laid off. Other crafts and workers faced the same consequences. The rest of those with family, parents, or friends in the concentration camps saw a ray of hope. Yes, they knew there was a future for them, for all of them.

*****

Colonel Duncan's aide called Tork along with several other officers into the colonel's office. As they waited for him, they all sat in silence, each to their own thoughts.

Tork was thinking back through the last day's events. Seeing it all come into view, each piece fell into place forming a large puzzle. The colonel's aide interrupted his thoughts when he entered the room and called them to attention. The colonel and Senator Forthright entered.

Colonel Duncan said, "Gentlemen, you have all been called here and chosen for a very special job. We have just learned the president has been moved to a secret and secure location. Our intelligence operatives at the White House has reported the location and we have it on file. This mission can stop a great deal of fighting and death to our misguided brothers and sisters. We were unable to pick up the secretary of defense or the attorney general.

"However, we were fortunate to have them call up the military units we control. Unfortunately, we were unable to move any of our men into the one command post the president picked to operate. This is where you come in. It will be your job to devise a way to neutralize the defending group without a fight. Now, let's come up with a plan."

Tork sat quietly thinking of a ploy that would divert the defenders and allow a strong force to enter the command post and take it over without any bloodshed. With most of the leaders sitting in New Mexico under guard, it would be to their advantage to have the president with them. Tork walked up to the table looking over the photos and then the blueprints of the compound. After looking at its defenses, he realized the safest way in was through the use of a diversion.

"Sir, I think I see a way to enter and possibly take over without firing a shot. Look, we can send in a chopper with dispatches showing the number of the administrations people we have in New Mexico and who they are. Also, we can have a dispatch from one of the military commanders that is in custody but unknown to them that he is sending a detachment of Delta troops to ensure the president's safety. The group would be moving in by aircraft on C-17 Globemaster II transports to the closest major airport and then to the command post by convoy. The officers at the CP could meet our troops at the airport and escort them to the president's compound. After arriving, and they have set up a bivouac area, and we have taken all of the normal procedures, a change of guard can be made. As we make the change, we can take out the existing force. After we are in full control, we can bring in a chopper to fly the president and his advisers out to our holding area. It will take a couple of days to set up, and the troops should be in place a week before we take control or whenever the time is right. That will give us time to secure the country by giving the people the essence of the freedom they need. What do you think, sir?"

Colonel Duncan thought for a moment and said, "It looks good, but I think we need a contingency plan. When we make our move, it will be imperative we hold all the aces. We mustn't leave anything to chance. Set up your secondary plan and a third as well. Present them to the entire council when we meet again. Get on it now, and make sure all the men, materials, and equipment are available."

"Yes, sir." Tork thought his plan was well merited, and they would have a problem with a second plan, let alone a third. On the other hand, putting his mind into it, he started to think. It was coming slowly, but it looked like a second way in. Yes, it may just work as well.

He started to write. Logistics and transportation were first, weapons second, and personnel third. As he thought, his plans started to appear. He was sure of the president's bodyguard numbers, both military and Secret Service. Next, he needed to know how many medical personnel were there and what their status was. How many domestic personnel and close relatives were there and any unknowns were essential. When he had this information, he would have the two contingency plans he needed. He also needed help and went to the phone to call Colonel Duncan.

"Duncan here," he answered.

"Colonel, this is Captain Albertson. I need a moment with you, sir." A minute later, Tork entered the colonel's office and saluted.

"Please have a seat, Captain."

Tork moved to the table. "Sorry to disturb you, sir, but I have the second and third plans ready for you to look over. Although I still prefer the original plan and think it will be to our advantage, these will do just as well."

The colonel moved to the table and picked up the diagram that Tork had placed on it. It was a detailed plan of the president's compound, complete with the underground tunnel complex, war-ready room, exits, garages, warehouse network, outhouses, and sentry positions. Two helicopter pads were evident, with a large group of trees to the north of the compound.

In the dead center of the trees was a clearing, large enough for a chopper to land. Tork had circled the tree area. At each position on the drawing were symbols Tork had made in red, yellow, and blue.

Tork picked up a pencil, looked at the colonel, and stated, "Colonel, the president has only about two hundred men at the compound. That includes his Secret Service guards. Now we don't know how many of them are loyal to him or if they can persuade them to surrender. Chances are, they won't. So it's my opinion that they will need a commando strike using either Navy SEAL or a Delta team to get him. Now here, you can see the trees are only about three hundred yards from the tunnel exit over here." Tork moved his pencil down from the tree line to the exit so the colonel could follow.

"You see, sir," Tork continued, "the exit is only a few steps from the door. I believe we can open the door and grab the president before any of his guards could respond. We take him out the door to the woods. As we move out from the bunker, we have several gunships come in close to the compound with their heavy searchlights on with blaring speakers calling for the defenders to throw down their weapons and surrender. At this point, we must divert everyone's attention from the outer perimeter to our choppers. Because of the noise level, they shouldn't hear a single presidential marine chopper come in just over the trees and settle down in the center of this clearing. It shouldn't take much time for the presidential party to reach the trees. The chopper can keep his power up, and when the president is on board, the ship can take off and fly to a transfer field here."

Tork pulled out a map of the area. Circled on the map about twenty miles to the west was an old airstrip. Pointing to the point on the map, Tork said, "This is an old emergency strip kept up to par during the Cold War days. It's still in excellent condition. I've had a team visit it, and it will take a Lear or Falcon. I can have one standing by with a C-130 to act as a decoy. Once both planes are airborne, anyone seeing them leave will add to the confusion. Both planes can then separate and head for their destinations. Flying low will divert them from any radar in the area that's not under our control. The C-130 can fly to ceiling and drop chafe. As the chafe drops both planes can descend to an altitude below radar and then fly where they want without detection.

"What do you think, sir?"

The colonel looked at him for several minutes. "Captain, have you coordinated this with anyone else?"

"Yes, sir. The whole team was involved in it. The only reservation I have is the Germans at Holloman. They could be a problem."

"Don't worry about them. They will be eliminated prior to our mission. Two squadrons of F-22 Raptors will hit them on the ground before they can be launched. Our men their will kill all power on the base and destroy the emergency feeds to the base. It's been arranged that all foreign bases will be hit within the next forty-eight hours. We have not forgotten the innocent men and women who were killed by their gun-gathering expeditions or the thousands of our people in the concentration camps all over North America. They will be freed."

Looking at Tork, the colonel added, "That's plan 2, Tork. What's plan 3 going to do for us?"

Tork smiled. "Sir, we are all in agreement. The third plan is a direct assault from all sides. We feel this will cause heavy casualties and may even cause the president's death. We have a complete plan of attack, using Special Forces. Still, we advise against it in favor of plan one or two. We feel plan one would be to our advantage, and we have set their wheels in to motion. The president's hotline has been opened and communication set up between General Tibias and us. The president is sounding him out about reinforcements. The time is now, sir."

The colonel stood looking at the drawings, mulling over in his mind all that Tork had said. "Tork, I need photo recon shots of the compound. I need to know for sure everything there is to know about the place. Can you get them for us?"

Tork smiled. "Sir, we have flown a stealth drone over the compound and should have the photos here within the hour. Time is short. That's why we felt that presenting this to you was necessary before the photos arrived."

"Okay, Captain. We use your first choice with the second one ready to move if it looks like we're in trouble, but I want all involved to be at their staging points ready to go within arranged time frames. Agreed?"

Tork picked up the plans and left Colonel Duncan. He had a lot to do and not much time to do it in. With that, Tork knew time was short and the time to extract the president and his staff was now. Tork could only hope that they would pick his plan, since he knew it would bring success. On the off chance they would pick his plan, he decided to start the ball rolling and prepare. If he was right, it would save valuable time and they needed the time now.

Tork knew there were obstacles and danger ahead. He also knew that there were still British, Russian, German, and French forces still in the country. After an invitation from the president, the French had moved their most elite Foreign Legion troops into Fort Polk.

Tork thought, *It's a good thing we have control over Barksdale Air Force Base. The taking of Polk will be hard but possible. Yes, very possible.*

CHAPTER 15

Wars and Rumors of Wars

New York City, New York

At the precise moment they made the declaration on the network news that special troops had moved into position around the UN building and had sealed it off, the new government UN ambassador had called and informed the secretary-general that the people had seized the US government. Withdrawal from the United Nations was in effect until further notice. No further UN activity would be permitted within the borders of the United States until the new government was stable. All communications between the United Nations and all other international countries would cease. And all ambassadors to the United Nations were to leave the country immediately.

As they were sealing the United Nations, the new government ordered the city to cut all power to the building; troops entered the building and went to prearranged destinations where they disabled satellite dishes and communication antennas.

As the building power dropped off line, the building's emergency generators tried to come up automatically. After starting and switching over to emergency power, they suddenly went off line too. The troops had completed their goals. As members of the United Nations realized what had happened, they tried in desperation to reach their consulates or embassies, only to find the phones there were not working, cell phones were being jammed, and the army was jamming their radio transmissions.

Just before the UN building was taken over, the new government in the New York City areas closed down all other communication services. The troops inside the building continued to move through it, room by room, moving people to the stairwells. Several people were disabled and confined to wheelchairs or were unable to walk down the stairs. They moved them to the elevator locations to wait until they declared the building was clear of all other personnel. The elevators would move them down after the power was restored.

The secretary-general, after receiving his call, raced to his embassy. He knew they would not allow him into the UN building, at least not until they restored the government and the president was back in power. He had to let the world know what was happening. The world could not afford to have a powerful democratic government in power in the United States or all would be lost in establishing the new world order.

London, Bonn, Paris, and Moscow—throughout the world, special dignitaries or members of US embassies or consulates notified the host governments of the military coup d'état and what it meant. Most of them were part of the council and would play a very important role in returning America to its people, quietly feeding valuable information to the new government about European activities.

When they had signed the North American Free Trade Agreement (NAFTA) between the United States, Mexico, and Canada, it became a one-way street, everything coming in and nothing going out except for American industries, another lie of which they had burned into the minds of Americans. The passing of the Central American Trade Agreement (CAFTA) was supposed to have been the end of the United States and the beginning of the new North America and the erasure of the Canadian and Mexican borders. They had duped the American public once again. Political infighting had delayed the border erasing temporarily. Some of the politicians were fearful of having to bid for jobs that were all service-oriented. Large-scale manufacturing was all but gone.

At the onset of the takeover, all border crossings were seized by special units of the army and closed. No manufactured goods would be flowing into the country until after the government, and the country, was secured. Naval units patrolled the US coastal borders in the Atlantic and Pacific regions to ensure security and national integrity.

*****

"Gentlemen, I have just received word from Command. Third corps commanders have just notified us they are behind us and want instructions. We have sent transportation to bring the corps commanders to our closest command centers for debriefing. If all checks out, we will commit them to duty."

The revolutionary council had convened and opened the floor to debate over present conditions.

Senator Forthright looked out over his contemporaries. "Any questions?"

A hand went up. "Senator, if you please. I understand we have or are having problems from several northern states and there are reports of heavy fighting and some National Guard units have taken up arms against us. What have you to report on this?"

The senator reached down in front of him and pulled a folder from his brief case. "Yes, sir. What you have heard is true. We have had reaction from several states not only in the north but also in the west and two in the south. New York State has called up its National Guard units, both army and air force. The people living in New York City have rioted and are attempting to burn anything and everything they can. Looting is running rampant. The police are powerless, and most of the rioters are chanting down with the revolution. They are yelling for the president to save them. Seems they don't want to lose their welfare payments. Some governors have pledged allegiance to the president and his cabinet. We have pledges of military support from thirty-six states so far. Two states have arrested the governors we missed and have ordered the National Guard to maintain order. They're two of the thirty-six states. California's state's legislature is in session now, and our men are there trying to convince all of them. This could be a split state.

"At this time, we are not sure yet where it's going. The commander of the National Guard is one of ours and is ready to move if the state decides to go with the president. We have enough men in command positions to control any adverse situations. Let's hope it doesn't come to that scenario. The state split into two regions could cause problems later. With our underground command post in the desert and in control of other military installations, we have the edge to secure our borders. We have put two divisions of troops on the Mexican, Texas, New Mexico, Arizona, and California borders. Border guards are cooperating at this time. As we secure other areas, we will have both our northern and southern borders blocked from any intruders or attacks. We have ordered all foreign troops in the country to disarm and prepare for evacuation to their home countries."

Senator Singleton raised his hand. "What arrangements have been made for anyone fleeing the country, trying to cross the Canadian or Mexican borders?"

"We have thought of that, Senator. Anyone wanting to leave the country that is a citizen of that country or any alien may do so. If not, we will detain them at two desert concentration camps the government had our people confined in located in New Mexico. If I may add, sir, they will be well taken care of."

Before the senator could continue, an aide stepped up to him and whispered a short message to him.

"Gentlemen, good news. We have ships on patrol on both the Atlantic and Pacific coasts, and they are diverting all incoming ships to ports we control. Pier J, Long Beach, has been secured by Special Forces, though the Chinese had tried to defend it. An inventory of the warehouses revealed vast amounts of Chinese weapons. For our protection, we will put all incoming and static cargos in quarantine until we release them to their respective customers. Illegal cargo will be confiscated and sponsoring governments warned.

"Custom personnel will ensure all our interests are satisfied. As members of this council and of the Senate and House, you know how this is going to affect our international affairs. It, no doubt, may inspire some unscrupulous countries or the United States of Europe to try to make a deal with the president and his administration. With outside help, the president may feel he can salvage his administration and defeat us. With the country divided in the early stages, one or more of these countries may try to intervene with their troops. Therefore, we have sent emissaries to all of our major trading countries with an outstretched hand and with a warning to not intervene.

"Should any try to intervene, we will retaliate with every means available to us. They are to consider us completely unstable. As all of you know, we are in the position now to move in and place the president under house arrest. We will notify all of you as this phase progresses. Also, we have all agreed on the newscast at six o'clock this evening. We have notified the networks that we will be cutting into their newscast with news update. So far, we have the situation well in hand over here. Outside the country, we are hearing a beat of war drums and rattling of sabers. To win, we must all pull together as one."

CHAPTER 16

The Clouds of War Gather

10 Downing Street,
London, England

The prime minister had called his cabinet together upon hearing the news from the British Embassy in Washington. The news looked grim to him, and a decision on what they had to do was imminent. His alliance with the president was well known and the help he received from the United States strongly influenced his party defeating the opposition party in the last elections. This had been paramount in cementing Britain completely to the new United States of Europe. At all costs, he knew to remain in power, they had to remain aligned with Europe. The road to the new world order was well underway and with a successful socialist movement guiding it. With the Soviet Union long gone, it was time now for Europe to show the Russians how socialism is done and include them as players. With the buildup in wealth and power, the Chinese could be a pickle in the sugar jar.

A question now on the prime minister's mind was what Europe could do to save the movement in America. First, he had to sell his idea to his cabinet. Then to Europe, maybe they could all end up with a piece of the United States. That might be a way to gain the allegiance of the rest of Europe and the entire union, although they were all trying to reconcile after some countries failed to accept the change in monies from their own currency to the euro and promises made were broken. He felt this might just make a difference. If all of

Europe had a piece of the United States and the dollar became useless, than all EU nations, including North and South America, could use the euro. With this control, the European Union could control the world economy. Still, some people were unwilling to accept the union. They would deal with the freedom-loving zealots in Europe that wanted complete freedom. What fools they were.

His secretary interrupted the prime minister's thoughts. "Sir, everyone is here and waiting for you. Is there anything I can get you?"

"Thank you, Pierce. Everything is set up in the conference room, is it not?"

"Yes, sir. All is ready."

The prime minister opened his meeting with a recording from the British ambassador in Washington DC. It was short and to the point. The prime minister then addressed them. "Gentlemen, we are at a historical point. We have the opportunity to help our American friends and ourselves. I have been in contact with several governments that agree we have the golden opportunity to move against the American rebels.

"With the country engaged in a civil war, we can move in to support the president and gain a foothold. We can tell our people we are moving against the rebel forces in solidarity with the US government. After we have helped the US government regain the country, we can move our troops into position and take over. Now, let us discuss our strategy and let's hear any negative comments. I want to hear anything that could possibly go wrong. Gentlemen, if you please."

*****

Colonel Duncan, Captain Albertson, and Calvin Varner deplaned at the assault assembly base. The committee had agreed on the method of assault on the president's headquarters. Everyone was ready. Colonel Duncan had planned for the committee to meet Tork. It was his plan and they all wanted to meet this young captain.

As they landed, there were eight F-22 Raptor fighters scrambling on the adjacent runway. As their plane taxied to the terminal, the F-22s were airborne. Cal could see them from his seat in the airliner. They all gained their altitude and then made a turn toward the northwest. Tork thought they were in one hell of a hurry.

"Colonel Duncan. Good to see you, sir." Senator Mac Elroy stepped forward with his hand outstretched, grasped the colonel's hand firmly, and smiled at Tork and Cal. He then shook their hands too. "Gentlemen, please this way," he said, turning to the three men.

"Did you see those fighters taking off as you landed?"

Cal nodded.

Tork smiled at the senator. "Yes, Senator. I watched them as we were landing. Is there anything wrong?"

The senator looked troubled. "Yes, Captain, there is. They have dispatched them to help a National Guard unit that has sworn allegiance to us and are presently under heavy fire from troops loyal to the president. It makes us all sad to think we must resort to firing on our own people, but at this time, we have no choice."

The four men reached their destination and entered an air force staff car. The driver saluted, slid in behind the wheel, and pulled away from the operations building. The senator said to the driver, "Sergeant, Command Center, pronto!"

The car took only minutes to reach its destination. They ushered the men into the briefing room and settled them down. At the head of the room were six men sitting behind a long table. Tork recognized several of them as members of the Senate and the House of Representatives.

The colonel leaned over and whispered into Tork's ear, "Everything is ready for the mission. I have asked that you participate in the assault. They will give us their answer at this briefing."

Before Tork could answer, three men entered from the curtain and were behind the men at the table. One was a high-ranking admiral. The other two were generals, one from the army and the other from the air force.

The admiral went up to the podium and looked over to the men at the table, and as if by magic, a video appeared on the screen to the left of the committee and the audience. The video showed a troop staging area, and the admiral explained the troops, their locations, reported strengths, and possible destinations. Everyone listened intently.

The admiral continued, "As you can, see gentlemen, we have to contend with not only our opponents here but also their allies in Europe. The Asian nations have talked with us and have assured us they do not intend to attempt to intervene in the war. However, we have not heard a word from Europe. We recently took the pictures you see, and they are from England, France, and Germany. Our intelligence has revealed they may attempt to land troops to save the president from us and to establish a beachhead here for other reasons. What these other reasons represent is unknown to us at this time. We can only speculate the European Union may be trying to slice our country up between them.

"To short-circuit this situation, we have deployed troops around the president's compound, and our troops are standing by in strategic marshaling areas about ten miles from him. Our first attempt will be to use the plan, code named Friendly. A battalion of our men will arrive at the compound around 0330 hours. The president and his defenders are expecting them. When they are in place and have taken on guard duties, our men will take control and, hopefully, without bloodshed. We anticipate about three days making our move. However, should the opportunity arise, we will move much sooner. Our second plan, if this one should fail, will be a direct assault using helicopters and members of the Delta Force. We don't want to use this one, but we will if necessary. Are there any questions?"

A member of the committee looked over to the air force general and said, "General Hotchkins, what defenses have you set up to monitor any incoming missiles or aircraft? And where are the foreign troops that the president has on our soil?"

The general looked over to the committee member. "Sir, we have satellites monitoring all aircraft crossing the Atlantic and the Pacific shores. We have notified all foreign countries we will not hesitate to fire on any ships or aircraft violating American sovereignty. We have diverted any ships coming into the country to holding ports. We also know that the United Kingdom has mobilized her SAS forces and their army, navy, and marines. We have told each embassy here of the consequences should they try to intervene. As for the foreign forces here, we have ordered them out of the country, and they have crossed into Canada. We have our sources there that will monitor their movements."

The general felt a tug on his coat, turned, and was handed a piece of paper. He read it and looked up and over to the men and women listening. "Is Captain Albertson in the briefing?"

Tork raised his hand. "Yes, sir."

The general smiled at him. "We thought you might be interested in going with the Friendly team, Captain, seeing it's your plan we are using."

Tork brightened up. "Yes, sir," he said.

The general pointed to the exit door. "Gunn is outside waiting for you. He will take you to the marshaling area for equipment. We have a company for you, Captain. Good luck."

Tork was pleased with the assignment and knew what lay ahead. He thought, *With this caper in motion, we might be able to end this civil war earlier than planned and bring the peace and sanity back to the people. A new beginning would mean a lot to the people, a new America without outsiders in control, a free America. Yes, a free America.*

Learning he was receiving a company to command, Tork had to bone up on his command structure and look for the specialists he would need. He immediately put out feelers for men he worked with in his last assignment. It would be necessary for him to have tried and true men that were used to him and his command style.

Tork sat with pen in hand and jotted down personnel names, ranks, and skills he needed. Next, he made out a special equipment list, different than his normal unit equipment. By the nature of the mission, special weapons and explosives would be necessary, and each of them went on the list. He also noted to ask Colonel Duncan if there were any F-35 available from the air force if he needed them for tactical support.

CHAPTER 17

Predicted Involvement

RAF Station Brize Norton
Oxon, England

Air Marshal Hollingsworth had called his command leaders together. He could see real trouble ahead; even with the United States divided, he knew any attempt to interfere could be catastrophic. He had all the British air force transports on standby, and Whitehall had invoked the War Act to commandeer aircraft from the airlines to transport troops. His tankers were loaded and ready to fly. The government had been in communication with the president of the United States, bases loyal to him were identified, and clearances were obtained from the president. It looked good, but he still felt a numbing feeling in his stomach. He knew from embassy messages that things weren't going well for US government forces.

He knew from experience that the rebel forces in the United States would not hesitate to fire on anyone interceding in their cause. No. Although he was ready, he knew the winds of defeat could be blowing toward Britain and the new United States of Europe. He also knew that many of his men had friends and relatives living in the United States and may not fight at all when they arrived. Commando units and marines were bivouacking on the base, and all civilian traffic was forbidden to enter the base perimeter; he was waiting for orders he hoped would not come. They did not question his loyalty to the government, but deep inside, he felt what was going on was very questionable. He thought to himself, *Am I doing the right thing? Are the European leaders right? Is the British government right?* Although Britain had left the European Union, she was still tied tightly to them as trade partners and hoping to cash in on the advantages promised them for their participation.

*****

The general was in the lead vehicle as it approached the president's compound; they had sent messages using the presidential codes that help was coming. Everything looked good. It looked almost too easy. Tork's company was in the lead vehicles, and everyone was ready to act or react to any hostilities they might encounter. The battalion was at full strength, and each man was a volunteer, each knowing what he was there for, each a highly trained professional soldier. If it troubled them that the government branded them as traitors and probably many people, they didn't show it.

The general had sent out a hold message to the column. They were to hold at Highway X before continuing on to the adjacent access highway until they received confirmation that all was well. The Secret Service and the army contingent group loyal to the president had it closed, and the prearranged passwords had to be recognized before anyone could enter the area. They evacuated the local resident that lived in the area in a five-mile radius to secure the compound. They told the residents a serious natural gas leak had occurred and they evacuated the area for safety. It was this area that could become a gauntlet of death if anyone slipped up, and they expected to be stopped and challenged all the way to the compound. The high command had the secondary attack team in place. The choppers were ready to come in when ready. Should plan one fail, plan two would go into effect immediately. Stopping any heavy fighting was imperative before it got started. They considered it; capture of the president and perhaps the factions loyal to him might throw in the towel and surrender. They reached Highway X and they contacted the compound. After an hour of waiting, two Secret Service agents approached the convoy and were taken to the command vehicle. They exchanged passwords, and the meeting began.

"Sir, I'm agent McDuff. This is agent Haroldson." Both men showed their identification cards. "They have sent us to meet you, sir. Did you run into any rebel forces on your way here?"

The commander casually welcomed both men as he dismounted from his vehicle and explained. "We ran into two motor patrols. Our orders convinced them we were moving to a bivouac area to support the National Guard. We have orders from the field commander in this area to seek out any federal troops and to dislodge or capture them. They were very trusting. Didn't take the time or try to check out our orders with their headquarters to see if we were legitimate or not. Shall we leave, Agent McDuff, or do you wish to confirm who we are?"

"I only have one question, sir. If you are the troops we are waiting for, then only you can answer the special presidential password."

"When you're ready, McDuff."

"The president will ask you for the word, sir. Have your radio operator switch to the prearranged frequency you and the president agreed on."

The commander walked over to the radio unit and whispered the frequency number into the operator's ear. An operator set the frequency, keyed his mic, and called out the call sign to the compound the general had given to him.

"Rebel Motor One to Rebel Base One. Over." The radio was silent. The commander nodded his head and the operator repeated the call. Still, silence. The general went over to the radioman and told him to add "leader" to the call after base one.

The operator called out, "Rebel Motor One to Rebel Base One Leader. Over."

Back came, "Rebel Base One Leader. Over."

The operator was about to answer when the commander stopped him. Seconds passed. They heard a second call. "Rebel Base One Leader. Over." Still the general would not allow an answer. A third call came in from the compound. "Rebel Base One Leader. Torch by."

The commander smiled. All was going well. Torch was the correct answer. He told the radioman to acknowledge with his reply.

"Rebel Motor One, Kennedy. Over."

A short answer came back. "Rebel Motor One, enter." The general looked to the two Secret Service agents. "Gentlemen, shall we proceed?"

McDuff was pleased; he knew the final code word to the president would be Kennedy. The agents mounted the vehicle with the general, and they started on toward the first checkpoint.

Tork was pleased. They had made and passed the first encounter with government agents. He knew there would be several more before they could enter the compound, set up camp, and take up their guard positions. The next few miles were careful miles. They had evacuated the local population, so the roads were virtually empty. Only patrols were out running around. Most people in the country were glued to their TV sets and radios. What was happening in other countries was happening there. Most of the country was glad at what was going on. Many young men and women had joined with the rebels for freedom.

The column came up to the first roadblock approaching the main compound as the vehicles slowed. Tork noticed a figure drop off one of the vehicles and race toward a set of trees to the right of the column. He tapped Lieutenant Foreman on the arm. "Lieutenant, I just saw one of our men slip out and run to the trees on our right. I'm going after him. Let the general know without alerting the two agents of what's going down. This guy is either a deserter or he could be a federal loyalist. Tell the general I'll catch up with you later if you move out before I return."

The lieutenant only nodded.

Tork dismounted and walked over to the woods. One agent saw him walking away and jumped down and started to follow him. Tork walked over to the trees and slipped behind one. He unbuckled his belt and was about to unzip his pants when the agent came around and saw what he was about to do.

"Sorry, Captain. Saw you leave and couldn't take the chance of anything happening. See you back at the column."

Tork waved and said, "I'll be right there."

The agent walked back to the column. When he was out of sight, Tork moved fast. He headed out where he thought the man had gone he saw leaving the truck. Moving silently, Tork heard some low voices. He moved in closer and found the man from the truck, a sergeant, talking with another man. He could barely hear what they were saying. As quietly as possible, he moved close enough to hear them both.

"Let me get this straight, Sergeant. The column is a rebel brigade from a battalion that they sent from the committee to seize the president and fly him out to an undisclosed location. Their main objective is to set up a takeover at the main compound with rebel troops. Is that right? Allowing them to take over without firing a shot, ingenious. Very good. Okay, Sergeant. Get back to the column. Tell them you had a bad nature call. Then see what you can do to hold up the column for as long as you can. I need the time. Now get going."

The sergeant moved out to meet the column, and the agent moved toward the other side of the tree line. Tork followed him, staying back out of sight. The trees broke into a clearing, and the agent started walking toward a four-wheel vehicle sitting there. Tork pulled out his 9 mm and called to the agent.

"Hey, buddy. What are you doing out here? Don't you know this is a restricted area?" As he was speaking, Tork had the automatic trained on him.

The agent could see this man and knew what he was doing. Fine time to have this happen. He had to get this information to the president. *Damn!*

Tork walked up to within ten feet of the agent and stopped. "Flat on the round, pal, or you're dead."

The agent dropped to the ground and looked up. "You're making a bad mistake, Captain. I'm a Secret Service agent."

Tork said, "Yes, I know you are. Too bad you chose the socialist way of life, pal. Reach down and pull the gun out of your holster with two fingers. One twitch and you're history. Throw the gun to your left, then undo your belt, and throw it over to your right."

Very carefully the gun and then the belt were thrown over.

Tork picked them both up and moved behind the agent. "Get up and walk over to the vehicle."

The agent moved carefully to the vehicle.

"Get in the position in front of the car."

"What position?" the agent asked.

"Let's not play games," Tork replied.

"You know."

The agent turned around and placed his hands in front of him. Tork moved up behind him and kicked his feet back. "Spread 'em apart!"

The agent moved his feet apart and Tork searched him and found the agent's pocket radio and his handcuffs. "Nice radio, pal." Tork reached over, grabbed the agent's left hand, and pulled it back, slapping the handcuff on. Then reaching over and grabbing his other hand, he brought it around and cuffed his hands with the bracelet, securing both of them.

He forced the agent around to the front of the vehicle and had him kneel down, slipped the belt around the bumper, and pulled it up tight, tying it as hard as he could get it. "Stay still. I'll have you picked up soon." Tork looked at his watch. Ten minutes was almost up, and the column would be moving soon. He raced out to the edge of the tree line and moved casually toward the front of the column. Catching up with his vehicle, he mounted and told the platoon sergeant where the agent was and instructed him to take two men and bring the man back to the rear of the column. Caution was important now.

It was imperative that they had the president before the UN new world order could bring in troops through Canada or Mexico. At this time and place, they were the only ones in the world willing to go up against them. The administration had already turned their satellites over to the United Nations, and they were now tracking everything down here.

The best part was what they had learned from Desert Storm, Afghanistan, and Iraq. The satellites were limited to their fixed positions. What they needed was a couple of SR-71s. *Yeah*, Tork thought, *we need to take them out of mothballs and use them if we can. I believe there's one in a museum in Utah. I should have Duncan look into it. Might be able to use one from Davis-Monthan Air Force Base if there's one there.*

The column had passed the last checkpoint without any further challenges and was moving into position in the presidential compound. The convoy moved in and the A team dropped out and deployed to their positions, relieving the president's men, giving them what they thought were well-needed rests from loyal federal troops.

The president and his security personnel came out to meet the general. "Ah, General, it's good to see you. We have been concerned our codes had been broken, so we have not communicated with anyone outside this area except you. What news have you for us?"

"Mr. President, unfortunately, your code was broken. Well, not broken. The rebels have all the codes available and they know the United Nations would try to intervene, so they have closed down the UN building in New York and have deployed loyal troops around the five bases you gave to the United Nations. They gave the UN commanders forty-eight hours to destroy all their weapons and to leave. Communications at the bases were jammed. Most of them have moved into Canada. We doubt if they've been able to confirm what is going on at this time."

The president smiled. "Don't worry, General. We have sent agents to both Canada and Mexico to let the world know that we will not give into these so-called patriots. They can wave the flag all they want. We are all under the UN flag now, and our friends will come, just as you have. Come, General. Let's get into the communication center and let the country know we have a conquering force here now. And all is well."

The president held a dinner for the commander and his officers. All were there except the handpicked groups that were out neutralizing the Secret Service and replacing them with Delta Forces. All was well, everyone was in position, and the other Secret Service personnel were in with the president.

Tork looked at his watch and was counting seconds, 8, 7, 6, 5, 4, 3, 2, 1. He pushed the button on the remote control he was holding, and the beeper the general had on his belt started to vibrate. The time had come. Everything and everyone were in place.

The general looked up at the president and smiled. "Mr. President," he said as he stood, "we have nullified your security personnel. All have been at this time disarmed and are being moved to the trucks for transport. You are all under arrest."

The president was in shock. He looked at the general and couldn't see him. Slowly his gaze became reality. The general continued, "Gentlemen of the Secret Service, if you will look out the doors, you will find machine guns have been set up, and if you choose to implant a confrontation at this time, my men have orders to open fire on everyone. We will permit no one in this room to leave. It's your choice."

One Secret Service agent with a gun in hand walked to the door opening it a crack, looked out, turned, and nodded his head.

A second man got up from the table and went to the window and peered out, turned, and said, "Damn, they're all rebels, Mr. President. They've swallowed us up. Damn."

The president focused on the general. The general returned his gaze and stated. "Sir, the UN troops in Canada have crossed the border and have engaged the Michigan National Guard. The Guard is holding them at this time, and General Armatage has dispatched troops from our northeast group to assist them. The air force from Nebraska is airborne with orders to destroy the UN bases in Canada."

The president looked up and smiled. "Well, General, it looks like the new world order is going to take you on, and I'm willing to bet we are going to win."

The general looked at the president. "Mr. President, our intelligence tells us the Canadian people want their freedom back as well. The world is not ready for what you people have planned for them. No one wants to be a number or be corralled like a bunch of cattle. We know your next step was to start on the chip implants here, and we'll be damned if we're going to let you people put us into slavery, no matter what you call it. No, sir. We will defeat the sign of the beast and the whole damn world if necessary. But then who is to say the world is willing to live in the same misery you have planned for us.

No, sir. We refuse to be made slaves. By the way, sir, we have released thousands of Americans you confined to your concentration camps, the criminals have been placed in prisons, and the rest are working for the new America and the constitution you circumvented with the executive orders that were meant for war use only."

Congressional Holding Camp, No. 11
New Mexico

The congressional detainees held at the facility were called to a formation in the recreation hall. Each of them mumbled together, wondering what news was brought forth. They only knew what they were being told, that their incarceration was due to their excessive liberal views. They were told they were being held until the people voted a national referendum to join in the new world order and to surrender the United States to the United Nations unconditionally. All but a few thought the people would vote yes. The meeting they were called to attend was to inform them of the results of the referendum. Getting any information from there captures was difficult. They all seemed to be handpicked men. Although they were all treated well and with the utmost respect, they found it difficult to get even the time of day from their guards.

They all knew the other members of Congress would be moving to find them and to get them out soon. Maybe this meeting, if all went well with the voting, would force a release.

Gen. Alexander Bartholomew, commanding general, entered the room. His aide, Major Tolbert, sang out in a commanding tone, "Attention." All personnel came to attention. The general waved his hand and the captain called them to ease.

General Bartholomew addressed the detainees. "All of you will be brought to justices by trial." The general looked out at the unsmiling faces, the grayness in their eyes, the look of dismay. They all now knew the reason for their incarceration.

The general continued, "All of you were selected and arrested for your acts of treason against the people of the United States, the selling out of the country to the United Nations, and the resulting decay of freedom we have all fought so hard to preserve since our Founding Fathers provided it. The wars and acts of terrorism through the years have proven how important it is to all of us. We, the American people, have fought to preserve our constitution. Therefore your future will be left in the hands of the people when this is over. All of you here are only a small part of those governing bodies that have been detained and will stand in judgment. Now, gentlemen, for some of you, my next words will be pleasing, and a ray of hope may very well rise up inside of you. Others may see the folly of what they have been a part of and will no doubt have sorrow in their hearts."

The general stood tall, erect, and proud. Looking out over the heads of the deposed members of Congress, he said, "Your friends from the United Nations have invaded the United States and have met with heavy resistance from the National Guard, reserve forces, and the regular military that is under our control." With that statement, the general turned and left the building, leaving all of them to ponder their fate and that of the country.

One senator looked around at his colleagues. "Well, gentlemen, what do we do now?"

Each man in silence looked to one and then to the other. Dismay and unbelief had stunned them. They all knew that something was wrong when they were picked up and placed under arrest and taken to Andrews Air Force Base where they were whisked away by helicopter to holding areas and then flown to this hellhole, wherever it was. Some said it was in the far West, while others thought it was in Texas or Arizona, but no one knew for sure. They had everything they wanted or needed with few exceptions. News and telephones were out of the question. US soldiers guarded them and they arrived on air force transport planes under guard. And now the truth, a coup had taken place and the rebel forces had arrested them. Without the necessary leadership to unite the loyal forces, all could be lost.

"Well, I for one," the senator said, "would like to talk to this general or his commander. I don't believe one damn word he told us except that we are here now. I see only a small number of senators and members of the House here, so I don't think they have the numbers he claims. I think if we put pressure on him, he'll break down."

The senator walked to the captain standing at a casual parade rest.

"Captain, get that traitor down here now."

The captain smiled, pulled the radio off his belt, keyed the mic, and spoke, "BBS-1 to Command-1. Over."

"Command-1. Over," they replied.

"I have Senator Copeland demanding our traitorous general meet him as soon as possible. Over."

The radio was silent for what seemed like minutes, and then one word came back, "Secure."

The captain smiled, waved two guards over from the opposite wall, and told them, "Secure the prisoner."

The men grabbed the senator, and before he could shout, they had him moving toward the doorway. In less than three minutes, he was in a detention room with the door closed and bolted. He looked around the room, bed, television, a small bathroom with a toilet, and a small refrigerator. *Well,* he thought, *at least a senator has some privileges.* He sat on the bed and noticed a speaker in the ceiling. *Looks like solitary confinement,* he thought.

Suddenly out of the speaker came the general's voice. "Senator, be advised you won't be telling the American people what to do from now on. We are taking back the country, and we'll be damned if we're going to let anyone steal this republic again.

"For your information, this country is under attack by foreign troops that you and your party had garrisoned here. They have been forced moved into the Canadian provinces. The president's use of them to confiscate our people's guns and to wontedly kill disinters was barbaric. We know you kept them here to enforce the chip implants on us all. I want you to know that we will fight to the last man to guarantee the constitution will stand and no time in the future will an executive order be used to disregard the constitution as congress has permitted it to happen. Your TV is tuned to CNN and Fox News so you can see the wrought of war that all of you and the administration has brought upon this great country. Good night, Senator. Pleasant dreams."

The speaker went silent. The senator looked over to the television set, hesitated for a moment, and switched it on. The announcer was detailing movement of UN troops in Canada and telling the listeners of the transports that were arriving there.

The senator's thoughts were of encouragement. The friends of the new world order were responding and sending help; it wouldn't take long to restore order once the world's troops were in command. In no time, the president would be back in power, and then they could go on to fully establish complete world peace and control. These misfits would learn that the old constitution was archaic, completely out of date. *Yes*, he thought, *our friends would soon be here and the sheep would follow the shepherd and the shepherd would be the new world order and I would be one of its leaders. All others would be serfs in a new world.*

CHAPTER 18

Treachery

Cal Varner entered the air base and was escorted to the facilities information services press lounge.

As he walked in, a guard stopped him and asked for his credentials. Cal pulled out his press card for the *LA Times* and handed it to the guard.

"Thank you, sir," he said. "You must sign in at the desk, sir. Just over there to your right, sir." He pointed the way for Cal, smiled, turned, and left.

Cal looked around the room for anyone that he might know; he had to be careful. Although they took great care to obtain the credentials he carried, he knew the wrong person could mean death for him. The room looked clean, and he went up to the registrar and signed in.

The desk clerk assigned him a room and a clearance badge after confirming his credentials. "You'll be in building 1046, room 292, sir, with two other correspondents. Hope you don't mind, sir."

Cal thanked the clerk and walked up to the makeshift bar they had provided.

"Cola, please." He started to pay for the drink and the clerk smiled.

"No need, sir. It's all been paid."

Cal walked over to the window and looked out on the taxiway and the aircraft approach aprons. They were filled with both military and commercial aircraft, landing and taking off, all in a steady stream. The transports were being moved out of sight to the hangars, while troop carriers were being docked at the main terminals.

Soldiers from Europe were being processed in. It was obvious what was going on, and it was Cal's job to see and remember and then to report it. Much was to be done, and they had little time to do it in.

As he stood looking at the traffic, a voice next to him said, "Well, it looks like the US rebels have chewed off more than they can swallow this time, huh?"

Cal looked at a very stunning woman, thirties, blonde hair, and blue eyes, with a slight touch of an accent. "What makes you say that?" he asked.

"Well, I've been here three days now and it hasn't stopped yet, and they tell me ships are on the way with tanks and all the rest. It's just a matter of time before they're ready for a full-scale invasion. Right now, they are only going into specific areas on rescue missions or to harass the rebel troops."

With a smile on her face and a twinkle in her eye, she continued, "Well, big guy, where're ya from? How goes the revolution in your neck of the woods? By the way, what's your name?"

"Cal. Cal Varner. What's yours?"

"Sybil Conner."

"Well, Sybil, to answer your question, the rebels are kicking ass. Almost all the states have joined forces with them and activated their National Guard units. Fighting in several states is heavy, and the federal forces are losing ground. Foreign troops are meeting stiff resistance in several areas. In Michigan and Wisconsin, both French and British troops have taken heavy casualties. Rebel troops have driven Russian troops back across the border in some areas, and it looks like the end is no closer today than it was before all this started. What news do you have of these events?"

Sybil replied, "Well, I work for the new European News Agency (ENA), and we are getting just the opposite reports. The Canadian broadcasters have all been reporting the rebel forces are in retreat in most eastern states. The Midwest states and southwest states have the strongest following but lack the population to support the rebels.

All in all, we are told the UN forces are driving deep into the United States and are being welcomed in every city. It's said the United Nations is taking light casualties."

Cal thought for a moment. He didn't want to blow his cover, at least not yet. "Well, I haven't been east of the Mississippi River, so I can't comment on the war in those areas. Perhaps we should see if we can accompany one of the UN brigades or companies so we can report their progress. What ya say, Sybil? Want to try?"

"Why not, Cal? I'm game."

Over the next several weeks, Cal had worked himself into the heart of the news command post and was privy to all the military dispatches being received. Nothing had been coming in about the raids on the European bases in Canada that had been hit at the offset of hostilities. Cal knew they were hit hard and devastating damage to buildings, aircraft, and runways had been made. It was obvious that the federal government and their allies were keeping vital information away from the public. The newscasters here were being pumped full of disinformation, and those going out on missions were being taken to mediocre targets of little value. Cal knew the Canadian targets were hit and with devastating results.

The news pool had been given a tour of the base and was impressed with the size and number of foreign troops that were there. The giant Russian An-225 Mriya transports had been ferrying in heavy weapons, tanks, big guns, and assault helicopters. As they arrived, they were moved to undisclosed locations for arming and staging. No doubt the United Nations was getting ready for a big push. The question was, when and where?

"Oh, Cal, there you are. I've been looking all over for you. Hurry up. I have a flight for us. One of the UN aircraft has consented to take us with them on a raid. Come on now. Let's go." Sybil was pushing Cal with eagerness. She had an opportunity, a real opportunity, to go on a real raid and wanted Cal to go along.

Cal was surprised she was that thoughtful. "Let me grab a coat and a hat and we can go."

Cal and Sybil entered the other room. "Tell me about this deal of yours," Cal said. "How in the world did you manage it?"

Sybil went on to tell Cal how she had met one of the officers leading the raid at the club and with a little persuasion had talked him into taking her and Cal. It seemed they were going to hit one of the rebel headquarters.

*****

Ten Royal Air Force (RAF) A380 Airbus transports with Tornado escorts were heading toward the US coast line when they received an urgent message from their air group. They ordered them to abandon their primary destination and to proceed to a secondary destination. No explanation was given.

The lead aircraft banked to the right and picked up a new heading for Canada. Just as the turn was made by all aircraft, eight F-16C Eagles appeared, four on each of their wings.

The lead Tornado was about to maneuver away from them and take up a defensive posture when he saw four more sitting above and behind them. No doubt there were more below him, not the right odds to take on America's finest, especially when you can see the Sidewinders on their wingtips. All of them carried US naval markings, so he decided to test the water for friend or foe. "Good morning, gentlemen. Jolly good of you to escort us to our destination. Hope you like Canadian beer. Will buy when we land. Over."

The American group leader came back with a very short and to the point reply. "Change your heading to south by southwest twenty-five degrees or we will lock on and put you all in the Atlantic. Any hostile move at this point and we will open fire."

Just as he keyed off the transmission, the Tornado had a missile locked onto it. The Yanks were not playing games; the transports and their air cover made their turn to the southwest. *Well, hell, this was better than fighting old friends*, he thought.

At least the Yanks were willing to fight for their freedom and were unwilling to give it away like they had. The Eagles were escorting them to God knows where and who knows what fate awaited them. *Well, maybe they can use a good pilot looking for freedom too*, he thought.

"Victor Charlie One, this is Victor Charlie Two. We are escorting ten British transports and six Tornado fighters to your destination. ETA is one hour ten minutes. Over."

"Victor Charlie Two, this is Victor Charlie One. Proceed to destination six eight two four for touchdown. We are unable to receive your group at this location. Over."

"Roger, Victor Charlie One. Over and out."

The navy squadron with its English transports and fighters turned to their new compass heading. Each navy aircraft had its target and orders to lock on and fire if the target tried to take evasive action or changed course. The formation flew southwest for two hours when the lead aircraft called his destination.

"Six eight two four, this is Victor Charlie Two, requesting permission for ten British transports and six Tornado fighters. Over."

"Roger, Victor Charlie Two. Northwest runway is open. The Tornado fighters will land first followed by the transports. We have locked on with ground-to-air missiles until all EU aircraft are down. Over."

With that, the leading British Tornado keyed in. "Roger, we are starting our descent now. Over." And as an afterthought, he added, "Please keep your fingers off the launch button. Thank you very much."

Each plane descended in order, landed, and was escorted to a secluded hardstand where they were met by armed troops. It was obvious they were going to be considered as prisoners of war.

One flight officer spoke out load, not to himself or to anyone else, just a remark, "The bloody fool who dreamed up this stupid bloody union and new world order should be right here right now."

The pilots in the Tornado fighters raised their canopies and started to dismount. An officer in one of the vehicles raised a bullhorn to his mouth and spoke.

"Hold there. Do not attempt to leave your aircraft at this time. Shortly you will disembark and be transported to a holding and processing area. Repeat, do not attempt to leave your aircraft at this time."

They shuttled all to processing under heavy guard and debriefed the British EU transport crews. Their cargos were unloaded and a thorough inventory was made.

CHAPTER 19

Heating up the Tamales

Carswell Air Force Base, New Mexico
Rebel Combat Planning, Southern Command

Gen. Cyrus Tique entered the conference room. In his hand, he carried a folder marked *Top Secret*. He held it over his head waving it in a circular motion for assembly. He strode to the podium, turned to the officers assembled, and looked out over them. Silence fell upon the men. The general's face was gray, unsmiling.

After a long pause, the general cleared his throat. "Gentlemen, I have here a communiqué from our agents in Mexico. As you are aware, European troops have been pouring into Canada and Mexico. We have been containing them inside our borders for two weeks now, and we have also been fighting federal and National Guard troops from states that have remained federal politically.

"Although we have reports of insurrection in some of them, they still confront us with strong opposition. Our agents in Mexico have informed us there are two divisions of troops getting ready to move up on our border. They comprise German, French, Italian, Mexican, and Spanish troops with Harrier support aircraft and German and French fighter-bombers using newly constructed airfields. We think they will move within seventy-two hours. Throwing them off-balance is therefore necessary for a preemptive air strike to weaken their resolve."

Air force general, Billy Kincaid, raised his hand interrupting the general and spoke, "Cyrus, we have the capability to hit them with cruise missiles coming in from the west. Why don't we hit them now before they can gain an offensive posture?"

Cyrus smiled and with a little chuckle in his voice continued, "At 0330 hours, the Second and Eighth Air Cavalry battalions will fly into Mexico from Texas. The Sixth and Fourteenth will move in from the southwest. They will then move around to the southern corridor and at ground level will move north. It is imperative that we strike them from the south. At this time, it is essential we demoralize the population. We must establish fear in all of them. We want them to push the Europeans out. Before we start our combat run, we will launch our aircraft from here and move them to the border and their attack positions. It is necessary we stay out of their missile range until our AH-64 and AH-64D Apache attack helicopters and the RAH-66 Comanche helicopters are ready to hit. As the choppers make their first attack run, we will drop chaff and fire starburst flares. The enemy should have all their radar and missile batteries trained on the border in anticipation of an attack. Our choppers can then move in and hit their ammo dumps and airfields before they can get anything up into the air.

"Targets will be primarily ammo dumps, aircraft, and ware-houses. Keep collateral damage to a minimum. After our initial attack, the helicopters will be returning home. Now, this is where you come in, Billy. Your boys will be the final blow on this mission. We will give the enemy an hour after our choppers are back, and you will hit them again with stealth fighter-bombers and B-52s you have taken out of retirement. Your latest reports state they're ready to go. Before your fighter-bomber attack, you will launch the AGM-86C cruise missiles from the Pacific region, approaching the targets from the southwest. The B-52s will do the cleanup approximately one hour after the B-52s have returned to their home bases. Billy, please remain for all planning details and have your entire crews meet with your aircraft commanders immediately after your final mission briefing. Now here are the details and the launch times for your aircraft. Good luck, and remember, freedom is earned."

General Kincaid nodded, turned to his aide, and gave him instructions. "Ready when you are, General." Both men returned to

General Tigue's office and prepared for one of the most damaging raids on the enemy. Within hours, it would begin.

*****

The United Nations deployed their combined European command and fully prepared for the invasion. The first real test of the new world order and the United States of Europe was about to begin. With the civil war going on in the United States and the movement of UN troops in the United States moving south, Field Marshal Von Volkinstead would move north. The United Nations, within hours of its invasion, expected to capture or destroy all American radar sites or any military activity he encountered.

After his initial attack, he expected to have troops occupying Carswell Air Force Base, and before midday, the rebel southern command headquarters would be his. *Thank God*, he thought, *for the American merger erasing the borders between all three countries, making infiltration simple.*

The troop carriers were ready and he had two thousand foreign legionaries due in before the invasion. He felt good. No, he felt pride, and he knew he would prevail. His intelligence from the area was excellent. The Mexican nationals living in the United States had been providing him with badly needed US troop movements and aircraft arrivals and departures.

The field marshal was very confident that he could destroy the mighty rebel war machine. Yes, he thought, glory would be his. He would receive the highest UN medal and no doubt the first USE Meritorious Honor Award.

He had two divisions of troops and assault helicopters and Harriers and ground-to-air missiles. Yes, he felt very cocky. Yes, he was going to teach these Yanks a lesson.

The field commanders and flight commanders were gathered for their daily briefing. Tension was high; they all knew how well trained the American troops were, and they knew they would be fighting on American soil—a hard combination to beat. They were told with the fighting going on in the north and with federal states fighting the bulk of the US Army, they were undoubtedly too busy to handle an invasion by two European divisions. Many of them had been trained with Americans in the old days and knew how they would react to different situations. They too, like the field marshal, felt they could walk in and take over without anything more than token opposition.

The briefing officer pulled back the curtain hanging behind him. As the curtain parted, a huge map of the United States came into view. The officer walked up to the map with a pointer in his hand and made a circling motion on the map with a red laser.

"This is our present location." As the red laser light circled the area, he continued, "We will move out in three separate directions going north, northeast, and northwest. Your objective? Towns, cities, hamlets, and all in the way must be destroyed. Try to move all civilians to the rear and burn everything. Destruction must be complete. We must demoralize all. Our objective is to move north and cut the United States into two halves, creating a corridor for troops and supplies to move in and divide the country. After reaching the Canadian border, we will be able to bring troops into the corridor and move in both east and westerly directions. As we move into other states, the capitulations should be rapid. The high command expects a complete victory within ten days. Any questions?"

A young captain raised his hand. "Sir, I spent six months undergoing training in an US Army unit before this revolution took place, and I know that many of these men are good. They're damn good, sir. We learned that in Afghanistan and Iraq. Unless we run into loyal federal troops, I doubt we will be able to finish this in ten very short days. To help ensure our victory, what do we have available for air support other than the Harriers, sir?"

The briefing officer glared at the young officer. "We need nothing other than the Harriers. They can move with us. They need no landing fields and can carry heavy bomb loads as well as low-level tactical support. Assault helicopters are no match for them. With their missile control system, we are counting on them to prevail. But to put your mind at rest, we have several squadrons of Mirage fighter-bombers for our long-range missions."

The young officer looked perplexed, for he knew the US Army's capabilities and cunning nature and dreaded the confrontation.

Now the field marshal only had to wait for his legionaries and they would be ready.

There was little activity over the border from the Americans; however they were getting a day-by-day report on all American rebel movements and everyday life. To him, it all looked simple enough.

*****

At Carswell Air Force Base, hangar 8, two companies of Delta Force personnel were packing gear. All of them were dressed in black; not a bit of light-colored material clothing was visible. Night vision headgear was being cleaned and special weapons were being assembled. Capt. Tork Albertson was going over details with his platoon leaders. Each move had to be precise. They were going to go in quickly, make their mark, and get out. There would be no time for a second chance. Three French helicopters with USE markings were in the hangar. They had mounted special guns in pods outside the ship, adding more firepower than the ship's original weapons systems.

The targets' locations were confirmed by satellite. It was a good move to have loyal informants giving them needed information from their satellite tracking stations as well as information from loyal Mexican Americans. True patriots working in Mexico provided badly needed intel. It was unfortunate they had no control over their own satellites. Eventually this would change.

Soon Tork knew they would have complete control. *Special Forces are moving into position to ensure we have control. Until then, field marshal what's his name would have information that would convince him that all is well.*

It was imperative the United Nations believe the satellites were providing them with aircraft and troop intel. Soon the satellites would no longer be controlled by the United Nations. They would soon control their own southern areas bordering Mexico and the northern areas of Mexico from Baja California to the Gulf of Mexico. Tork's mind reeled with thoughts and information.

They had already charted the area with U-2 aircraft a few days before the revolution started, and they knew every inch of ground and its environment. Captain Albertson had used this information well. In just a few short hours, his Delta Force would be moving in, just before the main raid by the gunships to spirit away the field marshal.

Tork's mind cleared, and he called over his pilots and addressed them. "One more time, men, from the top. Unit 1, go."

Lieutenant Baker responded, "We come in low below radar and land in the canyon a mile behind their lines. We'll set up our camp and make like French troops, bored and waiting for something to happen. We will be wearing French uniforms with the Velcro fasteners so we can pull them off if needed. Our main purpose is to deliver the main assault team to the canyon and stay there until pickup time. Hopefully, with the French choppers and markings, they won't notice us. At your signal from the command plane, we will pull off our French uniforms and take off for our assembly point at the targets. Never during the pickup, unless they fire on us, are we to engage the enemy. At all costs, we are to speak only in French."

Tork looked pleased. "Very good, Lieutenant Baker. Okay, Lieutenant Olson, your turn."

"When the first group is down, we will overfly them and hit our targets, setting off secondary explosions and creating panic among their troops. This is paramount. We will leave the field marshal's compound and chopper pad free of any open fire, and we'll try to ring it to give the impression that everyone down there is getting hit. We will engage the enemy as long as possible, giving Lieutenant Baker's flight the chance to come in low and land. Question, sir. Seems they will try to kill us and we are only going to respond if fired upon, except for the initial engagement. May I ask why, sir?"

Tork looked at his men, thought for a moment, and then said, "Gentlemen, we want all of those men to think twice about why they are over here, and if possible, we want to convince them to desert and join us in ridding the world of the malignancy of the new world order. We feel by sparing them, we can partially achieve this goal.

Now, if they follow orders and open fire, you are authorized to reply in kind. Is that clear? What's next, Sergeant?"

"After engaging and destroying the targets, we are to return to our pickup point. Should we miss it or they destroy the choppers, we are to move to the east and the gulf for a pickup by a naval unit. We're talking night travel only, and we'll be in radio contact, provided, of course, the air force will have a repeater plane in the air for us. If not, hope the Mexican phone company cellular systems are still operating."

Tork grinned. "Very funny, Sergeant. Don't forget your satellite phones are safe. A few more hours and we should have all the rough spots smoothed out and the teams will be moving out on Operation Fastback."

With that said, Tork looked over his team members and saw the dedication, resolve, and patriotism assembled and knew they would succeed. He was pleased and proud of each of them and could see victory and a new America in the making.

CHAPTER 20

Proven in Battle

Command had called Tork into the commanding general's office and was informed he would be leading the group to capture the field marshal. They gave him last-minute details and the alternate assembly points, if the original pickup had to be abandoned. Command had given him new communication frequencies to use and the code for radio transmissions. A hot key would be used instead of the radio. No verbiage was to be used; they didn't want any voice modulation. He had wondered if he would be going along, so to ensure success in the raid, Tork elected thorough training so each team would be self-sufficient. He was pleased of his forethought and preparation.

He had instructed his men that he may not be going and had trained each of them to act and to react as individuals, if they were broken away from the main party. Tork knew his men. He knew they were all exceptional in each of their specialties and could be counted on to win. They were handpicked from Delta Forces, rangers, Special Forces, and air force special ops.

All the talents were there. The slightest chances of a screwup were minimal but still there. Tork knew the importance of this mission. With the loss of their top commander, the United Nations would have to rethink its invasion plans. It would give the rebels time to move additional troops in and counter the enemy invasion. The UN troops had moved all the way down to the Idaho, Wyoming, and Utah border and were being held at bay by the Utah National Guard. Their experience in the mountains and the training they had made them a fierce force to deal with. The occupation of Montana, North Dakota, and Minnesota had been a prize for the United Nations. They thought Utah would be easy to take. The Canadian Armed Forces and UN troops engaged them and were being fought by a tiger.

"Ten-hut!" the sergeant called out as Captain Albertson walked into the briefing hall.

"At ease." Tork looked out at the team. "Be seated, men." Tork stood for a moment looking at the team. All in black, black makeup, uniforms, webbing, leather, and guns. There was no bright metal or anything light-colored that would reflect light itself. Even the casings on the rounds were burnished black in color.

"Men, tonight we will attempt to enter the command head-quarters of Field Marshal Von Volkinstead, commander of the Joint Chiefs of Staff of the USE and UN forces located in Mexico. This mission is highly important in maintaining our national integrity. The world must know we have the power and the resolve to over-come anyone who thinks they can take away our rights and subject us to foreign domination. We are Americans, and we will preserve the constitution at all costs. As outlined, we will move in under the cover of darkness while we are making diversionary strikes. As you move to the points of confrontation, our choppers will move in on the command post. The lead attack commander will radio the French command using only French, informing them that you are reinforce-ments. We will be giving French recognition passwords, and as we land, each of you must respond instantly to your designated assign-ments and return within the prescribed time frames. We cannot wait for you. If you are late, wounded, or unable to return, you must try to reach your secondary assembly point. If you are compromised or capture is imminent, set off your capture beeper and destroy your radio. Remember, we will be monitoring all of your frequencies, and we'll try to pinpoint your position. If possible, we will attempt to locate you and pull you out. If not, you are on your own. Are there any questions?"

The men looked from one to the other, but no one made a sound. Tork smiled. "Remember everything you have learned. We must move precisely as we have planned and practiced. Very good, let's go. Mount up and raise hell."

With that, all of them went out and mounted their choppers. The engines started and the black birds lifted up into the heavens. That night, all of the United States of Europe would learn what freedom meant to the oppressed and what they considered a ragtag army of a falling nation. That night, they would learn a valuable lesson from a free fighting group of Americans.

The choppers had moved in as planned. They dropped off the troops at their locations and assembly points. Two choppers flew into the French approach corridor giving the recognition signals. As they approached, all hell broke loose on the line. The aggressor force was pulling UN forces to them. Gunships hit them in lightning raids. It looked like a full-scale attack. The French commanders started replying, with everything they had. They thought the Americans were going to make a drive into the Mexican states. Pandemonium broke out among all of them. The field marshal's headquarter was alive with officers rushing to him for information and command. As the commanders entered the conference tent for their briefing, two SA 321 Super Frelon French choppers landed. No one paid any attention to the ships. Both had French markings, and through the windows, the pilots could clearly be seen wearing French uniforms and could be seen clearly waving at the men from the birds until the officers entered the tent.

Then, silently, the doors on the side of the birds slid open and the assault team moved to the tent. Several men circled it and all entered by command at the same time. Those that noticed assumed they were French troops put in place to protect the field marshal and his command post.

The French UN forces were moving men and equipment to the attack area. They stockpiled ammunition, while the sergeants barked orders. All things were chaotic, so much so no one was paying any attention to the helicopters or the men in them. They were all concerned about the fighting that had just started. Very soon they would feel the power of freedom from those willing to die for it.

Without warning, Tork moved into position. He whispered into the microphone attached to his helmet. "We're in position. On the count of fifteen, move in. Do not fire unless it's obvious they fire on us. If they do, leave no one alive, including the field marshal." Tork started counting. "One, two, three"—he gave his men fifteen seconds to get ready—"thirteen, fourteen, fifteen. Go!"

They all entered the large tent within seconds. Tork moved behind the field marshal and his staff. As he entered, he called out in French, "Attention, you are all prisoners of the US Freedom Army. Do not move and drop your weapons. Now!"

The startled men looked dumbfounded. Failing to understand what had happened, one French major pulled his sidearm. Before he could aim it, a steel bolt from a crossbow entered his chest on the right side, pinning him to one of the tent poles.

Tork yelled out in English. "Hold your fire!" He then swung his automatic on the field marshal. "Sir, if you wish to save your officers' lives, you will accompany us now. Otherwise we will be forced to kill you all. We have no time for debate."

The field marshal looked at the silencer on Tork's weapon and glanced at the others. They were all equipped for silent killing. One of his foolish officers was either dead or dying from a crossbow bolt in his chest. In English, the field marshal replied, "Yes, Captain. I agree."

The captain spoke into his mic one word, "Return." As they started to move, several of the men in black pulled out canisters from their packs and threw them into the tent. Bellows of smoke erupted. The men all returned to their birds, and in unison, they lifted off with the pilots shouting into their mics to the French below, "Americans have entered the compound and are using smoke to cover their entry. Quickly, quickly, move in before they kill the field marshal."

At these words, the outlying guards returned to the compound to find bellows of smoke and officers running around, firing weapons at anything that moved. Chaos was everywhere. The French troops were in disarray and were shooting at one another. They were dying from their own weapons. It would be morning before they realized they had caused their own casualties.

The flight was without incident, and the choppers landed safely. They escorted the field marshal to the commanding general's office where they received him.

The general saluted the field marshal as he entered the room. "Sir, they will move you in the morning to our revolutionary head-quarters, where you will remain until the North American continent is free from USE troops and the United Nations is gone. Until then, sir, you will be treated as a prisoner of war befitting your rank. Captain, escort the field marshal to the quarters arranged for him."

With a wave of the hand, they removed him from the office and the realism of what happened to him sank in. It was the most devastating and embarrassing thing that could have happened. The field marshal felt he had lost everything he possessed. They had stripped him of his dignity, self-assurance, and will to command. He went with his captor like a lamb to slaughter.

Captain Albertson upon arrival to the briefing room ran into an old friend. Standing and directing the debriefing of the raid was none other than Det. Sgt. Roland Tempelton from the San Francisco Police Department, now apparently a major in the new army.

Tork, in shock, exclaimed, "Tempelton, what in the hell are you doing here?" Noticing his rank, Tork corrected himself. "Or should I say Major Tempelton? The last time I saw you, we were in Frisco. What happened?"

The major, surprised to see Tork, said, "Well, Tork, it's good to see you too. What happened to me? Well, it happened like this. Many others and I had been waiting for something to happen. When it came, we were ready to move. I was a reserve officer in the army, so when it happened, I left Frisco and headed east with my family. I contacted the revolutionary forces in Utah. I have family there and they were glad to see us. Well, the rest is history and here I am. Tork, the whole country is behind us. In Utah, they all are working on methods to revamp the government and to improve the constitution, so nothing like the takeover of the government could happen again. It will prohibit the systematic dissection of the constitution by the Congress and put limits on presidential orders or anyone else. The

Utah National Guard Special Forces are working behind enemy lines as I speak, so don't be surprised to see me, for I'm glad to see you."

Tork was happy to see the major and wanted to know everything that was going on in the bay area. He needed to know how Di's family was and if Cal's girl was okay. He had loads of questions for Roland. This chance meeting of an old friend was a blessing he hadn't expected.

CHAPTER 21

Killing People and Breaking Things

Cal and Sybil had met with Lt. Col. Sean Doran of the Irish air force, Special Forces group, United States of Europe. The colonel had promised Sybil the chance to accompany him on a commando raid to an undisclosed rebel headquarters.

Both of them were to ride in an attack helicopter and would be put down after the initial attack. They thought it would get them firsthand pictures of the raid and they would be on hand to see a rebel headquarters destroyed.

Sean was an overbearing and pompous officer with little regard for the rebel's intelligence, let alone their military abilities. He had not yet had the opportunity to fight American soldiers. Cal took an instant dislike to him, but knew he could get valuable information on the European's military strategy that could help the rebel forces. The colonel wanted to equip the two correspondents with camouflage clothing so they would blend in with his men.

He did not impress Cal. "Sorry, Colonel. I can't wear your uniform or camouflage myself. If we are taken as enemy soldiers, we could be shot. It's my intention to report on your raid to show the country how our brothers from Europe and around the world have come to our aide to help us regain our country. I can't do that if I'm dead." Cal hated the words he had just spoken, but knew it was the only way to remain "hidden" in these circumstances.

Sybil spoke up, "Speak for yourself, Cal. I'll take the makeup job, Colonel. I'd like to go in with one of your assault teams. Cal can stay in the chopper until all is secured. He's a real Clark Kent, isn't he?"

The colonel smiled, pleased with her response. "Right you are then. We leave in twenty minutes. Both of you be here for boarding. Sergeant, take this young lady and get her into battle dress and camouflage makeup. Remember, we leave in twenty minutes."

Eight assault AS 532 Cougar helicopters lifted into the air and picked up their heading, south by southeast, staying just above the trees. They continued on their heading for two hours and twenty-two minutes and then turned due south. All choppers were in camouflage with a full complement of commandos and had USE markings. Cal had curled up in the corner of his bird and was looking out the window of the aircraft, wondering what target they were headed for. Sybil and the colonel were getting along very well; Sybil knew how to treat the men she needed. The soldiers with them were checking their weapons and talking about home and why they were there. They didn't seem to be in a big hurry to confront the rebel forces.

The European Union had trained some of them in techniques and weapons the rebels were using. It could be a standoff or a massacre. Any event, they would rather leave it for the politicians.

Being professional soldiers, they all knew they were in it, like it or not. Sybil and the colonel were in the middle of a debate when the pilot tapped the colonel on the shoulder and motioned for him to put on his earphones. "Yes, what is it?"

"Sir, we are twenty minutes out from our assault pattern. You need to get your men ready. The other birds will be notifying your group leaders of our ETA."

The colonel acknowledged and the men double-checked their weapons, preparing for the impending assault.

Maj. Beau Desmond, Kentucky National Guard, had received a message from a ground surveillance team that a group of helicopters with USE markings had passed over their position flying at about a hundred feet and was heading toward them. He reported they were loaded with troops and totaled eight in number.

"Sergeant Pringle, get on the hotline to the area air support coordinator. Looks like we have company coming, and I do not want to see them get out of here."

"Yes, sir." The sergeant keyed his mic and transmitted on a closed frequency. "Ground-K-One to Hawk Strike One. Over."

Almost immediately, an answer came back. "Hawk Strike One."

The sergeant replied with a possible intervention strike from the United Nations and requested immediate air support. He relayed the message that eight copters were incoming, possibly heavily armed. "Roger, Ground-K-One. Will implement. Over and out."

The choppers dropped down in a clearing about one mile from the target. They assembled the men and identified their targets. Part of the attacking force went to the east and west flanks. They were to hold at a predesignated position. The main group would make a frontal attack. The colonel knew the holding force was a National Guard unit stationed at a rebel-held weapons depot. It was the colonel's job to destroy the depot and to take no prisoners.

Sergeant Pringle reported to Major Desmond that he had contacted Hawk and they would be responding. Major Desmond felt much better. He had mostly green guardsmen assigned to the depot, and with little training under their belt, he felt they might be a liability, although they were all dedicated to freedom.

"Sergeant, you had better make sure our perimeter guards are alert. We can't take any chances. Only forty-two men to secure the depot and now we have a bunch of European bandits heading our way. Be alert, Sarge."

Pringle walked out of the headquarters building and started for the closest guard post. Just as he turned down the side of a building, a small hole appeared in the upper right side of his head, just above his right eye. He felt nothing when he fell facedown in the green Kentucky grass.

Silently, the colonel's commando unit stalked each sentry and dispatched them one by one. Before the last defender was eliminated, the colonel, Sybil, and Cal entered the major's office.

The major looked up expecting to see Sergeant Pringle, only to see the colonel raise his pistol and silently fire a round. The bullet was true and entered the major's head. The Irish colonel looked at his work and said, "That's one rebel officer that we won't have to worry about any longer."

Cal was heartbroken and furious about what he had just seen. He had been taking pictures of each atrocity and had gotten as many names of the commando unit he could, promising a real story for the men's home papers. He was appalled at the callous nature of the men. Sybil too had been frightened at what she had witnessed and was holding back tears.

She turned to the colonel and screamed at him. "How can you be so heartless, so murderous? Why have you killed him? Why didn't you just capture the depot? Why? Why? Why?" she shouted.

With a smirk on his face and his back straight as a rod, the Irish colonel replied, "My dear Sybil, it's my job to kill and break things. As for the depot, it is in the process now of being destroyed. As for you and your story, well, I'm afraid they will put it on hold until after the censors have gone over it. We can't have any unnecessary news going out to the masses, you know."

Cal quickly removed his camera's digital memory disk when Sybil and the colonel were arguing. He slipped it out of the camera and into the top of his waistband where they couldn't see it. He then inserted a spare one into his camera and spoke, "Colonel, if you don't mind, I would like to get a few pictures of the depot as it's blown up and a few pictures of your men as they work, if you don't mind, of course."

The colonel for a few minutes had forgotten Cal. "Sorry, but for the moment, I'll need all of your camera. They will return it when we're back at base headquarters and the censors have had a chance to go over them. Now, if you do not mind, Cal, I will take both the cameras."

Cal put his camera in the bag and handed it to the colonel—with one exception and it was safely under his belt. "Yes, sir, here it is. I hope you will take good care of it for me so it doesn't get lost. I've got some great shots of this raid."

The buildings were in flames and the team was ready to leave. The colonel ordered the choppers to land in the parking lot in front of the depot. Upon landing, each team boarded their machine. When the last bird was about to take off, Cal asked if he could slip behind a hedge running alongside the parking lot. With all the excitement, he needed to relieve himself.

"Go ahead, Varner. But mind you, you only have a few minutes. Then we're gone. We can't wait. You'll have to take your chances with the rebels. I'm sure they have troops on the way."

Cal ran to the hedgerow, stooped down, and ran toward the destruction and heat of the flames. The heat was becoming unbearable and the secondary explosions from the underground munitions bunkers were going off, showering the depot with shrapnel and debris. He found himself running into hell. He looked over his shoulder and saw the choppers lifting up and heading north. Their mission completed. He turned and ran toward the field to his right when he suddenly stumbled and fell facedown into the field. His unconscious body was waiting silently to be awakened by friendly forces.

*****

The rebel column had arrived way too late to help. The depot was in flames and with no evidence of an aggressor force. Captain Hopkins looked over the burning warehouses and the destroyed depot.

A lieutenant emerged from the shattered headquarters building. "Sir, we've found the major. He was shot in the head. They've murdered all the assigned personnel. Looks like each of them was disarmed and then shot. It appears to be systematic, post by post. Looks like a really professional commando job." Then as an afterthought, he added, "Oh yes, we found a civilian in the field with a knot on his head and no ID. Could be a victim or someone they left behind. What do we do with him, sir?"

"Take him with us. He might be able to tell us who they were and where they came from, what unit it was, and who the commander was. That's the guy I want."

Cal was placed aboard a Humvee and the group left after picking up the dead. There was no point in fighting the fire for there was no danger to any of the local people in the area, and besides, it would burn itself out. The depot was far enough out in the country to be considered safe for its ordinance.

Cal came to just as the column reached the rebel base. His head was splitting and he felt sick to his stomach. He wasn't sure who he was with, whether he'd been picked up by the colonel's men or was in the hands of the rebels.

"Hey, Sarge, this guy's coming around. Want me to put this turkey away again?"

"No, no, Bobo. Leave him be. We need him to talk." The sergeant waited until the column pulled up to the barracks area. He then called a formation, cautioned the men about loose talk, and dismissed them. He and two squad leaders escorted Cal to the provost marshal's office and interrogation.

Lt. Col. Arlington Jones-Bankman, West Point graduate, security chief, and provost marshal, welcomed Cal in. "Come in, come in, sir. I'm afraid I don't know your name."

Cal looked up at him his head still a mass of pain. "Could I have some aspirin please? I was hit while running from the fire."

The colonel looked at Cal and could see the pain in his face. He thought he could see something deeper, a pain that he hadn't heard about yet. "Tell me, what is your name? Where are you from? Why were you at the depot? Were you part of the attacking force? If you were, why were you left behind?"

A medic gave Cal a shot of Demerol and cleaned his head wound. Cal looked at the faces around him. The Demerol was working, his pain was gone, and he could think much better now. "My name is Cal Varner. The rebel command sent me to Wright-Patterson Air Force Base as an infiltrator to size up the base and what was going on. I was sent in as a correspondent from California as my cover. At this time, only those members of the press that are loyal to the federal government and to the United Nations are permitted news coverage and write only what they tell them to write.

"I hooked up with another reporter, and we were able to infiltrate the news command post where all the dispatches came through. They tell them the rebels are done for and the UN troops are moving through. They have released no news of rebel victories to the public. Sybil, the reporter I was with, managed to get us hooked up with a commando outfit that raided the depot where you found me. I was able to get pictures of the killings and the destruction." Cal reached into his waistband and handed the memory disk to the colonel.

"Here, sir, check these out and you will have a picture of each one of those bastards as they murdered unarmed men."

The colonel took the disk and tossed it to a lieutenant standing by the door. "Get this printed. I need to get this to command fast."

The man left the room. As he left, another entered, walked up to the colonel, and handed him a folder. The colonel opened the folder and looked at it for a few minutes. Then he looked at Cal. "Well, Mr. Varner, your prints and story have checked out with command. We have received instructions to get you to Carswell Air Force Base immediately. Seems they have another job for you, and thanks for the pictures. We will be looking for that group, and we'll need your help with names and such before you leave. Thanks again, Cal."

*****

Sybil and the UN forces had flown back to the base. She was appalled at what she witnessed on the strike. She tried to hide her thoughts and feelings from the men, and when she closed the door to her room, she burst into tears. Sybil lay on her bed with her head under her pillow trying to muffle the sobs.

She didn't know what had happened to Cal. Just as he went behind the hedge, one of the warehouses exploded and the colonel ordered the choppers up and out of there. He had no compassion for Cal and mentioned, as if it were nothing, that the explosion probably caught Cal with his pants down. If not, the rebel column coming in would find him and probably shoot him. "No loss," he said.

Sybil had decided no government could be right when they resorted to turning over the country to the United Nations and then selling out the last vestige of their freedom to them. The UN articles of the new world order would become the country's constitution. Liberty and justice for all would no longer exist.

Seeing it would enslave the world through control and dominance by the United Nations was obvious to her. No. Sybil Conner would now fight for freedom, but how?

*****

They put Cal aboard the C-130 aircraft, and he was airborne for Carswell. As the plane leveled off and just as he was about to relax, Cal looked out through a small window in the plane's fuselage. He saw two escort aircraft pull up to his left, just to the rear of the aircraft. He was amazed to see them. Then panic hit. They were not US aircraft; they were British Tornados. *Damn*, he thought. *We'll be forced down or shot down.* He stood up and rushed to the aircraft door leading to the cockpit.

As he opened it, an officer put out his hand. "Whoa, what's the hurry? What's the problem?"

Cal looked at him and pointed to the side of the aircraft bulkhead. "There's two British aircraft that have come up behind us. You need to let the pilot know."

The officer smiled and started to chuckle. It's okay, sir. They're ours. We'll be flying close to a federal-held area, and we need to make sure if they see us, they'll think twice about shooting at us. We were fortunate to pick up these birds when they were escorting cargo aircraft from the United Nations into the country. The pilots and crews are working to help liberate both of our countries."

Cal looked silently for a moment. Then he asked, "Just how do you plan to have the pilots of those aircraft respond to radio calls in the good old traditional American language. What about their accents?"

"Well, sir, it's like this. Seems the Brits don't really care about what's going on at home any better than we do here. Come with me, sir."

Cal and the officer entered the cockpit and the officer introduced Cal. He then reached over and keyed a mic. "Apple Tart One to Devon Cream. Over."

Several seconds went by and then a reply. "Devon Cream. Over."

The officer looked at Cal and smiled. "Complete with pilots, sir. As you can see, we are prepared."

"Devon Cream. Over."

The officer keyed his mic and answered, "Devon Cream, routine check. Keep your eyes open for any rebel aircraft. Over and out."

With that, Cal rested easily. He then went back to the cargo hold and sat down to think about all that had happened and wondered what had become of Sybil. Cal thought it would be smart if the council would send in another agent to act as a reporter. Working with Sybil could be helpful. They did not convince Cal that Sybil was a dedicated federalist. The many talks they had indicated a turn toward the rebels and what they were trying to do. Yes, he thought. He would have to bring this up when he got to Carswell.

The Tornados circled above the base until the C-130 had landed and was off the runway. They, in turn, landed and were escorted to outlying hardstands and put under camouflaged netting.

The pilots were picked up by vehicles and driven to the base debriefing room in Operations. The ground crew had unloaded their cameras, and the film was being processed at the lab as they brought them in. It seems their primary mission was to photograph strategic areas and then to escort the C-130 to Carswell. Photographs and the details given by the British pilots were invaluable. The UN forces were building up for what may be a big push into the central states. The concentration of UN forces in Mexico and the loss of Wyoming and Nebraska would indicate a push from the northern and southern regions was in the making.

Intelligence indicated the United Nations was planning on moving into the interior from the north and south at the exact same time. Word was out that they wanted to move fast, so they were going to try to avoid any mountainous routes they could. The only problem was their equipment. They needed information on the equipment. If they had it, they could be sure of the United Nations' plans and plan their defenses. It was imperative that they send a second reporter into the UN base immediately.

The command decided to send Cal back in. He would be given a cover story with backup information from loyal American citizens living around the depot where he was picked up by federal forces and brought back to the base. The so-called federal forces would be rebel troops. With their resources, they could make it a convincing story. Yes, Cal would need to go back in. He knew the base, and he had contacts there. His ability to move as a known person would make it possible for him to get around better than a new agent would.

*****

Major Tempelton keyed his intercom.

"Yes, sir," the clerk replied.

"Get me Captain Albertson and Cal Varner immediately and have them report to me."

"Yes, sir."

Within twenty minutes, both Tork and Cal were standing before their old friend and now a trusted one. Tork was overjoyed to see Cal was safe, and Cal was grateful Tork was there for him. He needed his support after his ordeal at the depot.

"You called, sir?"

"Yes, Tork. Because of intelligence reports, it has become necessary to send Cal back into the fire."

"Where to this time, sir?" asked Cal.

"We have to send you back to the base, Cal. It's necessary we know what type of equipment has been coming in and what type of munitions they have. They expect a big push from the United Nations, and we will need to be prepared. We need your eyes and ears?"

"Yes, sir, I understand. When do I leave?" Cal was ready and eager to return—only this time, he would be taking back help.

CHAPTER 22

Return from the Dead

Sybil had decided to try and find the rebel forces. After what she had seen at the depot and not knowing what had happened to Cal Varner, she knew she had to do something. After returning to the base, she went in immediately and wrote the best story of her life; no doubt it would have won the Pulitzer Prize, if they had allowed it to be published. Sybil had taken her story to the information officer coordinating for review and editing, expecting to have it approved and sent out to the news agencies. After all, she knew the Irish colonel had killed a fellow reporter. The truth had to be told.

They took her behind closed doors and she learned the truth about the new world order and freedom of the press. Harry Truman had a policy of the "Buck stops here" well, so did the new world order. That's where her story stopped, only it wasn't the buck. It was the truth.

The government, she was told, could not permit any information that would allow the rebels to distort it for their own propaganda efforts. The information officer couldn't allow the story on the raid to go out at all. He felt the rebels would use it to misinform the people. They would no doubt distort the truth and turn more of the people against the government and the United Nations. Besides it would be unfair to the thousands of UN troops that had volunteered to come over here to help them in their hour of need.

Boy, Sybil thought, *what a snow job. Hell no, it's a blizzard. If that officer had seen what those troops had done to the men at the depot*

145

and how they had callously left Cal there to die, he too would have second thoughts about the civil war.

After being rebuked by the information officer, Sybil went out and investigated the base and its soldiers. She had managed to get a date with several of the UN officers. By using a human-interest line with them, she was able to pump them for information on where they were from, what raids and battles they had been in, and what they thought of the war. Some of them were pompous, self-indulging egomaniacs and, once asked, wouldn't shut up on their exploits. Those were where she gained the most information. The full story of defeat and butchery came into play. The truth was slowly coming out, piece by piece, until Sybil had a vivid picture that the revolution was just and needed to free America from the grip the government had on it. She wondered just who the leaders were. She knew members of both parties made the initial broadcast. But just who they were and how deep in Congress and the Senate it went, she or anyone else didn't seem to know. Sybil had learned about the heavy weapons flown in and marshaled on the opposite side of the base and then shipped out to a staging area where the federal government and the United Nations were preparing for a big offensive. The only thing she hadn't found out yet was where it was to start or where it was going. This she had to find out.

They had almost caught her in a restricted area; only her small size saved her. She was able to hide in areas that concealed her. Now, if she could only find someone, anyone, that could get her and the information out and to the rebel command unit.

*****

It was just past seven in the evening when Sybil entered the base news room. Everyone jabbered at once, excited about something. She spotted a companion from her home office and pulled him aside.

"What's going on, Charlie? Why is everyone excited? What's the news?"

"You haven't heard, Sybil. An army unit found that guy that went out with you on the depot raid just south of here. They just brought him in. Seems the guy has been trying to get back since you guys left him there to die."

Charlie's words stung Sybil like a thousand hornets. "Now, wait just a minute, pal! I wasn't the one that left him there. If it bothers you so much, you go give that Irish lieutenant colonel hell, not me."

"Take it easy, Sybil. I didn't mean to say you were at fault. We just want you to know we won't be taking any trips with you or that colonel. Get my drift?"

With that, Charlie turned and walked off to talk with other reporters about Cal. It was obvious they felt Sybil had sent Cal down the river to get the story. They didn't know the story never made it past the information officer or that it was critical of the raid and the officer in charge. Sybil couldn't wait for Cal to come to the news room, so she went on over to the headquarters building to find out where he was. She wanted desperately to let him know how sorry she was about what had happened at the depot.

"May I help you, ma'am?" the young lieutenant wanted to be helpful too. *Such a very pretty woman*, he thought. He was eager to help.

"Thank you, Lieutenant. I'm looking for the reporter the army brought in this evening. Do you know where he is or if he's returned to the press quarters?"

"No, ma'am. That is, no, he hasn't returned to his quarters. He's still in debriefing. The unit that brought him in is in the lounge. If you would like to talk with them, go right in. I'm sure it will be all right."

"Thank, you." Sybil turned and walked toward the double doors to her left. The lounge was a waiting room in the headquarters building. They had furnished it with vending machines and tuned a large television set to the federal and UN channels. Nine men were lying around the room in chairs and on sofas, some munching on snacks while a few with eyes closed but not really sleeping. A captain sat in front of the TV set, engrossed in what was going on. The news was in full swing. The commentator was telling how the UN troops were moving south at a rapid rate and would soon reach the gulf, cutting off the rebel forces.

RONALD PRICE

Sybil looked around and saw a sergeant laid back, eyes closed but not yet asleep. She walked up and touched him on the shoulder. "Excuse me, Sarge. Have you seen Mr. Varner?"

The sergeant looked up, startled to see such a lovely lady standing there. "Who's that Mr. Verner?"

"No. No, Sergeant. Mr. Varner, Cal Varner."

"Oh, Cal. Yeah, he's in for a debriefing. We ran into a squad of rebels that had taken Cal prisoner and they were on their way back to their lines when we showed up. Got them cold turkey. Might say we caught some of them with their pants down. It was a real break, smoke and eat break. Couldn't take any prisoners, so we had to leave them there soaking up the ground. Not a pretty picture, ma'am, but then they were just a bunch of rebels."

Sybil felt suddenly ill. The thought of another obvious slaughter by federal troops shamed her. They couldn't take prisoners, so they murdered them. What had the world come to?

"Do you know when Cal will be out?" she asked, smiling.

"No, ma'am. Captain just told us to wait here until he came back."

Sybil picked an empty chair by the window and waited for Cal and looked at the killing sergeant watching TV. She was rapidly building up a hatred for this man, for this killing sergeant.

The words the sergeant had spoken continued to burn deeper and deeper into her mind. The more she thought of it, the madder she became.

Suddenly the air was shattered with a loud command. "Ten-hut!" Sybil looked over to the sergeant and the door. A colonel had entered the room, followed by Cal. She jumped up and called out, "Cal! Cal!"

Cal looked over and broke into a big smile. "Syb, good to see you, hon. Come on over here and meet someone."

Sybil, by this time, had thrown her arms around Cal and hugged him. "I thought they killed you on that damn raid, Cal. What happened? How did you get out?"

"Easy girl, one thing at a time, huh. I want you to meet—"

Before he could finish, Sybil had turned to the captain that had walked up and slapped him across the face as hard as she could. They all heard a solid whack.

All heads turned to see what had happened. Cal grabbed Sybil and pulled her away.

"Easy, Syb. What the hell was that for?"

Sybil burst into tears trying to explain the hate she had built up from the conversation she had with the sergeant.

The captain rubbed his face and hollered, "At ease," to the men. They all jumped up and moved toward the girl. "It's all right, men. Take it easy. She's upset about something. Go on over and sit." He turned to the girl and Cal. "Now, young lady, just what was that all about?"

Cal grabbed the girl and the captain and pulled them both toward the door. "Let's go outside, Captain, and find out what's going on."

All three of them walked down to the exit door at the end of the corridor, and there Sybil explained her attitude in a tearful voice. "I'm sorry, Captain. I had been talking with your men and the sergeant told me about the rebel group and Cal. After the depot raid and what I had seen there, I, well, I just broke down. Not a very good soldier, am I?"

Cal looked at Sybil and then at the captain. "Look, Syb, things don't always seem as they are. Sometimes soldiers stretch the truth, and things get twisted around. Just what did the sergeant say to you?"

Sybil told them both what she had heard and what she felt. After seeing the men at the depot murdered by the USE troops, she believed what the sergeant told her and she felt the country needed to know. The biggest problem was she was unable to get her story past the news desk. Seems the government didn't want any negative stories about the federal or United Nations going out to anyone.

After telling her story, it struck her. Cal had not introduced her to the captain. "Well, Cal, who's your friend? Aren't you going to introduce us?"

"Who? I'm so sorry. Sybil, I would like you to meet Capt. Timothy Allen. He and his company found me with a rebel squad that was taking me in for interrogation." Cal then explained to her what happened after she left.

"Well, Captain, what happened to the rest of your company?" Sybil was trying to figure out in her mind if there was a company of men. Then why only about a squad was here now? She didn't see any others outside waiting for them.

"Well, ma'am, on our way here, we were caught in a firefight with a rebel battalion and separated. We managed to slip by them. My guess is the rest of the company either got away or are now prisoners. I understand the rebels get ugly with federal prisoners, so we're not sure what happened to them."

"Excuse me, Captain. May I have a word with Cal in private, please?"

The captain nodded and walked back to the lounge.

"What's this all about, Sybil?"

"Cal, I had to tell you what happened at the depot. I think you have a right to know and I didn't want the captain to hear."

"Well, he's gone. What is it?"

"That monstrous colonel deliberately left you there to die or to be captured. He ordered the helicopters up and refused to send anyone out to see if you were hurt or dead."

Cal's eyes narrowed, his face turning red with anger. What he experienced flashed across his mind. The hate for what the Irish colonel had done to those soldiers and himself would be with him forever.

"After the killing and our leaving, what happened to you, I've been trying to get stories out, but they're all stopping me. It's obvious we can't get our stories to the people. We've lost our rights to write our copy and have it published without it being censored, to the point you can't print the truth. From what you've said to me and how I think you feel, well, I feel I can trust you, Cal. I want to get out of here and join up with the rebels. They're right you know. I couldn't see it before but now I can."

Cal looked at her for a long moment, silently trying to pick up some inkling of a trap. She seemed to be sincere; however, he's willing to gamble. So he took the gamble.

"Syb, I have been with the rebels since the depot and the stories we are hearing are not true. I have seen nothing that leads me to believe the stories about the atrocities we've heard about are fact. From what I've seen and heard, they can't be true."

After Sybil left, Cal and Tork discussed the incident between Cal and Sybil. Tork was concerned about it and didn't really trust her. Cal felt she was sincere and wanted to believe her.

Tork, on the other hand, said, "We'll need to gather as much info about her as we can, and if she's on the level, then maybe she could be invaluable to us."

Cal said, "I think she is a very honest person that has seen the light and wants to help. I'm in favor of trusting her."

Tork turned to Cal after listening for a few minutes. "Okay, Cal. We don't have much time, so we need to set up a little test for her. If she comes through, we take a chance. It won't be long before these guys find out we're not part of the federal forces. So we'll start tonight gathering the intelligence we need. Shouldn't take more than a couple of days. The men know what to do and some of them have already started. They've assigned us a barracks and some of the men were put on work details. We should be ready to move out of here within forty-eight hours. If she is legit, well, what the hell? We may as well take her with us. Until then, we go as planned."

Tork left for the bachelor officer's quarters and Cal went back over to the newsroom to see if he still had a room.

CHAPTER 23

New Ground, New Direction

Headquarters, Congressional Holding Camp in Exile
New Mexico

Sen. Robert Anderson had just convened the committee and was in the process of informing them about the impending invasion from both Canada and Mexico.

"Gentlemen, as you can see by the briefs given to you, the UN forces have taken Montana, Wyoming, and North Dakota, although at great expense to them. We have them under control at these points," he said pointing to a large wall map of the United States, filled with colored flags. "At each of these locations, we have brought in heavy artillery and missile launchers. You can see the estimated number of foreign troops and the nationality of each force. Our people tell us this can be a good thing. Using age-old rivalry and prejudices, we think we can divide them or create distrust between them.

"To do this, we have prepared flyers and we will airdrop them during the night from high-flying bombers. They will drop them in canisters that will open at a predetermined altitude by parachute so they can float down silently. The UN commander was pleasant enough to stage his divisions so we could take advantage of a good clean distribution."

Congressman John Meadows, New York, one of eight black members raised his hand.

"Yes, Congressman Meadows?"

"Senator, I was told there was a raid not too long ago in Mexico on a French headquarters and they took a high-ranking officer prisoner. What are the facts? Did this take place or is it a rumor?"

"Yes, Congressman, the raid took place and we removed Field Marshal Von Volkinstead. He was taken prisoner and is here at this headquarters now. He's a French officer from an old Dutch family line. His losses to the UN forces have been devastating to them. Our men and women that coordinated and took part in this raid have been commended for a job well done. To infiltrate behind their lines, we used a group of all black troops, and the devastating results allowed the mainstream of their forces to concentrate on the infiltration this gave our helicopters the time to land and extract the field marshal. We're very proud of all of them. Without that commando team's great risk, we wouldn't have pulled it off as we did. You might say Americans helping Americans save America. Does that answer your question, Congressman?"

"Yes, and thank you. We knew nothing about the raid and feel we should have been involved or informed."

"Yes, sir. However, when you include all of us in strategic and military planning, it becomes inconceivable, so we leave it up to the military, although all plans of a political nature come before the council for approval by each designated committee. To put your mind at ease, sir, two members of the Black Caucus suggested using an all-black force for this assignment. They felt an all-black force dressed in black could get through the enemy lines without detection. Because of the limited black members in the French army, the men that penetrated the French headquarters were white. To gain entry could not have been possible without the main core. We would not have entered the compound when we did without their diversion and would have had a poor chance of getting out as well. We are proud of all of our men.

"They were right. The mission was highly successful with only minimal casualties taken and they were brought back with their units, although several teams had to move inland and were picked up by naval helicopters. They are all back now and safe. They're

American, each of them, and that's why we're here. Remember, freedom is earned by being loyal to God, the constitution, and freedom."

Congressman Meadows looked at his contemporaries. He knew then that his prejudice was unfounded. It was apparent they were all working together for a better America and maybe a better world. "I apologize, Senator, if I sounded out of line. I want you to know I'm with all of you, 100 percent."

The senator smiled and went on to other business. "We have sent a small team into one of the federal forces staging areas where we believe they are building up for a strike into the Central United States. Our intelligence people tell us a big push is on the way to drive straight down to Mexico to gain an open corridor. They hope this will allow them to push east and west, forcing us to fight on two fronts. They expect us to run low on supplies and to capitulate due to the lack of munitions and food. The enemy believes the majority of people are against us, and as they move in, the conflict will cease from town to town and state to state. Florida and Puerto Rico have joined in with the federal forces and are now in their hands. You can see on the map. The red areas represent the federal government, and the blues represent the new government. The yellow line from point A down to point B indicates the suspected direction the UN and Canadian troops will take. The green areas are the routes we believe the federal troops will take to link up with the UN troops in Mexico. We know what, where, and why, but not when. Hopefully, our team can provide this information soon. They only have about forty-eight hours before they are compromised. Any questions?"

One of the senators present said, "Yes, I have one, sir. What is the status on our detained colleagues and the president and his cabinet? I would like to know how they are being kept and if we are making them aware of the situation we're in. Have you made any effort to inform them why all of this was necessary?"

Sen. Robert Anderson looked at him silently for a moment and thought to himself, *Why would a member of the council ask such a question unless he might be getting cold feet?*

Joseph Principle, member of the Senate for ten years, one of the founders of the revolution and a dedicated American, had asked questions that seemed out of place for any of them to ask.

Senator Anderson looked over to his colleague. "Joe, the president is being well cared for and has been briefed on every action that both parties have been taking. The United Nations will never again be located in the United States, so we need not contend with them now. After hostilities cease and we have won the day, we intend to expand our markets within the north and south American continents, provided they break away from the United Nations and form a new coalition of states, from Canada to the tip of Chile.

"I believe the people of the Americas can share in the same way as we have. When the politicians decided what was best for this country and the new world and turned us over to the United Nations, all was lost. Well, I for one will never allow this country to be dominated by the rest of the world. As you all know, the domination came slowly, with each president failing to act in our best interest because the United Nations must first request it, condone it, or authorize it. No, gentlemen. A world dominated by the United Nations must never control us again. All borders must be reestablished and made impregnable.

"We will not arbitrarily surrender ourselves again to a world group of countries who cannot yet control themselves, let alone tell one of the most advanced countries how they must live. American heritage and traditions must be reestablished too. Look what happened to Great Britain. She is a state of little importance within the United States of Europe, completely dominated by countries that could never beat her in battle. She was turned over to them by their politicians, a state within a country playing at being important, our mother country dissolved, a monarchy no more, a state controlled by Germany, France, and Russia, the new socialists of the world in control."

The members of the council looked at Joe, agreeing but not agreeing, wanting to acknowledge his statements, but not sure. A United States of America encompassing both North and South

America, well, that was a hard one to swallow, but Joe raised his hand to hold their attention and said "Senator Anderson has had his say.

"Now gentlemen, not too many weeks ago, a squadron of navy jets picked up a flight of RAF aircraft flying into our airspace. They were heavily laden transports carrying munitions to UN troops that had moved into our northern states. British fighters escorted those transports. We caught them by surprise and routed them to one of our bases. Gentlemen, as some of you know, most of the pilots and crewman on the aircrafts requested asylum and wished to join our struggle. When we asked them why, they all had the same answer. They wanted their country back too.

"They felt if our struggle was successful, then maybe they could count on us to help them return Britain to the British. They did not have any great love for the rest of Europe or its new USE image. To them, there would always be a United Kingdom, an England, Scotland, and Wales, not the United States of Europe where they became nothing.

"I believe that there are other states in the world that feel the same way. They don't want any part of the new world order either. The revolution for the planet has started with us."

Looking at everyone, seeing agreement in their eyes, he continued, "Gentlemen, I feel we've started the third-world war, and we must prevail or the world's biggest dictatorship will result. It's for these reasons I want to get through to the president and his cabinet. They must realize what they have done and how far it has reached.

"First, I would like to make a worldwide broadcast telling all the people what our goals are and ask all of them the same questions. Are you free? Do you still have the national identity of your fathers? Can you still call yourself by that nationality? Or are you just a member of the United States of Europe that lives in the states of France or of Britain, Spain, or Germany or wherever? Let's ask them all if they want to be part of a united nations of earth where others decide their fate and make their laws and decide how they will live or where they will live. Well, I don't think they will appreciate it any more than we have right here in this country. Let's let them know that we will inflict great pain upon them and their sons and daughters that come here to fight us. Let them know that our struggle may one day become theirs, and as we decide our fate, we may be deciding theirs as well."

The council sat quietly for a few moments. "Yes, yes, I agree," a member replied. "Yes, we should be doing everything we can to create a free Europe. Let the people decide for themselves. I recall during the treaty negotiations many countries would not allow the people to interfere. The government found out that those that did interfere were not in favor of the treaty. That's when their government prepared the treaty in what they considered 'in the best interest of the country,' thus destroying all of their national pride. The politicians then went into promised positions within the new government, leaving their own countries in disarray, seeing them only as members of a new united order. As we fight now for our independence, we should tell them the truth so they can decide their own fate. Yes, gentlemen, I too agree with Joe."

Joe looked pleased that he had made his point. "Thank you, Senator Paulson, for your support. If the council is in agreement, I have set up a time and date for a broadcast. I propose we invite the president to address the country and let him tell them that we are capable, that we have resolve to free our country from all foreign aggressors, and he must agree to our terms. If not, we can show the president and the other members of the House and Senate living in their quarters to let the people know we have not harmed them in any way. We have several that have asked for meetings with us. Seems some of them agree with us now. That brings up a second request. I would like a committee from this body to meet with these men to see if they are sincere and want to join us in our efforts for freedom. Gentlemen, with a show of hands, do we show the president and the others to the people and the world?"

First one and then another hand was raised. Within seconds, all hands had raised to the affirmative.

"Next, do we form a committee to interview each of the House members and senators that have been incarcerated?"

All hands went up to the affirmative.

"I thank you all for your indulgences, and I thank God for our new chance at freedom. God bless us all. God bless America."

*****

Cal called Sybil around 0100 hours. The phone rang for several minutes before she picked up the receiver.

"Hello," a very sleepy voice said.

"Cal here, Sybil. Are you still interested in a good story?"

"Yeah, Cal, if I can take it out of here on my own. I'm interested because they sure in hell won't let me send anything out. What do I have to do?"

"Just meet me in half an hour in the back hallway. Wear black clothing and bring a camera with the highest-speed film you have. No flash equipment. Understand?"

"Okay, I'll be there. Don't go without me, please."

"Syb, this could be very dangerous for us all. You have time to back out." With that, Cal hung up and looked at Tork. "Well, what test do you have in mind?"

Tork answered, "The USE forces are having a party in an unrestricted area tonight. It won't end until about 5:00 a.m. We'll tell her we'll be taking pictures of documents in their headquarters building. If she isn't on the level, she'll find a way to notify with some excuse to leave us so she can make a call. That's when we'll know."

"What happens then, Tork? What will you do?"

"If she calls, we won't have much time to get out of here. So we'll take her with us and try her when we get back to our own lines."

"What about the information we need for the council?"

"We've picked up what we need. The last three nights, I've had the men working overtime to get it—detailed equipment lists, aircraft, fording equipment, portable bridges, tank strength, and more. Our intelligence group should do well with it. Sybil's line is tapped and I have two men watching her. If she calls or leaves the room other than to meet us, we'll know. Now let's go and see if she shows as planned."

Both men and two of the team were waiting for Sybil when she showed up. Soon after her arrival, one team member and then another showed. As they entered, they gave a silent signal to Tork. As the last man approached and gave his signal, Tork smiled, turned to Cal, slapped him on the back, and said in a hushed voice, "All is well, my friend. We can trust her."

Cal smiled. He was right. He knew she couldn't have been spying on them. It was time to gather the last bit of information and get out of there. Tork had assigned the men to complete their mission and to meet with him and Cal outside the barracks area. They were to move all their equipment and stack it as if they were going out on a mission. Everything was to be prepared to show they would be moving out. They backed up a truck and placed the equipment on board. One of them would standby to answer any questions that may arise. If asked, he would tell them the men were eating and would be moving out in an hour. He would then bring the truck over to their assembly point and standby until they returned.

Tork was confident this would satisfy any nosy officer or non-com that came around. It would give them the time they needed to make their final arrangements and meet at the northeast side of the field. They would move together as a team for the pickup when the aircraft was in position. It would take teamwork and coordination to board a moving aircraft through a slightly open rear-loading door on the aircraft.

Tork and Cal had informed Sybil who they were and why they were there. She was delighted to know the rebels had come to her, and she informed them of the information she'd gathered. Tork was amazed of the quality information she had gotten on her own and realized the impact it would have on the war.

Tork, Cal, Sybil, and the team had moved to the flight line through the northeast sector that they'd assigned two of the teams to observe earlier in the night. They had bridged the sensors and cut out a section of the fence. It was neatly wired back in place.

At night and at a distance, it couldn't be seen. They had received the last bit of information they needed. It was here they would board a very special aircraft.

As the team slipped through the fence, two of the team went ahead silently. The guards never knew what hit them. As they entered the waiting area, Cal turned to Sybil and asked, "What happened to that Irish colonel that left me behind at the depot?" Cal had not yet gotten over the depot and what had happened to him or to the men they had slaughtered.

"He's still here. As a matter of fact, I think he's probably at the UN party tonight. Most of them are probably bragging about the depot. The guy is a real loser."

Cal turned to Tork. "Any idea where they're having the party?"

Tork could see that Cal was still upset with what happened to him at the depot. He pondered what he should do about Cal's question, knowing he was going to get drawn into a situation and knowing he was going to have to make a choice. Tork also knew what he would do in the same situation. He replied, "You really want to try to get this guy before we leave?" Still he had to smile. Here was passive Cal, with a vendetta.

Times had really changed since Cal's intrusion that night not so very long ago. All of them had become the new Americans, dedicated to true freedom and a just cause. Thinking back, Tork had concluded it all started with the country's acceptance of NAFTA and GATT. It was there they started losing their sovereignty.

As they say, the road to hell is paved with good intentions, and God only knows how many were made to pave the road they were on then. Surely they were in a war to fight and to win at all costs. Not since the terrorist attacks on the country had they been fighting on their soil for such an important principle—freedom. Tork felt they were going to win, and the fight must go on.

Cal looked at his friend and said, "I would give anything to see that justice is done with him and the rest of his team. What they did was not warfare. It was cold-blooded murder. Yes, sir, I would love to get him."

Tork looked at Sybil. "Want to go to a party?"

Sybil looked at both of them, one at a time. Then she threw her head back, looked up at the stars, and sighed. "Yes, you're damn right I would, and I know what he looks like."

The plane was due in less than forty-five minutes. They had little time to get to the party, find the colonel, and get him outside and back to the pickup point before the plane arrived. They all had to be in position and ready to move when the C-130 was taxiing by. Time and coordination were paramount.

The plane would be moving slowly with her cabin lights out and the tail section opened enough for them to crawl in. They all had to be in place before the plane reached the next guard position or they could be caught. Taking the colonel from the party could jeopardize the whole mission.

Tork knew the danger. "Okay, Sibyl, let's go," said Tork. Tork took Sybil and two of the team. They left as quietly as they had come. It took them almost ten minutes to reach the checkpoint.

"Good evening, Sergeant. The festivities still going on?" Tork said to the host at the door.

"Yes, sir. They've been coming out all night. Most of them are being carried out. Looks like there might be a big blow coming up soon. Only wish I could go, but I'll get off duty after it's all over."

Tork looked him over and winked. "Well, Sergeant, I have to pick one of the team members up, get him back, and sober him up for a big mission. Do you have a vehicle available?"

"Yes, sir. There's a Land Rover parked behind you, sir. You can use that if you can find your man."

"Thanks, Sergeant."

Upon arrival, Tork and Sybil walked over to the hangar. The music was loud and there was plenty of food and drinks. The other two had moved in ahead of Tork and Sybil and were there ready to help if they needed them. Sybil scanned the faces for the colonel. Time was running short, and they had just about given up hope. Tork was about to call it off and leave when Sybil turned and bumped into Lt. Col. Sean Doran.

"Oops, sorry, sir."

"Well, well, well, I wondered what happened to you Sybil. Where have you been hiding?"

"Well, Colonel, considering I haven't been able to send any of my copy out, I've been sleeping, writing, or reading. Would you know anything about it, sir?"

"I'm afraid I can't help you, Sybil. You probably have to learn how to censor your copies. Maybe then you can send it out right."

"Look, Colonel, I'm sorry, but it's just frustrating not being able to do my job. Could I have an interview with you now?"

"Why not? Let's go outside and get away from this noise, and I'll give you an interview right now."

The two of them walked out of the hangar. Sybil looked over to the parking lot where several vehicles were parked out of sight and poorly lit. She pointed to them and said, "How about over there, Colonel? We can sit in one of the trucks and you can give me the facts, okay?"

The two of them walked over to the Land Rover and got in. The colonel lit a cigarette, leaned back, and blew out a straight line of smoke. "Okay, Miss Reporter, shoot."

Before Sybil could respond, a needle penetrated the colonel's jacket collar and entered his neck. The serum worked instantly and the colonel collapsed, falling forward. Tork caught him before he could hit the horn. Two of his men helped him pull the colonel to the back of the vehicle, sat him up, and pulled his cap down over his eyes. One man got behind the wheel, started the vehicle, and drove to the gate.

Tork looked on from the back. "Well, we found him, Sergeant, three sheets to the wind, but I think we can sober him up in time for the mission. Thanks again for the help." Tork nudged the driver and they moved ahead as he returned the sergeant's salute.

*****

"Morning Star One to Morning Star Base. Over." The crisp British accent boomed out over the tower speaker. The air traffic controller picked it up and answered, "Morning Star Base to Morning Star One. We've been expecting you, Morning Star. Over."

"Thank you, Morning Base. Requesting landing instructions. Over."

"Roger. Proceed to runway NE42. Winds at two knots. It's clear all the way to the stars. Over."

"Roger, Morning Star, and thanks."

The Hercules C-130, with British markings, circled over the field. He came in on his landing pattern, the wheels were lowered, and the crew was waiting for their special cargo. As the bird touched down, all was ready.

Tork abandoned the vehicle about two hundred yards from the fence. They had just cleared the fence when they heard Cal's, "Over here." They made their way to the edge of the taxiway.

Cal, relieved at seeing them, said, "They just landed. You guys got back just in time. I thought we were going to have to leave without you."

The team was ready. Four men had the unconscious colonel ready to lift and run to the aircraft. The plan was to put him on board first and then they would enter behind him. The rest would follow. Once inside, they would put on USE uniforms, and when the plane docked, they would start unloading. Base operations thought the plane was scheduled for an immediate return flight to Canada. In-flight rations would be picked up, and the fueling would take place during unloading. The C-130 moved slowly through the night following the escort vehicle.

As the plane passed their position, Tork and the others moved out. By the time they reached the aircraft, the rear doors had opened enough for them to move the colonel inside and to enter themselves.

They took the colonel forward and quickly put a flight suit on him and put him under guard. They didn't want anyone coming up front. The pilot, a smiling English man, started supervising the unloading. Sybil was up front, out of sight with the colonel. All the others were staying busy.

The plane was empty, the fueling was finished, and the in-flight rations were on board. They radioed for a takeoff clearance and sat there for almost half hour before the clearance came. Even Tork started wondering what was going on. Maybe they found out the plane was a ruse. The rebels had sent the information on the mission, and he feared they were about to descend on them. They were all relieved when the tower gave them the go-ahead. The engines revved up, and the bird made a turn on the hardstand and slowly moved forward toward the taxiway. In minutes, they were in line for a takeoff.

The throttles were pulled back and gently the plane rolled forward. It soon picked up speed, and as the airflow increased over the wings, the giant bird started to lift itself up. Within minutes, it was climbing and turning as it gained altitude until it was on its prescribed course heading north toward Canada. It was over an hour when the plane started to descend. The pilot knew as their altitude dropped, the UN forces would monitor them on radar. When he was under radar surveillance, he turned west flying low, just above the trees, his ground search radar alerting them of any obstructions.

For over an hour, they hugged the ground and then started a steady climb. As they gained altitude, four Raptor F-22 fighters picked them up, two on each side.

The pilot looked over to the nearest plane and waved. The F-22 pilot pointed to his helmet and the C-130 pilot keyed his mic. "Good morning, Yanks. Glad to see you're on time."

"Always on time and ready to save your tail should some federal decide to smoke it with a Sidewinder. Everything go okay? Over."

"Right. We've got them all tucked in and even picked up two extra guests for dinner, although one will be served in the crossbar hotel. Have mother set the table for one more. The other would be great to take home."

With salutations over, all planes proceeded to their destinations and all landed safely.

CHAPTER 24

America under New Flags

The Hague Headquarters
Supreme UN Expeditionary Forces
United States of Europe

The orderlies were just putting the finishing touches on the conference table. A young German officer of the UN Elite Protocol Honor Group was inspecting it, making sure that each setting was correct—pens, tablets, recorders, phone jacks, and computer hookups for laptops and tablets all had to be at each chair and all working.

This was the biggest conference since the revolution in the United States started. Europe was getting raves about the war. They were telling everyone the federal forces were winning the battles with total victory just around the corner.

This conference, they were told, would put the finishing touches on it. Some even said they would divide the United States up among the world powers. Rumor had it that Mexico would get all of California, New Mexico, Texas, Colorado, Utah, and Nevada and that France would be permitted to occupy and administer Louisiana, Alabama, and Kentucky. Spain, it was said, would inherit Florida, Georgia, and South Carolina. England would get all of the New England states, and Canada would have all the bordering states west of the Great Lakes. All other states would be under control and monitored by the United Nations.

He looked around, checking each area one by one. Something was missing. *Ah, yes, the coffee cups.* Yes, they needed to bring in the small stands of china. This could be a long and tiring day for everyone. Perhaps, he thought, maybe he too could be part of the occupation forces. Yes, that would be fitting. He wondered about the occupation of the United States of America by foreign troops. *Yeah,* he thought, *I could be a part of that.*

The members of the Supreme Allied Command had been arriving since early morning, each with his briefcase overflowing with plans of occupation. Many already made plans in their own countries to move specialists into the areas they would be occupying. They knew it would mean tough shock troops to weed out the general populace that would take up arms against them. These troops would have to be hard, willing to shoot first and ask questions later. The American people were to be fully disarmed. Nevertheless, the council knew that many reported weapons had never been turned in or found. Although the UN forces had moved from house to house by presidential invitation and many, many guns had been found, they knew not all of them were confiscated and they could cause unnecessary casualties among the occupation forces.

Those in charge were groups of men, generals, admirals, politicians, administrators, and the heads of most nation's police forces, all comparing notes and purposely forgetting that most of their countries owed their very existence and prosperity to the United States. Notes were taken, and they were making deals that the men who would carve the freest nation the earth had ever seen into small occupied states under the new world order. Computers and mobile phones hummed.

They all felt the giant eagle was soon to fall and to rise no more. Soon they would clip those mighty wings forever, and in her place would stand the new world order and a new eagle holding the world in her talons.

A very stately gentleman walked up to the podium that stood off to the left side at the head of the table. He reached over and pushed the button on the side of the stand. They heard a little squawk over a speaker. The man looked out at the milling heads of states and their generals and admirals.

He then made an announcement. "Gentlemen, please, please, if I may have a moment. Our president has arrived and will be coming in soon. Please take your seats. We have much to do this day, and we need to get started. Thank you."

Everyone took their places. One by one, they found their seats and started pulling from briefcases or loading disks the material they would need to justify their demands.

As if on command, the room fell silent, and each of their eyes turned to the twelve-foot-high double oak doors at the end of the room. Silently, they opened and the president, flanked by his body-guards, entered the room and went directly to the head of the table. He sat down, his bodyguards taking positions around the room, each holding tightly a submachine gun.

The president looked out before him and spoke, "Gentlemen, it is time for the rebirth of the United States. We are about to embark on a military venture that will divide the United States in half, from Canada to Mexico. Our military chiefs have informed us that every-thing is in place, and the rebel forces have no idea what has been going on over the last few months. Although they have kidnapped one of our field marshals, our intelligence has reported they were unable to get any information from him. Within seventy-two hours, we will begin our plans to conquer the United States. Code named Dead Eagle."

*****

The C-130 was pulling into the unloading docks at the main terminal. Tork, Cal, Sybil, and the others were getting ready to disem-bark. Lt. Col. Sean Doran was handcuffed and ready to be escorted by two guards to the stockade. Sybil looked up and met his eyes. Two cold calculating points of hate and shivers ran down her spine, but she held her gaze and spoke, "Well, Colonel, looks like it's time to pay the piper. Seems these inept Yankee rebels were able to pick you right out of the United Nations' most secure base and transport you here for trial, doesn't it, sir?"

The colonel smiled. "It's war, and war is pain, suffering, and death. We do what we must to win. I'm a warrior, Sybil, and warriors are prepared to die."

The door of the airplane was fully opened and the three men disembarked from the aircraft and left, duty for all but Sean. His fate was to be judged by his enemies and God.

Captain Albertson looked at Sybil. "You know, Syb, he's right. We do what we have to do. Every soldier knows that. We kill and they kill us. What more can any soldier say? It's our job to kill people and break things."

Sybil looked at the men there. "I guess I'm not ready for all of this. I found it hard to see those men at the depot openly killed when it was not necessary. Am I supposed to throw away my principles and religious beliefs because a soldier is a soldier? I think not, Captain. I think not."

*****

"Capt. Marion Albertson reporting, sir." The captain saluted the general.

The general was happy to see Tork and returned his salute and offered him a chair. "Sit down, Captain. Sit down. Good to see you."

"It's good to see you, General, and congratulations on your promotion."

"Thanks, Captain. Now let's get down to business, shall we?"

"Yes, sir. How can I help? What assignment do you have for me now?"

"Captain, as you know, many American corporations have built and are now producing a great deal of products sold in the United States. They are second only to China. We are now using up our surplus faster than we anticipated. The federal government has been bringing in large quantities of equipment and munitions that we have managed to intercept in the United States. Most of these shipments are coming in through our southern borders by sea. More of it is coming in by air in other parts of the country."

Tork looking concerned spoke, "General, I have experience in interdiction. How can I help to stem this flow?"

"Captain, let me finish and you'll see the big picture, and I promise you, you will fit in. The trade agreement is now in full accord and, as we speak, more of our corporations are building or have started operating in Mexico. To stem this, it has become necessary for us to initiate attacks on their factories and to disrupt or destroy what we can. If possible, we will need to locate, confiscate, or destroy the federal supplies, whatever they may be and wherever they are. Any questions, Captain?"

Tork looked at the new star on General Duncan's collar, studying it for almost a minute. "Yes, sir, I have a few. First, many of the corporations in Mexico are American-owned, so would we want to attack our own people? Second, wouldn't it be an attack on our own values? Many of these same companies are supplying us. Won't that cause a breach in the supply lines we have now? Can we afford to cut off the hand that feeds us?"

Duncan smiled. He had a sharp man here and one he knew they could rely on to do the right things the right way. "Yes, son. In a sense, we can. If the corporation wants to supply both sides, it's only for one reason, money! If they don't, then we'll be forcing them to pick sides. They will decide what side of this war is going to be the winning side and what side they will want to deal with. Only the next few weeks or months will tell."

"Yes, sir. What do you want me to do?"

"Captain, there is a full battalion of Delta Force and rangers ready to move. We divide all of the company commanders into groups that will locate, capture, or destroy the incoming convoys or trains. Our intel has identified most of the routes and sea-lanes taken to supply the federal troops.

"The Special Forces battalion will work on them. What I have for you is commando strikes on the factories, any way that you can. We have set aside two Special Forces teams with air force special ops to assist you. Delta personnel will have all the special equipment you need to do the job. This will be well behind the enemy lines, and it will be dangerous. We must cut off the supplies and equipment coming in before the UN forces are prepared to strike.

"Any day now, they'll attempt to move north and south to cut the country in two. Intelligence from your last mission has been confirmed. Our men in Mexico have substantiated all of it, and at this time, we are not sure when they plan to move. We know it may be soon, very soon. Recently, we have received valuable information that the time is very close at hand. This confirms other intel we received, that they intend to take out anyone, military or civilian, that gets in their way. Any threat to them is punishable by death, so you can see your mission is crucial."

"Excuse me, sir, why don't you use the bombers on the plants? Why try to disrupt them or partially destroy them?"

"Captain, they are all well protected from air or missile strikes. They have the same countermeasures we do. You might say we are on a level playing field. So it's necessary for us to use guerilla tactics. Coming in at night, on foot, and taking out their sentries with stealth will enable us to set our explosives where they will do the most damage, lasting damage. This is very dangerous, but it's the best way we have to do what we need to do. Plus, it will be the most demoralizing act we can use."

Tork was busily making notes and scribbling ideas. He knew he would soon be engaged in serious attacks on the enemy. As he listened to the general, he planned.

"The Mexican army is guarding all the industrial targets," the general continued. "They have no combat experience and are poorly trained. They should be no match for your Delta troops. Now, you are to report to Maj. Jonathan Diamond for briefing and assignment areas. He will be your contact from here on out. His group will provide all radio frequencies and codes. After your briefing and you have met your troops, you will be on your own. Any additional transport you need, you will have to get off the land."

The general's pause gave Tork the opportunity to speak.

"Sir, I would like to have some Sikorsky CH-53E RH-65 made available if you can get them from the marines. We need them for their personnel capacities. If not, then something similar."

"Well, Captain, seems the major and you think alike. He too has asked for them. I authorized four pilots qualified in multiaircraft to be part of your team. With your qualifications, that should be ample. And that means you and your crew will have to take care of them. Oh, and good luck!"

The general knew the hell he was starting and the hell each of them would go through, not to mention the hell the enemy was going to get. Yes, you might say meeting the devil south of the border.

After being dismissed by General Duncan, Tork was ready for action. *The sooner, the better*, he thought. He was ready and the best place to start was at command headquarters.

Upon entering the building, Tork was stopped by two military policemen.

"May we help you, sir?"

"Yes, Corporal. I'm to report to special operations room 216."

The corporal picked up his phone and dialed a number. "Corporal Dennison here. I have Captain Albertson here to meet with you.… Yes, sir." He then turned to Tork and spoke, "Sir, take the stairs to your right. Second floor, right corridor. They're waiting for you."

The knock on the door was loud, firm, and in control. "Enter."

The door opened and Capt. Marion Albertson entered. "Sir, Captain Albertson reporting." He saluted the major as he spoke.

The major returned the salute. "Sit, Captain. Good to see you. I've heard quite a bit about you from General Duncan, and I have everything ready for you."

"Thank you, Major. I would like to get started, meet the group, and feel them out. Oh yes, I need to meet with the pilots and get an idea of their qualifications."

"Well, Captain, I think you will find them as well qualified as yourself and quite talented. You should have no problems with them. Come, let's go and meet them."

*****

Cal knocked three times on the office door, smiling at Sybil.

"Enter!" the general replied. Cal opened the door and entered a very military office.

"Come in, come in, both of you. What a pleasure it is to see you again, Cal. And this time, you brought us a new member of our revolution. Welcome, Miss, or is it Missus? Please be seated."

"Thank you, sir. Well, General, it's good to see you too. What can we do for you?"

General Duncan got right to the point. "Cal, I have a very special task for you and Sybil. We want you both to go into the San Francisco-Oakland Bay area. We need to know what the people are thinking, how they are seeing the war, you know. Are they accepting it, or is the media intimidating them? Being highly progressive, we need to know.

"It is our need to know if this area is still reliable. I can't tell you how important this is. With your knowledge of the area and the old friends you have there, well, we think you can get us a really reliable survey."

The general looked both of them over, waiting for his answer, knowing they were both civilians and under no obligation to go, and he knew there would be danger. He hadn't informed them the area was under federal and UN control and wanted to make sure they had a desire to go before he told them.

Cal looked at Sybil and smiled. "I see nothing wrong with it, sir. It will give me a chance to see my family. I would love to go, but one thing, sir. I understand from intelligence that federal troops have secured that region, and we will need some IDs and special papers to move freely."

"What about you, Sybil? Are you willing to go too?"

"Yes, sir. I could use the material. The people need to know what's going on and I can help by telling the country what the federal government is up to. I feel they have one hell of a disinformation program going on in all the areas they occupy."

"Good. You won't be alone. Diana is going with you. She's been under extensive training and will set up an underground cell in the Walnut Creek-Concord area. She'll have the communications and the codes. It's imperative that all of you work together and coordinate all activities. We will need to know the vessels that are coming into the San Francisco and Oakland area docks, the naval traffic to Mare Island, and the new activity at Port Chicago. Travis Air Force Base has been getting heavy transport traffic from Canada. It looks like they're getting ready for a Northern California buildup. They may try going south. We have control of some areas and they may want to secure the state or they may want to move east. Nevada and Utah are buffer areas now. Bringing in anything through that corridor is difficult for them. We need to know what's going on—the people, how they feel, local businesses, how they are surviving, how foreign military and merchant vessel traffic is dispersed, and what areas they control troop locations and consolidations. For the next two weeks, you will be undergoing special training."

The general touched his intercom button, and a voice instantly responded, "Yes, sir."

"Have Colonel Bovington come in. We have two more for training." The general looked over both of his new operatives, smiled, and said, "Good luck to both of you, and remember, it's *freedom earned*. If you can't work to preserve it, you can just as easily lose it."

The knock on the door was sharp and hard, the knock of someone in authority. "Enter," the general responded. The door opened and a stout man in a Special Forces uniform entered and saluted General Duncan.

"Thank you, Colonel," the general said. "Please take Sybil and Cal to your training center. It's imperative we get this started now."

The Colonel ushered them to a waiting car. Within minutes, they were on their way.

*****

Captain Albertson was released with his team; the pilots were more than he expected. The four men had extensive combat experience, and they were qualified on all helicopter aircraft and multiengine recip and jet transports.

His combat ground troops were also well trained and all had experience in special operational assaults. They were inventorying weapons and gear for the upcoming raids. Training had been extensive, and the men were all keyed up for the assignments to come. The first sergeant called out each item for verification. "Crossbows."

"Thirty-six."

"Sapper satchels."

"Twelve each of the 10 and 8 markhums."

"Markhums, what the hell is a markhum?" the first sergeant asked.

"It's a forty-pounder, Sergeant. When you set it off, it *marks 'em* big time." A few chuckles and smiles marked their faces, for they all knew what was coming.

All inventory items were checked and double-checked. Weapons, clothing, rations, munitions, communications, night gear, and vests were all checked. Everything was ready for the mission.

The men were ready. The gear was ready. The time was now, and the waiting continued.

Mexican Assembly Plant
No. 16, Heavy Truck
Military Design Unit

Captain Ortega and his junior officers were planning the upcoming festival on the coming weekend. The plant manager had promised to supply the food and drink for the village and to shut down all nonessential assembly lines so as many employees as possible could attend. Captain Ortega had been going over the United Nations' intelligence reports along the US border.

Captain Ortega was the camp commandant. With a full company of Mexican regulars, he was responsible for the assembly plant's security. The camp was a small well-equipped military compound with barracks, dining hall, and recreation facilities.

"Gentlemen, all indications are favorable for our festival. We have had no infiltrations or attempts of sabotage anywhere near our location. I can see no reason we shouldn't permit the garrison to attend the festival."

Looking over his officers, his eyes stopped on a newly assigned officer. "Lieutenant Quasada, I would like you to set up only a token guard Friday and Saturday. I think we will only need to man the front and rear perimeter guard posts. The factory will be completing their final inspections and loading the vehicles on transports for shipment Monday. The work should then be completed early Friday."

Captain Ortega was a dedicated regular army man with a thirst for fun and festivals. As a youngster, he was always the one to help plan the festivals with the village priest and elders. To him, this was a welcome diversion, one he could appreciate.

"We can all then enjoy the festival Friday night and through Saturday. Sunday, I want all the men back in the barracks, sober and ready for work Monday. Any questions?"

None of the officers had questions. All were planning for the festival and the girls. They all knew the rebel forces wouldn't dare attack the Mexican army because only an hour away was a UN army camp with heavy tanks, helicopters, and troops. No, they all felt safe. The day of festivals was due, and they were all tired from training and building up air defenses. The new missiles coming in from Europe would take care of any bombers the gringos may have. Germans that directed their installation told them that nothing could get past them. *Ah, let the Yankees come.*

*****

The briefing was in full swing. Tork had gone over the equipment lists and personnel rosters with the platoon leaders. He was about to lay out the strike force assignments when they heard the knock on the door.

"Get that, Sergeant. Thank you."

Tork looked up to see General Duncan, the major, and a civilian entering the room. The sergeant opened the door and yelled, "Ten-hut!" All of the men came to attention.

Tork saluted the general. "Good to see you, sir. What can we do for you?"

"You can give me those silver bars, Major. You are out of uniform congratulations, Tork, or should I say, Major Albertson?"

Tork was surprised. He had no inkling of this happening. "Thank you, sir. Thank you very much."

General Duncan and the others shook Tork's hand, wished him well, and departed.

Tork turned back to his men. "Let's get going. We still have a lot to do." With that, he put his finger on the chart. "Here, men, is the decoy. We will send in a quick response team to create a diversion. As soon as the Mexican army responds, we will hit our prime objective here." His finger once again came to rest on a different position on the map. "It is here that we must be thorough and decisive. It is here that we will sharpen the edge of our sword or blunt it."

UN Forces, Allied Headquarters
Brussels
United States of Europe

Dr. Hector Molonakov was at the podium. The elite members of the UN Mission on Population Control and Environmental Balance greeted the members of the mission.

"Gentlemen, it is a pleasure to have all of us meet together again. As all of you know, getting our esteemed colleagues here from the United States of America has been difficult. However, we have managed to have with us today one of the most renowned experts in population control, a scientist that has controlled the birth rate and more importantly the reduction of our elderly citizens in many parts of the world through the use of euthanasia. With his help, we should have no problems when the time arrives to eliminate the unproductive burdens of society, once we have secured the country and divided it for proper control and governing.

"When this happens, we can start the elimination of the aged in the sanatoriums and nursing homes. America's Affordable Care Act has worked well, but not well enough. We need to do more so we can then put those that are bedridden to sleep, and as others become bedridden, they too can be relieved of their burdens. Now let me introduce you to Dr. Paul Sebastian Toomay. Doctor Toomay."

Doctor Toomay was one of Europe's most knowledgeable experts on productivity and the disadvantages of aging. His work on the overall costs of supporting the aged and the disabled in a new world order versus their elimination was a paramount factor for the United Nations to start procedures in the new society. Doctor Toomay had high hopes for America where the costs were staggering due to the Affordable Care Act.

"Thank you, sir. First, gentlemen, let me say that over the past two years, we have reduced the cost that it takes to keep the aged and those individuals that are suffering with terminal illnesses by helping them to pass over. We have been able to open up thousands of beds and reduce the overall costs by billions. We have mandated the use of cremation in almost all countries, although we have several that still cling to the Christian and Islamic beliefs of burying their dead. It is our hope that we will be able to convince them of the necessity of what we do and the savings that they will realize. After all, the state of Oregon in the United States has been using euthanasia for years for mercy reasons. We are only taking it one step further, to eliminate those who have nothing to give. We consider it to be merciful. Plus, it is financially advantageous for the state.

"We have drawn up a divisional map of the United States that will give all of you an idea of what areas each of you will be getting. The circulars that are being distributed will give you the total population of the area, the estimated ages of the people, and the number of people that are terminal or bedridden. We want to ensure that everyone has the best medical care and that they can look to live long productive lives as long as they can provide. However, once again, should they become terminally ill or bedridden, then they will have to make room for others. Remember there is no room for sentiment.

"As we move into the rebel-held areas and the rebels are defeated, we expect each military commander to do their part and to secure the area so our teams may move rapidly in to start the new world order in America. Are there any questions?"

A minute passed and then a standing ovation was given by all. They knew the most productive country and the most powerful would now be under control of the United Nations and would become a glowing gem under each of their flags. It was now up to the field commanders and the elite troops they commanded. The US rebels would be no match for them. The next step is to find the US president. They would need him if all was to work as planned.

Congressional Holding Camp, No. 4

Two senators and one member of the House requested an audience with the camp commandant, and they had been taken to the headquarters building to Lt. Gen. Carl Fordham's office.

Sen. Otis Barkman (D) looked around the office at the certificates, diplomas, commendations, and medals with their citations enclosed in framed shadow boxes. They displayed a distinguished career in the army of the United States.

Otis turned to the others and spoke, "Why would such a highly decorated man involve himself in such a treasonable game as this?"

Sen. Louis Gionnone (R) looked at Senator Barkman and replied, "Maybe, Senator, we have gone too far and these men and women are trying to stop us. I don't know why you are really here, but I know why I am. I have been watching all the news reports from both the federal government and the ones from the rebels. You and many others might call me a traitor, most probably the president, if he is still alive.

"Nevertheless, as I see it, we have destroyed America as we know it. We have become nothing more than a colony of the world. We have turned over our lives to the United Nations and thus to the power of Europe. With NAFTA, CAFTA, and Asia sucking all the jobs out of the country and the Gun Control Act that we sanctioned allowing UN forces to enter the United States and confiscate our citizen's guns should have been enough. I think the straw that broke the camel's back was our attempt to legislate the implanting of individual chips into each citizen along with the use of euthanasia to eliminate the elderly and the bedridden. Senator, I think we went too far and caused this war.

"I plan to help the new government correct it, if it's not too late. For whatever reason we are here today is irrelevant. I want you to know how and where I stand. I want to see this country united again. I want to help put a stop to what's going on. And I intend to give the new government all the information I have."

Congressman Ralph Louder (I) stood, arms folded, listening intently, nodding in agreement to the words from Senator Gionnone. "I agree, Louie, and I'm with you. I was on the disinformation committee, and I felt at the time we needed to maximize control over everyone if we wanted to control crime, guns, and just about everything. It was our argument that we would need to divide the races to control them. We knew if we could keep the citizens separated by using the races and developing a phantasmagoria trend among the whites, blacks, and Hispanics, using their own prejudices, we could maximize control over them all. In short, we made laws prohibiting prejudice and then instigated situations that separated them all. Each group was then dependent on the party for guidance, control, and well-being.

"With the passing of the medical benefits, NAFTA, CAFTA, and Gun Control Act, we thought we had accomplished maximum control of the country. It appears we were wrong. I can now see the people want their freedom and couldn't get it in a free election because we had control of them. Gentlemen, the constitution is hanging by a thread, and we put it there. Our country has been invaded by foreign troops, and we helped pave the way. I, for one, do not think they are here to free us, but to conqueror us, divide us. I have a heavy heart at what I have done. I only hope it is not too late for me to help in this struggle. I'm looking forward to seeing General Fordham."

Otis looked at both men. "My comment was not intended to belittle the general. What he and all of the new government are doing is treason. It can only change if or when they are successful. I now think they will succeed. I have listened to our colleagues since they arrested us. Almost all of them are stout, dedicated men that feel the only way we can survive peacefully is through complete government control. Their liberal views are borderline anarchy, and their governmental beliefs are somewhere between totalitarian, socialism, and dictatorship. The people can sin all they want as long as they do what they are told. I have had plenty of time to think about all of this, and I can see now that the new world order wants to control the world by allowing everything that is immoral to be exploited. Play the game of drug control and at the same time reap the profits. We have all forsaken our national heritage. I agree we have started the beginning of the end unless the new government is successful in driving out the United Nations and reestablishing our constitutional rights.

"We must teach everyone that we are Americans. The fact that our ancestors came from different lands should be seen as heritage and nothing more. By putting a tag on America, we are only dividing ourselves. There should not be Anglo American or Irish-American or African-American. We should eliminate the words white, black, Hispanic, and Oriental from our spoken language and replace them with only one word, American. We all have the same chance for our place in life and it's based on our abilities. Cut out the things that make us bad and maybe the good can come out. Put our wealth into training, education, and jobs. Mandate to the world that we will buy only American-made products, and if they want to sell to us, they will need to manufacture here. I will do my best to reach an accord with the new government, if they will have me."

The general looked over his staff. They'd all been observing the three members of Congress over a closed TV circuit and closely listened to every word.

"Well, gentlemen, what do you think? Are they telling the truth? Or are they trying to play with us? Let's look at the facts. All three of these men were tightly entrenched in the new world order. They were all members of committees that sold us to the world, divided our nation, and created a presidential dictatorship. Let's go let the cat play with the three blind mice."

The guard at the door snapped to attention and saluted the general as he approached. He turned and opened the door for the general and his staff. As they entered the room, each acknowledged the presence of the three members of the now defunct government.

The general motioned them to be seated. He walked to a small panel that was mounted in the wall and opened it with a key. Inside was an array of LED lights and buttons. He pushed several of them, and on the far walls, the sound of motors could be heard, as two panels moved apart. Inside was a large screen and directly above the screen was what appeared to be a TV camera lens. The general pushed a third button and the screen flooded to life with the great seal of the United States of America on it.

The general turned to the three men, and addressing them by name, he spoke, "Gentlemen, we have been observing you and we heard what you said to one another. Although we want to believe you, we remain doubtful of your sincerity. Therefore, we would like to show you what is taking place in the country today and in the world overall. If for any reason you feel compelled to return to your quarters, we will understand. On the other hand, should you remain steadfast in your resolve to become part of the revolution, we will reunite you with many of your congressional or Senate members, who are at this time an active part of our new government. I might add, they all have been with us from the beginning. For many of them were the true patriots of the new government and will one day take their place among the founders of the new republic. You see, gentlemen, we in the new government are still abiding by the constitution, and we will not allow any judicial body to make changes to it as you have done over the years to meet your own goals or those of your party. We have stopped abortions, as you know, and have refocused on the family. We have reinstituted the importance of the mother in the home and have enjoined with business in these areas to keep costs down and to pay wages that permit a one-breadwinner family.

"Where men are in the military and the wives must work, we have made it possible, if they support the war effort, for them to spend the quality time they need with their children. We have driven the enemy from our shores and have regained our government. Congress will enact constitutional amendments that will guarantee the family protection and that the remainder of US corporations will not be permitted to sell out to foreign investors without congressional approval and that no business within the Unites States or its territories will be less than 51 percent American-owned. Gentlemen, that means the foreign-owned companies will have to divest themselves of their controlling interest of ownership or leave the country. We are going to guarantee jobs for our people and that we will control all imports and that Congress will address all custom factors with a committee dealing with foreign imports. We know that it will mean retaliation by them. Nevertheless, with us fighting a civil war here and an international war on our own soil, we feel when the time comes, we can prevail. We will ensure that the moral fiber of the country is restored.

"The immoral factors that the Supreme Court has thrust on the nation will not happen again. We will make constitutional changes that will ensure they cannot be removed. The anarchy in our school system still runs rampant. Although the Gun Control Act took the guns from the people, it made a new black market in them. The guns are still there, along with the ones hidden when the United Nations came in at your invitation.

"Based on these and other facts, you can see our reluctance when it comes to trusting those who were responsible for our condition. Gentlemen, freedom is earned, not guaranteed, and so is trust. If you want us to trust you, then you must be prepared to earn that trust."

The general reached up and pushed a button, and the screen instantly focused on a meeting of members of the new congressional and senatorial government in session. When the TV transmission was made, the speaker of the House directed the members to the camera and announced they were on camera and it was being transmitted to the Congressional Holding Camp, No. 4. Three senators incarcerated there waited to plead to the committee for a part in the revolution. The committee wanted each of those members of the House and Senate that were under arrest to see that they had defectors willing to join the revolution.

The general addressed the assembly. "Members of the House and Senate, I have three of your colleagues that were architects of the new world order. Each of them has recanted their previous beliefs and has asked to become a part of the new government. I have asked them to address you by way of closed-circuit television so that you may decide if they should take their places beside you. Gentlemen, I give you Sen. Otis Barkman (D). Senator, if you please."

Senator Barkman spoke, "Gentlemen, I have been highly visible in the new world order and I thought, most sincerely, that I was going to help this country by eliminating the crime, suffering, and poverty that exist. I thought in all sincerity that the people would understand and feel the same way. I felt the loss of a few rights would enhance the country and the people would endeavor to become part of it. When we implemented NAFTA, many of my colleagues and I felt we would be creating new jobs in all three countries. When CAFTA was passed, we expected to move into South America with no opposition. It was disappointing when we were unable to bring them into the new America.

"We knew without doubt that South America would respond and we could once again open up closed factories. When this didn't happen and the factories started closing and reopening in Canada, China, and Mexico, I had second thoughts. But I was still convinced that sometime down the road, we would reach our goal of eliminating the borders. I thought this would put us on the right track, and when we allowed the United Nations to enter the country and confiscate the weapons held by our citizens, I thought no more crime. I was wrong. The guns came in the country from the back door, and there are just as many out there as there were when we passed the law. When we decided on the implants, I knew for sure we could control everyone and guarantee their rights. I was wrong there too. We did nothing more than seal upon ourselves the same fate as the old Soviet Union and present-day China.

"These months in the camps have opened my eyes. The TV newscasts and the information we are receiving I thought at first was pure fabrication, complete disinformation. I have learned from some of the new arrivals that it is true. The United Nations has or is embarking on the complete dismantlement of the United States and the division of our states to certain member countries. With this in mind, my colleagues and I have what we feel is the right course of action to take the presence of mind to join with all of you, no matter what the outcome, and fight for the constitution and for our liberties. We all want to see every one of them that has been taken returned.

"The letter of the constitution must prevail. We cannot allow anyone to read into it what he or she thinks the framers said. We must interpret it as it is written. It says freedom of speech, and we feel that's what they meant. All of you have every right to deny us this request, and I cannot blame you in any way should you decide against us. I, for myself, would welcome any job no matter how small it might be. Gentlemen, I would say I am sorry, but at the time, I thought I was doing this for the country and for the people. I can only say now, please let me help to rebuild. Thank you."

There was no recognition or applause to what Senator Barkman had said. Instead, each member of the committee turned to the other and discussed the man, his past record of sincerity, and most of all his dedication to a cause and to what end he might go to achieve his goals. The murmuring went on. The discussions were lengthy and well defined.

As the committee discussed and evaluated the senator, he was quietly taken to the anteroom with the others to wait for an answer.

Two hours had dragged by before the second man was called in to the committee for his dissertation and his hope to fulfillment. He too wanted to become a part of the new revolution, since he could see the failure the administration and Congress had caused. He had been a part of the failure and could see the only redeeming way he could help was to be a part of the change. Sincerity was his only ally; he knew he had to convince the committee. All of the men had been called and heard, and the committee had taken great care to evaluate them all. The question foremost in each of their minds was the final answer to the most critical question they had—would each of these men be willing to make the same sacrifices they had made to put their lives on the line for God and country, or would they backpedal at the right time should the revolution fail and the United Nations win? For each of them knew they would either kill or confine them for life if this were to happen.

The discussions went well into the night with each argument being thoroughly examined. The final vote on each would be decided soon, each man to be judged on his merits. Following a short recess, the chairman called for final votes on each man. As they voted, each committee member wrote the man's name on a slip of paper with a yea or a nay. It was a simple vote with a simple majority to accept or deny the request. For the yea, the man would be returned to the revolutionary council committee as a full-fledged senator or member of Congress, when again he would pick up the gauntlet of government by the people and for the people. For the nays, he would be returned to the camp from whence he came and there to wait for the end of the conflict and final judgment if the revolution was a success or to return to the government that they had created and to be judged by their peers for their alleged defection. For each of them knew as the council knew that they could not escape what they had elected to do. Success or failure, it was their decision. Each of them waited, knowing that it was destiny to move forward and right a wrong and fight to preserve the union and safeguard the constitution. They hoped and prayed they would be accepted to become a part of the new America, a free America.

It was daybreak, and the morning sun was coming up behind the mountains when the chairman looked out of the window and remarked, "Those purple mountain's majesty." The heads of those who heard him looked to the windows and smiled. Yes, they thought, the revolution was the only course clear to them. Time passed and the word finally came.

"Gentlemen, I have the results of your vote. I know it was a hard thing for each of you to do. To judge three of our peers that we knew had been a contributor to what the country has gone through and to judge them without prejudice was a very difficult thing for each of you. I want all of you to know that as the committee chairman, it would have been my duty to vote if a deadlock had occurred. It is with pleasure that I tell you now that it will not be necessary. The vote favored returning these men to their elected positions. The yeas have it, gentlemen. We will return them to Congress as members in good standing in the new republic, and we will institute all security factors to assure they are welcomed aboard.

"Perhaps we may see others return as well. It would be good for the country to know that we are uniting against a common enemy. It will be our pleasure to broadcast in both the free and occupied areas of the nation that two of the nation's senators and one House member have joined with us to return the country to the people."

It was midafternoon before the committee's decision reached the three men. They were taken by guard to the committee chambers. As they entered, the guards stopped at the door, closed it, and left. The three men looked to one another. The chamber was silent and empty. As they looked out the windows of the rooms, they could see the sun shining on the mountains in the east. The deep blue of the sky highlighted the beauty of the desert and gray from the rocks and granite.

Each man was with his own thoughts when the door opened from the opposite side of the room. The chairman and the committee members filed in. They had obviously been up all night contemplating the three men's fate.

The chairman spoke, "Gentlemen, the committee has considered your request, and they took a vote this morning on your petition to join with us and the American people in building a better America. Gentlemen, it is with great pleasure that my colleagues and I welcome you back. You will take your place among us, assigned to committees with your contemporaries. Your new quarters are being prepared, and we have dispatched teams to pick up your wives and children and to bring them here to reside with you until we have won this conflict. Be assured we will not harm them. Although they are living in occupied areas, we do have the ability to get them safely out."

The three men looked at one another with smiles that could only come from sincerity and love. They each knew that they could not turn back now. They all would be dedicated to the revolution and to the people. Each of them thanked the committee and assured them they were willing and able to move forward.

The chairman thanked all for the session and he made a statement. "Gentlemen, this session is hereby closed."

*****

The first gunship had moved into position and was waiting across the border. All troops were dressed in black and equipped for silent killing. The choppers would move south flying low and would land a mile north of the plant. The route had been well planned, and the agents in the area had made every effort to provide a safe corridor to the plant and back. Once the target had been hit, they would return and move to support the primary objective sixty kilometers to the west. They should arrive at the same time as the assault team. The engine of the choppers lay silent, switches turned on; the lamps of the instrument panel lights reflected a mysterious glow around them. The troops checked and rechecked their weapons. There was no talking; silence and contemplation were the rule. Three words came across the earphones in Morse code—tic-tac-toe.

The mission was on. The pilot turned to the team commander, gave him the thumbs-up, and waited for a nod. He reached over and flipped his start switch and watched his instruments for the engines to come to full power. In seconds, the bird lifted off, and just above the trees, it moved south, sitting down in a small clearing. As the chopper landed, the men were off the bird and deployed in a defensive manner.

It was a black night, clear skies, and no moon. Within seconds, a red signal light was seen from the southwest corner of the clearing, a recognition signal was returned, and a second one was seen. A team of four men came into view. As they came closer, the team could see they were Mexicans.

"*Alto!*" shouted one of the team members.

They heard a reply. "Hang on, pal. We're your contact party. Let's not get trigger-happy."

It was not hard to tell the full-blooded American there. They were Americans of Mexican descent, born and raised in the United States, from Texas to California. They were all good and dedicated

Americans. They were some of the first to join the fight. Knowing what was going on in Mexico and seeing the destruction of their mother country were enough for them to fight for the democracy denied the people in Mexico and to remind them of their flight to the United States and a new life. They and their fellow Americans would now fight for its freedom.

They had been urged by their families to fight this time for the American way of life. The language they had learned now came to good use. It made it possible for them to enter the Mexican areas and merge within the country of their fathers and to seek out relatives still living there. It was important to see how they felt about the changes and to work among them without arousing any suspicion and collect the needed intelligence the special teams needed to make their strikes. It was a dangerous game they played. If caught, it could mean certain death. Each man knew the dangers the goals of the revolution would bring.

The first attack against a foreign invader was about to be made. The enemy would soon receive their response to the UN intervention. They would see, feel, and know what *made in America* really meant.

"I'm Lt. Jerry Martinez, Special Forces Infiltration Team. Password is Coney Island. We have the route and layout for you guys, but you'll have to hurry. We have to mingle at the festival."

The team leader smiled and said, "Brooklyn." The he waited for a reply.

Lieutenant Martinez quickly answered, "Hot dog."

"Okay, Jerry, show us the way."

The team moved out, and within forty-five minutes, they were at their destination. Jerry laid out the plans for them. His sketches of the perimeter fences and guard posts corresponded with the briefing plans they had already seen. The first objective was to skirt the guard posts and destroy the power stations and substations, set fire to the buildings, and set time fuses with C-4 on the trucks ready for shipment. It was interesting that American-owned truck manufacturers were building trucks for the enemy with United Nations and foreign markings on them. The team leader checked his watch and dispatched the Mexican team to the festival. It was to take them fifteen minutes to reach the festivities. When the time limit expired, the team would set off their explosives and get out. Everything had been done.

One guard had grown tired of standing in his guard shack and walked out to stretch his legs. He walked toward the plant looking at the night sky and wishing he was at the festival. He turned and started back toward the shack when a black clad figure stepped up behind him. In flawless Spanish, he said, "Hey, *amigo*. Got a match?"

The guard's knees almost buckled under him from fright. He turned to see a man dressed in black, carrying an M16 and wearing black makeup. He reached for his sidearm only to feel a sting in his left leg. Then he was unconscious. He was seized before he could hit the ground and carried back to his post. The man in black muttered, "Those knockout darts are fast and effective. He won't wake up for an hour."

The time was up and the war began. It was fast and full of fire. Both the main power station and substation went up in flames. Next the petroleum storage exploded and the warehouse and main power substation that controlled the assembly line were destroyed.

The team had completed their mission inside eight minutes after the explosives had been set off. They were all now moving back the way they had come.

The Mexican troops at the festival had heard the explosions and saw the night light up toward the plant. They quickly mounted their trucks and were on their way back. As they approached the plant, the guards ran toward them yelling, "The Yankee Army has come! The Yankee Army has come! They are destroying everything."

The column of men had stopped. Confusion was running wild. The commandant arrived and had the men form two lines. He was going to move in from both sides and try to determine the strength of the enemy. Buildings were burning and the power plant and power stations had been destroyed. Astonished, he could find no sign of the enemy. The firefight ended, and devastation was everywhere. Back into the night, the team members watched the devastations and were overcome with the size of the inferno. It had spread throughout the complex. The lack of fire codes and safety laws in Mexico made it possible for the plant to be built without an adequate fire system or sprinklers. As the firemen worked to bring it under control, the new trucks lined up and waiting to be transported began to explode.

When he heard the explosions, the commandant called his command headquarters for support. He had reported they were under attack by a division of US rebel troops.

The headquarters had immediately ordered reinforcements to the plant to intercept the American forces. The Mexicans requested a UN Infantry Brigade and a light-armored unit to support the Mexican troops.

They pulled them from the closest available unit, a UN command headquarters, leaving the center with only a token force to protect them. As the French units moved out, a chopper loaded with Delta troops was moving toward the headquarters at treetop level. East of them, a second helicopter just made mincemeat out of a truck plant that was taking off and heading northwest. The two choppers would meet as planned, one group coming in from the east, the other coming from the west.

They would be low and moving fast. As soon as they touched down, they would move their men inside the compound. They were ordered to take no prisoners and to be as silent as they could. Using knives or crossbows, silent killing could save lives. Where possible, they would use tranquilizing darts to sedate the targets.

Both copters almost landed at the same time. As the men came out of the choppers, they took out the guards with silent shafts of steel as crossbows released their deadly bolts of death. The men moved inside with speed. As they met the enemy, they ordered them down. If they refused, they too felt the sting of a dart or death as a bolt from hell embedded into their frail bodies.

Major Albertson moved quickly into the building and up to the second floor turned right. On the fifth set of doors on left, it was there. He placed a detonator on the door and set it off by remote control. The doors blew off in a blast of fire and noise. As he moved to the door, Tork pulled the pin on two grenades and chucked them both in, one after the other. They went off within seconds of each other. The team moved in to see several men lying in the debris, two trying to get up and move. Tork looked to the north wall. The cabinet had been opened and the force of the explosion had ripped it apart, revealing a large safe door standing open. He moved inside and gathered up all the paper he could find.

They left any monies they found and took only documents. In minutes, they were out and moving quickly. Again, Tork whispered into his mic, "A Team, B Team, load up. We're out of here."

Both teams responded instantly. Both the dead and wounded were picked up and placed on the choppers. It had been a good assault, but with heavy casualties, six dead and eight wounded. The price of freedom would be written in blood and the dead avenged.

The strike team was heading home. The documents were safe in the chopper, a real prize for the government and more proof for the people.

Sgt. Maj. Jonathan T. Bentley looked to the major. "Sir, we're ready for another assignment. That one was tough, but a winner. What's next on our itinerary?"

Tork looked up to meet the sergeant's eyes, smiled, and said, "Be rest assured all of you will see action very, very soon. Only next time, it may not be as easy. Sergeant, keep sharp and on alert. We can't expect all assignments to be simple. Our training and equipment will tell the tale. So let's stay on it, keep it tight, and lean."

"Yes, sir. It will be done," the sergeant replied.

They were homeward bound. The night was done the morrow waited. The choppers returned to the base, and they turned over the documents to the council, more proof of the deceit and dishonesty the president and his cabinet hid from the people. This and all information had to be brought before America so they could see what the new world government and the president had been up to.

The council had made it clear that when the time had come, full documented disclosure would be made across the world by satellite. Maybe the rest of the world would like to see what their governments were up to too.

*****

Sybil, Di, and Cal had come to concord by separate routes. Diana had arranged with her mother for the other two to stay with them until a safe house could be set up in Oakland or Contra Costa County area. It was imperative that all activity was secured among the three of them. They planned their goals in advance and all were dangerous, even life-threatening.

Never were they to divulge their mission to anyone without direction from the desert. Sybil was to get a job on a county newspaper as a cover, if possible as a local reporter. This would give her a press pass and open needed doors. Di was to involve herself in local church groups to test the mood of the people, to see just where the Northern Californians stood in this civil war. The reports from agents in the area were good but not accurate. They were constantly on the move, making it difficult for them to ascertain anything of the general population's attitude. One of the reasons Cal and the others were sent was to learn and report on local conditions and to funnel UN and federal forces activities to the rebel command.

Cal contacted some old buddies that could set him up with a good job at the ports in Oakland. This made it possible for him to see firsthand what was coming in and where it was going to from the docks. With the other agents feeding them information on UN and federal forces activities in Northern California, Cal could now send it onto the rebels. All of them were in place, communications set, and lines open. It was time.

CHAPTER 25

Envy and Jealousy

UN Command Headquarters
Chicago, Illinois

The little man stood to address a group of ardent generals all gathered around a large table that had a mock-up of the United States on it. They had divided the states with a flag of a United Nations to denote which one had claimed or had been assigned a state or states as its own. Through the center was a red cord that they had laid carefully through each state from Chicago to Mexico. It ran diagonally to show the direction the UN armies were moving or planned to move. The little man turned to a USE field marshal from Britain and in broken English demanded to know why the heavy-armored division under his command had not moved forward.

"Sir," Brig.-Gen. Cecil Evans, British liaison, said, "We are not French troops fighting Germans in this war!" His words cut deep into the French officer's ego. He looked upon the British commander with contempt.

Before he could answer, the British continued to speak. "Not only do I have the American rebel army to fight, but also the local population is causing problems, not to mention we have a big desertion rate among our own troops. From what we learned, our men are going south to fight with those damn rebel forces. I called in air strikes and their missiles knocked us down. It's all piddly stuff that's slowing us up, and we haven't been able to engage the real army yet. Plus, we need more troops to hold the areas we've already taken. It would be a good idea if we could get the rest of the implants done quicker. It would make things simple to locate everyone in the areas we've been through so we can monitor their movements and see where they're going. With the new satellites we've put up, there's no place we can't track them. The Jones chip gives us the infinite tracking capability."

Gen. Esperanza de la Diego, Spanish military adviser, spoke up before anyone else could. "Yes, General. I will have a team start today. We now have the latest type of implant. Let me explain about the new Jones chip. It has a very long-range signal we can monitor via satellite and tune them to each individual's own biological system. If they remove them or make an attempt to, they will send out a signal that will pinpoint their location and identify the person. If they remove them, we will eliminate the individual upon capture. We tell each of them what will happen if they have the device removed. It is working very well in the occupied areas. Chicago is like a large valley of lambs, and we have eliminated crime. Of course, we had to purge those that thought they could beat the system. Now, all is serene."

The little general pointed his stick at the Mexican border and spoke, "Why have we not been able to break through the rebel lines in this quadrant?"

General Quasada spun his seat and looked at the little general with contempt in his eyes. The Mexican chief of staff, a native of California and a graduate of West Point, had returned to Mexico to fight for the return of the western states, California, Nevada, Utah, Arizona, Texas, and New Mexico. He was a dedicated Mexican. He addressed the little general in flawless English.

"The rebel forces are too strong at this point. We continue to get hit with commando raids that have slowed our staging efforts, and we have lost a great deal of munitions due to the heavy bombardments. The B-52s and B-2s are too damn high to reach. Remember, we are fighting some American elite forces, and they don't play fair. They have some kind of a Special Forces group out there that's way ahead of us. We act and they react, only not when we are expecting it. If it wasn't for the illegal men and women agents we sent in to the

United States, we wouldn't control what we do. They are our eyes and ears, and we can't rely on all of them."

His idea of the US infiltrators reminded him of the large number of illegal Mexicans that had crossed the border and had exemplified the number of Mexican terrorists he had sleeping in rebel areas waiting for their orders to strike.

He continued, "The American forces move mostly at night. Our agents can't find them, nor do they have information on them. Plus, they are operating very silently. We suspect they are also behind the sabotage that's been hitting the plants in the Mexican states. This activity is costing a fortune. All the manufactures are screaming at us for security, and this is tying up needed forces for our push north. We are presently in the process of bringing in more troops from Europe, and we have started building in Northern California for our move east and south. We feel we can thin them out by opening additional fronts."

Slamming his fist down on the table and with a raised voice, he continued, "Gentlemen, soon the flags of the United Nations will be flying over a once proud United States, and the flags will be ours. Mexico will regain her property, and the new world order will be complete in North America. Then we shall move into South America. They spurned the Yankee agreements, setting it up for us."

The generals applauded, knowing soon the United Nations would control all of Europe and North and South America. Asia and the Orient were almost in control. After the United States, they would be in full control of the world's economy. Japan had only a self-defense force and had to rely on the United States for defense, and that would soon end. China was building, but did not have the full capability yet to move. First the United States and then one world—only the foolish little people would resist, and they would be found and eliminated one by one.

The men broke into planning groups, each group having a set objective to complete and a timetable to meet. Time was running short; the president had to be found and freed. It was imperative the unoccupied areas see and hear the president. They felt sure they would no longer resist if he were to reassure them the new world order would give them peace of mind, no criminals, health care, and jobs and provide them with everything they could need and ensure the children would get a state education.

*****

Tork whispered into his helmet mic, "Sergeant Glatz." The sergeant was a big man, happy-go-lucky, easy, and warm when not on duty, but hard as tempered steel when on the job.

"Yes, sir," he answered. "We are ready and the men are in position, and demos have set the charges along the perimeter fence line. We have three naturals with crossbows set to hit the active sentry posts. The enemy has only three operational tonight, so it should be an easy hit, sir. Tyrone has reported all the posts will be manned by either French or German troops. Guess they just don't trust the Mexican or British troops stationed here."

"Right," Tork replied. "Too many Brits have crossed the line and joined up with us." Tork motioned a platoon leader over. "Lieutenant, I've been watching the lights in the northwest assembly building, second floor. Looks like some kind of meeting going on in there. Bring us over a high power and let's take a look."

The lieutenant picked up a high-powered set of night glasses and brought them over to Tork. They set them up, adjusted them, and pulled the window and the room's contents into full view. There were about ten men. Some uniformed, mostly civilian, all intently observing what was on a table in the center of the room. The meeting had been going on for some time, and it had to be something special. Tork studied them, watching each man's expressions and gestures. He looked for what was in there that would be necessary for the group. Maybe they'd take back a prisoner or two.

Tork looked over to the lieutenant. "What's on your mind?" he asked.

"Sir, ah, well, I was just looking at one of the greatest logos in history. I never imagined it would desert us, but there it is! They are forsaking the men and women who made it famous and a household name, not to mention the country. That big blue sign meant everything to me. I would argue over its good and bad points with the best of them, and now it's an enemy of the people. For what, I wonder?"

"Maybe survival," replied Tork, looking at the lieutenant. "Yes, Lieutenant, maybe just to survive."

The lieutenant, not seeing the reason behind Tork's comment, asked, "Why?"

Tork's answer was strong and comprehensive. "The liberals," he said, "forced most of the big companies to move into Mexico and China because of the controls the government was placing on them. The cost of products was escalating to the point no one could make a profit. When foreign governments made big promises, the companies moved out of the country, east, west, and south. You might say the industrial migration began.

"The government didn't mind because it allowed them to do what they wanted to do all along, control the people from the cradle to the grave. Each inch they took brought more and more of the people closer to revolution. It has taken years for us to build up to this. It took insiders throughout the government on every level to succeed. Being in the right place to cover up mistakes was necessary to obtain the correct results for us to be successful. That was done. Well, we're ready to hit another one of those famous trademarks and destroy it if we can." Tork keyed his mic. "Code Yellow. Get ready, Sergeant Glatz. Main building, far corner to your right, see it?"

"Yes, sir. Looks like a party."

"You got it, Sarge. That's the one. Have your naturals move in. I want them going in fast. Have them move to the floor above, no lights on. They'll need to come in through the windows and take out any guards inside. I want you're A team to go inside when they hear the naturals enter. Try to take them all alive if possible. Don't let anything get destroyed. I want to know what's so important in there. Affirmative?"

"Yes, sir. Affirmative."

"Good. I'll be on your heels. I have a few other jobs to take care of first."

The time had come. All the men were ready to move, and they were only waiting for the command. The major keyed his mic and uttered one word to all, "Freedom."

Each man moved to his target. The naturals were black troops. Dressed in black and wearing night-vision glasses, they moved silently, invisible in the night. The elite guard saw nothing. One had just entered the gatehouse when a silent steel shaft penetrated the glass window and struck him in the center of his chest, pinning him to the wall. The shaft held him up like a limp rag doll nailed in place. Before the other guard could reach for an alarm or stand and draw a weapon, he was hit in the head by a second silent bolt. He fell as if asleep, head on the desk.

The team went to their assigned target areas. Silently they put the explosives in position, guards eliminated, workers evaded, and detonators programmed and armed.

Tork and his group moved into position. The outside team slithered up the side of the building to the roof and moved over to the section of the building where they needed to drop down to enter the targeted meeting room. They set up their gear and dropped the lines over the side, hooked themselves to their rappelling gear, and silently lowered themselves down to just above the windows of the target floor.

The four men were in place. Ty whispered into his mic that they were ready to move. A whispered reply was heard, and as if a silent command were given, they all moved together. Pushing themselves out from the wall, they dropped and swung into the windows breaking through the glass as they entered. They dropped from their lines, released their gear, and instantly picked out any armed guards that were there. You couldn't hear the phaaat, phaaat of the silenced automatics over the shouting of the men. The guards and those who drew weapons were cut down instantly. The inside group had moved through the building, checking each office as they went and eliminating any armed opposition they found.

As the main team entered the conference room, the inside team was at the door. As the message came over their helmet earphones, they acted instinctively, unlocking the door to the conference room. Entering it was simple, and within minutes, the room was secure.

Tork ordered pictures of the table and the charts on the walls be taken. Orders were given. It was time to leave. Explosions mixed with the charges as they went off. It was complete chaos. Firefighters were hesitant to start on a fire for fear there would be another explosion. The commander of the local troops immediately contacted UN headquarters and gave them the directions he thought the enemy had gone.

For five minutes, Tork and the group looked at the factory as it blazed. He turned to his captives. "Gentlemen, if you understand English, understand this. We will prevail. The United States of America will survive, and we will never forget the treachery of this planet. Pray to God we do not launch nuclear missiles on your capitols. They have contemplated and discussed it. As yet a decision has not been made. But if this madness continues, who can tell?"

Tork had no idea what the revolutionary command had discussed, but it wouldn't hurt to scare the hell out of them. If they ever returned to their lines, it may be something for them all to consider.

UN Command Headquarters
Southwestern region of Mexico

The UN commander spoke to his executive officer. "Get me the Third Army Group commander."

Within minutes, an officer from the group was on the phone. A German officer from Berlin answered, "Yes, sir. What can I do for you?"

"We have a serious attack underway at plant K-26. American rebel forces are engaged with the garrison there. We need your air support unit immediately. You will need full firepower, with gunships and infantry. I don't want to let them get away this time. Do you understand?"

"Yes, sir. As we speak, I have ordered the immediate dispatch of the group. They should be in the air in minutes, sir."

The elite German response group was one of the new world order's best commando groups. They had moved in and out of the rebel-held areas on several occasions causing damage and death to many loyal civilian Americans. In one incident, they destroyed a full, and potentially dangerous, weapons depot, eliminating all enemy forces, a real ribbon in their bonnets.

They knew their enemy well. The group was airborne within minutes. The response crews had the choppers ready and running when the troops boarded them.

The gunships were up and en route to the plant long before the troops were. As the lead ship first sighted the plant and the small town, the commander of the group could see the blazing sky. It looked like the entire plant was on fire. Secondary explosions were going off, and it could almost be heard over the roar of the engines.

The commander keyed his mic. "All ships, descend to attack altitudes and look for any groups on the ground. Fire at will. I suspect only rebel troops will be in the vicinity."

The eight gunships dropped low over the trees. As they descended, the birds separated and started a sweep moving east and to the west. Both flights circled to the north expecting to engage the enemy at any time. The sky in and around the plant was lit up from the fires, making it difficult for those on the ground to identify the aircraft overhead. As the UN gunships came in close to the plant, the Mexican anticraft batteries opened fire, and missile launches were made against the UN ships sent to help them, causing several direct hits. Two German ships exploded in midair. The German commander screamed into his mic, but he was so aggravated it was in German and only confused the Mexicans below. They, in turn, ignored the commands to cease-fire.

The Germans turned back toward the incoming troop carriers. To avoid any in-flight collisions, the German commander ordered the troop carriers to land in the desert below to reorganize.

The gunships remained aloft until the carriers were down, and then they landed too. The German commander contacted the UN command headquarters advising them of their present position and requested the Mexican garrison at plant K-26 hold his fire. He then advised them they had just shot down two German gunships.

*****

Major Albertson looked at his platoon leader. "Did you see where they landed?"

"Yes, sir. About a thousand meters to our left. We no sooner got our netting up when they returned and started to land. I don't think they know we're here, sir."

"I don't think so either, Lieutenant. How many choppers in the field?"

"Don't know, sir, but I'll see if we can get a count on them."

"Lieutenant, get me as many personnel you have with TOW missiles. I doubt if the Germans have posted a perimeter guard, so let's take a chance to move in as close as we can, as the enemy choppers move out, and they probably will very soon. I would guess just as soon as they get clearance from the plant garrison, they will move hoping to catch up with us. When they start their engines, I want ours started up. They won't be able to hear ours over their own. And when they start their climb, launch our TOW missiles. Fire on the gunships. If we have enough missiles for the others, get them as they lift off. Got it?"

"Yes, sir." Within minutes, the men had started moving into positions, each carrying one or two Black Mamba missiles and newly updated and superior TWO missiles, ten times more accurate, faster, and lighter than the old TWO missiles.

The major was right. It took the Mexicans more than twenty minutes to radio the group they could come in. There had been great confusion at the plant. They had thought the Americans had returned to bomb them.

The German commander acknowledged the message and ordered all engines started. Each of the chopper commanders reported their machine as it came up online and was ready to fly. The commander then ordered his gunships up. As they lifted up, they moved into their attack formation and held in place waiting for the command to proceed.

As the last ship entered his position, Tork's men launched their missiles. Within seconds, the birds started exploding. None of the men aboard them had a chance to survive. As they exploded, fiery debris fell on the waiting ships below. The men in the ships panicked and vaulted from them, running away from the dropping, exploding ships. Most of them left their weapons on board. As they ran, the burning choppers fell on the ships below.

Tork looked at the flames shooting up. The ammunition on the ships was exploding, creating even greater danger. Not wanting to get caught in the aftermath, Tork ordered the netting pulled down and left behind and then ordered the assault teams back into their choppers. The engines were running and all were back on board. The ships rose from their place in the night, black in color, no lights save the instrument panels. Onboard radar told the pilots what was ahead of them. They cleared the treetops and moved north toward their base. It had been a bad night for mankind, but a good night for Americans fighting the new world order.

It pained each of them as they left. They had been forced again to kill others. *Leave us alone, return to your shores, and there will be peace again*, thought Tork. *What a waste it was to destroy so many young people.*

"But we must prevail," said Tork.

The sergeant sitting behind him tapped him on the shoulder. "What was that, sir? I couldn't hear you."

"Oh, nothing, Sergeant. I was just thinking out loud."

It took several hours before they arrived at the base. They gave clearance codes and escort fighters arrived to see them safely home.

Tork entered the briefing room, saluted the officer in charge, and said, "Major Albertson reporting, sir."

"Please have seat, Major. We need to go over your assault on plant K-26 yesterday. We know you are still tired, but we need some important data. If you can, could you tell us what types of vehicles they were building at the plant, what nationalities were the troops there, and what were the markings on the aircraft you shot down?

We need to know if our intelligence reports coming in from those sectors are correct."

Tork went through each of the requests in detail. "I was surprised to see they had brought in special troops for this one plant. That's when I decided to look closer at what was going on. Did the prisoners and the information we brought back, did that help you any?"

"Oh yes, it was invaluable to us. You may have saved half the country with the information we have. Your group should feel proud of this mission."

Tork looked at him. "Sir, we had to kill many young men last night. We know it was necessary, and I couldn't take the chance. The enemy choppers would have spotted us as they took off. I felt if they had seen us, we would have been like targets in a shooting gallery. We surely wouldn't have made it out of there and probably would have lost most of our men. Sir, could we use this incident to tell the people of Europe to keep their governments from this foolish war? Is there any way to communicate to let the world know just how devastating this war is to all of us?"

The man looked at the major with compassion. "I wish there was a way that we could give them details of the raid and tell them how their sons have died. Nevertheless, I don't think it would help. You see, they are all in the new world order and must be completely loyal to the government where they live or perish. The burden they carry with them will not allow any dissidents. Should they remove the chips implanted in them, they can be executed. They must remain loyal or die. This is why so many of their troops have deserted and come to us. They too want freedom, and they are willing to fight and die for it, even if it means fighting against their own people. I doubt if even the UN commanders realize that. When we have beaten them and driven them from our shores, we will then try to bring peace and reasoning to the rest of the planet. Until then, Major, we need all of you to fight for our freedom. Remember freedom is earned."

Tork listening intently replied, "I and my men agree, sir. However, no matter the risk, we will prevail for we know freedom is within our reach."

"Major, you cannot take it for granted. Each member of society should know they are the ones responsible for it by voting those that will make decisions on their behalf. If each of us had done our homework and looked at those candidates a little closer, we wouldn't be in this fix now. We wouldn't be holding members of our government in camps for treason, and we wouldn't have the rest of the world dividing us up. Yes, Major, some information brought back from plant K-26 detailed the states that would be governed by certain foreign countries. Should we fail, this land will no longer be our land nor will those spacious skies we have sung about for generations. We will become economic slaves to the new world order."

Tork was impressed. He too had admonished many of his troops the same way, and yet the words just spoken really brought home the importance of individual freedoms within the confines of a decent, law-abiding social behavior. The whims of a few had turned the country over to others, with the disregard of the majority. His mind raced with thoughts of what they had done. They had dissolved their basic social responsibilities and abolished constitutional laws that govern the people. They lost their right to an open society and to be a law-abiding nation. Worse yet was the total disregard of God in their daily lives from a nation that promoted God in its houses of government and on its money. Then taking it away was the beginning of the end. The total disregard of their language and faith in their selves was enough for many.

Tork continued, "Well, if we fail, they'll all be speaking different languages and they will all have the privileges of owning and wearing their very own personal Jones chip."

As the speaker continued, his mind returned to the present, and he listened intently. "Major, go forward with the determination you have and win this war for all of us. We must prevail, or we will see warring forever, for no man or woman will tolerate total domination, and that's the new world order. If we fail, eventually there will be uprising throughout the world, and that means constant domination and killings. It's the only way to control the disobedience of the people."

The man got up, shook Tork's hand, and left. Tork looked at him as he walked out the door. He thought about life, liberty, and the pursuit of happiness, how all of us must and want to live a much simpler way of life. They, the greatest nation on earth, slowly destroyed from within. *We'll put a stop on it and we'll earn our freedom again—only this time, we'll make changes that will safeguard us from anyone taking away our freedoms. No judge can circumvent the law by making a law. They will be limited to the law as written. No more assumptions or opinion. How the law is written is how they will judge the law.*

The president will not have the power to appoint a member of their family to a position within their administration. There will be no room in the government for nepotism. They would restrict the House and the Senate to no more than two consecutive terms in office and each elected to no less than or more than a four-year term, not to exceed the two-term limit. No one would have the opportunity to use the people for their own reasons. All laws passed by both Houses would be given to the American people on a referendum vote to make them into law. If the proposal failed to pass, it would go back to both Houses for review. The power of veto would remain up to the referendum, but not beyond.

These were thoughts that Tork had often contemplated himself and debated with others, with most of them being in agreement. Some still clung to the past. All knew they could never go back to the liberal open anarchy that led to this war and the domination of the new world order by socialists.

Tork couldn't wait for his next assignment; he headed for the commander's office. He knew he had to get his group back into the war if they expected to win. Yes, he knew that.

*****

The United Nations' new world order forces had been pouring into the country from Canada, through Northern California, and on eastern ports held by the federal and UN troops. They held the threat from Mexico at bay in Mexico. All goods manufactured in Mexico by transplanted American companies had to deliver them from Mexico to federal-held territory by air or sea. Rebel forces in

Mexico destroyed much of it in place or as it landed in federal ports. More of the country was swinging toward the rebel government.

To counter the increase in hostilities toward the UN forces, the United States of Europe had been building up their forces for a full invasion into the United States. They built up the French and German contingencies along the southern Mexican border where they were safe from rebel harassment. They were assembling the British, Canadian, and Russian armies in Canada for a southern strike. On the West Coast, in northern California, Oregon, and Washington, the UN invasion force was building up for an eastern push into Idaho, Nevada, Utah, and Colorado. Canadian troops would be pushing south and the French and Germans in Northern California pushing south into Southern California. It was expected they would then move east into Arizona, New Mexico, and Texas where they would meet UN troops moving north from the Mexican territories.

The UN commander expected his troops in Southern Mexico to rapidly move north, and they expected new arrivals to dock in Mexican ports along the east and west coasts of Mexico very soon.

The UN high command expected to secure the West Coast and the mountain states before the rebels could build up sufficient troop strength to challenge them. They expected rebel forces in the occupied areas to withdraw from the western areas they had under their control. Alaska had been taken and secured by Russian troops, and the oil from the wellheads there was delivered to the United Nations.

The Jones chips in the occupied areas had proven highly successful in keeping the people in order. Should the rebels gain control of these areas, the United Nations felt they would lose complete control of the war and more stringent matters may prevail. They considered using nuclear weapons if their losses where to high. What worried them was the retaliation factor. Would the rebel forces capitulate or would they respond in kind?

The fact was that if these areas were vulnerable, the chips removed could provide additional troops for the rebel cause. Moving their timetable up was therefore necessary for the United Nations to correlate the western invasion with the push from Canada in the north to move south. It would require troops from Mexico to move northeast to meet with the invading UN troops from northern and eastern Canada. If successful, they would cut the country in half with the western and mountain areas under control. This would leave only parts of Texas, Louisiana, Alabama, Georgia, the Carolinas, and some pocket resistance in Florida to worry about. They felt once the mainstream rebel forces had been eliminated, the remainder would throw down their weapons and surrender.

*****

"Gentlemen, the information retrieved from plant K-26 has shown a vast invasion undertaking by the federal troops and their UN allies." The secretary of war addressed the joint members of the Congress and the military high command. "It is imperative that we counter these coordinated attacks."

As he spoke, pictures of the information seized on a recent raid were shown on a high-tech TV. "You can see by this map the extent of the forces being massed in the areas marked in red. The arrow moving up from Mexico and down from Canada is the route they are going to take. The arrows moving east from California and down from Canada into their neighboring states and driving east to meet troops going northeast from Mexico are the UN troops. The arrow moving southwest from the occupied northern states is going to link and assist Mexican and UN troops. With this information, we can meet them on our terms. The blue markers represent the federal troops under UN command that will be used to garrison the newly occupied areas. Seems the United Nations feels they will have less resistance if the US federal forces garrison the occupied areas.

"With this in mind, gentlemen, we must exercise the utmost care in our strategy. Where we strike, it must give us time to consolidate our troops and to meet the invasion head on. Are there any questions?"

They heard murmuring from within the group, and then a senator stood up.

"Mr. Secretary, we believe that we are presently engaged in a great war, greater than any the American people have had to face. For the third time in our history, we are confronted with hostile foreign troops on our soil. It is time, therefore, for us as members of the new Congress and Senate to allow our military planners to do their jobs and give us an offensive plan that will defeat the United Nations before they strangle our country and divide us among themselves.

"In the occupied areas, we know they are implanting the people with the Jones chip. The people are powerless to help us or to themselves. Reports have come in of men and women being executed for removing the chips. One family saw their parents shot in front of them when they were stopped at a UN roadblock. It's essential we gain control of those areas and remove the chips. My suggestion is to assign a committee of four members of the government to the Armed Forces Planning Group, to work hand in hand with them in learning a firm forward battle element that will stop them before they can destroy any more areas. At all costs, we must obliterate the munitions and supplies building up along the West Coast and incite civil unrest in the most heavily populated areas.

"We must start intensive guerrilla warfare within all held areas. The people need to know we are here, and we will fight for each of them. Their freedom is as sacred as our own. Gentlemen, we as a governing group, and at this point of time, must let the military do their jobs without hindrance from us. Our group should do no more than act as liaison between them, the Senate, and the House. We have changed the name and the status of the defense department to the war department because we no longer are united. We have on our hands a war, a civil war, an international war that must be won at all costs. Therefore, before the Asians decide to get involved, we must free our country from European dominance and return to honoring the constitution of old. We must fight, gentlemen, for we can no longer permit the amendments that they have repealed to stand. They have made the most honored document in history ineffectual in an effort to create a world socialist government, a government controlled by only a few wealthy families that make drones out of the people who made this country great. Our brothers and sisters need our help, and by the good grace of God, we will help them all.

"I, therefore, respectfully urge the Congress and Senate to pass a resolution reinstating the amendments to the constitution and give the military full powers to meet and defeat the enemy with a no less nor more than four members of the government to act as liaison between the military and the government. They would be working directly with the secretary of war, and each of the service secretaries. Could I have a vote on this please, gentlemen?"

They carried the vote in the affirmative. The security committee assigned the four members, two from both parties. Immediately they contacted the secretary of war and the planning started.

The committee set up their working headquarters at the desert base in Southern California with all intelligence information routed directly to them. With hot information coming out of the bay area, it was considered paramount that immediate steps be taken to destroy the heavily armed region. They would send in sabotage teams and guerilla fighters to disrupt troops and destroy munitions wherever they were located.

Major Albertson had just returned from his latest mission—low losses and high gains in disruption and destruction. All was going well with the team, so much so they had to put fourteen additional teams into the field. They were wreak havoc with the big corporations and the foreign combat troops stationed in Mexico. The adversaries were getting better. The teams were running into higher trained and skilled troops. It seemed the United Nations was sending its best into Mexico and that was good. It also meant they had to be pulled from top-rated combat outfits. Tork was elated over the prospects— it meant he was doing his job right and the men were doing theirs even better.

When Tork entered the debriefing, a lieutenant colonel signaled him over to the side.

Tork saluted and spoke, "Yes, what can I do for you, sir?"

The lieutenant colonel returned the salute and pointing the way said, "Major, you have an appointment with General Duncan. Please follow me."

The two of them left the building, entered a vehicle, and within minutes were on the way to the field. Without cleaning up or being permitted to shower and change into a decent uniform, they whisked

Tork to base operations where a C-17 was waiting with engines running for immediate takeoff.

Both men entered the aircraft. No sooner where they in their seats than the plane started rolling. Within minutes, they were airborne. The plane circled the field and headed due west.

Tork looked at the lieutenant colonel. "Well, sir, nice day for a cruise."

"Yes, it is," replied the lieutenant colonel. "Indeed, it is."

Time went fast. Tork and the crew joked over past events and experiences they had. One incident would bring up another story or deed, a smile, a laugh, or a tear.

They all felt and heard the engines change as the pilot started his descent in what looked like a deserted part of New Mexico. Tork could see nothing from the plane's window except mountains, desert, Mexican cactus, and sagebrush. As the plane leveled off at a low altitude, they could hear its hydraulics kicking in, and the landing gear started down. The plane was approaching a landing field or something. The crew chief entered from the cockpit and motioned for Tork to be seated and to put on his seat belt. Tork heard the lock snap in place on the belt, and the plane's wheels squealed when they touched the runway and landed. The landing was soft, Tork thought, a nice smooth return to mother earth.

Tork considered it would be smart to get this pilot's name and unit number; he might come in handy on a mission one day.

The lieutenant colonel unlatched his belt and started gathering his things together. "Major, we will go directly to our quarters where you will have time to clean up, take a shower, and get into a clean uniform before we see General Duncan. By the way, they sent your gear ahead before you returned from your mission, so everything you need should be here. Are there any questions?"

"Only one, sir. Do we have time to dine in this unit's most probable gourmet dining facility? I'm starved."

The lieutenant colonel was not amused. "Major, food based on Freedom Earned will always be a gourmet meal to me. Understand?"

What a pompous fool this guy is, Tork thought. *Wonder if he's seen any combat.*

CHAPTER 26

Northern California in Jeopardy

General Duncan and several men meeting with him had just finished going over the latest intelligence report, and it was not good. The United Nations was concentrating the buildup in the Northern California region and that had started to escalate. The bases in the area had their hardstands and grassed areas loaded with bombers, refueling aircraft, and fighters from Europe. With the reports coming in from the northern and southern areas of occupation, they knew an offensive was being readied for a summer launch.

They also knew that stopping it would be necessary to slow the offensive until they could get their troops in place and prepare to move first, forcing the enemy into a defensive position. They all had agreed on using the same hit-and-run method they used in Mexico using only the best men for the job.

One of the senior officers spoke. "Well, General, when do we meet this man of the hour to lead our minuteman brigade? Time is short."

The general smiled. "Yes, sir. He's on base and hopefully rested, showered, and will be with us shortly. I have scheduled a meeting with him immediately after we've eaten tonight. That should give all of us time to dine and return here for our meeting. Do you, gentlemen, have any questions?"

*****

Tork had found his gear all laid out for him. His dress uniform had been cleaned, pressed, and hung up in his locker. *Royal treatment*, he thought. *Must be something very important for all this attention.* He'd showered, shaved, and just finished dressing when there was a knock on the door.

"Enter," he replied to the knock.

The door swung open and a grizzled sergeant major entered. "Sir, General Duncan requests your presence at dinner. Sir, if you will follow me, I'll take you to the officer's mess."

"Well, well, well, Sergeant Piper, I thought by now you would be retired, not in a rebel army. How are you, Sergeant? It's been a long time."

Sergeant Piper, US Army, served with Tork during the first invasion of Iraq in Desert Storm. He was a decorated NCO with a reputation of honesty and heroics, an NCO Tork was happy to see.

"Yes, sir, it has been," Piper said. "But then you were just another officer during Desert Storm that someone had to look after, right, sir?"

"Well, Sergeant Piper, how did you get tangled up with us? Thought for sure you would be out West living a nice retired life. What happened?"

"Well, Major, by the way, sir, those oak leaves look good on you. I was doing just as you figured, living up in the High Sierras, minding my own business, doing a little fishing and what not, when the feds caught up with us. They wanted to move us into a retirement complex for retired military personnel. Well, sir, we kind of figured they were up to no good and had decided to run when the takeover occurred. Apparently they put the move to the retirement home on hold when the takeover occurred, so it gave us time to evaluate the situation. It didn't take long to realize what was going on and what side of the stream we belonged.

"Joanne and I knew we had to be part of it, so we headed toward the rebel-occupied areas. It didn't take them long to verify who we were and get their hands on my records. Still don't know how they did that. Once they saw them, they instantly recruited me, and here I am. Also, sir, we have others from our old outfit here. There's Bremer,

Hotchkiss, Southerland, Brodnick, and Fifer. They were all active duty when it happened, and one by one, they ended up here. So you might say we have one of the best Special Forces groups here. Any idea why you're here, sir, and will we see some action soon?"

"You know as much as I do, Sergeant. I certainly hope we'll know something tonight or in the morning. They pulled me away from a top unit for this, and I'm still in the dark. Well, Sarge, where's that mess? I'm starved!"

The sergeant escorted the major into a private dining room in the officer's mess. As they entered, Tork noticed the extra security. A few men in civilian clothing were standing together in conversation. One of them looked up and an instant smile crossed Tork's face.

"Well, I'll be damned, Cal. What are you doing here?" Grabbing Cal's right hand with a firm grasp and giving him a big hug, he asked, "Is Di with you? What's going on, boy? You better fill me in."

"Love to, Tork, but that's not up to me. You'll get an earful after the meeting, and no, Di's not with me. But she's fine and doing very well for the cause. You should be very proud of her. She's one in a million."

Before Tork could respond, the door opened and General Duncan, his aides, and several men entered. Before anyone could call attention, the general said, "Please, gentlemen, be seated and let's eat. We have a long night ahead of us, and we can all think better on a full stomach."

The dinner went well. Cal brought Tork up on everything that was going on in California—the massive buildup and the increased bomber activity at Travis and the commercial airports in the area converted to military use. UN ships we're laying in anchor in San Francisco Bay, and the United Nations was using Alcatraz for political prisoners. There we're high numbers of ground troops in special staging areas that indicated a thrust either south or to the east very soon.

They permitted no locals near them, nor we're they allowed off the bases for any reason. They're all being kept away from the public. "Their agents in the United Nations have let us know they can't trust all of them so they are making sure no one gets loose. They don't want any deserters going over to the rebels and providing information or enabling propaganda for us to use."

The rebel high command had summoned Cal to special meeting only hours after his last transmission to command. So he felt the meeting was to establish some kind of special team to gather more intelligence than his cells could provide. He had just finished telling Tork his opinion when General Duncan moved all of them to another secured meeting room.

General Duncan waved all of them to their seats and then spoke, "Please, all of you, take your seat. We will be going over the chain of events that has brought all of you here today."

The general waited until all had been seated, and then he sat down. The lights dimmed, a large-screen TV projector came on, and within seconds, they were looking at the enemy buildup. The narrator was concise and to the point. The information they we're seeing we're actual pictures taken and smuggled out of occupied areas. It was obvious the buildup was nearing completion and the UN offensive would begin soon and in earnest.

"As you can see"—the general was ready to lay on the cream and sugar for all of them—"the USE troop buildup and concentrations have nearly finished. Since these pictures were taken, they completed the buildup in key locations and will soon start their march from the occupied states in the east and from those bordering Canada. They will soon move west where we expect the forces occupying Wyoming to move southwest into Utah and Colorado. There, they hope to link up with their troops that have moved in from their intended invasion of Nevada and Utah. They'll be coming in from California at the same time we expect a pushout of the Mexican territories.

"We expect them to cross the borders and enter Arizona, New Mexico, and Texas. We are waiting for intelligence reports that should give us the exact locations for these crossings. We will best know how to meet these demands when we receive this information. It appears to us they hope to break the Central United States and the West Coast into four theaters of operations, making it easier for them to supply their forces and to keep watch over the occupied zones. Remember, they want to control us, but to do that, they have to defeat us. To counter this, we've been moving troops and Special Forces groups into these possible positions of engagement. The intelligence we received from our Night Hawks in Mexico has allowed us to ascertain their possible routes and to set up teams along these routes to harass them. We have moved our main battle troops into positions to meet the large advancing armies coming up from Mexico. However, those coming in from the north and the east are a problem. We have no large opposing troops available now in those regions. Our army units in the Southern California areas and some National Guard units loyal to us from Nevada, Utah, and Colorado are in position. We can count on those states for their tenacity and courage and their loyalty.

"In anticipation of their possible routes, we have started moving forces into the Central states to link up with partisan units and National Guard and reserve units that are faithful to us. The naval units we have at sea are ready to move when given the orders. We have most of the active fleets that are with us, including those in the Pacific fleet. We have moved them within a day of our west coast, because of the intense buildup by the United Nations. We must not overlook any possible threatened areas. In addition, attack—" General Duncan paused as he looked over his audience. All were taking notes.

"Are there any questions?" he asked.

No one answered him.

Satisfied there were no questions, he continued, "Submarines are not able to attack UN convoys in both the Atlantic and Pacific oceans, so we are concentrating on the Atlantic areas. Our submarines in the Pacific are safeguarding our interests in and around Japan, where they are keeping an eye on China. As the UN troops move into our regions, we are prepared to hit them in the most remote areas to keep the fighting away from the cities. We have already made preparations to hit them the hardest in the mountains and on the plains. For the past two months, we have deployed troops into those areas we expect them to move through, plus we have anticipated alternate routes they may take to reach their objectives. If the information we have received is correct, we can expect them to move on Reno, Salt

Lake, and Denver. To improve our odds, we have elected to redeploy several of our Night Hawk units from Mexico to California where they will do everything they can to harass the enemy. We want them hit hard before they start their offensive.

"If we can demoralize the troops before they engage us, we can expect an easier encounter. It is paramount we hold them back from reaching their objectives. Once we have them slowed, we are counting on the assigned army units moving into Northern California to thin out their lines. It is then we will attack with our main battle forces. Until their line is thinned out, we will be engaging them in a hit-and-run battle plan. This should lead them to believe we are weak and outnumbered. We will withhold heavy bomber activity and let them have air superiority until the line is as thin as a banjo string. Then we'll hit them with everything we have.

"Now that you have an overview of our intentions, I want all of you to join together for the California plan of attack. What units to employ, the size of the units, the number of MH-47E Chinook and AH-64 Apache and RAH-66 Comanche gunships for attack support. Your attack points are defined in the pink-covered folders. You will find troop strength and possible commando unit locations as well. We're not too sure of their true locations. The United Nations has been moving them frequently, and it's been a job keeping track of them all. These units could give us real trouble, so try to take them out first if you can substantiate their exact locations. If you can't demoralize them, the others will become uneasy, so work on it. You will find the basic outlines in the blue-covered folder. We will need a firm plan no later than 2100 hours. We are on a tight leash now and we can't afford any extra time. We must hit them soon. Do you have any questions?"

All of them sat thinking. Several minutes went by without comment.

"Fine, fine. Now let's break down into teams representing the areas you have been assigned. You'll find them in the envelopes being passed out to you now."

An air force chief master sergeant handed Tork an envelope. "Thank you, Sergeant." As he took the envelope, he noticed first it was heavy and had something loose in it. He started to open it and was unaware that the general had held up his hand to the others, silencing them. Everybody watched as Tork opened the envelope and pulled out several sheets of paper. He opened them up and examined them. The first sheet was a complete list of hard sites to hit. The second sheet was the available hardware for the entire operation in his sectors and the third was a set of orders. He assumed the orders were the orders for the assaults and didn't bother reading them. Instead, he set them down and started to discard the envelope when he realized there was something else inside. He tipped the envelope over, and two new blackened oak leaves fell into his open hand. He looked at them for a second and looked up to find a silent smiling group of men and women watching him intently. He picked up the orders, glanced at them, and held them up for all to see with a smile that couldn't be missed and a "thank you, sir," for the general.

The general had a smile on his face too and a chuckle in his voice when he said, "Congratulations, Lieutenant Colonel Albertson!" The entire group broke up and applauded Tork.

What a day this is, he thought. *Yes, what a day.*

The teams joined together and the battle plans for the east were in motion. They put great detail into their plan of attacks. The planning group was assessing the locations of each site to be hit, the type of equipment to be used on each incursion, and the route to be taken upon departure.

None of them were alike. They didn't want the UN command to establish a pattern, therefore anticipating their next move. They had just completed the last plan when the door opened and General Duncan returned. All the teams were as ready as they would ever be.

"I have established the teams, the men who will lead them, and their second-in-command. As I call out the last names of the team leaders, I want you to move over to my left and enter the door for a special briefing. Albertson, Clifford, Ford, Freedman, Howard."

As the general called, the men got up and moved to the designated room; shortly after, the general and his aide entered the briefing room.

"Each of you was chosen because of your Blackhawk activities or your Special Forces training and accomplishments," the general said. "These factors are paramount to our success. Each of you knows your teams and your men better than we do, so we are letting you pick your second-in-command from your present groups or someone that you know will fit in better and who may now be on another assignment. The only exception will be the San Francisco-Oakland Bay area group. That's yours, Tork. I have a special assignment for you and your team. We have just recently added to our group a new captain who will—and I'm sure you will agree—be invaluable to you on this assignment. His knowledge of the area and the location of the munition dumps and troop concentrations will make your mission much easier for you and your team. I'll have him report to you at the briefing at 2000 hours.

"By the way men, we have put on alert and transported your troops here. They are equipped and waiting for you. They have been reoutfitted with new equipment and arms. Now, let's go over these plans and timetables. It's important we hit the enemy while they rest. Unusual time frames are important to our strategy. Remember, no patterns must be evident for future attacks for them to see or to speculate on."

The group had just finished the timetables and had ironed out the errors in the plans. The general's aide entered. "Gentlemen, the 2200-hour briefings is about to begin. If you please, follow me."

The group followed the aide out and they entered a large bus, dressed in its best camouflage. Within minutes, they arrived at a large hangar on the flight line. In the dark of the night and with only a minimum of light, Tork could see the silhouettes of helicopters and gunships sitting on the hardstands. He could see slight movement, knowing there were armed guards watching them closely. As the bus moved into the building, Tork could hear the doors on the building starting to close as giant motors hummed their song of strength and power.

The bus stopped and sat in silence until the doors had closed and the lights came on.

The mercury-vapor lamps came up at a slow rate, a dim light at first and then a rose color. As they brightened, they changed to a white light. The operator opened the bus door. As the men exited, they could see they were in a windowless building, more of a garage than a hangar. At the end of the building, a door slid open and a colonel came forward. "Gentlemen, please follow me."

They all entered through an adjoining corridor into a large hangar, well-lighted and full of troops, complete with gear and weapons, all ready to go. A young female soldier dressed in fatigue battle dress called out names and gave directions to the team locations. The general's planners had been thorough. The teams were in grids and numbered for assignment locations and departure date and times. Each group had been reoutfitted for the area they would be fighting in. The officers and NCOs were fully briefed and waiting for their commander's arrival.

Tork had no problem finding his group. They were all there, including several additional companies. His promotion put him in charge of four groups that would be working in his assigned area. *Well,* he wondered, *who is this special captain he was getting, and how would he fit in with the others?*

As he walked up, a platoon leader saluted him. "We're all present, sir, and may I congratulate you on your promotion."

"Thank you, Lieutenant. I understand I have a new officer waiting. Have you seen him?"

"Yes, sir. You'll find him with one of the new units, sir. I saw him ten minutes ago talking with the company commander over there. Just go straight ahead, about twenty feet. You'll find them both, sir."

Tork talked with the men as he walked, stopped, and accepted the congratulations from all. He finished talking with a platoon sergeant and looked up to see the back of a tall helmeted man in black battle dress attack uniform, a back that looked familiar somehow. He was dressed correctly, with a sidearm hanging from his belt. Tork just couldn't put his finger on it, but he knew the back of this man from someplace, somewhere.

Tork reached the back of the man and tapped him on the shoulder. "Excuse me, Captain, may I have a word with you?"

The captain replied in a very familiar voice. "Certainly, Colonel," and turned to Tork smiling.

Tork, with a shocked look on his face seeing Cal in uniform, blurted out, "What the hell are you doing here, Cal?"

"I'm your new man, Tork. It's a long story, but a very important one. To put it simply, I have a better chance of surviving in uniform than I would have in civilian clothing. General Duncan had me commissioned prior to my last assignment. I've been in charge of the underground cells operating in Central California, and I'll be needed on this assignment to communicate with them, if we expect to do our job. Sorry I couldn't tell you earlier, Tork, but orders are orders. I guess this war taught me to grow up since our night in the desert."

Cal snapped to attention and in a loud and military manner announced, "All companies and personnel are accounted for, sir, and waiting for your command."

Just then the general mounted the stage at the end of the building and spoke to all of them. As he spoke, he emphasized the importance of their missions and what was at stake. Then he called out the groups in order of departure. Each group left twenty minutes apart.

As they exited the building, they could hear the choppers running, waiting for each of them to board for their meeting with destiny. After being dismissed and as each man walked out, they were given a paper with two words on it, "Freedom earned." They all knew the beginning of the end, be it liberty or slavery, one or the other, was at hand. Liberty was what they were fighting for. Yes, they all knew what it meant to be free and how easy it was to trust those liberal-minded fanatics who promised the world and then put them into eternal servitude.

From birth to death, if you don't want to think for yourself, become a government robot and live a controlled life, take the implant, and live that way. Many had. Most regretted it. Yes, Freedom earned. Freedom, it was worth the fight.

Tork ordered his group to board the waiting helicopters. Each waited patiently to transport them to their new battle positions. As they moved in line to their assigned positions, a runner approached Tork, saluted, and handed him an envelope. Tork tore it open and read a brief message. He turned to Cal and said, "Captain, come with me. Lieutenant, have the men board and the company commanders stand ready for my return. We'll be right back."

"What's up, Colonel?"

Tork looked at Cal. "I don't know. Let's find out."

Both men returned to the main building, and the runner that had brought Tork the message met them. "Follow me please."

He ushered both men into an office on the opposite side of the building. General Duncan was present. "Ah, there you are. It's my fault. I failed to tell you what that special assignment was, didn't I? Have you heard of the Jones chip?"

Not waiting for a reply, the general went on. "The man who invented the chip has made several changes to it that made it difficult for us to remove it once they've planted it in the host. We have found out that any attempt to remove it causes instant death. Seems Mr. Jones has added an additional microchip that controls a small needle that has a very potent poison on it. Once it's implanted and activated, any attempt to remove it from its location causes the chip to sense the change and it injects the needle into surrounding tissue. Within seconds, the poison kills the host. He thinks he made it impossible to remove the thing without killing the host person. Now, however, we found he has a way it can be safely removed. There is a code that is directed to the implant's chip through a remote-control device that locks the needle in its inert position, disarms the needle, and turns off the chip, allowing its removal."

The general looked at both men, reading their expressions. "Men, our Mr. Jones is in the San Francisco-Oakland Bay area. They plan to start implanting everyone there within the week. Before our attack starts, and they start implanting the new chips, we want this man picked up and brought back here. We don't want the West Coast implanting to start, but if it does, we want the designer and his knowledge of how to disarm the chips. Your mission is to apprehend him and fly him here. We need the information for our commanders in the east and southern commands where the new implants have been made. If we can stop the implants on the West Coast or get the information we need, we can save many lives and valuable time.

You both know that they can inject the needles in the implants if the host is in range of the convergence beam. As we move into areas we liberate from the United Nations, we must be ready to remove the implants before the United Nations has time to activate them. Once we have the hosts, we should be able to remove the implants immediately. You can see the importance of the information that Mr. Jones can give us. Your mission is to bring him to us."

Tork looked over to Cal and then to the general. "Sir, what happens if Mr. Jones does not want to cooperate?"

"We don't expect him to cooperate. For that reason, we expect you to do what is necessary to bring him to us. Along with the gentleman you are to bring, some of the implants and any prints, drawings, or schematics you can find. Be systematic when you search. Get everything you can carry. You see, Tork, I plan to implant one in Mr. Jones. We'll see just how brave he is and how dedicated he will be to the new world order when his own life is on the line. Major Bradford will give you the location and the itinerary we have on him and the hotel he is staying, including the UN security team that has been assigned to protect him and their known bad habits so we can deal with them."

Turning to Cal, he said, "You should be proud of your team in the Frisco area, Cal. Since your arrival here, we have been able to obtain the information that should help you bag your prey. By the way, your attack teams will be held for only forty-eight hours. You must be back to lead them, understand?"

Tork saluted. "Yes, sir. Consider it done, sir."

Tork and Cal left the general's office, and Tork immediately called the operations officer of the day to prepare a Blackhawks for their special mission. He would need a small team, no more than himself, Cal, two NCOs, and four enlisted men, eight in all. They would have to go in with small arms and some special equipment, and they would need a sedative for Mr. Jones. They didn't need any fussing once they had him, and they would have to move him to a pickup point for air shipment.

Tork knew the forty-eight hours was a short time frame for this and it would be a close call if they managed to connect with the target within twenty-four hours—two days tops. Tork could only shake his head.

Tork wrote out the names of the men he would need and handed them to Cal, He said, "Captain, call the group and detach these two NCOs and four men. Have them change into civilian clothing. You too. Also check out some plastic C-4, and we'll want .45-caliber Glocks for everyone and several lightweight fully automatic weapons. We will all meet within forty-five minutes at Operations. I know it's not much time, but then the good general didn't give us much, did he?"

Cal nodded. "Yes, sir. I'm on my way."

Tork moved fast. He returned to his quarters and changed into a business suit and went directly to Special Operations. "Hi, Meg. Did General Duncan leave us any vouchers?"

The sergeant smiled. "Yes, sir. He said you would be in shortly, only no vouchers. Everything has been prepared. Here's the cash you'll need for the operation. Good luck," she said as she handed it to him.

"Thanks, Meg." Tork looked over the pile of bills and whistled. "Well, he didn't spare the expenses, did he?"

Tork had just entered Operations a few seconds before Cal did. Both the NCOs and men were waiting for them when they arrived. All of them had changed into casual clothing for the area, and each had a small bag with them.

"What's in the bags, men?" Tork hadn't instructed them to pack a lunch or plan on an extended vacation.

"The captain recommended we bring a suit and tie, sir. Thought maybe we would be going to church or something."

Tork laughed. "Good point, Cal. We might just do that." Tork pulled out a strategic assault map of the area they were going into.

All the members of the team were from the area. They would have to have the cell leader of the area they were going to be working in advised their drop-off point for pickup. It would be necessary to plan on at least three return locations. Once they picked this guy up, every member of the USE forces and the local police would be looking for them. They would have to move quickly at low level, late at night. They would probably need to have a Blackhawks ready to move to the primary pickup location at the precise time and fly at treetop level through the small ranges, south, and onto the desert base. To Tork and Cal, it would be like coming home again to where it all started. Then they would cross over the Nevada border and back to their main base for the big push and a new start for freedom. They all had pretty well decided on the three areas and the best primary return location; the southern route with the move east at a low level to stay out of radar range and then south was their best bet.

The information was passed onto the coordinator with instructions to confirm through the cells, via General Duncan's office. They had just finished and sat down on the lounge chairs to take a breather when the chopper pilot came in. "Time to go, sir. We have confirmation from your cell leader that all is well and they will be picking you up within three minutes of our departure after we drop you off."

The eight men boarded the chopper. The red light from the instrument panels and the interior lighting gave it a frightening glow.

The pilots had increased the throttles. The engines whined as the blades bit into the air and the bird lifted effortlessly into the night sky. Within minutes, they made flight corrections and they were on course for the big snatch. If successful, they could save thousands of lives. If they were unsuccessful, then many brave men, women, and children would die. The forces controlling the new world order had to maintain absolute control. The only way to do it was with a device that would control itself.

Tork worked on his basic plan, from time to time conferring with each of the team members on their specialty fields. Cal had been working throughout the San Francisco-Oakland Bay area with his cell chiefs. It would be his job as soon as they landed to set up the escape route, transfer points, and code words to be used.

They would need a van or enclosed vehicle to transport the subject. He would be sedated, so the vehicle would need to be something that would not draw attention. Maybe an ambulance for the first leg, transfer to a van, and then maybe to a school bus or a delivery truck carrying a large box with special markings, perhaps even using a portable oxygen mask and tank. They would need to mark the box as a highly toxic product. Tork's mind was moving in concise logical patterns, trying to make the kidnapping and transporting of the subject with little danger to them all. If all went well, they could do it. Yes, he knew they could do it.

Tork wrote down his initial plan, routes they could use to get to the primary pickup point, the number of vehicle changes to be made, and the type of vehicle they would need at each point. It would be the cell leader's responsibility to have the vehicle ready to roll when they arrived with the subject. The vehicle used would have to fit in with the area they would be working in. They couldn't take any chances of using something out of place. It must look like an everyday occurrence.

Cal tapped Tork on the shoulder. "We're almost there, Tork. Pilot said to get ready. When we deplane, hit the ground, he's going straight up to treetop level and he's out of there. Our contact should be waiting. We'll get a three-second low-volume beep on the ticker."

Tork looked up, "A three-second what on a what?"

"Oh, sorry, sir. A little device we designed in the field to warn or to identify ourselves to each other. It's a low-frequency transmitter that puts out a signal that gives the receiver a low-sounding beep on audio or a vibration on silent, a green LED lights up at the same time. If the red LED is on, it's a warning they've been compromised and to abort the mission. I have one with me."

The chopper touched down and all men deplaned and ran toward the woods to stop and wait.

Cal had taken out his ticker to check it and was holding it in his hand when the green LED lit up briefly. "They're here. Let's go," he said. Cal turned to the northwest heading, and in the darkness of the night, they ran close to the ground, making as low a silhouette as possible. Within a few minutes, they entered the trees.

"Sego lilies," said a voice in the darkness.

Tork turned to the voice. "Are mountain dwellers," he responded.

"Over here," came the reply.

The group moved to the sound of the voice. There in the night stood two men, both in black with black faces wearing night glasses. They could see the group as if it were daylight.

"Good to see you again, Cal. Are you home to stay?"

"Good to see you, Dwight. No, we have a mission to do and not much time to do it. We'll need your help to succeed."

The man nodded. "What can we do, Cal?"

Cal said, "Dwight, this is Lieutenant Colonel Albertson. He's in charge and will fill you in."

"The first thing we need to do," said Tork, "is to get us out of here. If anyone spotted the chopper, they'll have reported it by now."

"Not likely, sir. This area hates the UN forces. Doubt if they'll tell them anything. That's why we coordinated this landing location for you."

The group moved through the area to a dirt road. There they drove northwest into a small town southeast of Sacramento. They had landed about ten miles northeast of the town.

The driver pulled into a garage on the outskirts. The door to the garage was open, and as they entered, the doors shut silently. As the driver opened his door and the lights in the garage came on, a tall man stepped out of an office.

Charles Drake smiled and said, "Come in. We'll lay out your route close to what you ordered, sir. Only had to make a few changes to keep us away from the UN checkpoints. Within an hour, we'll have you on the freeway to San Francisco. Once there, the next cell group will pick you up."

The group went over the itinerary together. Tork was pleased with the routes. The cell knew what they were doing. Cal could be proud of them.

"Good. Very good. Thank you all. Now let's get going. We don't have much time and lots to do."

The group started back to the vehicle when Drake stopped them. "Not that one, sir. Out back. We have another vehicle for you."

Behind the garage was a new Suburban SUV. "Isn't that a little bit of an attention-grabber?" Tork asked.

"No, sir," Drake replied. "It was rented in the name of a UN Agriculture minister. That's here to assess the California farms. We have all the papers and permits allowing him and his group to inspect everything in Northern California between the Nevada border and the Pacific Ocean. You should have no problem if they stop you. Just let them know you have been collecting data for the minister and you are on your way back to San Francisco with it for his meeting. With the credentials we have for you, there should be no problem with the checkpoints. If traffic is busy, chances are they'll wave you right through anyway."

Tork nodded. Cal slapped him on the back and in a low voice said, "Well done."

Tork pointed toward the van. "Let's go."

The team entered the SUV, and within minutes, they were on their way. The trip to San Francisco was uneventful. Everything went well. The checkpoints waved all cars through without hesitation. They arrived in Fresco and went straight to the safe house where they showered and grabbed a few hours' sleep.

Tork woke up sleepy eyed and with a strong desire to go back to sleep and stay there forever. He tried to focus on Cal standing by the door to the living room. "Our info come in yet, Cal?" Sleepily he rose and sat on the edge of the bed getting his thoughts together.

"Yeah, we're all set. Mr. J. will be at his hotel at 7:00 p.m. for a lecture on implants. Immediately after, he will attend a dinner with a few media potentates and then to bed. He has a meeting tomorrow morning at 11:00 a.m. at the Old Presidio. The federal government took it away from the Parks Service and is using it for a headquarters now, so we should have until then to find and transport him before they miss him. One hitch, he does have a body guard with him, and we don't know what, if any, call in reports he has to make or what times are required. Plus, they have a guard outside his suite to make sure no one bothers him. Our problem now is, how do we get past the guard outside and outfox the body guard inside?"

Tork thought for a minute, running his fingers through his hair, and then asked, "Does he have any snacks before retiring at night, any late drinks or any prostitutes brought in during the evening?"

Cal reached for the phone and dialed a number. He let it ring four times and hung up. It was ten minutes before the phone rang.

"Chin's Chop Shop. May I help you?"

Cal replied, "Do you chop at Chin's Shop?"

The answer came, "Chin's chops are the best chops."

"Could I order your number 12 and number 19, please?"

"Yes, sir. And where may I deliver it to you?"

Cal gave him an address and instructed him to bring it over within the hour. Twenty minutes later, a knock was heard at the door. "Yes," Cal called out. "Who is it?"

"Chin's Chop Shop with your order, sir."

Cal opened the door and let Gordon Chin in. "I need to know if Mr. J has any special guest brought up to his rooms in the evening or any special meals or snacks?"

Gordy Chin nodded, turned, and started to leave. Cal stopped him and said, "When you find out, we need this yesterday. Thanks, Gordy." Chin smiled and left.

Tork now showered and refreshed was waiting for Cal's report.

Cal after seeing Gordy safely out turned to Tork and said, "Sir, we should have an answer in ten to twenty minutes. Gordy will have everything we need for us by then."

"Good. Thanks, Cal. As soon as you find out or when he returns, we want to plan on having one or two men ready to go. Have sergeants Carter and Brock get the waiter uniforms and the largest delivery cart they have. Have two others ready to assist in the hotel and have the other two ready with the ambulance."

*****

"We'll need something we can put him under after we've sedated him. When we remove him from the room, we want to pass by the guard without arousing his suspicion. If we use the prostitute angle, we want one of our girls dressed properly and seductive. She will have to get past the guard outside and the bodyguard inside. In fact, let's get a real hooker for him. That will keep him busy for a while. Once we have him out of there, they'll have a hard time finding us. Remember, when the bodyguard wakes up and finds Mr. J is gone, we have to be out of the city and hopefully at our final departure point. Are there any questions or suggestions?"

Cal shook his head. Sergeants Carter and Brock and the others all nodded in agreement.

"Let's get with it then!"

When Gordy's reply came, all questions were answered, putting everything into motion. Sergeants Brock and Carter went to attend to their assignments. Two men left to pick up the ambulance, and two others started preparing for the next step in the hotel. They would arrange for the prostitute, tell her what she needed to do, and how much they would pay her.

Tork went over the plan again. *Yes*, he thought, *getting in with the champagne and plenty of food after the girl has warmed his heart would be the way to get him. As he's getting to the hot and passionate parts, we could hit him with the sedative, put him under the cart, and get him out. It should work, but what am I missing?*

Then it struck him. They would need two carts and plenty of food for both of the guards and champagne for the bodyguard inside and a little beer and food for the guard outside and another prostitute for the bodyguard to keep him busy for the rest of the night. They would have to be well paid after they leave at, say, 5:00 a.m. The money would be left at the desk with their names on it from Mr. J. The desk clerk would understand.

Tork could see the only thing not covered would be the trip home and that should be relatively easy. *Yes*, he thought, *should be a piece of cake.*

"Cal, get Brock. Let him know we'll need two carts and three prostitutes for the caper. Tell him we'll need plenty of champagne and beer to go with the food. This has to be just right."

"Yes, sir. Consider it done."

*****

The girls had waited at the bar as instructed, and the one for Mr. Jones made her move when he entered. She was a stunning woman, one of the best Frisco had to offer and a true patriot. After a few drinks, he asked her up to his room for some champagne. She readily accepted. As Jones was entertaining her, the other girl was teasing the guards, getting them ready for the right time. Everything was going as planned. The cart was in the bedroom with Jones. Tork was sandwiched in the small compartment underneath, waiting for the signal from the women. He could see only the light from the lamps shining under the curtain around the service cart, but heard everything. In his hand, he held his Glock pistol equipped with a silencer, just in case.

The party was warming up. Mr. Jones was starting to talk. The alcohol was taking hold, and he was becoming uninhibited. Tork heard the ooh from Jones and the sigh from his lips. He could only imagine what she was doing. Whatever it was, she had to act soon or he would never get out from under the table in time to get Jones.

Tork condemned everyone as his legs started to cramp; he almost didn't hear the women as she asked Mr. J to help her remove her blouse—the cue Tork had been waiting for. She had Jones ready for him.

He pulled back the tablecloth slowly, facing the opposite wall from the bed. He slipped quietly onto the floor. Silently he peered around the edge of the cart to the bed.

Both were half clothed, and Jones was working hard to remove rest of it. He was completely occupied. Tork thought, *What a rotten thing to do to him, but then when you think of what he did to the people and what could happen to them.* Tork disregarded the thought and pulled the protector cap off the syringe, knelt, and crawled to the bed. He drove the needle into Mr. Jones's buttock.

Mr. Jones stiffened from the pain and looked back over his shoulder, and the last thing he saw was Tork smiling at him saying, "Pleasant dreams." Tork quickly pulled him up off the woman and laid him on the floor. He rolled the cart around and lifted him up. The woman raised the curtain on the opposite side and reached through to grab Jones. Within a few minutes, he was neatly in place and taped up, secure for his trip downstairs.

Suddenly there was a loud rapping on the door. "You okay in there, sir?"

The woman quickly pulled back the rumpled cover on the bed and laid down. She whispered, "Lay on top of me and pull the covers up." She reached over and turned off the lights. Tork had just pulled the covers up and the woman started to moan. Tork caught on and started moving his rear end up and down.

The door opened and the bodyguard looked in, saw what was going on, and quickly closed the door.

The girl looked up at him as he closed the door. "Well, honey, what's going on in there? They got the hots or sumthin'."

"Yeah, he's getting his and I got nothin'."

"Well, honey, I wouldn't say you got nothing. I'm game if you are. Any place around here we can be alone?"

The guard looked at her, looked to the bedroom door, and looked back at her. "Sure, he's going to be busy all night like always. Let's go to my room. It's through here. He opened the connecting door and they slipped in. The hooker was doing her job as expected.

The guard outside had fallen for his small bit earlier and had fallen asleep. He was curled up with peroxide blonde. The sex and the alcohol had been too much for him, not to mention the Mickey Finn in his last nightcap. The girl had waited a half hour before dressing and leaving. They had told her to pick up her money at the desk and to disappear, or she might be in danger of being arrested by the feds. When she left, she was on her way out of town. With what they had paid her, she could well afford to disappear. She was gone.

When Tork opened the door from the bedroom, he could hear the others in the adjoining suite making love. It wouldn't be long before he too would take a last drink for the night and sleep till noon the next day. Tork had just opened the door to push the cart out. Dressed as a waiter, he could move freely. Just as he started to move, the adjourning room door opened and the bodyguard standing their naked asked him what the hell he was doing.

"Sorry, sir, just removing the cart. Mr. Jones called down for more champagne and asked me to remove the cart. He said it was in his way."

The guard looked him over. "Don't move, buddy. Understand?"

"Yes, sir," replied Tork.

The guard started to open the bedroom door.

"I wouldn't do that, sir. He was kind of engaged, if you know what I mean."

The guard hesitated. "Yeah, you're right. He wouldn't like any interference right now." He turned to go back into the bedroom and then turned to Tork. "You got a drink left on that cart, bud?"

The girl answered for Tork. "I got one, baby, just for you."

Tork snickered to himself. He didn't have to worry about a thing. In an hour, the girl would be gone, and so would they.

The two men dressed as housekeeping attendants pushed two laundry carts to the service elevator, entered, and pushed the garage button.

The elevator moved silently down. At 0300 hours, it was doubtful anyone would be using the service elevator. Both men were ready when the elevator doors opened. Cal and Tork wheeled the carts to the laundry van and lifted both carts up and into the back. The two sergeants shut the van doors and walked back to the elevator, closed the doors, and pushed the third-floor button. As the elevator raised, they pulled off their coveralls and straightened their ties.

Quickly Brock climbed the handrail and moved the access panel in the ceiling, and Carter handed him the coveralls. He slipped them through the panel opening and shut it.

He just dropped down when the service elevator stopped and the door opened. Both men left the service elevator and walked to the guest's elevators. "Where to, Jeeves?" asked Carter when they entered the elevator.

"Why, to the lobby, old man."

The two left the elevator and walked up to the desk. Brock smiled at the sleepy attendant. "We have an early meeting at the navy yards this morning. Could you call us a cab please?"

The attendant pointed to the hotel entrance. "Cab stands are right out there, sir. Should be a cabby waiting."

"Thank you, sir."

Brock and Carter walked out. One turned left, and the other right. Carter had gone about a hundred yards when a van pulled up alongside of him. "Like a lift, mister?"

"Thanks. Don't mind if I do."

Tork asked Carter where Brock had gone. "He went down the street. Said he would cross over and walk south on the third side street."

Tork turned to the right and drove to the next side street. They made a left turn to the next right. He turned and went back to the main street, turned left, and drove past the hotel entrance.

Tork counted the streets from there. It was the third side street to the right. *Yeah, right here.* He turned right. One tall figure was walking south about four or five blocks ahead. Within minutes, they were all in the van.

Cal asked Tork to go over to Johnny Trumble's garage.

"Johnny Trumble's garage, what's over there, Cal?"

"I set up a vehicle swap over there this morning. When we pull in, drive up to the left-hand door. You remember, it's the paint shop door."

Tork turned into the parking lot and toward the door. Cal pulled out a garage door opener and pushed the button. Just as they drove through, Cal pushed the button to close the door.

When the door had closed, the lights came on. Johnny was standing by his office waving at Tork. "Come on in, Colonel, and say hello."

Tork looked over at Cal. Cal anticipated his words. "Relax, Tork. He's one of our operators, one of our best operators."

Tork felt relief and wiped the sweat off his hands. "Let me in on your little secrets next time, Captain. Please."

Johnny pointed to the back of the garage at a new ambulance and said, "There she is, ready and fully equipped for ya."

Seeing the ambulance, Tork nodded his head and said, "Well done, Johnny."

The men moved Jones into the ambulance and set him up with the usual oxygen, and Tork gave him another shot to keep him down. The other men were there waiting for them when they arrived. They had the ambulance ready with all documents for the trip.

Both vehicles, the ambulance and the SUV, moved out at 0400 hours. The roads would start getting busy as soon as the defense workers went to work. They had to be on their way or they could get trapped in early morning traffic.

It took them three hours to move west toward their departure point. It was too late for them to bring in the bird, so they would have to stay over one more night. The forty-eight hours was almost up, and the enemy would be looking high and low for them.

Tork decided to play a long shot. They reached their departure point and he called home for a special bird.

As arranged, they had planned to hide the ambulance and SUV in the barn when they left. It was planned they would abandon this safe house. If the authorities found it, demolition explosives were wired in and motion sensors were set if the house or barn were broken into. The cell in the area would observe it. If all went well and its location was not compromised, the cell could use it again. The SUV and the ambulance might come in handy again someday.

Tork had figured if they had gotten this far with the ambulance, maybe they could go one step further.

"Brock, you, Carter, and the others disconnect the charges from the ambulance, get it, and meet us at the local airport. Go to the Operations lounge and tell them you're waiting for a UN air vac unit that's picking up a VIP for medical evacuation to Sacramento. Hopefully our bird will be coming in on time."

Brock and Carter entered the lounge at the airport, and Brock walked up to the desk.

"You get word on a UN air vac coming in soon, bud?"

"Yep, we just got word not more than five minutes ago that they were on their way in."

Suddenly the radio behind him crackled, and a limey voice was calling, "UN Air Vac seven eight four three niner approaching from the southwest. Request landing instructions. Over."

The desk clerk grabbed the mic. "UN Air Vac seven eight four three niner, you are cleared to land runway SW2. Wind at four knots. Weather clear. Over."

Before he received an answer, they could hear the wheels screeching on the runway. The bird was down and taxing to the operations building. It turned and the side doors opened when they'd barely stopped. When the ambulance had backed up to the plane, two attendants dressed in MedTech white and wearing the insignia of the USE forces were busy moving the gurney out of the ambulance and into the aircraft. Four men dressed in UN fatigue battle dress and a medical team escorted them onto the aircraft. Within minutes, they had finished, the plane's engines started, and Brock turned to the desk operator.

"The ambulance will be picked up in an hour. The doctor and the attendant that brought the injured minister will be attending to him. If no one shows up by noon, call this number and let them know they need to pick up the ambulance. Okay?"

"Sure, buddy. Hope this minister gets better."

Brock and Carter ran out to the waiting plane, boarded her, and the pilot moved his throttles to increase power and the bird picked up speed. He throttled back at the end of the runway and turned into the wind.

Tork went forward and patted the aircraft commander on the shoulder. "Good to see you again, Flight Leader. Thanks for the lift."

"You're welcome, Yank," he replied. Within minutes, they were airborne and on their way. Climbing to an acceptable altitude, he turned toward the southeast.

Tork checked on their passenger. All was well; he was still sedated. Tork felt the tension melt away. For first time in the past forty-eight hours, he was comfortable, and they were on their way back well within the time the general had given them. Tork would be back with his men in time for the offensive and the fight to regain the country. Once they had the answer to remove the new chips, they could move ahead.

Tork had made sure all was well with his special passenger and his men. He then went up to the cockpit to thank the pilots and the crew for their pickup.

"Well, Flight Leader, it's been a while since we met last. How goes your war?"

"Well, mate, it's top-notch. Bit of a wacko. You know, since coming on board with you, chaps, more and more of our boys have been dropping in. Seems things are getting sticky back home. This chip thing has them going too. The people want to see Britain free again, just as much as you want to see this country free from the

United Nations and the new world order dead and buried. It reminds us of the Eagle Squadron during World War II. You, chaps, came over and flew for us. Now we can return the favor."

Tork looked at the British officer flying them home. It took real courage for all of them to desert their forces and fight for the United States—no, to fight for a free world. Tork had real admiration for them all.

Tork smiled at the pilot and said, "Give us the time, the weapons, the resolve, and we shall conquer all of our foes. Let no man think we are capable of defeat, nor will we meekly standby and surrender our freedom without a fight."

"Bravo, bravo, old boy. I jolly well couldn't have said it better myself. We're with you chaps, all the way. Long live a free America and a free Britain. But first things first, let's give them all what for. Righto."

Tork smiled again. He knew the new world order was in real trouble now and winning had to be in the future and soon.

*****

General Duncan reached over and pushed the dial button for his aide. "Yes, sir," he replied.

"Has Lieutenant Colonel Albertson returned yet?"

"No, sir, but I do have a one-hour ETA on his return, sir."

"As soon as he returns, I want him here. No breathers. Straight to me. Understand?"

"Yes, sir. I'll alert Special Operations and have him report directly to you, sir."

The general ended the call and dialed the Security and Special Operations commander. He instructed them to meet in his office in one hour with the details for Operation Close Door. The general pulled out the file he had been studying earlier and went over it detail by detail. It was hard to believe the South American countries of Argentina, Brazil, and Chile had joined with the United Nations to invade the United States. It was rumored the United States of Europe had pressured them into it and they had no other choice.

With the Mexican territories firmly in the UN commitment, the other big three had been faced with the loss of the United States as a trading partner. With the war on, it was almost impossible for the United States to deliver. Mexico had closed its borders with them, and the European market had closed their ports and cut off relations with them too. It was obvious. They had no other choice. Cuba, after being freed from Castro, was aligned with the United States and was no problem to the federal forces.

With the big three southern countries now aligned with the new world order, it was necessary for an offensive thrust into the region to stop their troops from moving north under a UN flag. Intelligence had reported USE troopships moving toward South America. More troops for the UN offensive in the United States were being sent south to support the Latin countries. They would be training the Latin Americans in the latest equipment and methods of war.

The rebel high command had decided on Operation Close Door to slow the troop movement or to stop it if necessary. They felt the South American troops would need training and full equipment issue prior to their commitment to the US campaign and subsequent embarkation. This time period would give the US Special Forces time to infiltrate and destroy docking and staging areas. It might also require possible high-altitude bombing of concentrated troop staging areas.

General Duncan pondered the question in his mind. *A lot of troops would be killed for the new world order. What a waste of youth for the power of a few. Yes, the war has become deadlier and now it is worldwide.*

*****

The load master motioned Colonel Albertson to the cockpit. Tork stood, stretched, and walked to the sergeant.

"What is it, Sergeant?"

"Sir, we just received a coded message from General Duncan. You are to go directly to his office upon arrival. No detours, sir. Seems they have something brewing and your team is involved."

Tork thought about the sergeant's comment and said, "How would you know that, Sergeant?"

"Well, sir, before you left, your team was pulled from their assigned quarters and moved to a special compound. They have had special teams like yours coming in for the past twenty-four hours. Looks like something big is going on. We had just moved in special supplies when they sent us on this mission to pick you up. I'm guessing, sir, but it looks like you might be going right back out again."

"You might be right, Sergeant, and then it may be nothing more than site assignments."

Tork left it at that. If something was going on, fueling it was not necessary any more than it had been before. But Tork felt the sergeant was right. Something was going on.

The plane had started its approach for landing. He would know very soon. They were almost on home plate.

*****

Tork entered the outer office of General Duncan. He smiled at the general's secretary and asked, "Where's the ole man?"

She smiled back and announced, "He's inside and waiting for you. It's a hot one, Colonel. I'll have everything ready for you when you come out, so see me first after the general's meeting."

Tork knocked on the door and entered. Stepping up to the general, he saluted and then reported his mission was complete and Mister Jones was at interrogation.

General Duncan waved Tork to a chair and walked to the large wall map, picked up a laser pointer, and spoke, "Colonel, we have reports. The United Nations has three sea transport ships docking in South America with more on the way. We are tracking them now and should have their destinations soon. We believe they have convinced or pressured these three countries"—Tork followed the red dot on the map as it moved from country to country—"into joining them for the final stages of the US invasion. We also think the ships have tanks, APCs, and heavy artillery on board for the buildup in the south."

Tork sat quietly as the general spoke. He envisioned what his goals were likely to be and studied the map, three of the largest countries in South America, vast in size. It seemed like an impossible task that the general was suggesting until he made it clear.

"Tork, we've assembled twenty-four. Yes, Tork, two dozen assault teams to engage the enemy on their own turf. We had to make changes after your departure. We knew you were planning to take your teams into the main engagements. Unfortunately, we will need your team's special talents in these countries before we can send you into the fight up here. It's imperative we create as much havoc as we can."

Tork's mind was working hard to keep up with the general and still formulate and understand. Raising his hand, he said, "Sir, I understand the mission. I don't understand why."

The general was quick to reply. "Colonel, it's become essential to stop or slow down the entry of these nations into United States. To help us fight the United Nations, we have called on the president and his incarcerated cabinet to make an announcement to the country asking all citizens to fight the UN forces. He, however, has refused. He believes the UN forces will find and free him and it will be business as usual. We have won over some of the senators and members of the House, and they have joined forces with us and have taken their places on the committee. It's too bad they are few in number. When we've won, many noble but misled Americans will have to face the people. God help them all.

"The rest have sided with the president and are contemptuous of us, believing our days are numbered and the UN forces will liberate them soon. If we hope to shorten this war and drive the UN forces out of the United States, we will need to start our offensive as planned. But to be successful, we will need to stop the United Nations from bringing Brazil, Argentina, and Chile into this war. To do this, we will need to hit their staging areas, docks, supply and munitions dumps, and their heavy equipment motor pools. Their tanks, artillery depots, and heavy weapons must be destroyed before they can be used against us. We are very sure the United Nations plans to train the South American troops prior to moving them north. So it's very important, Tork, that your eight teams are ready to hit each of your areas, hard, fast, and thoroughly. You will command eight teams and the other sixteen are ready to go. It is imperative that we put the fear of God into them all."

Tork put up his hand, stopping the general. "I have a question, sir."

"Yes, Colonel?"

"I can see pretty much what you have in mind, sir. My first question is, how do we move our equipment through Mexico and all points south? Every country down there will be on alert for something. My guess is they would just love to shoot us down. Most of those countries would like nothing better than to see the great United States destroyed."

General Duncan smiled. "Simple, Colonel. We put them on board an aircraft carrier and sail down. Colonel, I have all of your team commanders and top NCOs in the conference room. They have all been briefed and all teams have been completely reoutfitted. All helios have been serviced and new armor and guns installed. We've also added additional flack and small arms Kevlar padding to each bird, like the vests against ground fire and light shrapnel you wear, only more effective. We have everything you will need for the job. The navy will get you there and will resupply you through airdrops or submarine supply. Now, Colonel, let's go into the conference room and lay out the targets and your itinerary. I want this show on the road within forty-eight hours."

Tork couldn't help thinking about how freedom is earned. It's not a privilege, a right of birth, or a gift from God. If you want it, you must earn it, and to keep it, you must fight for it. To preserve it, you must stay within the bounds of its constitution. His thoughts were vivid and precise. *Let no man take it from you by changing it to suit their own values or reach their goals at the expense of the people.*

Tork looked to the general and said, "General, God-fearing men founded this country. When this war is over, the return to sanity will begin and a new and stronger nation will be born. Sir, we will be ready to move out as planned."

The door opened and General Duncan's staff officer called the room to attention. "Be seated, gentlemen. Sergeant Bowers, the DVD presentation please."

The large projection screen was lowered, and at the general's command, the DVD projector heads came to life and the group orientation briefing was underway. Colonel Albertson heard everything. He jotted down notes on his kneepad along with questions for the general after they ran the tape and concluded the oral briefing. Tork could see flaws that could get them into trouble, maybe even failure.

The tape ended and Lieutenant Colonel Brighten took the rostrum, pulled down a map from the overhead, and with a pointer in hand started laying out the initial strike points in three South American countries.

"Gentlemen, the initial strike must be in complete unison at precisely the same time. Surprise must coincide with confusion. We believe the enemy will immediately announce the hits to one another. It's imperative we create the confusion to give our departing troops time to move out and reach their destinations without, we hope, being found out. To do this, we will need the communication nets buzzing with strikes from all three countries at the same time. This should confuse the UN command and deter them from committing strike forces to anyone in the attacked area until they have confirmed which of the reported attacked areas are for real. It should give us some needed time to withdraw.

"Colonel Albertson's group will hit four troop staging areas in Brazil. Colonel Madison's group will hit the three in Argentina, and Colonel Hernandez will hit four in Chile. The withdrawal routes are as indicated in the tape you have just seen, plus the routing maps will be issued just prior to deployment. Remember, all units must move out after the raid as planned. It's important the pursuing enemy notes the withdrawal direction. You must make your course changes precisely if we hope to recover all the strike teams. Any questions, men?"

Tork stood up. "Yes, Colonel. I have an updated equipment list here and have only a token number of silencers for small arms. No crossbows or limpets. I want all of my men fully equipped with silencers on small arms and sniper rifles. Also, I want every squad to be carrying a crossbow with at least twelve shafts each with explosive tips and twelve conventional armor-piercing. If we are going to take out such a heavily occupied area, we will need to eliminate the on-duty guards and dispose of the commanders before they can call a full-scale alert. General Duncan, we all must resort to a lot of silent quick kills to accomplish this mission. It means a lot of men, and maybe women, will be silently killed to accomplish the destruction of these staging areas. We cannot afford to advertise the attack unless we are spotted. Then and only then can we afford to make our presence known. Each unit must have these items before departure."

"Yes, Colonel. I see your point, and I agree. Your strike units will be so equipped. All commanders will give Major Johnston your additional equipment list at the conclusion of this meeting. Major Johnston, you will provide all equipment requisitioned. If there are shortages, pull them from forward staging areas. These teams come first. Gentlemen, I'm sorry, but at the conclusion of your raids and at the time of your return, we will have additional orders for all of you. So don't plan on any vacations or rest time when you get back. Now let's all get our teams together, go over your areas of responsibility, and please leave nothing to chance.

"The success of these missions could make the difference between a new America and a free America. Let's make it free. Remember, freedom cannot be taken from you unless you let it happen. Let's go take it back."

Upon leaving, Tork called his team commanders and platoon leaders together. The briefing room was quiet as he spoke, "I've laid out our targets on these four tables, designated Gored, Sidewinder, Scorpion, and Firewood. I have assigned four companies to each target with two companies on standby at designated areas. Should a team be caught in a bind and the cavalry has to come to the rescue, let's make sure our passwords and coded signals are recorded and beacons are activated at the moment the message for help is transmitted. The rescue teams must be able to find you as quickly as possible.

"Remember, silence is our friend. You must take out the sentries as quickly and silently as possible. Make sure that each guard post has one of our replacement personnel in place after the guard is taken out. Okay, right, now, demolition teams, listen closely. I want all transports, be it light or heavy transportation, including tanks, hit at precisely ten minutes prior to our departure time. I want them to go up at the last minute. When they go, the whole country will know it.

"After the guards and sentries are out, I want the armories opened and the weapons mined to go off first, the ammo dumps second, the warehouses third, and the food supplies fourth. It's not going to be easy, but we must try to demoralize these governments, intimidate them so they will think twice about shipping north. If we can stop them in their own countries, we can increase our chances of success in our own country."

Captain Alred raised his hand and said, "Sir!"

"Yes, Captain."

"You haven't given us the go-ahead to enter the barracks and dispatch the troops there."

"Captain, we have set up one unit that will take care of the barracks. We will hit only a few designated areas. If we disarm them and destroy their weapons, they might just figure it's better to stay home and thank God they're still alive. However, should you meet resistance and they manage to get arms, well, then you're soldiers, so fight as soldiers, fight to win. We leave in forty-eight hours. Be ready."

Tork retired to his quarters and went through each attack plan he was assigned. He then reviewed each of his commanders and units, looking for any weak link that might be there. He knew if they were to win in the north, they would have to neutralize the south. It was a shame that so many young men would have to die for the new world order.

Tork was tired and knew what to expect. He knew the where, why, and when of this war but had problems of who really started it way back when. It was time now for rest, for tomorrow was going to be a busy day.

CHAPTER 27

Rivers of Red

UN Allied Supreme Headquarters
Canada

General Fitzimmons stood before the map of the United States of America. He called for an orderly to place a blue flag on another large American city. He turned to his colleagues sitting around a conference table, all of them military leaders representing all the UN forces occupying American cities and towns. Each of them was eager to report their area's accomplishments and to announce their fervor to move forward. Although they were having continued battles with the American rebels, they all felt it would be to the United Nations' advantage to begin their offensive now.

The last flag on the map signified their advancements. Most of them were unaware of the turmoil in Mexico and the bitter fighting in other areas of the country they were trying to defeat. The high command had not informed them of the defeats or advances made by the Americans or the terror they were spreading in South America. Only the victories or the disinformation was released to the commander. They all thought all was well with the invasion and victory was at hand. The high command knew the truth, and they were not willing to release it until the invasion forces had secured more states and had control over a larger population. They were moving slowly but they were advancing. They thought by bringing Argentina, Brazil, and Chile into the fight, it could swing the American people to their side,

FREEDOM EARNED

thus using the combined armies of these nations and Mexico, and by moving into the states from the south, they would break the backs of the rebel forces. Victory would be theirs.

While this was going on in the west and southern areas of the United States, the northern forces of the United States of Europe would continue their move in a southeast direction, moving troops into areas that had little or no rebel activity. They felt they could wrap this up in less than six months. Upon defeat of the rebels, they could implement the capitulate or face destruction plan for world-wide domination. They would then control two thirds of the world's population and would have defeated the world's greatest super power. Having seen their strength, the rest of the world would capitulate to the new world order and the world would be united under one ruler, the United Nations.

"Now, gentlemen," General Fitzimmons continued, "I would like a complete report from each army commander. Include please your operational readiness and equipment lists. Also, add your present engagements and loses to date. Make sure upon completion that all new equipment requirements are in so immediate shipment from Europe can be made. Remember, we must have everything ready within fifty days. It is imperative we move as planned. General Zukov, let's start with your training of the South American forces."

General Zukov, a general of the old Soviet persuasion, was a tough and thorough commander. He had moved his training cadre, composed of the best Russian and European training cadre, to all three South American countries.

He spoke, "We have started our training and expect to meet our completion dates as planned. At this time, we are very pleased with the enthusiasm of the units undergoing training. It appears they all have a very strong dislike for the Americans. They see great rewards for themselves and all are eager to move north. The Mexicans expect to have California, New Mexico, Arizona, Nevada, Utah, and Texas returned to them. We have a very educated and dedicated group of fliers there that have taken to our aircraft as if they were born in them. I see no reason why we can't meet our deadline and move north as planned. The Americans have no way to move a sufficient number of troops south to engage us. Though, if they do, we will be ready."

General Fitzimmons looked pleased. The report he just heard was reassuring. Gen. Rene Picard, a proud pompous French commander, was next. "General, it is with great jubilation that I announce to you we also are ready now. My troops hold key American cities, and we have the populations in these areas compromised, that is, they all have had the Jones implants.

"They are all very cooperative. As we have moved into and taken over our areas, we immediately eliminated the criminal elements and implanted the population with the Jones chips. They are very willing to assist us. Knowing what happens to them if they tamper with the chips has put them completely under our control. We feel the people are not willing to fight. Only a few have gone over to the rebels. I can see we'll have no problem meeting our deadlines and feel we should have this wrapped up long before your target date, sir."

As each army commander made their reports, General Fitzimmons felt very comfortable. It was obvious the intelligence reports were accurate and the present plans would lead them to victory. It would be much easier, however, if they could find the US president and his incarcerated cabinet, not to mention the House members and senators being held by the rebels. If they had them, the quest would be over. The people would throw the rebels out.

The general held up his hand, palm out, and said, "Well done, well done. Let's all get back to our areas and prepare for the end. Remember, in sixty days, we will start the biggest invasion of a nation since D-Day and then we can celebrate the return of a long-lost piece of our past."

*****

The Argentine general was not impressed with the British commander training his troops. Since the humiliating defeat in the Falklands War, the Argentine army felt it should have been a fully Argentine initiative. Cadre training could have been done in Europe. But the United Nations had insisted on shipping in the equipment and then training the army there. To add insult to injury, they had insisted on the British army training them, like rubbing salt into their wounds.

Gen. Xavier Von Stronhiem, commander, Third Corps, Argentine army, was a descendent of the Third Reich. His father held a high military and political office in Germany during the World War II and had escaped with his family in a German submarine to Argentina. With the great wealth he had brought with him enabled him to get Xavier into the best military schools in Argentina and other South American institutions. His father had helped him up the ladder. At his passing, the ninety-six-year-old wanted to see the end of the United States and Britain. His and other Nazi influence and money had paved the way for them all these many years, and he now felt the time had come to see the end of the United States. He knew in time that Britain would become nothing more than a state within the European Union. The failed Falklands venture was the end for him, and he passed quietly after learning of the Argentine defeat. He and his son felt it was due to the lack of fully trained soldiers and sailors. But thanks to the new world order, this would change.

With the integration of Europe, the one thorn that needed to be removed was the United States. With it being brought into the fold, the rest of the world would be easy. Britain had been the only worry, but with their greed satisfied, it left only the one thorn to be plucked and that was imminent. It would be then a new Reich. The Fourth Reich should have no problem taking command.

The general sat looking out his office window when a knock on his door disturbed his thoughts. "Enter!"

"General, Colonel Vaughan of the British training group is here, sir. Said it was urgent."

Reluctantly the general responded. To deal with the British commander was distasteful, but part of the scheme, a part he had to play. The party required it and who knows, he might even get a US state of his own to rule.

"Send him in, Captain."

The colonel entered, came to attention, and saluted. "Sir, we need to talk."

"Well, go ahead, Colonel. What's on your mind that's so urgent you couldn't send me memo on this?" His voice was sharp and critical, biting hard, and forceful.

"Your troops are not responding well to the training. They fail to show up for night training and we have found them more interested in other pursuits than their programs. General, if you expect to move your units north on schedule, we will need all of their attention and participation. The success of the invasion into the southwest United States must be coordinated, be precise, and with fully trained troops. We cannot allow for any mistakes.

"Right now, you have only infantry with outdated weapons—no match for a well-trained and equipped army. Your air forces and navy are using antiques compared with the United States. Remember, the American rebels are well prepared and equipped. The majority of the states and the people are supporting them.

"The Allied command in Brussels has informed your government that they will cut off all monetary considerations, and Argentina will be isolated if your command does not cooperate. Also, General, the other two units have similar problems. It would be a shame if your country's lack of cooperation forced the new world order to consider you as hostiles, wouldn't it, sir?"

"Colonel!" he shouted, his face contorted in rage. "I tolerate your insolence only because we have a common goal. I tolerate your presence here for the same reason. Do not, sir, underestimate our resolve. We will meet our commitments and we will move into the United States as planned and on schedule.

"I will instruct all commanders to intensify training on a twenty-four-hour basis. I expect your cadre to set up training schedules on a twenty-four-hour basis to meet our schedules. We shall see, Colonel, who has the resolve to meet the deadline, you or I." The general dismissed the colonel with a wave of his hand. He looked at the man leave and thought, *What a pompous British officer*. Well, he would show all of them what his army could do.

With the new equipment and arms, the American rebels would be no match for them. Within sixty days, they would enter the United States.

Allied Headquarters
Brasilia, Brazil

"Ah, General Quasada, good you could make it. Did you have a pleasant flight from Chicago?"

"Yes, Mr. President."

The president of Brazil and commander in chief of the Brazilian Armed Forces was a short man of Portuguese descent, a very intelligent man of wealth and a foe of the United States. "Very good, excellent, excellent."

While speaking to the president, the general picked up a steel shaft from the president's desk and examined it, and then laid the shaft and replaced it on the table. "Very ugly-looking shaft, Mr. President."

"It's what the American rebels are using in Mexico. Seems they may be getting low on small arms or ammunition. We're checking on it now. Could be they're weaker than we think. In any case, we don't expect any problems this far south. Our intelligence tells us they are harassing our troops along the industrial line in northern Mexico. However, we should be ready on time."

The general looked over the other weapons on the table. He recognized them all, the latest small arms in the inventory. He could see no reason they could not obtain success once they had trained the Brazilian and Argentine armies in their uses.

The general smiled at the president and spoke, "Mr. President, we have moved up the invasion date by two weeks. We must accelerate our training schedules."

The president was in silent contemplation for over five minutes. The security of his nation and the bases were more important to him. The nation's security was at stake.

He looked up at the general, slowly shaking his head from side to side. "No no no, we can't do it. I must maintain constant security on our bases. We can't afford to have American forces hit us. We can't do it. No, sir, it cannot be done."

General Quasada removed an envelope from his inside uniform coat pocket and handed it to the president. "I think, sir. This will motivate you to do as you're told."

The message was short and to the point. It read,

> It is imperative your training be accelerated to meet our present invasion schedule. Your troops will be in place no later than two weeks prior to the original assigned date. We will schedule air transports to meet this change. The completion of the equipment delivery will be made at the assembly areas in Mexico.

The president looked at it in disbelief. "This cannot be true, General. It will mean pulling in our security forces for early training. We will be left vulnerable. We cannot secure the training bases adequately and train the security forces at the same time. No, we must complete the troop training first so they can pick up on the security when we train our security forces."

"Mr. President, the rebel forces do not have the strength to commit forces here or in Argentina. You have nothing to fear. We assure you. The enemy cannot move their troops this far south. They don't have the capability."

The president was agitated at the lack of support he expected from the United Nations and said, "General, we will make these changes, and I will hold you responsible if anything happens because of this change. Agreed?"

"Mr. President, we know the rebel forces are cut thin and they are attempting to move troops into strategic areas to meet our thrust south. With our southern friends moving north, we will be able to complete our mission. To do it, we must have all of your troops and the other southern allies in place two weeks earlier than planned. We know you can do it. The acceleration should not hinder you that much. We have everything under control. All of you are safe here. Get the training finished and let's get those Yankees once and for all. Remember, you too will share in it. Maybe two or three states could be yours."

"General Quasada, we have no choice but to help. If it were up to me, I would close our borders to all of you."

"Yes, Mr. President, we know. Just remember what could happen to your country should you change your mind."

*****

A submarine surfaced off the coast of Argentina. It was a dark night, no moonlight to mark their presence. Quickly the naval crew put two rubber boats over the side. The SEAL team moved expertly away from the sub. As they moved toward shore, the sub silently slipped below the sea to wait.

"Over there, Commander. Just to your right. Did you see it, sir?"

The commander nodded. He had seen the small red light blinking the recognition signal and knew their advance party was on time.

The rubber boats silently reached shore and the team were out and deployed without a word being spoken, each man to his place.

A middle-aged man—American by birth, Hispanic by ancestry—was waiting for them when they landed. "Fremont," he said to the commander.

"Oak tree," the commander replied.

Recognition had been achieved.

Maj. Roger Hernandez, army Special Forces, was ready to pass on the most vital information in the war. "Commander, we have just learned this evening, the United Nations has given the Brazilian and Argentine armies new training schedules. Tomorrow they must begin accelerated training. The word is they must be ready and in place within two weeks of their previous scheduled dates. All security forces are being withdrawn and integrated into the training schedule. Within two days, the training bases will be like overripe plums, ready to be plucked. They are training at these bases here with their security force number three munitions layouts, including equipment areas, headquarters, barracks, and troops. With only four bases to contend with and training acceleration starting the day after tomorrow, it would be prudent to bring in those special troops tomorrow night. It may be the only chance we have to hit them while they sleep."

The commander nodded. He quickly pulled at a notepad and scribbled something on it, tore out the page, and turned to his radio operator. "Fax this message to the sub." It read, "Plan KA to go into effect now following information to all other units for immediate implementation. Must hit all areas as planned tonight. Changes to training agenda are critical. Can you do it?"

The fax came in on the radio modem from the battle computer the crew had on the beach. The operator looked at it briefly and sent the copy to the captain. Then he typed in a coded message for transmission to the other ships and submarines waiting for it. He waited then for the captain's reply. The intercom buzzed, and he keyed the receiver and spoke, "Yes, sir." The captain responded and hit the transmit key on his keyboard. Within seconds, all units had received the words, "KA now."

*****

Tork and his assault troops were on alert, each having been assigned their targets, each knowing this might be the last party for them. They all knew what had to be done and the death that would be wrought upon the Argentine troops and their own. Chances were, though, the enemy would not be fully armed and security would be light.

The word spread fast. All the troops boarded their assault choppers and the gunships lifted off first. They would escort the assault choppers and head for their target at treetop level.

The assault teams would hit their target areas first. The gunships would give full area support and knock out all light and helicopter aircraft on the base. If the teams hit their targets as planned and the gunships took out the enemy's aircraft, then there should be little danger to their troops. They were to hit hard and fast, inflict maximum damage, and meet their objectives. It was imperative that all three countries felt total destruction of their troops. Public attention had to be aroused and training had to be stopped.

The rebels would be moving against the United Nations within two weeks; they didn't need to worry about the South American troops crossing the US border and diverting them from their goals.

All heavy bombers would be needed for the final victory, not in South America. They needed them for their offensive.

As Tork sat in his chopper flying at treetop level with the terrain moving swiftly by, the ship's avionics flew and directed the aircraft, moving it up and down as it launched toward its final destination. Tork's thoughts wandered back in time to the spring of '95, the bombing of the Oklahoma federal building, and then in 2001 when the twin towers were destroyed. The changes that were made by the government were the result of the people that had demanded the change. It took time for them to change the laws, but the people were willing to give up their rights to control or stop the terrorists. Little did they know how important it was to the government. The golden opportunity had come and they and the media had jumped at the chance to start the takeover of the nation by the United Nations. The secret government unit was created to infiltrate and institute changes in the federal and state laws. It was then the new world order started their game in earnest.

The single-world government had been in existence for some years. It was now the time for the United States to start its part in the conspiracy. Troops had been trained from the famed SAS in Britain to the Delta Forces and the Navy SEAL in this country.

Cal and Tork, like so many others, failed to see it. Tork had opinions but always shrugged it off until all the evidence had been given him so many months ago, when he and Cal had been caught in the desert. Colonel Duncan had made it clear the Bureau of Alcohol Tobacco and Fire Arms, the US Attorney General's Office, and the Federal Emergency Management Agency all made part of the Home Security Administration were instrumental in securing control over state rights. It was clear that a new identity created from the trilateral commission was in full control of the world's economy. Tork was converted by facts supported by the government's actions. He thought to himself, *Had the people only had the insight to see that the changes to the constitution would deliver their most sacred rights to the enemy, none of what is happening now would have been possible. If only the people been responsible to themselves.*

Now Tork and hundreds of men were airborne in a foreign country, hell-bent on destroying a training attack force at four bases in the country, not only there but also in two other South American countries. Young men and women from three countries would lay dead in a few hours, and many rebel forces would be dying with them, committed to the restoration of the American dream and heritage. Tork knew they had to prevail. He vowed he would not return to be a slave of the United Nations.

Tork's thoughts were interrupted by the pilot. "Colonel, we're coming up on target in twenty minutes. I'll be putting you at the headquarters building, then move to the staging position at Charlie Delta 05, and will remain online for support or withdrawal."

Tork answered, "Affirmative. Contact all ships to be ready, no exceptions. If possible, pick up all dead and return to their pickup positions when called. New change from command. Leave no enemy living. Take no prisoners without authorization. Understood?"

"Yes, sir, understood."

Tork turned and silently looked at the men before him who were completely dressed in black; faces in black makeup, weapons, and webbing, everything were in black. Each man had his own transceiver in the back of his helmet, earphone in his left ear, and a mini mic sitting in front of his mouth. A whisper was all that was needed to communicate. No sounds should be heard if all went well. The crossbows, weapons with silencers, and even the automatic weapons were equipped with suppressors. The enemy would hear the choppers as they descended, but nothing more until the fighting started. If they hit hard and fast, they could minimize their initial contacts.

"Two minutes to go, sir."

"Thank you."

Tork gave the signal for all transceivers to be turned on and then whispered, "Acknowledge by the numbers, go!"

"One, two, three," they all replied, all in whispers. The birds in their silent mode descended at each assigned position. The men were eager to move to their designated targets, each one moving precisely and silently. Tork and his group moved fast to the headquarters building.

A night "officer of the day" was sitting with a sergeant at arms at the entry desk. Most offices were closed. They occupied the main conference room. However, an invasion planning team was going over destination targets and troop assignments. They heard nothing unusual.

Tork whispered into his mic, "Hogan, try the door."

"Locked, sir," he replied.

"Thomas, set a small charge to burn out the lock assembly. Brogan, have two bolts ready to hit the two men at the front desk. Go."

Sergeant Thomas silently moved to the door and slipped a magnesium charge to burn through the lock. They taped a small electrical detonator over it. It took less than three seconds. Thomas stepped back from the charge and pressed a button on his transmitter.

The lock was burned through and fell to the floor, and the door entry was clear. In a split second, the two men sitting at the desk looked up. No one knew if they saw anything before they died. Two bolts hit, first one and then the other, each in the heart, pinning them to their chairs.

Tork ordered the men to search for any significant personnel, officers, or meetings, planners, or NCOs. If found, they were to detain them and hold them for transport or elimination.

Tork's men entered the building, searching for personnel and setting explosives with timed detonators throughout, moving as fast as they could and eliminating personnel as they found them. These people had to learn that American freedom is earned and that each American soldier was a patriot first and would kill for his country and his freedom and die for it as well.

"Colonel, we found a group in a conference room going over plans and maps. We've shackled and gagged all of them, plus a couple of troublemakers, sir."

"Sedate those two and get them all out and on board a chopper. Go!"

The sergeant spoke quickly and his assigned medic injected both men. Within seconds, they moved rapidly to the choppers and stored them on board. They moved the others to the choppers and divided them among the teams, one or two to a bird. The mission was going well. Silently the guards were removed. The special teams quickly moved through the barracks.

Captain Cumbers called Tork. "Colonel, Cumbers here, sir. We're ready to enter the barracks."

The captain relayed the message to his group and they entered the barracks, stopping at every other bed and silently eliminating the sleeper. A waking soldier was quickly dispatched. They finished their task and returned to their pickup point. When the heavy stuff went off, the waking men would see half of their forces unmoving in their beds. The realization of their losses would be devastating. Either the will to fight would be greatly reduced or they would become very, very vengeful.

The high command was betting on fear to muddle the mind of each soldier. If the enemy could silently enter their barracks and kill every other man, how could they be defeated on the battlefield? Time would tell.

Tork glanced at his watch and in a low voice spoke, "All units, repeat, all units, clear and board as instructed now." Each man stopped where they were and retreated to their assembly area to board.

What was not completed was left. Munitions timers were set. Within minutes, the strike teams were in the birds and taking off. Noise was unavoidable, but then it made no difference. As the birds started, the timers clicked to zero in intervals of one to three minutes apart. Some were set to activate in thirty-minute intervals with several set to strike in one hour.

As the engines started, a school instructor looked at his watch. *Strange*, he thought, *there has been no notification of any night missions scheduled tonight. All training is to be in the classrooms.* The drone of the chopper's engines became louder and he realized that there were far too many choppers starting and taking off. His heart started to race as the thought hit him. *The Americans must be here.* Then he relaxed. *It couldn't be the Americans. They would be landing, not leaving.* He raced to the window to see what was happening. His students looking bewildered rushed outside to see the birds lifting off. Suddenly, from the warehouse area, there were explosions, one after another, seconds between, and then silence. He realized he was right. Somehow they had come and now they were leaving. The whole base was awake now. Men had awakened in their barracks only to find half of them lying in their blood-soaked beds, never to face another day. Fear had taken over. They looked at the carnage around them and knew what they were in for if they moved north against the American rebel army.

One man looked at his sergeant, crossed himself, and said, "God help us all, Sergeant, for we are doomed."

The commander was quick to order full battle alert and to have the high command notified of the attack. Confusion was everywhere. He called on his adjutant to order all assault choppers and fighter aircraft into the air. "I want those choppers caught and all shot down. Take no prisoners. Spare no one. Do you understand?"

"Yes, sir, but we can do nothing. All of our aircraft were destroyed in the first explosions, and then the warehouses went up."

A company commander, Major Rojus, entered the room, pale and unnerved. "Sir, we have just learned that every other sleeping man in the barracks was murdered in their sleep. Their throats were cut."

The general looked at the major in disbelief, shaking his head. "No no no, they couldn't do such a thing. It's not in their makeup. What of the damage to the base?"

The major's head hung down as he replied, "The explosions have stopped. The fires are out of control, but we hope to have them out soon. We can only hope that they will catch the Americans before they move north."

"General." A communication technician entered the room. "Sir, our communications are down. They have destroyed our telephone substation and the base radio, and microwave towers were blown up. The radios were shot to pieces. We've lost all communication and sent a messenger to the city to notify command by way of telephone to alert them of the attack."

The attack teams flew low, tree hopping and skirting around the villages and towns. They moved north for several hundred kilometers toward their pickup points. The jeep carriers would be waiting, and the Aircraft Warning and Control System would be circling, watching their movements and looking for any interceptors that may have been dispatched to look for them. Tork felt like he had been hit in the stomach by a two-thousand-pound bull. What they'd done tonight was unheard of by their standards, but it had been necessary. The enemy's fear of the American rebels was paramount. If they moved north, it would make them think twice before entering combat, maybe even stop the movement. Propaganda pamphlets had been printed telling the people what the United Nations had caused and why their soldiers had been attacked. The pamphlets would tell the people to save their soldiers' lives and keep them at home and no more assaults would be made.

Tork looked at his watch and ordered the final course change. They would be linking with their carrier soon, and then they'd be homeward bound.

The carriers had pulled silently into position with all lights out—mission accomplished. All birds landed safely. The wounded were rushed below deck to the emergency hospital that had been set up in advance. The next step was the debriefing and preparation for their return home. The task force was now underway, vigilant and prepared. All aspects of the raid were evaluated. Pictures taken of the bases and their equipment were scrutinized for detail. The warehouses were checked during the planting of the charges. Only special prisoners were taken. All were being interrogated.

Tork and his group mounted their choppers and waited until their turn to take off. Tork sat silently, thinking over the mission, the death and destruction they had caused on this venture. *What a waste of human kind. What a waste of humanity.*

A voice came over his earphone. "Colonel. We're ready, sir. We should be back in about two hours."

"Thank you," said Tork.

The chopper's engine whined as it lifted up. Tork looked out at the carrier as they steadily climbed. The bird made a turn to the northwest, leveled out, and picked up speed and they were on their way home. The wounded and the dead would follow later.

The briefing on the ship was long and tiring, every little detail taken down and analyzed. After their return, they would have to go through it all again. Hopefully it would reveal additional information, something they may have forgotten, something that they might recall that could help shorten the war.

The group needed rest, but Tork knew what was ahead and ordered additional training for the group. He wanted them in top shape, knowing that Duncan would call on them once again.

CHAPTER 28

Traitors and Heroes

UN Transport Command
Detroit, Michigan

General Surkov studied the map of the United States. Lines had been drawn to show UN forces and controlled areas. At other points on the map were thick vinyl arrows. Written on the arrows were destinations and dates. These were the invasion dates and times for units to move. General Surkov stepped down from the map stage and replaced the satin rope with a brass fastener to a polished brass stanchion.

The general looked up as the door closed. His smile mimicked that of the member Daniel B. Jackson.

"Well, General," Jackson said, "are we ready to move? My people are becoming impatient."

"Be patient, Daniel. We move closer to victory by the hour. It won't be long and you will have control of both Alabama and Florida. Maybe even Georgia. Have you a new name for it yet?"

"It will be known as New Africa, General. Have you spoken to the United Nations about our request yet, sir?"

"They are deciding on it now. I don't know if they'll go along with giving you three states. Maybe too much to ask for."

Throwing up his hands, Daniel said, "General, we need room for twenty seven million African-Americans. The two states will not support us. We'll need all three of them. You must try to convince them of this."

"Daniel, I'll do my best. Now, we're waiting for our transport order. What have you to report?"

"The factories are producing at maximum. You should have all the heavy troop transports you need and on time. We'll ship them when they clear final inspection. We've produced to date more than 21,000 vehicles, including light and medium tanks. At this time, we don't understand why your troops have not started to move yet. Enough equipment has been shipped from our factories and received by you."

"Well, Daniel, we were waiting for the troops from Argentina, Brazil, and Chile to arrive on site before moving north and invading the United States from the south. The rebels, however, have made preemptive strikes in all three countries. It has set us back several months, and we needed to finish this assignment as planned before we can help you with your dream."

General Surkov grimaced at what he had implied and a bead of sweat broke out on his forehead. He quickly wiped it off.

Realizing what the general had just said prompted Daniel to ask. "Did they hurt you that bad that you have been put in defensive position?"

"Well, they did give us a few bruises, but we can still move as planned, and we just might. However, right now, we're waiting on intelligence reports. We'll move ahead as soon as we've ascertained our position. The council is meeting today in Geneva and we should know within a few days, if not hours."

"General, the Detroit City Council has worked closely with you. Your promise for our own states has paved the way for complete cooperation. I must have better information now, not maybe or soon, but now. We grow impatient with every hour. We need a date."

The general looked long at this tall black councilman. He never realized how prejudiced they were until UN forces had moved into the Detroit area. Yes, he thought, it would be best if they had their own states.

"Daniel, come here." He reached down and unlatched the satin rope from the stanchion and let him through. "Let me show you how close we are."

Daniel looked at the map, the arrows and the dates; he studied them, each one. His mind was seeing, sorting, and storing them all. If the general ever knew, beside him stood a man with total recall.

"Well, General, it looks like we can sleep well tonight. The council will be pleased to know that we'll be moving south soon."

The general replied, "Yes, Daniel, very soon."

*****

Daniel arrived at the council meeting a few minutes late. He went straight in and took his seat. The city manager had just made his report to the council and was sitting as Daniel arrived.

The chairman looked at Daniel. "Well, Dan, what did that honky have to say?"

"Good news, Mr. Chairman and council members. The offensive starts in eighteen days. The United Nations was waiting for three South American countries to help them by moving north from Mexico. Seems the rebels went south first and spoiled the show. So now they are bringing in more French, German, and Eastern European troops instead. They figure they will have enough troops in place by their original date to start the offensive. They're convinced they will have no problem destroying the rebels and freeing our brothers from their imperialistic control. As for Georgia, well, he's still working on that one."

The council members looked pleased; they had convinced the United Nations that they were in the group and only wanted their own states to run and to control. He and all in the group played their parts well. Soon, they would have the means to inflict the utmost damage on the UN forces. They all knew a new Africa in the new world was not very likely. They were Americans—all American.

Daniel left for home after the meeting. His day was over. His report was ready to be transmitted and it needed to be done immediately. His driver dropped him off at his door.

As he entered his home, he called for his wife. With no answer, he knew she was still at the baby shower. The kids were still in school, so Daniel went straight to the basement to his darkroom. Daniel was an amateur photographer and did his own developing. He entered the room, closed, and locked the door. He turned on the light outside the door to warn anyone coming in that he was working on his film and printing.

He went over to the chemical cabinet and with the toe of his shoe depressed a small section of the baseboard next to the cabinet, and the cabinet silently moved out and to the left. Dan moved through the entranceway, and a sensor caught his body heat and the lights went on. He was in a well-hidden room. Along one wall was a very sophisticated shortwave radio system, state of the art. It had residual power on it and was warmed up and ready to go. Dan reached over and hit the active switch, bringing all of it alive.

He switched on *transmit* and then pushed a button marked ANT. Softly in the attic, a motor turned on and an antenna moved silently up through the center of a weather vane, unnoticed.

Dan sat down and grabbed the "bug" and started sending Morse code at a rapid pace. To most people, it would appear that some kid was playing around with a Morse code key, but in a rebel enclave several hundred miles south was a radio receiving a very sophisticated code. The operator had it going into a computer that was ingesting, decoding, and analyzing it as fast as it was received. The transmissions stopped, the operator tapped out received in code, and shut down. Daniel pushed the button, and the antenna silently descended into its place in the attic.

Dan turned, looked at the picture of Martin Luther King on the wall, and smiled. Under his breath, he said, "Freedom earned, brother."

*****

Tork had returned to the main objectives. His units were on the move. The final days to freedom lay ahead. The cells in California had proven very reliable; the resistance there was working to cripple the UN forces a little at a time. After delivering Mr. Jones to Duncan, they obtained invaluable information. It was now possible for the Jones chips to be safely removed. The removal of the chips would integrate new faces into the resistance movement. Volunteers would be everywhere—the push was on and they would all play a decisive part in implementing the final round of Freedom Earned.

*****

Fighting had been hard and decisive. Many foreign units had deserted to the freedom fighters and joined ranks with them. Most were from British and Canadian fighting units. Through interrogation, they'd learned that the majority of the commanders they had engaged were similar to the Irish colonel that Cal had learned firsthand about. It seemed a standard had been established on how a UN commander was trained. It was obvious to Cal that their own men couldn't wait to desert and join the forces for freedom. He still shuddered at what they had done. The hate, the malice, and the prejudice of the new world order had a lasting effect on him.

It would be a long time before the wounds would heal. It had made a better man out of the free-loving Cal Varner. Yes, he finally matured into a real American fighting man.

*****

Tork was studying the local maps when Corporal Clayton approached him. The corporal saluted. "Sir, we have a tank column taking a break about ten minutes north of us. The scouts have them under observation. It's the one we received word on."

"Thank you, Corporal. Who's the officer with the scouts?"

"Captain C, sir," the corporal replied.

"Good. Tell him to keep out of sight and to signal when they depart, got that?"

"Yes, sir."

Tork called for his platoon leaders and sergeants.

"Gentlemen, we have a column heading in our direction. Captain Varner is scouting it now and will alert us on their departure. I want your men deployed in the trees, both sides, and they are to allow the enemy to travel through until the lead tank is at this point here." Tork had each man observe the position on the map. "When it's at this point, the lead squad will knock out the leading tank by hitting the track with an antitank rocket. When this takes place, we'll call to the tank commander on his frequency to surrender.

"Remember, keep your heads down. They will most likely open fire. I want the last vehicle in the column hit as soon as the lead tank is stopped. You are to knock out the track or the rear-drive sprockets. Try not to take any lives if possible, understand?" They all nodded in unison. "Good. After the initial commotion is over, I want the antitank weapons zeroed in on each tank. If they refuse to surrender, take them out at once. I'll give the command on your helmet radios."

Captain Clark seemed puzzled and asked. "Colonel, why don't we take them out at once? Why are we going to toy with them, sir?"

"Captain, over the months, we have had a great number of defections from the UN forces. Like us, some of them are from nations that have been swallowed up by the United Nations. They can't stand the new world order any better than we can. I feel we owe it to those that would rather switch than fight us. If they choose to fight, well, then I guess we'll do what needs to be done and destroy the column. Now we don't have much time, so let's get into position."

The column commander lit his cigarette, took a swig from his canteen, and checked his watch. A few minutes more, he thought, won't hurt. The men could use the break and there had been no resistance and nothing in sight. The observation planes showed a clean road ahead. The only bad place was a few kilometers south a wooded area and he would send a scouting vehicle ahead to check it out.

Cal was watching every move they made. He was taking notes on their break habits, snacking, and conversations. The listening antennas were a big help. It seemed the malcontents hung together. *Could be a few friends in there.* Cal called over to the radio operator. "Pete, call the colonel. Give him this info now." He handed him the information for Colonel Albertson.

"Yes, sir!"

Since his recall by Duncan, Cal was pleased he was again serving with Tork. It was a good combination. Diana and Sybil were well in control of the cells in California, and they had sent others to work with them. Tork had asked for Cal and enjoyed working for freedom and with Tork again.

They relayed the incoming message to Tork immediately. Tork looked at it, smiled, and handed it to Captain Clark. The message read, "Have noted large number of men disgruntled. Eavesdropping shows defections among personnel likely."

Captain Clark looked at Tork, shook his head, and said, "Well, I'll be damned!"

The scout vehicle moved along the road and pulled off at the tree line. The four men got out and two moved across the road to the opposite side. One snuck in through the trees, knowing if anyone was there he could be killed instantly. When an enemy soldier moved out of the other's sight, Cal's men quietly took them prisoner. One by one, they took them to the command post and turned them over to Tork.

Tork was concentrating on his maps and looking for the best ambush position when the prisoners started arriving. One of the NCOs reported to Tork. "Sir, we have the enemy scouts."

"Thank you, Sergeant," Tork replied. Looking over the enemy soldiers, Tork commanded harshly, "Who's in charge here?" No one answered. Tork reached up and pulled the identification tag off one man's neck, looked at the name, and realized he had a Scandinavian trooper.

"Okay, let's pretend no one here understands English, in which case it won't matter if I have your throats cut, will it?" Tork nodded and the men were grabbed from behind and commando knives were pressed against their throats.

"Now, let's try it again. And remember, in most Scandinavian countries, English is a mandatory second language. Now who is in charge here?"

"I am, sir," one of them replied. "Karl Albertsen, lieutenant, army of the United Nations. You have no right to stop us. We have control of this country and you, sir, are our prisoners."

"Well, Lieutenant," Tork said, "you have plenty of gall, but no common sense. But you do have a choice—you can live or die here. To live, you only have to make a radio call and clear this area for your column. If you choose not to, well, then we'll just have to bury you here. Got that?"

Before he could answer, one of the other men spoke up, "Sir, I understand that you allow UN soldiers to defect and join you. Is this true, sir?"

"Yes, Private, it's true. Do you wish to defect?"

"Yes, sir. I do, sir."

Tork looked from one to the other, searching all their faces. "Anyone else want to defect?" he asked.

"Yes, sir," said the other two. "We do, sir."

"Very good," said Tork. "And who would like to send the all-clear signal to your commander?"

Three arms went up in unison.

Tork turned to the lieutenant. "Well, it looks like your neck's been saved, Lieutenant."

"Yes, sir," he replied, "and by three cowards."

"Or patriots," Tork said.

Tork called for Olson and Hakkenson to come forward. "I want you both to monitor this radio transmission. If it's not correct, tell me instantly. Got it?"

"Yes, sir."

The men returned to their scout vehicle. Private Sinkinson turned on the radio transceiver, and the UN trooper made his initial call, waited for confirmation, gave the column the all clear to proceed, and signed off.

Tork looked to his two men. "Well?"

"It was clean and aboveboard, sir. They're coming."

Within minutes, Tork received a message from Cal confirming the column's movements. All of Tork's men were in position. They only had to wait for the column to arrive. They moved off the road and covered the scout car with brush. They then removed the lieutenant and his men to the rear under guard.

The column started into the area unaware they were drawn into a trap. The lead tank moved through at a rapid pace. Just as it was to reach the end of the tree line, a rocket from the brush hit its left track and drive sprocket, ripping the track off the tank and stopping the column. The tanks had been following too close together and didn't have time to pivot out of the way. The best they could do was to stop short of hitting one another.

Seconds after the column stopped, each tank pivoted their turrets looking for a target and seeing nothing. The rear tank reversed itself and swung around. Halfway through its turning radius, a second rocket hit it in its right rear drive sprocket. It stopped, blocking the road.

Tork turned to his radioman. "You have their frequency yet?" he asked.

"Yes, sir, I've got it. When you're ready, sir." He held the mic up to Tork.

"Commander of the tank column," Tork said into the mic. "Acknowledge this transmission!"

The radio receiver remained silent. Tork repeated it a second time. No answer. Once again, Tork spoke. This time, however, he was more explicit. "Commander, you have thirty seconds to acknowledge this transmission or we will destroy your column completely and take no prisoners." Tork waited, counting.

Sergeant Colombo spoke, "Maybe he doesn't speak English, sir."

"No, Sarge. They require all battle commanders to speak English. Helps them to keep the people in line."

Corporal Hennessey called out, "Sir, maybe he's testing you."

Tork nodded and said, "Probably, Corporal." He spoke one last time. "You have less than ten seconds left, Commander. We have enough power to wipe all of you out within minutes. Please save the lives of your troops." No answer came. Tork keyed his mic and gave an order so the commander could hear.

"Prepare to fire. After the initial barrage, flamethrowers finish up. Leave no tank or equipment. Burn them all. Riflemen, take no prisoners!"

Suddenly over the speaker, pandemonium broke out. All the tank crews were begging the commander to surrender. Over the shouts, the commander was yelling out orders to fire into the woods. No one was listening. Tork keyed his mic and said, "Open your hatches and come out with your hands over your heads and move to the back of your column. Do it now!"

Tork looked over to Captain Clark. "Abe, prepare to destroy any tank that attempts to fire on their surrendering men."

"Yes, sir."

Within minutes, hatches were opening and men were coming out. They no longer hit the ground, then their hands were up, and they were running to the rear of the column.

Well, not bad, Tork thought, *we have a column of captured tanks and men.* "What do we do with them now?" he asked.

Suddenly, several of the men stopped, knelt, and pulled automatic weapons out from under their clothing. They started firing on their own men. Al Sanders saw what was happening and opened fire. Within seconds, the men firing on their comrades were cut down. Tork ordered the medics to help those that had been hit.

He then called on the commander to surrender or he would blow his tank back to the new world order, back to hell.

The column fell silent, as both sides watched the commander's tank. Seconds turned into minutes. Cal ordered the tank destroyed, and just as they were about to fire, the top hatch opened and a non-com pulled himself up into view. In a Norwegian accent came the words, "The commander is dead. Long live freedom!"

Tork ordered the crew out of the tank. Sergeant Bailey entered the tank and within seconds was out and reporting to Tork. "Sir, the tank commander and one other officer were knifed, sir. Seems the crew took care of the problem themselves."

Tork ordered his radio operator to contact command and have CH53 Sikorskys brought in to shuttle the prisoners back to base. Those men wanting to defect would be processed and evaluated.

The tanks would be destroyed where they sat after the intelligence sweep was completed. Every little thing in or on the vehicles would be picked up and sent back for evaluation. With the United Nations' big sweep on and the full-scale invasion getting ready to descend on the rebels, Tork knew they had to be ready to move at a moment's notice.

Tork ordered charges placed in the tank turrets and set the timers to go off after they were a safe distance away. He knew when the charges went, the magazine in each tank would go and the tank would end up nothing more than junk.

The Sikorskys arrived and started evacuating the prisoners. Tork was ordered to return to base with his unit, priority red. Something was happening. He called and had Captain Varner return to the unit and to report directly to him when he arrived.

Tork had just finished issuing orders for the withdrawal when Sergeant McKennsey ran up to Tork, saluted, and reported. "Sir, Captain Varner is retuning now, sir, from his patrol."

"Good, Sergeant. Meet him and bring him right hear. ASAP."

"Yes, sir."

Sergeant McKennsey was waiting for Cal when his recon vehicle pulled in.

"Sir, the colonel wants you to report to him immediately. Please follow me."

Cal followed the sergeant past the destroyed tanks to the head of the column where he met Tork. "What's up, Tork? Oh, sorry, sir, Colonel?"

"Captain, we have a hot one. Let's get these troops back. Call in all your scouts and get with Captain Clark. He has all the details. We need to assemble for immediate departure. Something is up, priority red."

Cal assembled the officers and NCOs, received his briefing from the men, and was informed by Clark the choppers were waiting in the clearing on the other side of the tree line. Cal gave the orders for the prisoner evacuation and the return back to the base. He informed Captain Clark that he would wait for his scouts to return and they would proceed upon their arrival. Something big was up, but there's no need to let everyone know now. He thought it best they get the information and assignment after their return and they had a chance to rest, shower, and eat.

Because of the emergency, Tork had called in additional choppers to carry his troops back to the base. They abandoned the vehicles they'd obtained after their drop-off in neutral territory. They had previously picked up several light trucks the scouts had been using. Tork ordered Cal to ditch them when the scouts came in and to leave immediately after. Tork left one chopper for their use to return them to the base after the scouts reported in.

The chopper Tork was in had no sooner touched the ground when a messenger was on hand to meet Tork. "Colonel, you are to report immediately to General Duncan's office. They are waiting for you, sir."

"Thank you, Sergeant. Do you have transportation?"

"Yes, sir. The Humvee to your left, sir, is waiting to transport you."

Tork entered Duncan's office and his aide was waiting for him. "This way, sir." Tork followed him out of the office and to the elevator where two MPs stood waiting.

"War room," said the aide to the MP standing just inside the elevator door. Minutes later the elevator stopped at the third-level basement conference area. The men and the two MPs entered the conference room.

Tork looked surprised when he saw it was full of revolutionary council members.

General Duncan heard the door close and looked up. "Ah, Colonel Albertson, please come in. You will find a seat to the left. Your name is on the table."

Tork moved to the empty seat and sat down, nodded to the general, and smiled. General Duncan went on with his presentation.

"As I was saying, gentlemen, our offensive has been gaining momentum. Although we have run into stiff resistance from UN troops, we have broken through in several areas.

"We are advancing at a slow but steady pace. As you know, the UN forces crossed the border into Nevada from the Northern California border and have moved down into the Lake Tahoe region, Reno, and Carson City where they met with stiff resistance from the Nevada National Guard units and US Marines from Fallon. The marine Raptor aircraft well placed back into the dessert areas attacked the UN troops as they moved east along the interstate, cutting off their supply system in the High Sierras.

"Locals that lived in the mountains hit them after the air attack, cutting into them badly. Those units that have moved into Reno and Carson City found both of them deserted. We managed to evacuate most of the population southeast to desert camps where they are digging in and making themselves useful.

"The UN troops that started into Southern California at the same time their units entered Nevada were met with stiff resistance near Salinas. There's been heavy fighting between Salinas and Fresno. Enemy ships have Monterey tied up and they have landed troops at Monterey. Transports have been arriving at the airport in that region since they started. We have alerted our B-2s to hit them early in the morning and have decided to destroy the main electrical power plants in the region including all high-voltage-carrying pylon towers. We know, gentlemen, that this will cause confusion among the civilian populace. This we feel will hinder the United Nations. The more they have to worry about, the better."

Pointing to the map with a laser pointer, he continued, "In addition, the B-52s will pound the runways of this field. We want it totally destroyed. We will endeavor to use the same tactics on the airfields at Fresno and Bishop. We hope to destroy all major and small airfields in the area. This will help to diminish the use of supply areas that can be used against us. To support our troops in these areas, we are rushing troops in from our Southern California, Arizona, and Nevada locations. Our underground cells in Northern California have been invaluable to us in providing UN troop movements and delaying them. They have been instrumental in blowing up major interchanges on the major freeways around the Oakland Bay area and in the Sacramento areas. This has slowed the enemy's supply and troop movements in this corridor and has hindered supplies moving east to the California-Nevada war zone.

"Our cells in the Placerville and Auburn areas have blown rail bridges and destroyed miles of track. It will take the UN weeks, if not months, to repair or replace bridges. Several highway and rail tunnels have been blocked with derailments in the tunnels and on the main roads. Several fuel tankers were blown up inside the tunnels. These disruptions have bottlenecked the supply and replacement of needed men and materials for the UN forces. Our tactical fighters are patrolling these areas and hitting any targets they encounter. Gentlemen, we are now at the point where we must declare war on our southern neighbors. First, though, we will give the Mexican government the option of closing their borders and bases to the United Nations. If they refuse, then a declaration of war must be made. When war is declared, we will further our attacks on their naval and port facilities. The time of commando raids and hit-and-run tactics is over. To win, we must start saturation bombing on all UN and Mexican bases there.

"Our troops in Texas have already entered Mexico at Juarez, Ojinaga, Boquila, Ciudad de Victoria, Piedras Negras, Mier Reyrose, Rio Bravo, and Matamoros. Our troops are moving on all UN strongholds and garrison bases. Our Harrier aircraft are targeting radar stations and UN helicopter bases. They will destroy any gunships or troop-carrying helicopter units they engage.

"We have enormous numbers of Mexican-American troops undercover across Mexico and we have identified and targeted all UN and Mexican bases. At this time, we expect to encounter heavy engagement with them and are hoping for a great deal of defections. Now for a little good news, Lieutenant Colonel Albertson's teams have been working in the Colorado-New Mexico area.

"We had intelligence reports that large tank battalions were moving south toward Mexico. Well, gentlemen, they encountered a large mechanized tank battalion en route, and through their American ingenuity, they set up and engineered a trap that enabled them to stop the UN battalion. They captured all enemy personnel and destroyed the tanks. I'll leave the details of this to Colonel Albertson. Please, Colonel, inform the committee of the incident."

Tork stood and walked to the podium and gazed out to the members of the committee and the general officers present. "Thank you, sir."

Tork looked at the faces of the men and women of the new Congress and Senate leaders of today, the men and women that would lead the new America back to the constitution and the bill of rights. His mind was reeling with the tank encounter. He had a difficult time with the battalion commander and was outraged at their men shooting down their own troops as they ran toward the rear of the column. Tork was at a loss for words. His mind reeled to say it the proper way. *Well, here goes*, he thought.

"Ladies and gentlemen, I can only say to each of you, that you. Thank you for the guts to stand among your peers, to continue with the government in exile, and to provide us with the leadership such as no one has seen since 1776. You are all now in the same league as Washington, Jefferson, Adams, Payne, and others who gave their lives and their fortunes for this great country. You are the ones that should be praised—not me, for I am only a soldier, among many thousands of soldiers that have heard your call to arms. We know that what awaits us is monumental global servitude, and we, like you, want no part of it. No, I am among many, only one soldier. You have airman, sailors, and marines that are at your call. All of us will serve this country with all that we have to give. For the tank engagement we encountered, this was an opportunity to save lives. But more importantly we're here to do our job. That job is to restore the republic and democracy to the American people. We will not give up."

With those words, Tork retreated and sat. The hall was silent. Everyone sat there listening, awed at what they had just heard. One, then a few, then the whole room stood and applauded Tork. General Duncan returned to the podium.

"Well, that was some speech, Colonel, and you shouldn't take your accomplishment so lightly. Your engagement was more of a victory than you think it was. You stopped badly needed tanks getting into Mexico. You also stopped, if only temporarily, a push that was expected by the United Nations to cross the border at Juarez. It gave us time to launch our own into that area and enabled us to push them farther south toward Monterrey. With our troops crossing at Laredo and Reynosa, it gave us the opportunity to hit them without getting hit by those tanks. We are going to herd them all back toward Monterey where we expect to hit them with B-52s armed with cruise missiles, and we plan at this time to concentrate on military targets only. It is our intent to free the Mexican people from the new world order and give them the stability they want and need. They are a courageous people."

With that said, General Duncan concluded the briefing with, "It's a new dawn tomorrow. All commanders be in here at 0500 hours."

With everything said, Tork could see his bunk waiting. It had been a stressful day and a long one, and he needed the rest. His thoughts were selfish. *Look out sheets. Here I come.*

CHAPTER 29

The Commitment

Supreme European Command Headquarters
London, England

Gen. Rudolph Wagner, British forces commander, opened his staff meeting with a shake of his fist.

"I want those American rebels defeated at all costs. We have injected five hundred thousand troops into the United States and have lost nearly a third of them to desertions, not to mention the loss of aircraft to the rebel forces. Intelligence has reported the costs may be higher. Aircraft that we thought were lost to combat have been reported seen at US installations. Unrest here in Britain has not been as alarming since the union took control of Britain in 2018. We thought we had the entire British Isles in complete control. The upheaval in the United States has given hope to the malcontents here. We must eliminate the rebel forces in the United States, or we may have upheavals within the union itself. It has taken us over thirty years to bring Britain to her knees. If the Americans prevail and the US constitution survives, it may be the beginning of a revolution spreading across the Atlantic. We cannot let this happen."

Jock Furnnier, minister of Foreign Affairs, European Union, stood facing General Wagner and said, "General Wagner, we have pushed the main battle offensive up and expect to move east from Nevada within hours. Our first objective will be the capture of Salt Lake City. It shouldn't take more than a day to move across Nevada to the Great Salt Lake where we should meet little resistance. The Mormons are a peaceful people. It is expected the National Guard and reserve units will put up a token fight that we can easily defeat.

"The fighters they have at Hill Air Force Base will be no match for us. We will eliminate the base they have established at Wendover before our initial move from Reno, so I'm not concerned there. To ensure success, we will introduce additional forces from Canada into Montana and Idaho to reinforce our troops there, bringing them south to meet with our forces moving east. At the same time, we have moved South American troops into positions in Mexico, just north of Mexico City. Our plan is to move them north, while our forces move east into Utah. Our troops will then engage the American forces that have gone into northern Mexico. Our intel tells us they are under strength and have little armor with them. The American forces will be engaged throughout their northern areas and will be unable to protect or move reinforcements to help their troops in Mexico. Once we have defeated the Americans there, we will move north to meet our advancing troops. When we have cut off the American forces between Canada and Mexico, we will move east. We should have victory within thirty days."

Jock Furnnier wiped the sweat from his brow. He reached down and poured himself a glass of water and slowly picked it up. He looked silently at the faces around him, weighing their expressions and reactions to his words and analyzing each of them there.

Setting down the glass, he continued, "We will not stop until each city is in our control. We will bomb any city that shelters or supports the rebel forces. The American federal forces will set up military controls in each state and city we take so our troops can continue their advances. Any questions, General?"

The general looked at the bureaucrat, anger in his eyes and hate for this pompous Englishman, one of those who so diligently helped deliver the United Kingdom into the European family. He thought, *What no country could do, the traitors from within and the greed of the people will be delivered.* The general looked into the eyes of this man and spoke, "Minister, in all respect, sir, the plans that have been formulated and are about to be implemented have many flaws. There are questions of intelligent matters that have not been answered that could have devastating consequences and could change the course of this conflict, a conflict we cannot afford to lose."

General Wagner continued, "Let me remind each of you that we have spent billions to bring down the Americans. With them out of the way, we can move forward, and the only country in our way that would prevent world domination would be Red China. We have forces on alert and naval vessels in and around the Chinese coast to prevent them from interfering. For this reason, we must bring down the United States as planned. Therefore, all planning committees within the union, both here and in America, will be meeting in Brussels a week from today, where we will bring all intelligence and planning factors together to ensure we are successful.

"All military high command commanders in both European and American theaters of operations will be there to participate. A tentative date has been set for our final invasion. They will announce this date at the conclusion of this meeting. Gentlemen, they will give those of you that will be participating in this strategy your assignments and locations upon leaving. Good luck. God bless the European Union and the future of the world—our world."

At the conclusion of the meeting, a British colonel silently put his memorandums in his briefcase, put on his overcoat, nodded at his superior, smiled, and left the room. What he had heard was of the utmost importance and had to be transmitted as soon as possible.

As he was entering his car, a hand fell on his shoulder. "Excuse me, sir," a voice rang out. "You dropped this." As the colonel turned, a young man handed him a glove and walked off so quickly he didn't see who it was. He entered the car and instructed his driver to take him back to his quarters. He shoved the glove into his pocket.

Upon arrival, he dismissed the driver and went to the Officer's Lounge and straight to the bar to order a glass of brandy. He casually looked about the lounge. Seeing all were engrossed in conversation or reading, he removed his coat and took the glove from his pocket. It was the one that had been given to him by the man at the conference center. He set it down in front of him and looked it over. Seeing nothing on the outside, he slipped his fingers inside and felt a piece of paper. He grasped it with his thumb and finger and pulled it out, opened it, and placed it in front of him, looking about to see if he was being observed. Feeling safe, he glanced down and read, "Daimler Chrysler Best Buy, Brussels. Contact Herr Schmidt for best deal in new autos."

The message was written in French. He knew then he was to meet his contact at the Brussels Museum just before closing at the entrance to the military exhibit. He would be contacted for debriefing. He picked up his cigarettes, lit one, and slipped the message into his pocket. He then walked to the men's toilet where he entered a stall, slipped the paper into the toilet, and waited five minutes. After flushing it, he returned to the lounge where he finished his brandy and left. He went to his quarters, changed his clothes, and proceeded to leave for the museum and his meeting.

He arrived an hour before the museum was scheduled to close and started through the galleries. Looking interested in most of the exhibits, he paid no attention to anyone around him. He had been looking for almost thirty-five or forty minutes when an elderly man approached him.

"Excuse me, sir," he said. "Could you tell me what this painting represents? I'm confused. It seems to be at war and at peace at the same time. It's very questionable, don't you think?"

The colonel smiled and said, "Yes, sir. It is a symbol of war and peace. Don't you agree?"

The man answered, "Yes, if peace is earned to regain freedom."

The colonel replied, "Freedom is earned."

The man looked around him and asked, "Do you have it?"

The colonel smiled and pulled a copy of his notes from his pocket, handed it to the elderly gentleman, and said, "Time is short. This must get to the high command immediately."

The man smiled, turned, and left. As he walked away, another man passed him. Unknown to the colonel, the elderly man had passed it along.

The information would be transmitted by satellite within the hour. The American rebel high command would be alerted to all that had been discussed at the conference. They would move troops to meet the new threat. Bombers would be readied and ships would be moved into position. Heavy tanks and artillery would be moved to advance on the enemy. US Rebel Special Forces would be prepared to move into remote positions behind enemy staging areas. They would parachute rebel air force special operations units behind their lines to direct air strikes, coordinated with other teams. The constant movement of enemy troops would always be in view. Should one team be found, another team would move in to continue the job. Bombers and tactical aircraft would be directed to intercept troop movements day and night.

Everywhere where there were troops or cells, the word would be spread. Plans to meet the enemy would be implemented. When the European Union started to move, they were going to meet resistance. A defense by Americans was in place designed to become a full-scale invasion to get rid of the invaders and drive them back in to the sea.

The rebel committee had made the decision to act on a new government when the new world order and the United Nations are defeated and to move on both the Mexican and Canadian governments through an occupation. They would be taken under control, and the people in each country would be given the opportunity through a referendum to be made a part of the United States after the American people voted on it. The new North America brought by the president's surrender to the world's elite would be dissolved; only the consolidation of all three countries under the American constitution would be permitted and only then after the American people voted on it. If this took place, the constitution would prevail within the borders of the North American continent and a new United States of America would emerge. All South American countries would be given the chance to create a new economic confederacy that would open all borders to economic trade but would not allow a union that created the same open borders and political controls that the European Union created. Safeguards to ensure each country's sovereignty would be left intact. No country within the confederacy could dictate to another. Agreement regarding trade would be controlled through a confederate congress composed of all member countries. Freedoms based on the confederacy would be guaranteed under a similar constitution to that of the United States. Once the US borders were secure, the country would consider the return of American corporations. Manufacturing would be mandatory in this country with all corporations being majorly American-owned. All foreign-owned corporations operating in America would have to sell their controlling interests to American stockholders.

The new revolution was about to bear fruit. All who opposed it were about to learn how well America responded to threats. The destruction of the twin towers, the terrorist threats upon the American people, and the removal of the Canadian and Mexican borders based on the Council of Foreign Affairs' report on building a North American community have led to the loss of freedom and the elimination of the constitution. Fear had strengthened the government's resolve to repeal rights. The defeat of Al-Qaeda terrorist groups and the release of the Iranian and Iraqi coalitions showed the power of the United States. After preemptive strikes on the Iranian nuclear facilities, the riots in the United States by illegal aliens in the country were thought to have been started by the government to incite them and force the implementation of the new North America country. It was thought by all it was copied from the Muslims in France when they rioted several years ago, and the European Union caved to all their demands.

The Iranian people overthrew the Islamic government and aligned itself with the new Iraq. These successes prompted the European Union to take over the United Nations and to create a quest for absolute world domination. They felt the United States had become too powerful. This, it was assumed, spurred the European desire to control the world through the United Nations. The United States and Japan met and defeated the North Korean invasion of South Korea in late 2018, this defeat and the realization that their worldwide commerce kept the Chinese from invading Formosa. They watched it with scrutiny, but left it alone. The Chinese had become the world's dominant industrial producer.

America was now going to win or they all were going to become puppets of the new world order. Nations from Arabia to the Balkans had fallen to the United Nations. America's new government and the cabinet said that was not going to happen, but with the American government's help, it did. The government fearing the use of private weapons allowed the United Nations to enter the country and confiscate all private weapons. Freedom is earned, and the rebels were now on the job. Freedom would be theirs once more, and it would spread to the rest of the world again, with a new America leading the way.

Rebel Forces Headquarters
New Mexico

General Duncan and his staff had received the satellite message from Brussels. They had studied the details and recon had been made in each area mentioned in the dispatch. Everything had been verified. The movements in Canada to reinforce the UN forces in Idaho and Montana were known. The information of troops moving north from Mexico City was not known and intel was needed for their exact locations. Their strengths and armor were necessary to formulate an offensive move to stop them from advancing.

General Duncan studied the area noted in Mexico, looked up, and said, "Get me Lieutenant Colonel Albertson now!"

His aide immediately exited, and within minutes two, military police sergeants were on their way to Tork's quarters. The march to freedom was about to begin.

The knock on the door was loud. Tork had just finished dressing and was looking forward to a good breakfast and a review of his battalion's training, equipment, replacements, and rest for his troops. He had informed the sergeant major to have his company commanders ready for briefing by 1300 hours. Captain Varner was preparing his reports on the last mission with the others for General Duncan's approval.

Tork had submitted his earlier and was going to take a few minutes to relax before the meeting took place. But the loud knock startled Tork. *Sheee—What is it now?* he said to himself. *No peace for the wicked*, he thought.

He opened the door to see two men standing at attention. "Sir, General Duncan requests your immediate presence at his staff meeting."

He looked at both men and smiled. "Must be important to send two of you so early in the morning. Hang on, men," he said, turning to put on his coat. He checked his appearance, turned back, and said, "Let's go and see what kind of mayhem and catastrophe the general has for me today."

Tork knew from experience when the general sent for him, something hot was about to happen. As they passed by Cal's room, Tork stopped and knocked on Cal's door. As the door opened, Tork said, "Alert the brigade and cancel the meeting at 1300 hours. Have all senior officers and company commanders in my office immediately."

"Yes, sir," Cal replied.

Tork looked to his escorts and said, "Shall we continue, Sergeants?"

General Duncan was briefing his staff and was about to introduce them to his basic plan of attack when Tork entered the room.

"Sir, Lieutenant Colonel Albertson reporting as ordered."

"Come in, Colonel. Please sit over there." The general pointed to the empty seat next to Colonel Thomas. Tork sat, nodded, and smiled at his old friend Col. Stew Thomas. Stew acknowledged him and slid a piece of paper over to him. Tork glanced down and read the note. Stew had been very thorough.

The general continued his briefing, showing on the war map the probable location of enemy troops that had been moving north of Mexico City heading toward Ciudad Victoria in Tamaulipas. If so, it would signify they were on their way to enter the United States at Brownsville. It could also mean the enemy could be divided there and part of them would move toward Monterrey to engage the rebel troops hoping to defeat them and then cross the border at Laredo. Word came in that another very large UN force had landed at Ciudad Obregon in Sonora and another at Mazatlan in Sinaloa. It indicated they were moving east toward Durango.

General Duncan looked at Tork and said, "Colonel, I want to separate the two forces. One group will head north toward Chihuahua and then up to El Paso. The other group will continue to Monterrey and join up with the group from Ciudad Victoria. If they do, it will give them a very large battle group. You must, and I repeat, you must confirm their locations, direction of movement, strength, and armor. You will be taking along with you Col. Stewart Thomas who will assist you in language support. We believe that these groups will be composed of troops from France, Holland, Belgium, Germany, and Mexico. Colonel Thomas and one other interpreter will be there for you and your specialists to recon this area."

The general paused and looked over each of them, before continuing, "Keep in mind, Colonel, the best way to gather information is to integrate into these areas and through prisoner intel. Get in, search, and grab any officers or NCOs. Any questions?"

Tork had written down the information received and slipped a note to Colonel Thomas that read, "Welcome aboard, Stew." He looked up at the general and said, "No, sir. We'll have our group ready to move out as soon as you conclude this briefing. Our transportation is ready and the brigade is eager to finish what we've started. We'll transmit all information gathered when we receive it."

The general dismissed the group and called Tork over. "Colonel, I have all the terrain, road maps, and aerial recon photos taken within the last eight hours. You can pick them up from my adjutant within the hour. Study them thoroughly and be careful. Get us this intel as soon as you can. We must know precisely their destinations. Before they arrive, we must have our troops in place and be ready to greet them in a way they'll understand."

Tork saluted, turned, and moved to the phones. His first call went to Cal, instructing him to inform all commanders that the briefing would be within fifteen minutes. Next, he called flight operations to ensure all birds were fully fueled and armed and that all support munitions and weapons were placed on board with rations and night glasses for personnel. He emphasized that all personnel were to be equipped with helmet radios and spare batteries for each unit, crossbows with explosive-tipped bolts, and bows with explosive arrows for the special operations personnel. They were going to go in silently, even if they came out loud. They would make their presence known and maybe keep them at home.

Tork completed his call and was about to address his men when they were interrupted by two men entering the meeting. Tork called the group to attention when Colonel Thomas and his other interpreter came in the room.

"Gentlemen," Tork addressed his group of officers and introduced Colonel Thomas and his companion, Mr. Arliss Dumas, foreign language expert from Vanderbilt University. Mr. Dumas was fluent in seven languages.

Colonel Thomas then spoke, "Gentlemen, it is a great privilege for me to be assigned to accompany you on this mission. I want all of you to understand I'm going only as a foreign language interpreter. Along with Arliss, we'll interrogate all personnel you pick up. Remember, the most important aspects of this mission are for intelligence gathering. Lieutenant Colonel Albertson and his officers are in complete command of this operation. I want to emphasize the importance of getting much needed information for the final showdown in this terrible war. Freedom is earned, and we are going to ensure this type of world dominance by any nation or group of nations will not happen again. Perhaps someday when we have secured our borders from all interlopers, we will move to support other nations in slipping the knot of oppression from around their necks as well."

The colonel turned to Arliss and asked if he wished to address the men. Arliss answered with a shake of his head.

Tork stood and addressed the officers in his command. "Gentlemen, your target locations have been given to you. Your troops have been alerted and at this time are presently waiting to board their ships and get underway. Therefore, man your ships and lift off. I'll see you in the field and God bless."

"Captain Varner, please escort Colonel Thomas and Mr. Dumas to the operations area for night clothing and equipment. Issue weapons to the colonel and night vision equipment for Mr. Dumas."

"Yes, sir," replied Cal as he walked off, motioning the two men to follow.

Colonel Thomas spoke up, "Colonel Albertson, Arliss is a reserve officer in the marine corps. General Duncan has requested authorization from the council to activate him to duty. Would you please provide him with the weapons of his choice?"

Tork nodded, turned, and left the room. On his way to finalize the mission before meeting with the others and boarding his chopper, he stopped at General Duncan's office. Tork went directly to the general's secretary. "I need to speak to the general before the mission starts. It's important."

The secretary keyed the intercom button and spoke, "Sir, it's Colonel Albertson to see you. Said it was important."

"Send him right in," was the reply.

Tork entered the office, saluted, and spoke quickly. The general nodded, picked up a pile of paper, and sorting through it handed several stapled together to Tork.

Tork looked it over, smiled, and saluted the general. Without a word, he left the office. Folding the information up, he put it in his top pocket and headed to the assembly point to board his ship. Upon arrival, he called over one of the senior NCOs. "Seen Mr. Dumas or Colonel Thomas?" he asked. "Yes, sir, I have. They just entered your ship, sir."

Tork walked over to the ship and called out to Arliss. "Mr. Dumas, if you would, sir. Please come with me. Tork turned and started to the operations building with Arliss right behind him. Both entered the building and Tork turned and handed him the papers he had taken from his pocket.

Arliss took the papers, opened them, and read. A slight grimace appeared on his face that turned to a smile. He looked at Tork and said, "Where in the world will I find marine corps insignia and gear here, sir?"

Tork smiled. "Come with me, Major. We'll find you something before we leave."

A short time later, after Tork had taken him to the supply building, they entered the ship and Tork instructed the pilot to prepare for takeoff. He plugged in his head mic and spoke, "Gentlemen, start your engines. Take off as instructed and contact me upon arrival at your destinations."

CHAPTER 30

Southern Exposure

UN Headquarters
Brussels, Belgium

The UN commander had entered his Mercedes sedan when his cell phone rang. The commander of the UN troops in Mexico, Gen. Ronaldo Cortez, answered it. "What is it?" he asked in an agitated voice.

"Sir, we just received a satellite transmission from the Mexican commander at Saltillo. He reports the rebel forces have dug in just north of Monterrey. Their troops are in place from Brownsville, across Bermejillo, and from there they have a defensive line north to Chihuahua and then west to Hermosillo. They have taken all the airfields within these areas, and intelligence reports they've moved Jump Jets to those fields for tactical hits against us.

"They claim the larger fields have support aircraft and fighters in place. We know there are heavy bomber groups in Texas, New Mexico, and Southern California. Our troops expect to make contact sometime tomorrow, if not before. They have asked what they can do to stop the gringos and push them back across the border. He says he has thirty thousand troops at his command between Monterrey and Esperanza and he has control of all airfields between the Gulf of Mexico and the Gulf of California. He says, sir, that he feels very confident that he can move against the American rebel forces without waiting for our troops to arrive. What's your order, sir?"

"Tell him our troops are moving cautiously. We are only hours away from his troops in the east and a day at most from his central positions. We have troops landing at Ciudad Madero now. Once they're ready, they'll be three hundred kilometers from his positions at Saltillo. Tell him to wait for us to reinforce him, and thank him for his support and we look forward to meeting the enemy with him at our side."

"Yes, sir. Will do."

The general smiled and said, "Well, it looks like we may be able to surprise the rebels for a change, and when we do, I want no prisoners. Pass the word to all field commanders and to the Mexican army commanders. No prisoners."

*****

Tork's ships were sitting down in their assigned areas when a coded message came through. It was from one of the special operations units that had been operating in Mexico. This unit had supported Tork before, and he was well aware of their capabilities and he trusted them. Major Whitehead had taken down the information and had it decoded. It was hot information and he called Tork as his ship was about to touch down.

"Sir, Major Whitehead here."

"Go ahead, Major. What is it?"

"Sir, we just received hard information on impending activity. It's most important you contact me upon touchdown. I'll be in the north end of our bivouac area waiting for you."

Tork knew something was up; most important he said. He looked down, and to the north, he could see a number of helicopters being moved to safe areas and some being covered with netting to conceal them. "Tony, don't sit down in our designated area. Look up to your right, north. No, northeast, near those other choppers, can you set it down in there?"

The pilot looked closely. "Looks like a tight spot, Colonel, but I think I can make it." As an afterthought, he said, "Want me to try, sir? It's your chopper."

"Don't need any levity, Tony. Park it."

The ship moved in and dropped safely between two others, tight fit but with room to spare. Tork exited his ship and moved up toward the others sitting in the north field.

"Hey, Soldier. Where's Major Whitehead's groups?"

"Straight ahead, sir," came the reply.

Ducking under the tail section of a ship, Tork looked up and saw Major Whitehead coming toward him. "What have you got for us, Major?"

Major Whitehead was alarmed at the intelligence report he held and the look on his face had alerted Tork to the importance of the major's report.

"What have you got?" Tork repeated.

"We have heavy troop movement coming up from the Gulf of California and others are coming up from Durango, moving toward Torreon. Looks like it may be a full division with heavy artillery and tanks. They'll try to intercept us, sir."

"Get that information over to crypto ASAP and call in all commanders for a briefing. I'll be over at my ship. Oh yes, find Colonel Thomas and Major Dumas and have them meet me there."

Tork went directly to his ship and pulled out the latest satellite photos of the area and the maps he had that could detail not only the roads but also the terrain. He had to know where they were heading and what he was getting into. He had to determine when, where, and if it would be advantageous for the United Nations to put their surveillance posts and where they might be now. Most of all, why, he wondered, were they moving in this direction?

After studying the area maps and the information they had received, Tork could now ascertain the what, when, where, and why the enemy was moving and with such great strength and what he had to do to stop them.

The commanders and their top NCOs were assembled and ready when Tork addressed them. "Men, it appears that the UN forces are moving to engage our troops at Monterrey up to Brownsville in the northeast and at Chihuahua. If I were their commander, I would start an offensive by moving north on Highway 18 at Chihuahua toward the Texas border, and at the same time I would engage our troops at Chihuahua and at Hermosillo. I would go after the airfields and invade them to help our aircraft land. It appears that the Mexican armies have at least a battalion, maybe even a division available to support the advancing UN forces. What we need now is hard intel from the enemy. Therefore, I want prisoners brought in from each of the advancing groups. Let's get in our EU uniforms with French and German insignia and meet our enemy on the move. We'll also need several Mexican American troops to move into the areas occupied by the Mexican army. Use seasoned men that may have families in the areas that can help them. If the enemy thinks they are loyal Mexicans that want these foreign troops out, we should be able to infiltrate their ranks. We need to pick out officers and high-ranking NCOs as our targets. Don't get into any firefights. We do not want them to know what we are up to. Remember, desertion rates are high among the UN troops. Hopefully, they will think any personnel missing are deserters. Any questions men?"

With no questions asked, Tork dismissed the groups and waited for the teams to return with, hopefully, the prisoners and the information needed. Time was running out.

General Duncan needed the information quickly so they could move additional troops into strategic positions so an offensive could be initiated to stop the movement. It was imperative the UN forces throughout Mexico were stopped from entering the United States from the south. They all knew the minute the UN troops crossed the Mexican-US border, the UN troops garrisoned in the northern United States would move farther south, hoping to drive a wedge through the country, dividing it in two so they could drive both east and west, separating the country into quarters and thus causing the rebel government to capitulate. If that were to happen, they would divide the country among the victors and many flags would fly over the United States. What was left of the constitution would be banned and most probably burned. Not since the liberals tried to destroy it in the late 1990s and early 2000s has the constitution been in danger. It started with the fall of the towers. The country went into an antiterrorist war footing, and several countries were invaded. Islam rose up and declared war on the West, and the Christian countries rose to meet the challenge. Peace was the vital goal of the Allies; world peace was America's paramount goal to live and let live with peace and prosperity for all mankind. As the final phases of the Great War started to cultivate, the United Nations decided that global peace on their terms must prevail. All political parties in power within the United Nations decided the United Nations should be the one and only controlling government over the earth—only then could there be peace. After several years of war, the liberals returned to power in the United States and accepted the UN mandate. Through their control, the Congress was able to open the doors of the country. UN troops moved in and confiscated all privately owned weapons, putting the United States of America solidly within the United Nations and destroying the amendments to the constitution.

The full restoration of the constitution and the removal of all UN troops and the United Nations itself were mandatory.

The rebel government would tolerate no options when it won its freedom. The perverted enemy would be removed and the global economy forced on the country would be stopped. American-owned corporations that refused to reinvest in new factories within the United States would be confiscated and reopened as American corporations with all American assets. The country would rebuild and would support, protect, and develop other countries that were willing to help themselves. They would ban Europe from doing business with the United States, and any country supporting them would be banned as well. Only those countries that removed themselves from the union would be protected.

The time was at hand. They had moved all troops to their primary positions. The forces were ready to move against the rebels, but unknown to them, the rebels were ready to fight.

The aircraft carriers in rebel control had been moved to their launch positions. Submarines were in the Atlantic and Pacific ready to move in on their prey. Nuclear subs in position around China were ready to launch at both UN ships in the area or the Chinese if the Red Chinese decided to enter the war with the United Nations.

The rebels were to support them if they chose to enter the war against the United Nations. Intel from China had shown the Chinese were ready to enter the conflict, but on whose side would they help? It was indicated through Chinese sources they may go with the United Nations so they would be in a position to start a heavy assault on Europe if the US rebels were defeated. Intel also revealed a plan the Chinese might use to move against the United Nations when all nations were fighting the rebels in the United States and their troops were scattered throughout North and South America. The rebel command had no choice other than be vigilant and ready for either of the plans to happen.

To be on the safe side, rebel submarines were ready to take out one or both of the two factions. It made no difference then, either the United Nations or China or both. The protectors of the people and the constitution were ready.

*****

US revolutionary government had joined in a meeting at a well-concealed new base. The military had set up presentations from each leading group to inform them of their plans the what, when, where, and why of the services. Their objectives and their initial battle plans were ready for presentation to the new Congress.

The briefings went well. All members of the House and the Senate were in agreement. The armed forces had been very detailed on both military and political events. The intel from the field had been very helpful. The information from Mexico had been a real eye-opener, and all had agreed that the initial strike should be there. The UN forces waiting to enter the United States from Mexico would have to be neutralized and held.

Mexico would be the first to feel the eradication of UN forces. The US rebels would give the Mexican people a second independence day to celebrate. Once again, foreign troops would be pushed out of its cities and sent home. Once again, French soldiers would be buried in Mexican soil. It was felt the Mexican people would join in earnest when the fighting started. Old memories could be rekindled.

All was set. Rebel troops had moved into vital spots. Sabotage and general harassment would start soon. The enemy would be pulling troops off line to protect their rear areas. Once they established confusion, the offensive to free America would begin. They planned that any foreign ships or convoys moving toward the United States or any South American country would be either stopped and sunk on the high seas or bombed while in port. They would not allow troops and equipment to arrive. It was time.

Tork and his command had all the information needed to stop the French and German troops before they reached the US border. The rebel high command had targeted regular Mexican army troops allied with them. US rebel forces of Mexican descent had been moved into critical areas to confuse and disrupt the Mexican army. As the Mexican army starts to mobilize, their radio frequencies would be broken into. Messages would be sent to them in their codes moving them into areas where they would be trapped and where American rebel troops would be waiting for them.

Twenty-Four Blackhawk VII assault helicopter troopships were waiting west of the Mexican-Pacific shoreline to bring in mountain troops and Special Forces when needed. These ships had been modified with special armor and were from Nevada, some thought from Area 51 or another secret area unknown to the people.

Additional Apache and Comanche helicopters were standing by, fully armed and ready to attack. The Comanches would be sent in first. With their stealth capabilities, they could hit quick and hard. They would be followed by the Apaches, and then the Blackhawks would be delivering the troops. Once they deployed, a corridor would open to allow the infantry to move south and cut the enemy off.

A push both east and west would then begin. Tactical fighter-bombers would be employed to cut off reinforcements and supplies from the United Nations' rear supply areas.

To meet the demands of the war, it was necessary for the rebel army to improve existing equipment. Many of the aircraft had been modified to meet these demands.

The specially equipped Blackhawk VII had been modified with new armor and specially equipped engines. The newly designed fuselage and rotor blades had made them the quietest helicopters in the world—so quiet the men called them the whisper's whisper. The Apache and Comanche helicopters had additional armor. Specially designed light cruise missiles were installed that allowed a prestrike to take place just prior to their arrival. It allowed for an all clear to be declared just prior to the gunship attack to catch the enemy completely by surprise. Hundreds of drones were going to be used.

Lieutenant Colonel Albertson looked up as an orderly entered his enclosure. "Sir, we have just received intel from our forward positions. Colonel Thomas sent me right over. Said to tell you it is hot."

Tork grabbed his radio and called his adjutant. "Have all commanders and senior NCOs report to the assembly area and wait for me there. This is an alert call."

On his way to the communication center, Tork's mind was reeling with assembly plans and target areas that may come up. The thought of their overall battle plan for each target area was racing through his mind. He entered the communication tent and saluted.

Colonel Thomas nodded to Major Dumas and said, "What do we have? Give us the what and when and our alert status."

Major Dumas grabbed Tork by the arm and said, "Over here, sir. I have it all mapped out."

Tork looked at the map that had been marked and could see the UN troops were moving in the direction they had calculated. It was time for the strike.

"Gentlemen, the time has come," Tork said. "Pass the word onto General Duncan. The enemy has been sighted and freedom will be earned for the Mexican people and ourselves. Operation Freedom Earned Mexico will commence at 0300 hours. Get your confirmation from command that the bomber targets are as anticipated and bombing should commence at 0001 hours.

"Saturate the depot and ammo dumps until 0230 hours. Inform them that we will be airborne at 0230 hours and will arrive behind enemy lines as planned. If all goes well, our forces should start their artillery barrages at 0230 hours. This should bring all UN troops to full alert as they move forward after the barrages stop. We will attack from the rear with our gunships.

"As the enemy turns to fight us the Special Forces, Blackhawks will hit both their flanks. This should force them to defend their flanks and their rear. We will then open our corridor and continue to defend the front of our attack. Hopefully this will allow us to move our French choppers into the center of activity. The French troops will believe they have reinforcement, and it will give us the chance to land and move on their command center. If we capture the center, we can stop them and end the fighting in this sector. If we pull this off, it will delay the United Nations' thrust from the north.

Oh yes, Major, make sure the Harriers from the fleet are ready to support us if we need them. We may have to burn them out if they refuse to surrender. They think we're a weak and undermanned group with no teeth. Intel has it they are of the opinion we have to use crossbows because we don't have the arms to resist. It's time, gentlemen. We start our attack precisely at 0230 hours."

CHAPTER 31

A New Century, a New Beginning

Oakland, California

Diana had taken over Cal's position when they reassigned and commissioned him in the army. It had been hard work and perilous coordinating intelligence and forwarding it onto the rebel high command.
They had dealt the UN forces a devastating blow from the underground, hitting them hard with hit-and-run tactics from Sacramento
all the way up to Reno. The UN troops had moved across Nevada
and were in the process of getting ready to go into Utah. They had
relocated the naval facilities at Fallon back into the southern desert area and had camouflaged it against prying eyes. The Nevada
National Guard had joined forces with the Utah National Guard and
had received reinforcements from rebel forces, federal army, and air
force units loyal to the rebel government. Along with them several
thousand UN deserters had been equipped and rearmed to fight with
them and for freedom. They all expected help in freeing their country after they defeated the United Nations here in the United States.

Diana was ordered to move their group south and interdiction
was imminent as the rebel troops were preparing to enter Northern
California from Monterey across to Fresno and east to Bishop.
Diana's cells were following, supporting, and servicing the enemy
troops. Each of her men and women were there collecting intelligence. The smell of the diesel engines was strong, and the heavy
tracks of the tanks were shaking the buildings, scaring the children,

and instilling hatred and vengeance in each of them. The UN troops had been moving into these positions, and when the offensive started in Mexico, the Southern California rebel troops would move north. Bombers from George and Edwards Air Force bases would hit Travis Air Force Base and radar facilities as well as missile sites in and around all strategic cities in the area. The San Francisco International Airport runways would be closed down with heavy bombing. Oakland airports would also have its runways closed. Heavy bombardments would hit them both at the same time. Although sabotage in the San Francisco and Oakland docks had been successful, more hits would come. Submarines in the Pacific would lay on the bottom for the first attacks to start. Then they would fire missiles at all UN bases in the San Francisco-Oakland Bay area. Depots would be first targets. Rebel forces and the underground knew collateral damage was inevitable, and many of their friends and relatives would be killed or wounded. The United Nations will repair them and they would include them too in the first-strike engagements, destroying all shipping in the bay. The underground had identified and targeted missile defenses around the bay area. All UN AWACS were to be destroyed on the ground at 0230 hours to ensure they could not scramble them to pinpoint rebel submarines. All aircraft in or near operating rebel ships were to be targeted and destroyed by missiles. No rebel aircraft would be airborne in these areas until after the navy completed its first strike to ensure their own ships would not inadvertently target one of them.

The United Nation's attempt to consolidate its forces had failed. Diana and her underground cells had done a marvelous job. It was time their knowledge should be used directly. Sister cells were to remain underground and inactive until called upon later. They were to be the ace up the sleeve when the time came. Although the United Nations had put an army on the north-south border, they had pulled a third of it to strengthen the troops they had committed for the invasion of Nevada. They'd experienced great losses from underground attacks on their train and convoy movements to the Nevada line. Though there was little resistance in Reno, Carson City, and Fallon, the United Nations had been hit hard in the mountains west of Tahoe. The United Nations felt they were being pulled west when they should have focused on the important move east. They left small governing garrisons in Reno, Carson City, and Fallon. Then the United Nations regrouped east of Reno for the big push toward Utah. The base at Fallon had been pretty well destroyed by the rebels when they moved everything into the desert and up into the mountain areas. The rebel forces had taken over a number of remote mines southeast of Fallon and were using them to store war supplies and troops. The marines had moved Harrier aircraft into remote areas that were concealed from prying satellite eyes. Hit-and-run skirmishes within the area were a nightly harassment activity by rebel night raiders. Their primary targets were the UN troop encampments west of Lovelock.

The enemy had started moving troops and equipment into Winnemucca and Battle Mountain to establish depots for their big push. The same type of tactics that proved so well in Mexico and South America was working even better against the UN troops in the north. The rebel forces were growing stronger and stronger as more and more federal troops deserted and members of the UN forces chose to fight against their own countries for freedom. It was rumored that a battalion of Canadian troops had deserted in Idaho and had moved south and had joined up with Utah forces. This seemed to be catching on with many that wanted to see freedom in their own lands once more.

Revolutionary Headquarters
New Mexico

The congressional and senate leadership had joined with the Rebel Armed Forces Joint Chiefs of Staff. General Duncan had given them the present status of events, and they knew the time had come to push the enemy back across the Canadian border and out to sea. General Duncan was now addressing the Armed Forces Senatorial Committee. "The South American forces were hit so badly they would not be able to intervene for several months because new equipment they received from the United Nations was lost to the attacks by rebel Special Forces. The people were outraged that our troops could move in silently, kill their sons, and destroy equipment in such a short amount of time. In major South American countries, the enemy saw us destroying and killing as we went. The military in those countries wanted blood, revenge. But their governments were in disarray and were holding the military at bay. This was going to give our forces the time we needed to vanquish the invaders. The United Nations had underestimated the American people in every city, in every state, that had not fallen to the United Nations. They had sent out their sons and daughters to fight. Saving the country and the constitution was paramount to each of them."

The words were on everyone's minds, in whispers in the occupied cities and states, and on the lips of those in rebel-held cities and states. You could hear them all, "Freedom earned," and they all knew what it meant. They knew that all must fight for the constitution, its principles, and its guaranteed rights. They learned the hard way. By giving in and surrendering a right, you give up a freedom. By allowing the removal of a right, you encourage further deceit and control. They now knew that you cannot have peace if you surrender those freedom. No, if the people had only said no. They could not allow any of the constitutional amendments to be changed or eliminated for the sake of peace. They took away their rights by telling them it was for their safety. They woke up one day looking at chips controlling their lives, their freedoms all gone, controlled by a foreign government with foreign troops invading their homes and taking their weapons. The United Nations sent people from countries that were still living in the Stone Age and told them how to live as they plundered the country and held people captive. They forced the people to work for them. The country was ready to fight and the fight was about to begin. The new American leadership knew what course had to be taken. A new Congress, fresh and alive, was in control.

All of them, each party, had made it clear. The nation, the people, all must be their goal. If feelings were hurt, so be it. It was time that political correctness was dismissed; adversity should make you stronger, not weaker. This nation had become weak to themselves and unresponsive to all others. The nation had fallen to believers in the new world order, and it had almost destroyed her. It was time to rebuild.

The committee chairman cleared his throat, and then thanking General Duncan, his gavel hit the desk. All looked to the chairman. "Gentlemen, the time has come. We will implement four major offensives simultaneously. First will be in Mexico. UN troops have massed troops across the northern top of Mexico were they believe we are weak and will be unable to meet their thrust. They are wrong. Second we are ready to move into Northern California and push through to the Washington-Canadian border and on when the time is right. Third, our troops are ready to move north, east, and west from Utah, Colorado, and Kansas. Fourth, we will converge on Illinois and retake Chicago. Our nation is now firmly behind the new government. The country now knows that our precious freedom is earned and not to be taken for granted. If they want to keep them, then fight they must."

General McKenny, chief of planning for the Rebel Armed Forces Joint Chiefs of Staff, stood up and addressed them. "Gentlemen, I have the charts available for you in the adjoining room. We have drawn our battle lines and show you where the UN troops are located, where our lines are, and how we plan to move against them. In each instance, we will illustrate how we are going to back door each element we are engaged in. You will see how we plan to use ground, air, and naval forces to bring us victory. All that you see here is classified and no notes or pictures or recordings can be made.

"To ensure complete secrecy, we will move you through scanners and any devices you have on will be taken, but they will be returned after the briefing is over. Are there any objections? No? Fine then. Let's go in. Remember, the officer at the door will take anything you have on and will keep it safe for you. Gentlemen, if you please."

With a wave of his hand, the large double doors to the right of them opened up, and the committee members went through. They willingly gave up their briefcases, laptops, electronic notepads, cell phones, and other devices.

The session lasted almost an hour and a half. All of them were amazed at the United Nations' advances into the country since they started their invasion and the mighty force the American people had built to repel them, all well located and built up to the largest American force since World War II. On one chart was the nuclear capability of the American forces.

"We are well armed and can use any number of them if necessary," explained the general. "But we will not unless the enemy uses them first. We will not be first response nuclear adversaries. As you can see, gentlemen, we are ready. We begin at 0230 hours tomorrow."

Many thoughts went through their minds as they left the meeting. Most of them found themselves going into the chapel. It was time for all to call on God for deliverance, strength, and victory.

Each committee member left the meeting knowing the outcome of each mission they would send these men and women into battle, the terror and killing they would commit to regain a great nation. Each would look into their own soul and feel the pain of sending these warriors into harm's way. Some of them knew the exploits of men like Tork and Cal and the women of the underground cells like Diana and others fighting secretly against bitter odds, knowing what they would face if caught.

The Battle Begins

Tork's troops were waiting in their ships and all were ready to fight. The hour was at hand. At 0220 hours, all engines were started and the ship's guns were checked. The troops reinspected their weapons for the tenth time. They could hardly hear the engines running; they were so silent on these birds. Each man in turn checked his helmet radio. Night glasses were adjusted. NCOs checked each of his men for their Kevlar vests. All of them were in full camouflage, their faces painted. Those with bows and crossbows checked their shafts, one calling off the list and each replying.

"Clean kill."

"Okay."

"Incendiary tip."

"Okay."

"High explosive."

"Okay."

Each was ready.

They knew they would be the ones to go first. It was up to them to take out the sentries and to silently hit the company munitions dumps. One high explosive shaft in the right place could cause extensive damage and set off ammo and fuel dumps. One in an open tank engine hatch would destroy the tank. An incendiary hitting a fuel drum could destroy a fuel dump. Let the enemy believe they were using outdated weapons because they were desperate. Little did the United Nations know of the weapon factories in use in rebel-held states and cities.

The silence of the running engines surprised the men; they were far quieter than the older ships they flew, and they all felt safer knowing their chances of arrival were better than they had ever been. Everyone knew what they had to do; all were veterans of the past. Mexico, Argentina, Brazil, Colombia, and Nicaragua—all had been part of the biggest raids in South America during the war. Now they'd be hitting one of the main French armies that had been sent by the United Nations to destroy them. Not since they captured the French field marshal had they been prepared for them. They would once again use French helicopters and uniforms and, yes, even their own language. Already a complete Mexican American unit was in the air to hit the supporting Mexican forces supporting the French. They would engage the enemy and then try to convince them they were fighting to lose their own freedoms to the United Nations. If they could not convince them to surrender or join forces with them, then they would fight to defeat them. The choice would be up to the Mexican commanders.

Tork looked out at the black shadows moving through the darkness—twenty-four silent ships. He felt hopeful this was the beginning of the end; the beginning of the resurrection of the constitution was in sight. The ships had swung out to sea and had circled well behind French and Mexican areas. The French helicopters that would be moving into the central-controlled French war zone had been moving with the main group. Should any radar contact be made on them, the French-speaking chopper pilots would run interference for the ships, explaining they were reinforcing the French troops in the north. However, at the moment, all was well; the rebels made no contacts. Because of the large amount of UN air traffic from the south to the north, the French and the Mexican forces thought they were routine aircraft supporting their troops.

Upon their arrival, Tork's battalion we're met by Special Forces and air force special operations personnel. The ground work had been well done, the enemy positions were identified, and the elite troops used in the past were sent out to eliminate the French rear guards. Silently and with stealth, they moved through the night. Quietly the guards feel one by one as the black-clothed Special Forces moved in among French sleeping troops, eliminating them as they had done in the South American campaign. Sleeping men had their throats cut.

The attack plan was in motion. Tork knew when the bombardments started and when the commanders would call for their troops. The silent deaths of the French soldiers might create enough panic to cause them to surrender. It was time for the rebel forces to move south on the French and Mexican troops. The flanking movements were about to start. Tork had ordered his men to begin their mortar attacks when word came that both flanks were under attack. This, they expected, would force the French to move troops from the south perimeter to stabilize their flanks, making the French rear positions weaker. When Tork's troops started their mortar attack, the gunships would be in a position to launch their cruise missiles. Next they would move in and start rocket and strafing runs on the French positions. With any luck, they just might figure it's too costly to die in Mexico and hopefully surrender. In any case, that was the plan. Tork knew that plans could go wrong and contingencies would be brought into play. If anything goes not according to plan, full saturation bombing and heavy artillery bombardments must be implemented to pull the heat off them. Tork felt confident the mission would be successful.

Through the night, the battle was hot, heavy, and costly for them all. But they moved on the French forces with devastating success, delivering heavy casualties. The French helicopters used by the American forces had entered the French central area and landed unopposed. They moved their forces into the command post and had taken the entire French command.

The French commanders refused to stand down and the fighting continued. When told of their commander's capture, they tried to rescue them and were beaten back. Tork ordered the French prisoners to be transported back to American lines where they could interrogate the French general and his staff. Tork was hoping the French officers—after seeing the command post deserted and the French high command leaving in French helicopters and moving south—would have second thoughts about continuing the battle. The American forces were moving south farther into Mexico, pushing the French ahead of them. The high command ordered Tork and his troops to move to the east and help mop up what was left of the Mexican forces. The Mexican American rebel forces had driven the Mexican army units back and away from supporting the French, allowing the east flank of the French forces to face the American forces and pushing the French southwest. With the rebel troops moving out with their French high command prisoners, both the east and west flanks were forced together. The American rebel forces coming in from the north forced the remaining French officers to surrender, permitting the American rebel forces to complete the invasion of Mexico from Mazatlan across to Torreon and east to Monterrey, south to Ciudad Victoria, and then to the gulf.

The UN ships that had been in the Mexican ports from Puerto Vallarta to the north on both the mainland and Baja California had been bombed. They had been either sunk or damaged and could not move out of port. Cities were spared from any bombing activity, and only those that had been used as military support had been bombed using surgical bombing techniques with smart bombs to hit their targets. The rebels tried not to hit villages or major cities unless they had firm hard targets. With the main ports under attack or destroyed and rebel American submarines attacking UN ships, the United Nations and the United States of Europe were now looking at disaster. With the capitulation of the UN troops and the capture of the French high command in Mexico, the outcome for the United Nations did not appear good.

With the Mexican army in full retreat, the American rebel government sent a message to the Mexican government and dropped pamphlets with the message to the people. It read,

> To the government of Mexico, you are to cease all hostilities and accept peace with the new US government now, or we will continue until we reach the Guatemalan border. You will accept peace or we will accept nothing less than unconditional surrender. If you do not, we will look upon your refusal as a full state of war.
>
> We are adamant in our quest to free the United States from foreign domination. We have started a massive thrust into our occupied states in the north and expect to realize complete victory. We will not stop until we have cleaned Canada and Mexico of our enemies, and our forces will soon retake Florida. Let it be known that the southern command of the new US Armed Forces have entered Northern California. The Nevada and Utah National Guard with regular army forces have pushed UN forces back into Canada. We have turned to the west and we will retake northern Nevada and California within the next one to two weeks. All support ships from the United Nations have been sunk or have turned around and headed back to their home ports.
>
> You have twenty-four hours to meet our demands or suffer the consequences.
>
> End of message.

The Mexican government received the communiqué with reservations. The president called his Joint Chiefs of Staff and demanded to know where the armed forces stood. Were they in jeopardy of losing? Was the United Nations failing to uphold their pledge to support them? Were the Americans truthful in their demand? Had they taken half of Mexico already? Had the French troops fallen to the American rebel forces? Had the Mexican Armed Forces failed their country? The president wanted answers.

General Quasada laughed at the president and the other members of the government there and said, "Gentlemen, you have nothing to worry about. I have been in touch with the United Nations, and they have assured me all is well with the French troops. Our battle lines are drawn and we have made great progress in our fight with the American forces. It is true. We have had to retreat to Saltillo south of Monterrey, but there we have dug in and are staying put. The Americans are just trying to force you to capitulate. We have heavy transports coming in from the United States of Europe this afternoon, and we expect a large USE convoy to dock at our gulf ports this week. We are prepared to provide air cover when they enter the gulf. Florida is in the hands of the United States of Europe, and we feel there should be no problem getting our war materials from Europe. It is essential that we must fight on. You need to order the conscription of men between the ages of sixteen to fifty to bolster our armed forces. The German army has started moving north and should meet the American forces within forty-eight hours. As you can see, you have no fear. All is well."

General Quasada turned to his aide and ordered him to follow him. They left the building and he ordered his driver to take them to the air base outside Mexico City.

Upon arrival, he went directly to the air force base commander and ordered a transport be made available for a secret meeting with the UN German commander in Southern Mexico. He then made calls to the chief of naval operations and the air force commander and had them bring their families to the air base. He then in turn sent plainclothes army personnel to his home in Mexico City to get his wife and children. Upon their arrival, he and the other officers with their families boarded a military Avro Regional Jet aircraft and ordered the pilots to take off. As the plane lifted off the ground, he ordered the pilot to fly south. It wasn't until they approached the Guatemalan border that General Quasada ordered the plane to change course to the east and then south along the South American shoreline toward Argentina where he felt they would given political asylum. The general knew all was lost, as did the others. He also knew if they had stayed, they would have been arrested and probably executed because they lost the war with the American rebels. It would have been hard to explain to the president and his cabinet that American and Mexican American troops had defeated them. The plan to retake the western states by infiltrating the illegal aliens before the merger of America and Mexico was a complete failure. They failed to see the illegals had accepted the United States and their customs as their own. *Maybe one day*, he thought. Yes, maybe one day they could all go home again, after the war was over and all had been forgotten.

San Francisco-Oakland Bay Area

Carol had stayed behind. While still working for the newspaper, she was able to contact the rebel forces using codes in her column. She sent the movement of troops, equipment, and aircraft in a daily newspaper to all the cells and to the rebel high command. The information was incalculable in helping to win the war. Not since she left the new world order had she been able to do so much for her country. The word had finally come. The fight for the United States was about to begin. She quickly formed the message required to start the final attack on the United Nations. Each cell had their targets and all were ready. Throughout Northern California and up in Oregon and Washington, the war would begin in earnest at 0230 hours Zulu (GMT, military and aviation time). Freedom would be earned and America set free again.

Next, Carol thought, *we need to free Europe and the rest of the countries the United Nations forced to join the new world order and then there could be global peace.* "Let's face it," she said. "Global economics has failed. The main benefactors were big business, manufactures, and the Chinese. Most other countries ended up as service countries dependent on the new world order." Looking around the office to see if anyone had overheard her, she thought, *Great, now I'm talking to myself out loud. Damn it. I need to watch it. Be more careful.*

At 0200 hours Zulu, Diana met with Carol and the cell leaders in the bay area. Targets were confirmed and all was ready. Explosives had been hidden several months ago in preparations for the coming offensive. Men and women were waiting for the hour to set off the start of a new era. At precisely 0230 hours Zulu, the offensive would begin throughout North America. Di knew that Tork would enter combat at the same time and all of America would set out to regain their freedom. He was only minutes away now. They waited.

Tick, tick, tick.

CHAPTER 32

The Beginning of the End

Command Headquarters
American Revolutionary Forces
New Mexico

General Duncan entered the conference room and quickly sat at the table to the right of Gen. Charles Ledgeman, ground forces commander.

General Ledgeman spoke. "Gentlemen, now that General Duncan has arrived, we can start. General Duncan, where do we stand now that the United Nations has started its major offensive? Please, if you will, all information is critical at this time."

General Duncan stood before the group. "Gentlemen, we have encountered heavy fighting in most of the UN occupied areas. First let me inform you of our advances. As of this morning, we have pushed the UN forces back from the western Utah border region to within forty to fifty miles east of Elko and within thirty miles of Austin, Nevada. We have moved marine Harriers up and additional troops are arriving to move both west and north. We expect to retake all areas in Nevada, Oregon, Idaho, and Montana within the next two weeks.

"At this moment, our troops should be moving into Bishop, California. To meet our advances, the enemy has sent troops from the Southern California engagement northeast to meet our advancing troops. We have employed heavy bombing of their supply dumps

and have destroyed all rail lines entering these areas. It's now necessary for them to move everything by truck or aircraft. Heavy bombing of military bases in these areas has disabled them. We have taken
control of the skies and have naval units in the Pacific region from
Acapulco, Mexico, to Seattle, Washington. These units include heavy
cruisers, missile platforms, destroyers, and aircraft carriers. We have
initiated a push north from Des Moines, Iowa, across to Akron,
Ohio, and have three divisions there moving north. Our goal is to
take Minnesota, Wisconsin, and Michigan."

General Duncan paused for a moment and sipped a glass of
water while observing those around him. They all knew the importance of this meeting. The general set the glass down, cleared his
throat, and continued, "Once we have taken Chicago and Benton
Harbor, we will start putting fast gunboats on the lake to harass all
foreign shipping and UN warships in the Great Lakes region. Before
our attack on these areas, we will use precise surgical bombing to
reduce collateral damage. Our intelligence tells us that the United
Nations will move their ships out of the docks at the first sign of
hostilities. Therefore, we have set up a watch group that will inform
us of their activities, giving us the ability to attack them when they
are underway.

"We still have control of Wyoming and all of our missile bases,
though our enemy has tried to force us out with great losses. The
troops we have moved into these locations have been instrumental in
keeping them in check. However, we have intelligence reports indi-
cating the United Nations has moved massive troops into position
and an attack is imminent.

"I have ordered eight air cavalry units into the area. They will be
using our newest gunships and cruise missiles to engage the enemy.
We have tactical aircraft ready to hit all their staging areas and airfields. If our information from the Canadian underground is correct,
we should hit them with a low-level attack just before they take off.
If we are successful, we can destroy their aircraft on the ground. The
underground will hit the radar and ground-to-air missile sites just
before our arrival. We have army and air force special ops units in
place, posing as Canadian citizens. They and the underground will

be our front-runners in this operation. Pray all is well, gentlemen, or we could lose our Wyoming missile sites.

"Our reserves in all locations are equipped and ready. We now have under arms more troops than we feel is needed. Federal troops and commanders are deserting in mass, and we have sent many of them to front-line positions. The country as a whole is again united. Not since the defeat of the Muslim radicals and rogue Islamic nations have we seen such a swing to a united country. The day of our victory will be a true dedication and tribute to Freedom Earned. The people will remember in the annals of history not only December 7, 1941, or September 11, 2001, but also the date of America's great victory over world domination. That day is about to happen."

General Ledgeman raised his palm forward and stretched out before him and quietly said, "What of our naval efforts? Where do we stand there? What of our Poseidon platforms? Where are they and what can we expect from them?"

Adm. Felix Metcalfe stood. "Gentlemen, I cannot tell you for security reasons exactly where they are or the number that is on station. However, I can tell you we are in position to protect and supply our forces from Mexico to Canada, and we can and will counter any Chinese or UN movements that could interfere in our struggle. In addition, we have placed them in positions that will inflict nuclear devastation on both the Chinese and European cities if they confront us with weapons of mass destruction. Rest assured, we as a nation will not be a first-strike aggressor. However, we will strike all major industrial centers in any country that—Let me make this clear! Any nation using nuclear or any weapons of mass destruction on us will be hit in kind. In addition, we will retaliate on any aggressor of an ally, though right now we seem to stand alone, except for, I might add, those men and women that have crossed over and joined us to fight for freedom. Theirs and ours will have our full support when this struggle has ended. We will endeavor to free their oppressed countries as well."

The meeting went on into the early hours of the morning. Planning was thorough and proficient. All members of the group were well pleased when they had finished. Plans were changed and others were formed to ensure a new and greater America would surface and the constitution would once again serve Americans as she had in the past. Safeguards would be in place to preserve the republic as intended, not how it had been changed to meet the desire and needs of a socialist group of politicians. The men and women of America, the members of Congress, the generals, the admirals, and the men and women who brought forth this new American revolution slept that night. Nevertheless, the men and women in uniform were ever vigilant.

The time was soon. The effort was real, and the bullets were waiting. The bombers were loaded. The ships were out to sea. The marines were ready and the beaches waited for them. As Europe slept, content in their belief they would soon control all of North America and then the entire world, America's strength grew stronger. A sleeping *eagle* was about to be wakened as a *titan* in the name of freedom.

*****

Tork's regiment had been moved into a holding area just south of the Wyoming and Montana border. The United Nations had built up forces in Montana and North and South Dakota and had brought in Harrier aircraft to hit rebel troop areas. The American forces had been building up for months in areas well selected and hidden. They were all fighting on their own turf now. They all knew the mountains and the prairies and how to fight in them.

The elite mountain divisions were in place and ready to move. The latest equipment was provided and all were ready to help in the liberation of the country and in restoring the constitution.

Tork had been equipped with the latest weapons. He would for the first time be commanding and piloting one of the newest gunships in the world. Targets were selected and the equipment was treated with the utmost care. Most of all, the crews were diligent, compromising, and faithful to those who would soon see combat.

The goal was to push the United Nations back across the border and force them to regroup so the bombers could destroy their will to fight. Everyone hoped they would see mass desertions as they had already. Many deserters had been reequipped and integrated into American battalions, and they would be fighting troops from their homelands. The rebel leaders hoped they could influence the opposing forces to lay down their arms and join with them. They all knew that after winning this war, the one at home would have to be won too.

Tork had influenced his commanders to strike at 0345 hours. Their strike would commence with a copter-launched cruise missile attack, followed up with the gunships hitting the targets soon after. Concentration would be on mopping up after the cruise missiles hit their targets. The underground would destroy radar and missile sites that were missed. The underground and air force special ops personnel would victor them in on their targets to ensure success. They would hit ground troop concentrations when the gunships and Harriers cleared the area. B-2 and B-52s and other bombers would hit them within minutes of the rebel aircraft departures. Everyone was ready; planes and ground troops were in the red waiting for the green to go.

All ships were in the air and well on their way toward their targets at 0300 hours.

Lt. Col. Marion "Tork" Albertson was directing his forces. All knew their targets and were eager to hit them.

At precisely 0345 hours, Tork's gunner had just finished entering his final targeting data on his two cruise missiles. He paused for a moment and then whispered into his mic, "Boss, freedom earned." He then pressed the firing button and the ship rose as the two missiles dropped below them, their short stubby flight wings extending, engines firing, and guidance systems directing them to their targets. At the same precise second, all missiles on the other craft were fired and heading to meet the United Nations head-on. America would be free or broken up and occupied by the world. The latter was not acceptable to Americans. They would defeat the enemy, and the traitors would be found and dealt with.

Each bird was on course. By the time they arrived, the cleanup would begin. First they would hit the missed missile sites, and second any birds trying to get airborne would be destroyed. Third, strafing all compounds would commence and building or gun emplacements targeted and destroyed. They would intercept any aircraft in the air with air-to-air missiles. In addition to the standard missile load of eighteen missiles, special stealth pods had been fitted to the sides of the ships. After the pods where emptied, they would eject them. The standard weapon carriages would be used as needed for any tank encounters or other targets the pilot may want to hit. With the lighter material and upgrades made to the ships, they could increase their endurance factors to three hours and thirty minutes.

As Tork started his run, the adrenalin was pumping and his eyes were focused on his helmet displays. As he maneuvered his ship in line to the target, the gunner was firing and hitting. His target area was a blaze and all hell was breaking loose. Below them, men were dying for a lost cause. Only a few sites were missed and later hit by the underground. The special ops guys were mopping up any loose cannons on the ground. The Blackhawks arrived and the move north was well on its way. As Tork moved around and lined up on a target, he received a loud, "Colonel, incoming three o'clock!"

Tork instantly increased power and pulled the ship back and, starting to climb, went into a loop as the ground-to-air missile flew by him. As he came around, he couldn't believe what he had just done. He brought the machine around and locked onto the position the missile was fired from. The gunner cut loose with two missiles and opened fire with his 20 mm Gait cannon. The secondary explosions confirmed they hit a hard position. As they started another pass, they received word from the bombers. It was time to leave. Tork ordered all his ships to move to their rear area assembly points where they could assess the damage and debrief the pilots and crews.

Tork and his squadron commanders had just finished their debriefings when word came in that the special operations teams confirmed the damage they had inflicted on the enemy. It was better than they had hoped. They had broken the buildup and forced the UN commanders to establish a tactical move north. They had the United Nations retreating.

The bombers had done their jobs. The heavy bombardment had been paramount in opening the lines for the US Rebel Forces to advance at a more rapid pace than hoped.

Tork and his regiment had refueled, rearmed, and were getting ready to hit the enemy a second time—only this time, they were to hit selected sites in Canada. The United Nations had moved additional reserve troops along the Canadian, Montana, and North Dakota borders ready to support the troops that were just hit by the United States. It was now time for a preeminent strike. With these troops hit hard, the retreating columns would be unable to receive replacements and needed supplies. The same tactics would be applied, first the cruise missiles and then the gunships—only this time, they would bring in the special ops troops behind them and on each flank as well. Tork had convened a planning briefing with his ground troops. They had given Cal a company and they were to converge on what was a suspected command position.

The Canadian underground had informed them of a very important UN meeting of both USE and UN commanders at a lodge on Lake Manitoba. The information received indicated it was the final meeting prior to the United Nations' main thrust into the United States. The rebels had blocked the corridor they hoped to push through to Mexico. The UN troop defeat there had made it impossible for them to achieve their entry into the country from the south. The rebel high command had indications from European sources the United States of Europe would now try to divide the country in two by moving down from Chicago, following the Mississippi River to New Orleans. They believed the United Nations could use the river to move equipment, men, and supplies, both up and down to augment their troop movements. They believed if they had control of the river and the docks from Chicago to New Orleans, then they could still fulfill their ambitions by moving both east and west once they had cut the country in two. It was going to be Cal's responsibility to capture the men and women at this conference and either confirm this information or provide other intelligence that would give the enemy's intentions. If necessary, they were to destroy the lodge and everyone there.

Rebel leaders were timing the raid on the troops massed in Canada along the border regions to hit thirty minutes after the strike at the UN conference at Lake Manitoba. After Cal and his troops had reported they had taken their objective, the gunships would launch their cruise missiles. It was hoped to be a stunning shock to the captured UN commanders or their superiors and a disastrous impact on them to learn their retreating troops would be running into heavy fighting. Bombardment of their reserve troops would be made. It was hoped they might realize the effort to fight was frivolous and that they might surrender. But knowing the history and arrogance of the UN commanders, both Tork and Cal knew they would fight to the end. Only their hope of mass desertions by the UN troops would help to bring the war to an end.

The Blackhawks had moved through the early hours of the night, slipping in behind enemy lines using Russian- and French-speaking troops. They entered the Canadian border between Minot and Devil's Lake, moving northeast of Brandon to their rendezvous point. It was there they would start Operation Snatch, a very perilous attack. The UN's conference areas were well guarded and all knew that they may not return. Tork ordered all commanders to gather for a final briefing before their departure. The leaders of the Canadian underground had met them on arrival, and they gave the latest intel to Cal.

Capt. Murray Flannagan, previously a member of the Irish army, reported to Cal, "Sir, I just left the lodge. All of the attendees are here. The conference goes as scheduled. They're anticipating the high command's blessing to start south. Although they've been pushed back by you, Yanks, they all feel confident they're ready to destroy the rebel army. I have listened to them explaining their strategy and describe the eagerness of their troops to move forward. I have also received information that many British troops may defect. The Russians are eager to fight. They still regret losing the Cold War and are bragging about their superiority over the rebel army. You should also know they have a battalion of US federal troops bivouacked in the northeast end of the lodge. They have been told they are in reserve. The truth is the UN commander doesn't trust them and he has them under silent guard. UN troops are between them and the lodge. They've set up mortars and are ready to fire into their positions if anything goes wrong. I would suggest you try to send in an emissary and let them know what they're up against. I've heard some of them talking about defecting to your side. See if you can convince them to make the change. They could be invaluable to you when you move in."

Cal looked at the Irish captain, his thoughts going back to what he had just heard, realizing he could have them attack from the north as he comes in from the south and the east. The enemy would be unable to fall back and they wouldn't be able to move west because of the lake. The UN forces would be trapped. (It might mean going in and cleaning the enemy out of the lodges, outbuildings, and cabins.)

"Captain, let's look over the maps and you can give me all the details. Leave nothing out. I'll need to know the safest way in so we can meet with the federal commander. We must answer these questions before we attempt a meeting. First, is this meeting possible? Will his troops follow him if he defects? Will there be any chance of loyalty for the United Nations within the battalion? Now, Captain, let's hear all the details!"

CHAPTER 33

Quietly, Silently They Moved

Cal waited until the remainder of his troops had arrived. Then using the information he received from Captain Flannagan and the layout of the lodge and outbuildings, he decided to send Flannagan in with two special operations groups through the northern underground corridors. If Flannagan was correct, there should be little if any personnel in this area early in the morning. Cal set the time for infiltration at 0330 hours. The UN troops had scheduled the changing of the guards at 0245 hours to ease the scheduled chow call. The new guards would complete their chow and be mustered and ready to change the guard at 0300 hours. They expected them to be entering the dining area at 0315 hours. If all went as planned, they should be eating at 0330 hours. It would be a simple and restful shift for the guards. Surprise should work in Cal's favor. Cal had assigned two other units to come in from the eastern side. They were to advance at 0100 hours and to move slowly and silently eliminating any sentries found. They were to be in place prior to the guard change at 0300 hours. It was imperative that all areas were covered and ready to strike at 0300 hours.

They did not expect the outer perimeter guards to return to the dining area until 0330 hours. Cal calculated he would be making their assault before anyone in the compound or the lodge would realize they were missing. By then he hoped they would be well inside the lodge and had taken the barrack areas and the outlying positions. He planned to round up the UN high command and dignitaries quartered in the main lodge and the cabins assigned to them. The information from Captain Flannagan had enabled them to pinpoint all the guard positions. The entrances to the buildings, motor pool area, tank positions, missile launch positions, and the main ammo dump for the entire area, now knowing their locations, Cal had sent a demolition team with two squads of rangers to destroy the dump. They were to set off their charges at precisely 0400 hours.

To ensure there would be no outside interference, he assigned a special hit team to take out the main communication center and to destroy the satellite uplink antennas. All radio-equipped vehicles were to be destroyed. All usable armored equipment would be commandeered for use. They would neutralize and take the airfield. Cal had given instructions to assemble all prisoners at the main helicopter assembly area. Then he would call in the Blackhawks, and the prisoners would be flown back to a transfer point for transportation to the command headquarters for interrogation. Cal knew that the success of this campaign could spell the end of the United Nations' control of western Canada. The troops were in their assigned areas, and infiltration had been made.

They all waited for Cal's command to go. Cal looked at his watch, the seconds ticking by. He keyed his helmet mic and whispered the go command to all, "Freedom earned." They moved forward.

Captain Flannagan, formerly of the Irish army, now captain of the US Revolutionary Army, and Captain Rogers moved forward as planned. Captain Flannagan moved quietly up to the first sentry position. He looked at the young soldier standing there shivering in the early morning hours, more interested in the warm dining hall he had just left. The captain idly looked out into the night knowing the UN army was in the United States kicking Yankee ass. He sighed, thinking of home in Dublin, wondering why he was here. Why had the United States of Europe decided to interfere in the United States? Many others in his unit felt the same way. Bewildered was the word he thought of. He decided to move around, maybe warm up a little. He had a four-hour tour to do and an hour before the corporal of the guard arrived to check on him. He slowly walked to the far end of his position, turned around, and started back.

Captain Flannagan tapped a sergeant on the shoulder and gave him the hand signal to dispatch the young guard. The hand signal was to disarm and disable. Flannagan knew they ordered many troops from Ireland here and they wanted no part of this war.

The sergeant and one other moved into position. As the guard moved past them, one would stand and grab him putting a hand over the mouth, while the other would hit him with a tranquilizer shot. One man would take his place and a second would standby to intercept the corporal of the guard when they came by to check on him. The order was to take them alive if possible—if not, dispatch using silent means. The guard moved by, not looking, just thinking of home, parents, friends, the local pub, and the fine Irish beer that was waiting for him. Suddenly, without warning, they grabbed him from behind, a hand over his mouth as they pulled him down. He felt a sharp sting in his thigh and then a relaxing feeling fell over him just before he silently slipped into a deep sleep. The sergeant and the soldier quickly removed his helmet, weapons belt, and jacket. The rebel soldier slipped the jacket and the belt on, picked up the man's weapon, and moved back to the starting point of the position. The sergeant grabbed the soldier, hefted him over one shoulder, and moved him back to the captain's position to lay him down.

"Only sedated him, sir," he said. The group moved up the next guard position and duplicated the move. There was only one sentry left before they entered the underground entryway and the tunnel to the main lodge building. Just inside the entrance to the right was the sergeant of the guard's office. Here the officer of the day and the sergeant of the guard had their office and conducted all guard duties.

Flannagan knew from experience there should only be about three men there at this time of night. The guards for replacement would be at the guard barracks room sleeping and wouldn't be wakened until just thirty minutes before changing the guard, so they had ample time.

The third guard was removed like those before him. Flannagan slipped off his field jacket and wore his Irish field dress underneath. He handed it to Rogers and then pulled out the automatic he was carrying and screwed a silencer onto its barrel. He concealed it down at his side and slightly behind his right leg before entering the tunnel's blackout door. Closing that, he opened the main inner tunnel door to a low-lit tunnel and walked to the open door twenty feet on the right side of the tunnel. He put his Irish berry on and walked up to the counter of the guard room.

The corporal of the guard looked up, seeing the Irish captain standing there. "Yes, sir. May I help you?"

"Yes, Corporal. Please ask the officer of the day and your sergeant of the guard if they could meet with me please," he replied.

"Yes, sir," the corporal replied. The corporal walked to the office door and saluted the officer of the day. "Sir, Captain Flannagan to see you and Sergeant O'Riley."

The captain acknowledged and told the corporal to show him in. The corporal then returned to the counter and said, "You may go in, sir."

Flannagan moved around the counter. As he moved behind him, he raised his gun hand up and brought the gun down hard on his head. The corporal slumped and started to fall. Flannagan caught him and laid him down softly on the floor and then entered the office, smiled at the officer in charge, and brought his pistol out from behind his leg. The shot killed him instantly. He looked over at the sergeant who was paralyzed for a second for what he had just witnessed. Suddenly the sergeant knew what was coming next and he grabbed for his sidearm.

Flannagan said, "Stop, sergeant, or I'll have to kill you."

The sergeant put up his hands and asked, "What do you want you, traitor?"

"Why, Sergeant, we want to save your life and as many others as we can. If you cooperate, you just might see Ireland again."

The sergeant looked at him. Reluctantly he said, "What do want from me, sir?"

"First, I want you to unhook your gun belt and drop it on the floor. Next slide it with your foot over toward me, then stand back two paces, turn around, and face the wall. Then place your hands on the wall and move your feet back two paces. Got that?"

"Yes, sir," he said.

As the sergeant did what he was told, Captain Flannagan pulled his ear and mic unit from his pocket and keyed his mic. "Everything is secured, Captain. First door on the right. Come in quietly and move your men to the end of the first tunnel. Also, send in two men with cuffs. I have two prisoners and one dead. Over."

Cal responded immediately, "Roger." Cal moved his men in and instructed them to go no farther than the next tunnel and to stay back and not show themselves. "If someone came along, take them out quietly and alive." He then went into the guardroom with two men. They handcuffed the two prisoners and moved the body out of the way, covering him up after taking his ID tags.

"Well, Captain," Flannagan said, while putting on his field jacket and replacing his berry with a Special Forces one. "Where to next, Cal?"

"You know the layout from here, Captain Flannagan. First the highest-ranking man here. Civilian or military, makes no difference. We want them all. Let's get going."

Captain Flannagan moved up the line of men with Cal. Turning to Cal, he said, "Okay, we move to the right here and then to the left at the next passage. It will take us up to the main lodge above. We'll come out at the north end. As you go up to the first floor, it is the main lodge area, meeting rooms, restaurant, main desk, and offices. They even have a gift shop for the lads. The stairs continue up to the next level where you will find the general officer's quarters. Next floor above that are suites. There you will find the high commissioners and political cadre from the E. European Union and the United Nations. Also the UN forces commander is on that floor. He has the presidential suite. I suggest, Cal, you post at least three men at each door. I have one of the master key cards for the entire lodge and outbuildings. Before we go up, you will find a key card machine in the office. We will need to make a master key card for each team member so each team could unlock and enter each room at the same time. I have the code and it shouldn't take more than a few minutes to make the cards. What say you?"

Cal responded immediately, "Let's do it. As soon as we move to the main hall, you and I will duplicate the key cards. How many rooms are there?"

"There's twenty-four on the second floor and only twelve on the third floor. Thirty-six rooms in all. Each of those is a suite, and they are twice the size of the others. Some are vacant, but we still need to enter each to make sure we don't miss anyone, agreed?"

Cal nodded and said, "Let's go!"

The troops moved fast and quietly through the hallways. It was almost time for the ammo dump to blow and they wanted to enter all the lodge rooms and the cabins at the same time. They would enter the barracks just before the dump blew up.

As they entered the office, Flannagan went straight to the lock up where the cards were kept. He then went to the computer terminal, entered his code, and brought up the key program and then entered the access code for the key system, followed by the code for the master key card. Set up for duplicating, he put the first card through the machine. He handed the card to Cal and asked him to try it out on the night door. Cal handed the card to a sergeant and instructed him, "Move to the west entrance door, exit it, make sure the door is fully closed and locked. Then try the card key on the card reader to see if it functions. If it doesn't, call me on my helmet radio immediately."

The sergeant nodded and hurried to the exit door. He looked around quickly to ensure there was no one around, opened the door, closed it quietly, made sure it was properly locked, and then ran the card through the card reader on the left side of the door assembly. The LED on the reader turned green, and the sergeant opened the door and entered. He then called softly into his mic. "All is well, sir. It's a go."

Before Cal could speak, Flannagan started running the cards through. They would need thirty-six plus an additional twenty for the cabin's outer buildings. All other keys that could be found where gathered up for possible use later. They quickly gave out the cards to each group leader. Each team then moved silently through the corridors, stopping at each door. When both floors were covered, Cal called his outside team leaders and received the all in place code, Freedom Earned. This meant all was ready. The time was checked. They had two minutes to wait. Everything was on track. Cal looked at his watch; the minutes ticked by slowly. He was counting seconds trying to make them go faster. Time had arrived.

Suddenly, from some distance the earth shuddered as tons of high explosives started detonating, raising huge plumes of fire and shrapnel that would be raining down shortly. The explosions were waking up everyone just as they entered their rooms. Some reached for their weapons only to find men in black holding M-16s and machine guns on them. One tried to reach a window, only to be a pulled back and handcuffed. Those with wives were separated. They permitted the women to dress. Several had small children with them. They were kept together and would be taken in separate helicopters from their fathers. Parents would be separated from each other. All the barracks were entered at the same time just a few minutes prior to the dump blowing up. Barrack guards were taken out quickly. Rebel troops dressed in USE battle dress uniforms entered each building with a thermos of hot coffee. As the European troops poured and drank the coffee, they were taken out with a strong sedative. If they turned down the coffee, they were killed swiftly. Fortunately, they all were pleased to see the hot coffee. They were getting sleepy from the sedative and it was a welcome sight for the rebels. Only a few had tried to fight off the effects, but they too fell silent. Most of them that tried to fight were dedicated officers, looking forward to being part of those who defeated the great United States. They died for their efforts. The rebel forces took the airfield intact. They wired the aircraft with explosives to be detonated upon departure. The field would be left intact for later use by rebel aircraft.

Cal called Lieutenant Colonel Albertson as soon as they had secured the complex and neutralized the garrison. He reported their success and requested the Blackhawks be sent in for the UN captors. They would evacuate them first. Then the big birds would come in on the main runway to pick up all other prisoners. Cal's Blackhawks would pick up the last of the rebel troops and fly them back to their regiment for the continuing invasion of Canada.

Tork waited for their return and plans were being finalized for the invasion of Canada. Fighting had pushed the UN forces northward to the outskirts of Milwaukee. Chicago was in the hands of the US Rebel Army. In the west, fighting was hard and furious. The American troops had forced the enemy both north and east. They had liberated Minneapolis and St. Paul and they were driving the United Nations east into Wisconsin. A corridor between Minneapolis and Duluth had forced them to drive northeast toward Sault Ste. Marie. The United States hoped to force them into the upper Michigan peninsula where they could cut them off.

The Mackinaw and Sault Ste. Marie bridges would be destroyed before they could use them. The rebels hoped this would cut off the UN forces' escape and they could then arrange surrender. If not, heavy bombing would commence. Strategic bombing of Canadian and UN bases were ongoing. The United States had gained air superiority and they would not relinquish it. The UN forces that had been cut off were being forced northwest toward International Falls. Highway 53 and Highway 71 were the only good roads able to move the UN forces and armor into Canada without getting bogged down. The tide had turned. Americans had seen and disliked the new world order and they were rallying around the rebel government. It was time.

CHAPTER 34

The Eagle Prepares

The Blackhawks had returned, and the enemy's high command was now completely incapacitated. Answers would shortly be coming forth, and the country would be free of the oppressors. The Jones chips were being safely removed thanks to Mr. Jones's cooperation. Many had applauded the use of the chips at first, but now the tide had turned, and even those who wanted peace and serenity could see what freedom really meant. It had come home to all that freedom was earned by attention to what went on in all legislation enactments—be it small towns, cities, or in Washington. It was each citizen's responsibility to search out the truth and to act accordingly. The vote was the most powerful weapon they had to defeat those who would take their most precious rights.

Tork's regiment was composed of four battalions. Three were special operations and one was air cavalry. This unit was equipped with the newest fighting assault helicopters in the world. They had already been showing their capabilities throughout the fight for freedom. The eastern command was moving rapidly northeast, pushing the enemy toward the St. Lawrence River. All bridges were in the process of being destroyed, making it far more difficult for them to cross. The rebel high command wanted to hit Ottawa first and then north to Montreal.

Tork's regiment was given the job of hitting the strategic UN bases in Ontario. The largest was in the process of mounting a full attack on the American forces moving north toward International

Falls. It was Tork's mission to move behind their lines and attack them using hit-and-run tactics with stealth and cunning. Tork had called in his battalion commanders and laid it out to them, assigning targets and rendezvous points for each. To be successful, the main plan incorporated both special ops personnel and gunships. The gunships would attack small targets to draw out men and equipment from the enemy's closest response base. As the enemy moved to encounter the rebel forces, special ops would enter the base and attack all supply and equipment holding areas.

Stealth was the key. As they had been so successful in Mexico and South America in the past, they would again be stalkers. Navy SEAL would infiltrate the docks at Thunder Bay and set off ordinance destroying ships and dock facilities. The word of this attack should pull needed troops from the UN base northwest of Thunder Bay. Expecting invasions, the United Nations would respond with a large force to protect the town and facilities there. Tork's gunships would then hit targets west of the UN base forcing reserve forces to respond. It was then the special operation forces would hit the base.

Tork called for Capt. Cal Varner to report. Cal was in the process of readying his troops. All Blackhawks had been fully reequipped, and troops were going through last-minute preparations. Junior officers were going over aerial recon pictures with the NCOs for explosive placement, guard positions, headquarter layouts, ammo dumps, and fuel dumps.

Cal knocked on the tent post and entered. "Sir, Captain Varner reporting as ordered."

Tork returned his salute and said, "Cal, you're out of uniform."

Cal looked down at himself, felt his head for his cap, looked into Tork's mirror hanging from a strap on the side of the tent, and could see nothing wrong. In bewilderment, he said, "Colonel, I can't see where I'm out of uniform, sir."

Tork smiled and retorted, "Major, you have the wrong rank on your battle dress."

It took a few seconds for the statement to sink in, and then Cal's frown changed to a bright new smile. "Major!" he exclaimed.

Took replied, "Yes, Major. The high command was so pleased with your accomplishments in bringing down the United Nations' high command conference and the intelligence you provided them that they felt it only fitting you should be advanced to the next grade. I heartily agreed."

Cal thanked Tork and said, "Yeah, and you didn't have anything to do with it either, did you?"

Tork just smiled and changed the subject. "Cal, this next hit on the United Nations is going to be a tough one, so I'll be commanding it. I want you and your troops to be the advance companies. I know them all from our days in Mexico and South America. With you leading them, I have no doubt we can fulfill our assignment. I'll set up a command center to maintain open and secure communications. We'll use our satellite communication headsets. Ensure all your personnel are equipped with them. This must be a quiet assault. As soon as you're in position to take the headquarters building, you are to notify me immediately. We believe there are very important documents there, along with other USE commanders. We need the documents and the commanders intact, that is, the men should be alive and the documents in one piece and readable. I'll join you when you are ready to make your attack on the building."

"Yes, sir," Cal replied. Cal returned to his battalion headquarters. Sergeant Major Owen was preparing site strike points for the gunship commanders when Cal entered. The sergeant looked up and called the others to attention. "Yes, sir. Can I help you, sir?"

"Yes, Sergeant. I need to see the commander right now."

The sergeant major smiled at Cal and replied, "Sir, you are our new commander. Major Hawthorn has moved to the regimental headquarters, and I received word from Lieutenant Colonel Albertson's headquarters you are our new commander. Congratulations, Major." Reaching down and picking up two objects from the desk, the sergeant said, "Oh, by the way, the Colonel sent these over for you, sir." The sergeant major held out his hand and dropped two blackened gold metal oak leaves into Cal's hand.

"Well, then, Sergeant," Cal exclaimed, "have all company commanders here within the half hour. We have changes to make."

*****

Heavy bombardments by the UN forces had been made throughout the United States, uniting the American people even closer. The advancing rebel forces had been shelled and bombed while in towns and cities. The enemy made no distinctions between military and civilian targets. UN forces wanted to completely disorient and kill the civilian population's moral and turn them against the rebelling factions. Nevertheless, the United Nations failed to realize the fear instilled in the people by using the Jones chips and the tyranny they used in the occupied areas. There were few liberal factions left to honor them.

The sergeant major entered Cal's tent. "Sir, all commanders and senior NCOs are present and waiting."

"Thank you, Sergeant Major. Give me two minutes and I'll be there."

Cal picked up the area maps he had been using, looked them over, and, satisfied with his assessment, left for the meeting.

Sergeant Owns was waiting when Cal arrived. "Ten-hut!" he barked, as Cal entered the area.

"At ease," Cal remarked as he moved to the front of the assembled men and women warriors. He was now in command of his own battalion.

Cal spoke for all to hear as he detailed the attack procedures. All Blackhawk helicopters were assigned specific areas of engagement. Troops would be dropped off, and while they moved to their strike points, the ships were to return for additional supplies. Stalkers would go out to eliminate sentries and prepare the way for the main force, the same tactics used in Mexico. Silently, they'd eliminate the guards and then move into the barracks, officer quarters, and the headquarters building before any alarm could be set off.

Satellite reconnaissance photos were passed around. A large one was set on a large easel, and Cal stepped forward with a laser pointer and pointed out the sentry locations, barracks, officers and NCO quarters, guardrooms, and the headquarters building. He moved his pointer to the northeast side of the building and circled where the main safe or vault was. He emphasized the penetration teams must hit this area simultaneously from the roof and from the inside. They would need to be cautious, as they were not sure what security would be in there. Cal was clear to point out that they had been given information a special guard unit was put in place in the event of an attack, and they were to set of explosives in the vault or safe. Intel did not know what was in there. It was suspected it was a vault, and if it was, the device in side could be an incendiary. If so, they could instantly destroy all information. He went on to explain the possibility of top war plans being secured there and the importance of its contents. If intelligence information was correct, it could mean total victory for America and the end to UN and EU dominance.

Cal spoke to Captain Summers. "Captain, you will inform me when your penetration team is in place. I'll contact Lieutenant Colonel Albertson. You will then wait for the colonel and me to arrive prior to your attack. You will enter through the windows with the roof assault team. Remember, both teams must enter the room precisely at the same time. All of you be cautious. It's imperative we maintain silence. No noise until you go through the windows and the doors. Got it? One gun shot, one call for help, or one cry out could blow this whole thing. Ensure that each penetration team is equipped with silencers and crossbows. Colonel Albertson will be commanding this engagement and will be with the stalkers to alert us if there are any problems. Do you have any questions?"

One company commander raised his hand. "Sir, if there is a problem with the guards prior to the headquarters penetration, what are our orders? Do we break off and regroup or stand and fight?"

"Captain, if for any reason we cannot penetrate the headquarters building before they blow it, we will take out the base. Air force will be waiting for us to give them the go-ahead. If this happens, we should be well clear of the assault area. All commanders will follow their order and will regroup at the predetermined assembly points for a pick up and return. Are there any other questions?"

"Yes, sir. What about prisoners? If taken, what do we do with them?"

"We will treat all prisoners accordingly. Secure them at our landing zone. We need the intel they can give us, so we will use the supply copters to transport them back to our lines. Remember, no harm must come to them. We will assemble anyone taken from the headquarters building separately from the others. All officers and the team sent to the commander's quarters will be kept separate and flown out in Blackhawks. Remember, each of them will be clothed in our army combat fatigues. No rank is to be displayed. Upon arrival, we will take them to our headquarters for interrogation. It is imperative we do not allow anyone to know that we have them. We cannot take the chance that we have no intruders among us. Now, let's go out and kick them off this continent."

CHAPTER 35

Silent Goes the Nightmare

Their ships had landed. All troops disembarked and the teams moved to their assault points. Colonel Albertson's group was in position. All were waiting for the command to move. Cal's group had moved to the headquarters building and had eliminated the guards. Team members had taken their places and were silently making their rounds. Should a change of the guard appear, others would be there to make that change also.

Tork had ordered the team to enter the commander's billets and silently remove them all. Wives and children, if there, would be taken to the departure point and moved out first. They would move the commanders and their assistants separately to ensure no communications between them.

Capt. Jason Hawthorne commanded the team. He and his men moved in through the front and rear windows. They cut the glass quietly, the windows were raised, and the men entered using night vision equipment. Each of them moved silently through the building until each was at the bedroom door, and as silently as possible, a stethoscope was placed on each door to listen for normal sleeping sounds. Next a small TV monitor camera was slipped under each door and moved into the room. The camera's night vision lenses enabled the operator to see clearly. They called back the results to Tork. When all reports were in, he gave the word. "Enter quietly," he whispered. "Wake everyone up, tape their mouths, secure them, and move them quickly out to the assembly points. Do not allow them to sound an alarm. Go."

Each group responded as directed and trained. They woke each person from the commanding general to the smallest child. The children were picked up and moved silently, some not even waking until they were at the assembly points. Each was united with his or her mother or a relative. The officers were separated and would be moved separately as planned. Cal's troops had moved through the night. As they moved ahead, they took each enemy guard position out. Cal had a special team formed to move on the main guard post. They moved silently up to the building where they could hear a radio playing. One ranger with his back to the wall of the building moved close to the window and removed a small mirror from his pocket. He slid the mirror out from its handle until it was a good eighteen inches long and then moved it slowly as he looked into the mirror so he could observe inside the room and then tilted the mirror slightly down so it wouldn't reflect any light. The ranger could see plainly the three men inside. One was at the counter making out a duty log. One was cleaning his weapon, disassembled it in several pieces, and laid it on the table before him. The third man was reading a book. The ranger slid to the ground, crawled back away from the building fifteen feet, and keyed his helmet mic. "Sir, I count three men. One is making out a duty log, one cleaning a weapon, and a third reading a book."

Cal nodded to what he had heard, turned to his sergeant, and gave the command. "Take it out."

The sergeant gave a signal to the others, and within minutes, four rangers entered the building from all sides. Before the young man standing at the counter could grab his weapon, he was struck down. The soldier cleaning his weapon grabbed for parts and was hit with a silent bullet. The third man threw up his hands and the book he was reading went sailing through the air, hitting the wall and falling to the floor.

The leading ranger keyed his mic and reported. "Sir, guard post is secure. One captured. Two down. Will report conditions shortly." He then checked the first man, who was alive with a shoulder wound. He waved to one of the others and had him dress the wound and then went to the young man that had been cleaning his weapon. He had a grazed wound on the right side of his head just above the ear and was out cold. The ranger secured his hands and taped his mouth and then dressed his wound. They would move these three to the embarkation point, and three rangers would take their places. The cleanup was fast and Cal's team moved to the headquarters building where they identified each guard post. Each was in place as indicated on the intelligence reports. They silently removed each man, and a ranger was left as a stand-in for each man they had removed.

The team had moved into the building and to the rooms shown on the reports. The roof team moved to the roof and found it empty. A deserted antiaircraft gun emplacement was sitting silent; the gun was in place with no ammunition. The team leader set a timer with C-4 attached and set the timer to go off two minutes after their planned departure time. Everything was set.

Cal called Tork and informed him they were in position. Tork told him to hold. He was in the process of securing the enlisted barracks and dining facilities. Tork's men had taken over the dining hall and had locked the cooks up in the walk-in refrigerators. Two rangers had walked through the barracks setting up explosives. They entered the gun rooms after removing the keys from the orderly rooms. They wired the gun rooms with remote-controlled detonators and high explosives. If they were discovered, the barracks and armories would be destroyed.

Word came to Tork that all areas were secured. Troops were sleeping and they had neutralized all guards. Tork turned to Major Thorn, left him in charge, and took three men to meet Cal at the headquarters building. Cal took Tork up to the area just outside the secure area where they had information where the safes were. Cal's men had listened and could not detect any movement or noise in the room. The TV cameras had shown an empty office with a second door that was closed and no lights or activity. Cal suggested they abandon the mission and return to base. It seemed to him it had all been moved elsewhere.

Tork looked at Cal silently for a few moments. "No," he whispered. "Our intelligence information has been perfect so far. It's in there. Tell the men on the roof to go in exactly thirty seconds from now."

Cal alerted his team and told them to go on his count. Tork was counting the seconds, 26, 27, 28, 29. His finger came down at thirty, and Cal announced in his radio mic, "Go." Instantly they breached the first door. The second door was forced open, and the windows in the second room burst apart as the men entered. They all stood there amazed. The room was empty of personnel. The safe was a large walk-in type. It was closed with a tag on it giving the name and rank of the man that had closed and locked it. Tork quickly called for Sergeant Matthews. He came in instantly.

"What can you do with this one, Sergeant?" he asked pointing to the safe.

The sergeant examined the safe and turned to the colonel. "Shouldn't take but a few minutes, sir, to open it, but it will require a little noise if you're in a hurry."

Tork radioed his teams and informed them to return to the embarkation point and to set the remote detonators to on. He then had all but a few of his men stand by for the return and then had the others return to the choppers for a clean getaway. Everything was ready. He ordered Sergeant Matthews to open her up. The sergeant had studied the safe and had decided to try to open it before he used any explosives. It was a very old safe, and he felt the equipment he brought with him would help. He had placed an electronic device on the safe next to the dial and was turning it slowly. As the tumbler fell, it showed a number on the dial. He had all but one or two numbers left, and shortly he would have the combination. When the colonel told him to blow it, he just smiled. The dial moved slowly and the seconds were long. Click, click, click went the dial as it moved from tumbler to tumbler and then the last one dropped into place. He had a complete combination. He quickly dialed in the combination— right one, full turn to twenty-seven; left, two turns to sixteen; right, one full turn to forty-two; and left, one turn to six. The sergeant looked up at the colonel, grabbed the wheel on the front of the safe, and started turning it. He could hear the mechanism pulling the door pins back. The wheel stopped turning and he pulled the huge door open. As it opened, the light inside came on.

Tork reached in and opened the inner gate and they entered. Everything in the safe was gathered up, including the money. It was quickly put into backpacks, and the men strapped them on. Tork then ordered all of them to return to the choppers. Tork stopped Cal from leaving with his men and they followed close behind them. When they were out of sight of the base, Tork removed a remote-controlled detonator from his pocket. "This should keep them busy while we move south." He pushed the button, and within seconds, the base started to explode. They entered their ships and all were on their way home, the noise from the explosions covering their move. Each could again know that freedom was earned.

Their choppers had just landed and word had come that they had taken Vancouver, and all of the west coast of the United States was back under control.

CHAPTER 36

The Final Solution: Quebec

American forces had pushed deep inside Quebec. They had taken Ottawa, and Montreal had been put under siege. They had destroyed the ports along the St. Lawrence and had pushed the UN forces east into New Brunswick. The UN forces were relying on reinforcements or hopes of rescue by the European Union, not knowing if their ships had been destroyed or was on their way to rescue them. Both American and British aircraft that had defected intercepted UN bombers coming in from the northeast. The country was growing stronger and stronger. As areas were liberated, construction began to rebuild homes and factories. They had moved American nuclear submarines to Europe, waiting for peace, knowing only the United States of Europe could end the war by surrendering and withdrawing its troops. Everyone had learned that freedom was earned and they had fought for it. The liberal movement had slipped into the shadows, hiding from the new American. A united country was emerging with only one race, the American race; one soul, the American soul; and one people, the American people. Color and race had no place among them. They all had learned there was more to an American than the color of his skin or where he was from.

*****

"Lieutenant Colonel Albertson reporting, sir." Tork lowered his hand from the salute he had just given to General Duncan.

General Duncan began, "Colonel, we have reached the final phase in regaining our country from the enemy. Our new Congress has authorized the restoration of the country, and the first act is to start protecting our borders. Our northern and southern borders are to be sealed by the army. We will permit foreign nationals entry only through designated entry points. The reestablishment of diplomatic relations will begin immediately after hostilities end and then only when we instigate it.

"Colonel, we are prepared to accept the surrender of the UN and USE forces. The surrender will be unconditional. Upon surrender, all troops will be moved to the camps in New Mexico, and we will not be repatriated until all the countries sign a nonaggression treaty. We will remove ourselves from the United Nations and will stand alone in sovereignty, dignity, and as a compassionate nation under god. We have all decided to stand by the Declaration of Independence and the constitution of the United States as amended, including the 27th Amendment. All articles passed and placed in law after the 27th Amendment are considered unlawful and will be removed from the constitution. Our troops have the remaining UN troops cut off in New Brunswick and Nova Scotia. All ports have been blockaded, and all airports have been bombed. We have killer subs in the area looking for any UN submarines that may be used to pick up troops or officers and remove them from the area. We have sent surrender terms to both the UN and European capitals. We have given them a warning. Any future attempts to overthrow, invade, or inflict economic harm to the United States of America or her new American allies will invite reprisals of the most horrendous means.

"Colonel Albertson, I have asked you here today to accept a new and challenging job, one that is dangerous and intriguing. The new government feels, to ensure our freedom, we must assure that other European nations will not continue to pursue a war with us or any other country if they too are free. Therefore, we feel it necessary to help others to regain their freedom as well. Our British cousins feel the need of freeing the United Kingdom from European domination. They, like us, know they were sold a bill of goods and they want to free their people from the same controls we've faced. The Congress has authorized funds to support them and men and materials to help them. We have already dispatched a submarine with British operatives home to set up the cells needed to infiltrate the armed forces and the government. Tork, we want you and a handpicked team to enter the United Kingdom and help them any way you can. You will be fully in command of our team and answerable only to this headquarters. We will supply you with whatever you need to free the British from the EU alliance and to support them in reorganizing it as a true common market, not part of a politically organized and controlled European nation. What say you?"

Tork looked to the general, thinking back to the day he and Diana sat on a bed in California listening to a general telling them about a new revolution. He never considered it would necessitate moving across oceans and freeing others as well. He knew what he had seen and what the Jones chips were capable of. He fully understood what freedom meant to the Americans.

Surely it would apply to others as well. He recalled what a British pilot had said to him when he and his crew defected to the rebel cause. He knew others—French, German, Irish, and many others—that sought freedom had joined forces with the rebels to fight the new world order and most of all for their own country's freedom.

With a smile on his face, Tork looked at the general saying, "When do we start, General, and where? I know the why."

CHAPTER 37

Final Solution

There was a rap on the door. The incarcerated president of the United States looked to the door from his sofa. He had been watching a DVD on his television and wasn't sure if he heard something. The rap repeated. He stood and walked to the door.

"Yes?" he asked.

The door bolts were slid back and the door opened in. General McGuire and General Armstrong stood together.

One spoke, "Mr. President, please come with us, sir."

The president saw a remarkable change in the men's demeanor; they were much more at ease. He wondered if his loyal forces and the UN troops had triumphed. Had the war ended and they were taking him to freedom and back to his presidency? A slight smile curled on his lips. *Yes,* he thought, *that is it.* The United Nations had won and he was returning to Washington.

The men entered the auditorium through the center doors. Beyond on the podium sat the revolutionary congress. Both senators and members of the House were present. Some of the men he recognized he thought were loyal to him and to the federal government. The others were the men and women he once thought of as members of the government that had perpetrated and entered into treasonous revolutionaries. His hopes began to fade as he approached the podium. He knew he would not be going home as president of the United States.

He stood before them all, a defeated man. He was a man who, with his cabinet, had invited foreign troops to disarm America, to enslave them with identification implants, to surrender their rights against their will by placing their country under control of the United Nations. He was a man trusted by his fellow Americans who accepted the United States of Europe as the leader of the United Nations. The president felt the bitterness in each man and woman there. Many Americans had died fighting for their lost freedom. Foreign troops had destroyed towns and cities, and the one man responsible stood before them.

The president was informed the revolutionary council had decided to impeach him and all others that were responsible for crimes against the people. Others in consort with him would be tried as well. Each of them would be tried individually. If impeachment were made, a trial for treason would follow. Each person would be tried as individuals and each would be given attorneys. All proceedings would be in accordance with constitutional law. They would hear appeals all the way to the Supreme Court if warranted. The world would see liberty in all its glory.

The speaker of the revolutionary council rose. "Mr. President, before we begin, it is paramount to each of us that you be informed of the charges against you and the general condition of the country. The United States of America is once again under full constitutional protection. The constitution and the original twenty-seven amendments are once again the law of the land. We stand once more under the protection of this great document. The changes made to enslave the citizens of this country have been eradicated from it. We have pushed the invaders out of the country and we have complete control of Mexico. She is a defeated nation. In Canada, European troops have been driven east into New Brunswick and Nova Scotia where we are presently negotiating surrender terms with their commanders. Our nuclear submarines stand off China and European shores to ensure peace. We have given the world an ultimatum, peace or death by nuclear devastation. We do not want war, but are prepared to protect ourselves and anyone else who would befriend us. You, sir, and your administration are responsible for all that has happened to us. Many of your party joined forces with the true spirit of freedom, and they, along with their opposing party, joined to plan and execute this revolution. The days ahead will be long and tiring, but they will be just, something you failed to address in your quest to sell us to the new world order. Sir, freedom is earned. And this country is free because we, the American people, are again free. The future will not stop here. Other nations and their people want to be free too. Already America is responding. We are building new factories. The armed forces are being enlarged for we cannot assume we are out of danger. Therefore, we will prepare for a free future by being prepared. No future president can reduce our capabilities to what you have done to us.

"Mr. President, your administration is responsible for what's happened not only here but also in Canada. You and those in Canada that bought the UN line of propaganda to both countries are fully responsible for this war. You should know, sir, Canada has fallen, and they are unable to protect themselves. Without the United Nations to protect them, they're vulnerable. It's our responsibility to protect them now. Their borders will be closed to all foreign commerce. All foreign diplomats will be removed from Canada and they will be invited to send observers to Congress. Eventually we will give all of their provinces statehood if they want it, and a referendum from both the American public and Canadian people will be required. The fate of both Canada and Mexico will be dependent on their cooperation. We have plans to invite all of the American nations to join us as a unified American market. But it must be to meet there own needs. Borders will be kept intact and only free trade will be open to all nations of the Americas, and they will have to abide by the treaties to be negotiated and provide the same guarantees, constitutionally, to their own people as we have to ours. Canada and Mexico will be under US occupation and will be absorbed eventually into the union. If they agree, we have considered a new name for the country, the United States of North America.

"The provinces of Canada will be made states and the Mexican states will remain as states in the new union. The will of the people will be accepted. Members of Congress will only have the responsibility to write the laws. The people will vote on them and make them laws through referendum voting.

"The Canadian and Mexican people deserve no less than our people do. Thousands were instrumental in bringing freedom back to us. We shall never forget the sacrifices made by them. Freedom is earned and they will have their share for they've earned it too."

The speaker of the revolutionary council felt sorrow and pain that a president of the United States had resorted to such treachery. He looked at the president with sorrow in his heart and addressed the president's escorts. "Return the prisoner to his quarters and place him on high security."

He then turned to the members of the revolutionary congress and addressed them. "Ladies and gentlemen, we have secured our borders and have control of both border nations that were parties of the United Nations that perpetrated the war against us and allowed foreign troops to enter the United States. Most of those in power in these countries have been located and are under arrest. Some of them were out of the country or managed to escape before we were able to apprehend them. The leaders of the drug cartels in both Canada and Mexico will be apprehended and tried, and all of their wealth will be confiscated and made available for remaking the economy. We know who they are and we will succeed in bringing them to justice. We are again a free nation and a strong one. We have the resources to move ahead and we will let no nation on earth believe they can conquer us or change our way of life. We are free and we intend to stay that way. God bless America and may God bless each and every one of us, for we are a free nation of all colors, creeds, and religions. Do not tread on us for we are one, free and independent."

CHAPTER 38

Preparation

Congressional House and Senate Oversight Committee
Washington DC

The war had been over for a year and the country was repairing itself. New business in all areas were growing, and the American people were very cautious, watching all local elections and demanding honesty from the electorate and demanding integrity in each member of the government.

The liberalism of the past was frowned on by all. The country hadn't seen such patriotism since the 1940s; few dared to speak out against the government, for all knew without the sacrifices made by them, they would all be slaves to the government controlled by the Jones implant identification chip. Even those with no religious affiliation thanked God for their deliverance.

Colonel Albertson and Major Varner had entered the New Homeland Security Headquarters Foreign Action Sections briefing room they were the last to arrive. Gen. Marshall Townsend, Admiral Pointer, and General Duncan were entering the stage as Tork and Cal sat.

General Townsend stood and addressed them. "Gentlemen and members of the Freedom for a Free World, our first foreign operation is now named Churchill. It is the name for our first strike against Europe and the United Nations on their soil.

"Our first force will be leaving within the next month. The exact date and strike area are classified. At this time, you only need to know we will be preparing the strike area over the next year. Our personnel and members of the underground in the strike area will be building new cells and establishing strike areas, recruiting new patriots, and stockpiling weapons, munitions, and financial safe house throughout the country.

"Targets have been identified and a wave of patriot hits on UN and USE installations will be carried out. We have for the past year infiltrated the government and armed forces in the target country. While we are busy creating havoc there, we will have teams entering other European countries and setting up cells and targeting areas that will be struck later. It is important we all work in harmony on the Fight for Freedom.

"In front of you are your instructions. Do not share this information with others that are not on your team. In each folder, you will find your orders and your team members, the mode of transportation and your destination, the day and hour of departure, arrival date, and your contacts. Each of you has been placed with local team members within your area of operation. The only member's name you will receive now, the man you will be reporting to, the one that will have full responsibility in the field is Colonel Albertson, commanding officer in charge of this expedition. Your orders lay out all channels that you must use to communicate in a hostile area and the procedures you are to take. All of you know what is expected of you and your teams and all of you have been thoroughly trained. We here salute all of you and know you will be successful. Remember you will be training and setting up the cells I've told you about."

Tork was busy going over his file; it was thick, well written, precise, and illustrated the responsibility he had been given. He felt elated about the responsibility he was entrusted with and knew the importance of the mission.

He and Cal would be the first of this group to land, and the game would start with them and friends across the Atlantic. The equipment was ready, boats had been loaded, and the first move for the fight for freedom in Europe was about to begin.

Admiral Pointer took the stand; he was quick and to the point. "Gentlemen, your boats are ready. In your file are your date of departure. Your destination will be given to you after departure in sealed orders. Only you and your boats captain will be aware of it. Upon opening your orders, you will discuss them with your officers and men. During your, ah, shall we say, cruise, you are to train your team over and over on your mission and its importance. We must not lose sight of our goal. A well-trained and cohesive mission will start the fight for freedom in Europe. One last thing, you will be receiving supplies on scheduled time frames. Understand each drop notification will be made by satellite on your receivers, and all messages will need to be screened by your crypto analyst, so take extra special care of him. He's worth his weight in gold to you. General Duncan will now address you. General Duncan."

General Duncan moved to the podium, smiled at the men and women before him, and spoke, "A year ago, we ended the one war we never expected to fight, the second war against our brother and sisters who tried to enslave us through the United Nations and the European Union. In our last engagement with the United Nations, it was a fight for freedom. We won the war and earned back our freedom. The constitution gave us our freedom and man took it away from us. We must always be vigilant, freedom is earned, and we must ensure our own safety by helping and supporting all nations to fight for theirs. It's for our own security and the welfare of Europe. We move forward and start Operation Churchill, code name Fight for Freedom. We as a people will never allow any foreign government or any religion to dominate any of our laws or people. We will ensure all are covered under the constitution and at no time will we allow any religious group to compromise the constitution by any means. You, all of you will become the new world freedom fighters. Good luck and God bless you all. Freedom is earned."

General Duncan came to attention and saluted them all and then dismissed them knowing the fight they had ahead of them and the long months of a silent war they would endure.

Tork and Cal gathered up their files and left with the other. Tork put his arm around Cal's shoulder and said, "Cal, get some rest.

Write a good letter to all your girlfriends for tomorrow we start a new day and a new life. Be in my office at 0800 hours tomorrow for a briefing on our new fight for freedom.

Cal saluted Tork and returned to his quarters. Tork returned to his headquarters and started preparing for the operational briefing at 0800 hours. Tomorrow would be the first step in his group, for they would be the first to move out and meet those sent ahead, and it was only a few days away. At this point in time, he was the only one in his group who knew the date and time of departure.

*****

It was 0400 hours when the group arrived at the boat. The USS Freedom Shark was ready to sail, all equipment and supplies had been loaded on board, and the captain had been waiting for the troops to arrive.

The busses arrived on time and the troop commander, Colonel Albertson, had them on board and ready to depart in less time than the captain had expected.

The captain called over the intercom for Colonel Albertson to report to the con. Within minutes, a master chief petty officer reported to the captain. "Sir, Colonel Albertson awaits your pleasure."

"Thank you, Master Chief." The captain followed the chief to the con and dismissed him.

"Colonel Albertson, we're happy to have you and your men on board. Welcome to the Freedom Shark."

Shaking hands, the two men became friends. The boats captain smiled at Tork and invited him to his cabin. Upon arriving, he went directly to the ship's safe and removed an envelope and handed it to Tork. "Your orders, Colonel, and good luck, sir."

Tork took the orders, opened the envelope, and read the orders. "Well, Captain, I hope you know the way to Scotland." He handed the orders back to him.

The captain read the orders, smiled, and said, "No sweat, Colonel. I know those waters well. We've already made several deliveries there for your group. Make yourself comfortable. Sorry we won't get a chance to surface until we arrive, but we do have other entertainments for you and your men."

Tork thanked him and told him they would be holding training classes until there arrival. The first group was underway, and within days, they would be setting up for the return of freedom to the British Isles and the restoration of the kingdom, if the people wanted it.

With the British free and cells working in the European Union, freedom would be won for all of Europe. Although it would involve a civil war, the European Union would be freed. Tork knew it could be done.

Tork's orders gave him his destination and his host, an old friend he met so long ago. Flight Leader John W. Walters, a true patriot and a loyal Brit. *God save the kingdom*, he thought. Well, he could only wait and train, for soon the new fight for freedom would begin.

The end.

CPSIA information can be obtained
at www.ICGtesting.com
Printed in the USA
BVHW031033160621
609528BV00001BA/91